Remember Summer

REMEMBER SUMMER

ELIZABETH LOWELL

THORNDIKE
CHIVERS

This Large Print edition is published by Thorndike Press, Waterville, Maine, USA and by AudioGO Ltd, Bath, England.

Thorndike Press, a part of Gale, Cengage Learning.

Remember Summer was previously published in an altered form entitled *Summer Games* by Silhouette Books in 1984.

The text of this Large Print edition is unabridged.
Other aspects of the book may vary from the original edition.
Set in 16 pt. Plantin.

LIBRARY OF CONGRESS CATALOGING-IN-PUBLICATION DATA

Lowell, Elizabeth, 1944–
   Remember summer / by Elizabeth Lowell. — Large print ed.
     p. cm. — (Thorndike Press large print famous authors)
   ISBN-13: 978-1-4104-4198-0 (hardcover)
   ISBN-10: 1-4104-4198-9 (hardcover)
   1. Large type books. I. Title.
PS3562.O8847R46 2011
813'.54—dc22   2011029961

BRITISH LIBRARY CATALOGUING-IN-PUBLICATION DATA AVAILABLE

Published in 2011 in the U.S. by arrangement with Avon, an imprint of HarperCollins Publishers.
Published in 2012 in the U.K. by arrangement with the author.

U.K. Hardcover: 978 1 445 87147 9 (Chivers Large Print)
U.K. Softcover: 978 1 445 87148 6 (Camden Large Print)

Printed in the United States of America
1 2 3 4 5 6 7 15 14 13 12 11

For
Karen Solem

who has supported my writing in
two very different fields

appreciation

PROLOGUE

Summer of 1984

She looked like hell.

Sallow, blotchy skin, pale lips, red eyes, and stringy brown hair. The woman's picture put the cherry on the cake of a day that had sucked from the instant a telephone call woke him up in a place halfway around the world.

But Robert Johnstone didn't share his thoughts. He was, after all, talking to the woman's father, who was also his boss. Justin Chandler-Smith IV — called Blue by those who knew him well enough — loved his family as much as he hated terrorists. It would take a stupid man to point out that the youngest of the Chandler-Smiths hadn't inherited her parents' good looks.

Johnstone was not a stupid man.

"How old is this picture?" he asked neutrally.

It was an effort to keep his voice calm. He

was still angry about being pulled off one project and dumped into the middle of another without any warning. So he looked at the passport-size photo and kept reminding himself that Blue wouldn't have asked for him by name if it wasn't important.

Whatever *it* was.

"Seven days, give or take," Chandler-Smith said. "It's Baby Lorraine's Olympic ID photo."

Johnstone's ice-blue glance shifted from the photo to his boss. Other than the girl's hazel eyes and a stubborn kind of chin, he didn't see much resemblance between Lorraine Chandler-Smith and her very handsome, hard-edged, and distinguished father. Though Chandler-Smith had no title worth mentioning, he had much more power than ninety-nine percent of the uniforms marching around the Pentagon. More brains, too.

"Who else?" Johnstone asked, passing the picture back over the big desk.

"Captain Jon. Trainer, coach, ass chewer, mother hen." Chandler-Smith pushed another photo over the desk. "He's reliable."

"Opinion or fact?"

"Fact. I had that man vetted all the way back to his great-grandfathers before I let Baby Lorraine train with him."

A fleeting smile changed the impassive lines of Johnstone's face. "I believe it."

"These are Baby's teammates, both long and short list." Chandler-Smith began laying out laminated ID photos. He tapped each photo, reciting names and outstanding physical characteristics.

Johnstone didn't interrupt. He simply sat with a predatory kind of stillness and memorized each face, each name, each fact that would help him to separate Olympic riders from Olympic terrorists.

"These are the stable help," Chandler-Smith continued, laying out more photos. "Pay particular attention to the females."

"Why? Do we have information on one of them?"

"No. But if anybody gets to Baby's horse, it will be through the girls. That stud won't tolerate men within kicking range."

Johnstone's black eyebrows rose. "Sounds dangerous."

"Her stallion? Yes. Make no mistake about it. Without Baby nearby, Devlin's Waterloo is as dangerous as a hand grenade with a loose pin."

"I'm surprised you let her ride a rogue."

" 'Let' has nothing to do with it. Baby is as stubborn as I am."

"And if you were any more proud of her,"

Johnstone said dryly, "you would strut sitting down."

Chandler-Smith laughed. "Guilty as charged. Baby has more brains and guts than most men I've worked with. Plenty of looks, too, but you'd never know it from that ID."

Wisely, Johnstone said nothing. Beauty was in the eye of the beholder. Obviously Chandler-Smith looked at his youngest daughter with a blinding kind of love.

"You'll be paired with Kentucky again," Chandler-Smith continued. "He'll guard the motor home when you're not inside."

Johnstone nodded. "He's a good man."

"He said the same about you."

"What about Bonner?"

"He's still undercover." Chandler-Smith hesitated, then almost smiled at the ingrained reflex of secrecy. If he couldn't trust the black-haired man sitting in front of the desk, Chandler-Smith was a dead man. Literally. "We're hearing rumors . . ."

Though Johnstone didn't move, he changed the same way a lion changes at the scent of game. "I'm listening."

Chandler-Smith didn't doubt it. The other man's eyes burned with an intensity that would have made most people uneasy. It didn't bother Chandler-Smith. He wouldn't

10

tolerate men around him unless they had the patience, intelligence, and concentration of a supreme predator.

"The man you call Barracuda has been making noises about killing me," Chandler-Smith said calmly.

"He's been doing that since you broke up his cozy little terrorist college in East Bumblefuck, Lebanon."

"Actually, you were the one doing the shooting."

"Shooters are a dime a dozen. Strategists aren't."

Johnstone was much more than a shooter, and no one knew it better than his boss. But Chandler-Smith didn't argue the point any more than he tried to convince Johnstone to give up the field for a desk job. For the past eight years, Johnstone had turned down every promotion that had come his way. When asked why, he simply said, *I'm no good at desks. If I ever get out, I'll get all the way out.*

Chandler-Smith knew that someday — if Johnstone survived — he would burn out. Everyone who stayed in the field did. But until that day came, he was the best agent Chandler-Smith had ever had.

"If you were Barracuda, how would you kill me?" Chandler-Smith asked.

"Do I want to live to tell the tale?"

"You must. I'm still alive."

Johnstone smiled thinly. He knew better than most people just how impossible it was to protect against a terrorist who was willing to give his life to take a life. Fortunately, very few of them were. They wanted to kill and brag, not kill and die.

"I'd grab one of your daughters," Johnstone said, "swap her for you, and kill you. Probably her, too."

Chandler-Smith nodded. "That's what I figured."

"Question is, has Barracuda figured it?" Johnstone retorted. "And is he willing to take the risk?"

"The answer to the first question is yes. As for the second . . ." Chandler-Smith shrugged. "I'm betting he is. He dropped out of sight six days ago."

"Not good," Johnstone said succinctly.

"Tell me about it. Lorraine and the older girls are under lock and key, but Baby Lorraine is different." He grimaced. "I can't take her out of the game without taking her out of the Olympics. I won't do that. Not on the evidence we have now."

"You have an asset in Barracuda's organization. Start twisting him."

"I am."

"Twist harder."

"Bonner is working on it, up close and very, very personal. But until I get something solid, I won't pull Baby out of the Summer Games. Hell, I'm not even sure I could. She's an adult."

"In that case she'll listen to you, weigh the danger to herself, and withdraw."

Chandler-Smith gave a crack of laughter. "She's an event rider, not a bloody dressage artist. The kind of riding she does is more dangerous than getting on a brahma bull at a rodeo."

"Then don't watch her."

"I'm not following you."

"Barracuda has wanted you for years. There are two reasons he hasn't gotten you. The first is that he doesn't want to die. The second is that your movements have never — repeat, *never* — been predictable. If you insist on being there for Baby's ride, he won't have to go to the trouble of kidnapping her. You'll be putting yourself right in his sniper scope."

"That's where you come in."

"You're taller than I am," Johnstone said matter-of-factly. "I'd make a lousy shield."

"Don't worry. I'm not planning to pull a Charles DeGaulle and surround myself with taller men. But you have the best eye for evaluating attack-ambush terrain that I've ever seen. I want you to go to California, reconnoiter the Olympic sites at Santa Anita and San Diego, and choose the safest place for me to watch my daughter ride."

"A motel room with a big TV. In London."

"No. Not this time. Come hell or high water, I'm going to be at the Olympics for Baby."

"Is it worth dying for?"

"It's worth *living* for," Chandler-Smith said simply. "I've missed too much of fatherhood, disappointed my kids too many times. Especially Baby. By the time she came along, most of my life required a security clearance for access. I owe the Olympics to her. I owe it to myself. I'm going."

Johnstone knew his boss too well to argue. He looked at his watch, subtracted three hours for West Coast time, and stood up. "I'll make plane reservations."

"Don't bother." Chandler-Smith pulled out a fat brown envelope and tossed it on the desk. "Tickets, new ID, everything you need is here."

"Who am I this time?"

"I didn't look. Does it matter?"

"No. When will Kentucky arrive in California?"

"He already has."

With a curt nod, Johnstone turned to leave.

"Robert?" Chandler-Smith said.

Johnstone turned back, and was treated to the rare sight of his boss's genuine, warm smile.

"Shave, would you?" Chandler-Smith asked. "Even without the brown contacts, you still look like a Lebanese terrorist. Baby will take one look at you and run screaming."

"She wouldn't be the first."

CHAPTER 1

Rancho Santa Fe

Rancho Santa Fe's tawny hills rolled gently up from the broad sand beaches of the Pacific Ocean. Many hills wore crowns of expensive houses whose windows and walls of glass were molten gold in the late-afternoon light. The cool salt smell of the sea mingled with the scent of wild grass cured by hot southern California days.

A riverbed that rarely held water twisted through dry hills and ravines, eucalyptus trees and granite outcroppings. Patches of the Fairbanks Ranch Country Club's emerald golf course remained along the riverbed, making a startling contrast with the brown hillsides. Manmade obstacles of wood, rock, and water crisscrossed the riverbed and climbed the hills.

It was the obstacles, not the quiet beauty of the land, that held Raine Chandler-Smith's attention.

Yesterday she had marched at the Los Angeles Coliseum, joining the colorful, uniformed ranks of athletes from around the world who had traveled thousands of miles to compete in the Summer Olympics. Yesterday she had been one among thousands surrounded by rippling multicolored flags and dazzling Hollywood-style ceremonies. Yesterday she had been enthralled, humbled, and excited to be part of a tradition that was as old as Western civilization.

Today Raine was alone.

Today she was measuring obstacles that had been created for the sole purpose of testing the skill, stamina, and trust that existed between herself and her horse. The three-day event was to riders what the pentathlon was to traditional athletes — the ultimate test.

Even while her eyes and mind traced the dangerous course, she breathed in deeply, savoring the strange scents of the land around her. Raised in Virginia and Europe, she found the dryness of a southern California summer both alien and compelling. The combination of odors was clean, haunting, older than civilization or man, as old as hills and sea and sunlight combined.

She looked over the countryside again, then stretched and shifted the weight of her

18

knapsack. The water bottle inside gurgled companionably. When she walked forward, her camera's long lens and binoculars knocked lightly against each other below her breasts. She took a few more steps, winced, and decided it was finally time to remove the pebble from her hiking shoe.

With a supple, easy movement she balanced on one foot while she removed one shoe and probed for the pebble that had been abusing her arch. She made a graceful line as she stood there like a beige flamingo at rest, but she would have been the last person to describe herself as graceful.

When she had been eleven years old and just becoming aware of herself as a woman, she was five feet, seven and three-quarters inches of angular female who despaired of ever being as at ease on the ground as she was on a horse's back. Because the picture in her mirror never seemed to change, no matter what efforts she made to be more like her gorgeous older sisters, Raine had stopped looking in the mirror. Instead, she concentrated on the one thing she was good at, the thing she had been born to do.

She rode horses over jumps that were taller and much harder than she was.

At twenty-seven, Raine was lithe and gently curved. She had a woman's smooth strength and the poise of a rider who regularly entered and won world-class competitions. Yet she still thought of herself as a little awkward and relentlessly average in looks. Medium brownish hair, medium brownish eyes, and medium brownish figure was the way she summed up herself when she thought about it.

Raine rarely thought about it anymore. She had spent too much of her youth trying to be as beautiful and as accomplished as her much older siblings. She had failed.

A gawky brown hen simply couldn't compete with the pair of tawny swans who were her sisters. One of them was a partner in a powerful law firm and a senator's wife. The other sister was a leading lady on Broadway. Her two older brothers were also successful. One was a diplomat and the other a neurosurgeon.

When Raine was five, she pleaded and demanded and persisted until her parents gave her riding lessons. After that, life became easier for the whole family. Riding was an elegant solution to the problem of what to do with Baby Lorraine. Or Raine, as she insisted on being called, as soon as she realized that her given name was "secondhand."

Horses gave her a way to be first.

There was an elemental rapport between her and the big animals. Horses were her life's work and love. When she was riding, she forgot to feel awkward and inadequate. She merged herself with the rhythms of her horse and the demands of the jumps. There was a fantastic exhilaration in flying over fences and obstacles on the back of her huge blood-bay stallion. Only then was she wholly free, wholly alive, wholly herself.

"But if I don't get to work instead of daydreaming," she told herself as she retied her shoe, "I'll end up flat on my back in the dirt, instead of flying over jumps. The cross-country part of this endurance event looks rougher than anything I've ever taken Dev over."

Picking up the binoculars again, she focused on the dry riverbed twisting along the base of the hill. After a few minutes she pulled a pad out of her rucksack, sketched in the line of river and hills, and scuffed at the ground beneath her feet. Nothing gave beneath her prodding toe.

She bent and yanked at a handful of grass until some of it pulled free. Beneath the thatch of tight, incredibly tough roots, the ground was rough and dry. It was made up of tight clods of clay and small stones. She sifted out some of the pebbles and kept them in her left hand, fiddling with them as she tried to absorb the reality of the ground through touch as well as sight and smell.

Dry, very dry, but not really hard going. Frowning, she made notes along the margin of the sketch. The surface would change radically if it rained. The clay looked like it would be lethally slick if it ever got wet. But no storms had been forecast for the Olympics. From the look of the land, she didn't doubt that it would stay the way it was. Dry.

After another long, slow look at the river-bed, she put the small sketch pad back in her rucksack. Absently juggling the pebbles she still held in her hand, she stood on the crest of the hill and thought about the Olympic Games to come, wondering how the hills would look wearing clusters of people as well as houses.

From time to time she threw away one of the small stones until finally all the pebbles were gone. Her palm felt dry from the thirsty rocks. As she rubbed her hand on her pants, she hoped it wouldn't be too hot for the three-day event. Heat sapped a horse's strength even more than a rider's. No matter how hot it became, the horse was stuck wearing a fur coat.

"At least it isn't humid," she muttered.

"That would be a killer. But this . . . I like this."

That surprised her. The arid land that should have been so alien to her felt instead like a home she had forgotten or never known.

Smiling at the odd thought, she brushed off her fingers, raised her camera, and went to work. Delicately she adjusted the very long telephoto lens and took a series of overlapping photos. Once developed, the slides would make a panorama of the part of the Fairbanks Ranch Country Club that had been torn up and given over to the Summer Games.

Frowning, far from satisfied, she lowered the camera. Photos were better than nothing, but not good enough. What she really needed was to walk the course itself. But she couldn't. All the endurance-event competitors would walk the course for the first time, together, the day before their ride.

Ten days from today. Just ten days until the event that would be both climax and close of a lifetime of work.

Raine didn't know what she would do after the Olympics. She only knew that it would be something different. She was ready to step off the glittering, grueling carousel of international competition. In the past three years, the idea of raising and training event horses had come to her more and more frequently. Devlin's Waterloo was a stallion to build a future on. Earning a medal in the Olympics would go a long way toward making her silent dreams come true.

Wind combed through the grass around her, whispering of rain that didn't come for months on end. She closed her eyes, trying to absorb the essence of the strange, beautiful land. Never in her life had she ridden over such dry ground. It worried her that she wouldn't have the same instinctive understanding of the terrain that she had on the East Coast or in Britain or France.

But there was no help for it. Until the day before the endurance event, she would have to be satisfied with learning what she could at a distance.

Her lips curved in an ironic smile. Somehow it was fitting that the most important contest of her life should find her on the outside looking in. She had spent her years like that, watching the world at a distance. Most of the time she preferred it that way. Sometimes, though, when she heard lovers laugh softly, saw them touch each other as though they were more precious than gold, a man bending down to his woman, smiling . . .

Abruptly Raine picked up the binoculars again. She had no illusions about her chance of finding a mate. As many men had told her with varying degrees of anger, she was too damned particular about her sex partners. The few times she finally had succumbed to loneliness had left her feeling worse about herself as a woman than before.

Get over it, she told herself coolly. *The only kind of riding you're good at is on a horse.*

For long minutes she scanned the land below the crest of the hill. She hardly saw the rich honey sheen of sunlight on grass or the blue-black dance of shadows beneath the wind. She concentrated on a grove of eucalyptus, deciding that the smooth-trunked trees were rather like horses, huge yet graceful, powerful yet elegant.

She wondered if the drifts of dried leaves and peeling bark she saw at the base of the trees would be slippery or if the ground itself would be damp. She couldn't tell from where she was and she couldn't get any closer without crossing the Olympic boundary markers.

Damn.

Raine looked through the glasses at the dense shadows and the gray-green leaves shimmering in the late-afternoon light. So near and yet so far . . .

Story of my life.
She lowered the glasses and turned away.

Deep in the eucalyptus grove, concealed by shadows and by the absolute stillness of his body, Cord Elliot waited for the woman's attention to pass over the grove.

Over him.

Even when she turned and disappeared beyond the crest of the hill, he didn't move. He crouched in the fragrant shadows and waited for a long sixty count.

When no one reappeared at the top of the hill, he stood in a smooth, controlled movement. Even standing, he was still concealed by trees. He listened with the concentration of a man whose life depended on the acuteness of his senses. He heard nothing but the slow sound of grass, breeze, and leaves.

After a moment Cord flowed out of the grove, moving with the silent ease of a shadow. His sand-colored bush jacket and jeans blended completely with the tawny grass. Even his binoculars were dun colored. He walked up the sloping hill, choosing a shallow ravine that would bring him out just behind the place his target had stood.

Using every bit of natural cover, he climbed swiftly until he was just below the crest of the hill. Then he dropped flat and eased up to the top. He made certain that his head never rose higher than ripe grass swaying in the wind. His black hair would be easily spotted against the golden hillside.

His pale blue glance raked the downhill side, searching for the woman who was entirely too curious about the site of the Olympic endurance event. A quick glance revealed no one moving over the land. A second slower glance didn't do any better.

All right, honey. Where did that nice smooth walk take you? he thought grimly. *Over by those boulders?*

No, not enough time. The next grove, then?

His eyes narrowed as he saw her on her knees in the grass. *Why are you kneeling there? What are you doing?*

Cord checked the location of the sun. No help there. If he lifted the binoculars, sunlight would flash off the lenses, giving his location away. For now he would have to be content with his own excellent vision.

Holes. She was digging holes.

Why? What choice piece of hell are you planting? And why there?

The tactician in Cord knew that the most effective place to put a bomb would be on the event course itself, where the horses would come thundering by, exhausted and yet still game, running their hearts out because they were born to do it and because their riders were there every step of the way, as tired and tough as their horses.

Is that what you're after? He watched the kneeling woman through narrowed, glittering eyes. *Do you ache to kill something that's stronger and better than you'll ever be? Or will you be happy just turning the spectators into a hell's kitchen of dead and dying?*

There was no answer to Cord's questions except the one given by his own experience.

It wasn't a comforting answer.

Motionless, he lay just below the crest of the hill, watching. Waiting. It was all he could do for the moment. As soon as the woman turned her back on him, he would come down off the hill and ask her some questions.

And she would answer every one of them.

Slowly Raine stood up. She let the last fragrant eucalyptus leaves crumble between her fingers and drift away in the fitful wind. Absently she brushed off her khaki slacks and faded chambray blouse. The pungent scent of eucalyptus still clung to her like an invisible shadow, mingling with the summer scent of grass and heat.

The good news, she decided, as she looked at the dusty earth, was that it wouldn't get

28

muddy under the trees, no matter how many horses galloped through. The land was dry all the way to its stony, enduring soul. With new respect and appreciation, she stared up into the towering crown of a nearby eucalyptus.

"It's a long time between drinks for you, isn't it?" she asked whimsically. "You could give lessons to a camel. Makes me thirsty just thinking about it."

Without looking away from the tree, she reached into her rucksack for her water bottle.

At the same instant something big slammed into her back, knocking her off her feet. Dazed, totally unprepared, she let her riding reflexes take over and fell loosely, rolling with the impact rather than fighting it. Even so, the breath was knocked out of her.

By the time she could breathe again, she was flat on her face in the leaves and dust, pinned to the ground by a heavy weight. Her binoculars, camera, and rucksack had been stripped away.

She tried to get up, only to be knocked flat again.

"Don't move." The male voice was cold, flat.

Instinctively she obeyed.

Then Raine felt hands moving over her body with a familiarity that no man had dared in years. Even as she stiffened, she realized that for all its intimacy, the man's touch was impersonal. He might have been feeling her, but he wasn't groping her.

Her world spun crazily when the man flipped her over and laid her flat again. She felt the hard muscular weight of his leg pinning her own legs to the ground, the iron power of his forearm against her throat. As long as she was utterly still, she could breathe.

If she moved at all she would choke.

Lying on her back, fighting panic, she stared up into the unyielding planes of her attacker's face. Swiftly his free hand moved over her shoulders, under her arms, over her breasts and her stomach, between her thighs. She made a guttural, involuntary sound, fear and anger and protest squeezed into one hoarse syllable.

A winter-blue glance raked over her face while the man's hand continued down her body to her right ankle and yanked off her shoe. He repeated the process on her left leg. Then he tossed both shoes beyond her reach. They landed on top of the knapsack, binoculars, and camera, which he had also thrown aside.

stunning as being knocked off her feet.

"You might not like my suggestions," she said, forcing herself to speak, to push away the sultry, drugging heat stealing through her body. "You hear a lot of names around the stables. Especially during competition."

"Olympic rider, hmmm?" Cord asked in a low voice, looking at the lithe body lying so quietly half beneath his. He was almost positive he knew who and what she was, but the difference between almost and positive had killed a lot of people.

"Yes," she said coolly. "My specialty is the three-day event."

"That explains why you fell all relaxed and controlled, yet you didn't know how to counter the simplest unarmed combat. You're a product of very civilized training, not Cuban or Lebanese commando camps."

"Commando camps?" she asked in a rising voice. The drugging intimacy vanished as though it had never existed. Suddenly she was afraid she was in the hands of a madman after all.

"Don't sound so shocked. They exist."

"What are you talking about?"

"Terrorism."

Cord answered almost absently. His attention had been caught by the soft swell of she's breasts when she breathed in

"Name."

It took her a moment to connect the man's curt command with the information he wanted from her. "Raine."

"Last name."

"Smith." She swallowed, trying to ease the dryness of her mouth.

"What are you doing here."

She closed her eyes and fought to control the chemical storm in her blood. She was used to dealing with adrenaline. The first thing any competitor learned was how to control the body's response to stress.

The second thing competitors learned was how to think under intense pressure. She began thinking very quickly, and just as quickly decided if the man was going to hurt her, he would be doing so, not asking her questions.

Fury replaced fear. Her eyes opened clear and very hard. "Who the hell are you?"

The man's powerful forearm moved slightly, cutting off her air. The pressure ended almost as soon as it began. Pale eyes watched her to see if she had taken the hint.

She had. The next time she spoke, it was to answer his question.

"I'm looking at the country," she said through clenched teeth.

"Why."

No inflection, just the same flat demand that had characterized the man's every word.

"I'm an Olympic rider."

Something flickered in the man's eyes. "Prove it."

His voice was still flat, yet even as he spoke, his body changed subtly, becoming somehow less . . . predatory.

"I left Dev at Santa Anita," Raine said curtly. Her voice was thinned by anger and the aftermath of fear.

"Dev?" For the first time, inflection and curiosity humanized the man's voice.

"Devlin's Waterloo. My horse."

"Describe it."

"Seventeen and a half hands high, stallion, blood-bay with no white, three-quarters thoroughbred and the rest either Irish or —"

"Good enough, Raine *Smith,*" the man broke in, giving an odd emphasis to her last name.

His body changed as he looked down at her, becoming less hard and more forgiving, less impersonal and more male. He moved his arm, releasing her neck from restraint.

But he didn't remove the weight of his leg across hers. Nor did his wariness vanish. It was as much a part of him as the darkness at the center of his ice-blue eyes.

"As for who the hell I am," he said, smiling slightly, "you can call me Cord Elliot."

He could have added that she barely resembled her Olympic ID photo. The photographer should have been shot. Or hanged. The photo had completely missed the intelligence and vulnerability in her extraordinary hazel eyes, the seductive curve of her lips, the feminine strength in the line of her jaw.

Close up, there was no doubt that this was Chandler-Smith's daughter. Well . . . not much doubt. In Cord's world, nothing was one hundred percent sure but death.

"If you don't want to call me Cord, I'm open to suggestion," he added, amused.

Raine stared up at him, fascinated by the countless warm glints of blue in his eye. When she breathed in, she smelled the the grass, and the heat of another life to her. A very masculine kind of life.

Suddenly she was aware of Cord a all man, and all of that man was out alongside her. His body wa warm, quick and dangerous, was as thick and black as mane.

The feeling of intense

sharply. Distantly he registered and approved — the resilient warmth of her legs pinned beneath his thigh.

"Terrorism? That's ridiculous! Do I look like a terrorist?" she demanded angrily.

"No fangs, huh?" He smiled with grim humor. "Honey, the last terrorist I had my hands on was dressed in a yellow silk ball gown and stank of hate and cordite." When he saw Raine's confusion, he added helpfully, "Cordite is explosive powder."

"*She?*" Raine repeated, her voice rising again. "The terrorist was a *woman?*"

"Men don't have a corner on violence."

"But —"

Cord continued talking as though she hadn't interrupted. "You don't smell like a terrorist."

His glance moved over her more intimately than his hands had when he frisked her for weapons. He brought his head closer to her neck and inhaled slowly. The scent of her went through him like sunrise, warm with promise.

"You smell of sunlight and dried grass and the shadows beneath eucalyptus trees," he said in a low voice. She smelled of other things too, sultry woman heat and the sweet musk of sexuality, but he doubted she would like hearing it right now.

Raine saw the small, sensual flare of his nostrils as he breathed in her scent. She found herself holding her breath like an amateur rider approaching a big fence. She felt defenseless, angry, utterly disturbed.

So she challenged Cord recklessly, willing to risk his anger in order to escape his consuming sensuality. "Even if some terrorists are women, what harm could I possibly be doing out here alone?"

"Setting bombs."

"That's ridiculous."

"What were you scattering around?"

The question was offhanded, as though he didn't really care about the answer. But his eyes were ice clear, ruthless as winter. The difference between almost sure and absolutely certain was never far from his mind. Death was damned final.

Raine sensed the intensity beneath Cord's casual pose. He was like Dev gathered for a blind jump, waiting for a signal from his rider.

"Little stones," she said quickly. "I was throwing little stones. It's a habit. I go for walks and pick up small stones and toss them as I think." Then she added hotly, "There was no reason to tackle me! I don't have room in my rucksack for bombs."

Even though Chandler-Smith's determination to protect his family from his work was legendary, Cord couldn't believe that Blue's daughter was so naive.

"Det cord and explosive caps don't take up much space," he said impatiently. "Neither does C4 or even phosphorus, for that matter. Your knapsack could even hold a stick or five of good old-fashioned dynamite. All the things that go boom in the night." His voice shifted, becoming clipped and hard. "Why were you digging?"

"To see what the going is like."

Cord's only response was a silence that had the effect of making her want to explain herself. That listening kind of silence was a very potent interrogation technique. He had used it often enough to value it. If Raine was as innocent as she seemed, she would hurry to explain what she meant.

"I wanted to know whether the ground is hard or soft," she said, "dry or wet, how stable the soil is, what to expect on a downhill run when Dev's hooves cut in deep. That sort of thing."

"You weren't going to set little explosives?"

"Why would anyone —"

"So that when the horses come down the hill they have a preview of hell," he cut in coldly.

Shocked, she could only stare. "Injure the horses? No one would be that sick!"

He looked at her for a long moment. If the horror and innocence in her eyes were faked, he was a dead man. If they weren't faked, Blue should have his butt kicked through every room in the Pentagon for sheltering his youngest child from too much of the dark side of reality.

When Cord finally spoke, his voice was both cynical and very tired. "If you believe that, little girl, you shouldn't be let out alone after dark. Remember the Munich Olympics? If you're too young to recall that bloodbath, how about the IRA bombing the Queen's Palace Guard? Great bleeding chunks of men and horses all over the place."

"Stop it!" she whispered in a strangled voice, horrified by his words.

"I'm trying to."

"By tackling strange women?"

"Whatever it takes," he said flatly.

Raine looked at his cold, measuring eyes and realized just how lucky she was that Cord's self-control matched his lethal skills. At least, she hoped it did. When all was said and done, she was still pinned like a butterfly to the hard earth.

And the man doing the pinning wasn't in any hurry to let her go.

CHAPTER 2

Cord gave Raine a long, searching look. His gut said she was telling the truth. Past experience wasn't nearly as trusting. There was still that three percent of error. Not very much, really.

Just enough to kill him.

He shifted his body, easing the weight of his leg over hers, but not quite freeing her. If she tensed for a sudden movement, he would feel it instantly.

Raine didn't take advantage of her apparent freedom. She simply waited, watching Cord's angular face. Beneath his impassive expression, she sensed a ruthless, sweeping intelligence. He was measuring her in a way that was totally unfamiliar to her.

After a few moments she saw the subtle shift of his heavy black eyebrows, the easing of the tension around his icy blue eyes, the relaxation of the hard line of his mouth. Whatever danger she might have been in from him was finally past.

In the wake of relief came the realization of just how terribly vulnerable she had been. If Cord Elliot had been another kind of man, she would have been another mutilated, violated body on the six o'clock news.

She began shaking, a reaction to being knocked off her feet and flattened helplessly beneath a stranger's merciless trained body. Though she fought to control herself, a small whimper escaped. She shuddered again and again, raging at her own lack of self-control but unable to do anything about it.

The trembling of Raine's body told Cord that her shock at being overwhelmed and held captive had worn off. She knew she was safe now, but she was thinking of what had just happened.

And what could have happened.

A fragile glimmer of tears magnified the green and gold of her dark hazel eyes. Her mouth trembled despite its flat line. Ripples of fear moved visibly over her clear skin.

An odd feeling of shame grew in him — odd because he had simply been doing his job in the safest, most efficient manner he knew. She could have been reaching for a weapon in her rucksack. That was why he had knocked her down.

Yet even though his act had been fully justified according to the terms of the world he lived in, Cord felt as though he had violated Raine in a fundamental way.

Because he had.

Between one instant and the next, he had given her a terrifying demonstration of just how frail her security and her world really were, how vulnerable she was, how unexpected and dangerous life could be. It was a cruelty that he regretted, however necessary it might have been at the time.

And now she was lying very close to him, her eyes wide and her lips pale, her hands clenched as she fought not to reveal how badly she had been shaken.

I'm sorry, Blue, Cord thought almost helplessly. *You were right. She's worth protecting. There's too much darkness already, too much cold.*

When Raine bit her lip against another cry, he couldn't take it anymore. Knowing he shouldn't, going ahead anyway, he gathered her close against his body. His hands were gentle rather than hard. His strength cherished rather than threatened her. Long, lean fingers stroked her hair. He spoke to her in a voice that was deep, calming, and his arms were a solid barrier protecting her from the vulnerability he had just demonstrated so graphically to her.

"It's all right," he murmured, smoothing her tangled hair with his palm. He tucked her head against his chest, holding her close without really confining her. Comfort, not captivity. "I won't hurt you. And I'm damned sorry I frightened you. You're safe with me, always. I promise you, Raine."

She could no more control her reaction to his offer of protection than she could control the shudders wracking her body. Her hands came up to his chest and her fingers dug into his skirt, seeking the resilience and strength beneath cloth. His words ran together, becoming a soothing, dark velvet sound that sank beneath her fear, reassuring her mind even as his strength reassured her body.

He had showed her how fragile her safe world really was. The knowledge that he would also protect her was a relief even greater than her fear had been.

With a last shuddering breath, Raine brought herself under control. As she looked up at Cord, tears made silver trails through the dust of her cheeks. She felt his sudden breath, saw his eyes change, dark centers expanding as he memorized her features and the shine of tears on her skin. Warm fingers slid beneath her tangled hair as he

43

bent and gently kissed the tears caught in her eyelashes.

"I'm so sorry." His voice was husky. "I wish to hell I hadn't frightened you. Raine . . . such a beautiful name, beautiful eyes, beautiful spirit . . ."

His mouth brushed over hers so lightly that she thought she had imagined it. But she didn't imagine the silver glimmer of her tears on his lips, the subtle tightening of his body against hers, and the warm flush of sensation spreading beneath her skin. Her breath caught in a way that had nothing to do with fear. A shiver snaked through her body, heat rather than chill.

He felt her involuntary tremor. He lifted his head and looked at her with pale, intent eyes. "Are you all right?"

She nodded, afraid to trust her voice. Then, hesitantly, she whispered, "I'm sorry."

He smoothed tendrils of rich brown hair away from her face. "For what?"

"Being such a — such a child."

"We're all children when we're taken by surprise."

"Not you."

Curiosity expanded the blue-black centers of Cord's eyes. She was so certain of him, as though she had read his file. Yet he knew she hadn't. "What do you mean?"

"No one has taken you by surprise in a long time." Her voice was soft, positive.

"You did, just now." He looked at her with an intensity that was almost tangible. "You're an unusual woman, Raine Smith. Very unusual. And very beautiful."

Automatically she shook her head. Chestnut hair slid forward, tickling her full lower lip. With an impatient movement, she pushed the hair behind her ears. She didn't think of herself as attractive, much less beautiful. As far as she was concerned, if a man complimented her, it was meaningless flattery. Worse, it irritated her, as if men thought she was too dumb to look in a mirror and see the truth.

When Cord felt the withdrawal stiffening her body, he slowly released her, even though he wanted to hold her closer. Yet he sensed if he tried to hold her, she would fight him. She had every right to. He had no excuse to hang onto her now, except his own unexpected, consuming need to keep her close.

Reluctantly he forced himself to let go of her completely. He already felt as though he had pulled the wings off the most intriguing butterfly he had ever seen. He didn't want to feel like a rapist in the bargain.

Carefully Raine sat up, telling herself that

45

she was relieved not to be held anymore. She didn't really believe it. It was one thing to be attacked. It was quite another to be held as though she was as delicate and precious as fire.

Cord made no move to stop her from sitting up. But when she reached for her rucksack, his hand shot out and locked around her wrist.

She gasped and spun toward him.

He was looking at the knapsack beneath her hand. In the instant that she had reached for it, he remembered that he hadn't really searched the shapeless sack. It easily could conceal a weapon.

"You still don't trust me, do you?" she asked, surprise and disappointment in her voice.

He looked into her startled hazel eyes for a long moment. Then he slowly released her wrist, letting the soft flesh and delicate bones slide away unharmed.

"I'm ninety-seven percent sure you're who and what you say you are. The other three percent," he added matter-of-factly, "could be the death of me."

She snatched her hand back from the rucksack as though it had burned her. "I just wanted my comb."

"Then get it."

"No. You get it. And take your time. We'll both feel safer if you're one hundred percent sure."

"Nothing is one hundred percent sure but death."

His long arm reached past her. He started with her shoes, flexing the soles as he gave them to her. Finally he lifted the rucksack onto his lap and opened it.

While Raine put on her shoes, he rummaged through the contents of the blue bag, looking for her comb. He didn't come across anything suspicious. Certainly nothing dangerous. What she carried was as innocent as she was. Or seemed to be.

That damned three percent.

Lean fingers brushed against the sketch pad he had seen her using. His training demanded that he examine what she had written or drawn on the sheets, but still he hesitated. He didn't want to invade her privacy any more than he already had.

His own reaction surprised him. More accurately, it stunned him. In the past he had never been particularly fastidious when it came to searching, and that included body cavity searches. He did whatever it took to get the job done.

When Cord turned back to Raine, he had her comb in his right hand. In his left he had the small pad of paper. He held out the comb to her. He noted — as he noted all details, however small — that the comb was worn, had no missing teeth, and was clean but for some lint from the rucksack.

"May I?" he asked, holding up the sketch pad.

"Of course."

"There's no 'of course' about it. But thank you for allowing me to snoop."

"Like I said," she retorted, "we'll both feel better."

She took the comb from his hand and began to unsnarl her shoulder-length hair. She combed carefully, favoring her right arm, which had taken the full force of her fall. She ignored the aching of her upper arm. When necessary, she had ridden over jumps with cracked ribs, a mild concussion, and a stress fracture in her foot. A few bruises were nothing.

With fast, efficient movements Cord finished searching the knapsack. Then he gave his attention to the sketch pad. He flipped through it quickly, seeing everything with brief, encompassing looks. What he saw impressed him. Blue's daughter couldn't draw worth a damn, but she had a fine appreciation of the impact of geography on man and animals.

Thoughtfully Cord closed the pad and looked at her. Her hair had just enough natural curl to give it thickness, body, and a mind of its own. The curl showed as a stubborn tendency to turn up at the ends no matter how hard she tried to make everything lie straight. The slanting light brought out gold and red highlights, giving her hair a sun-shot appearance that made the underlying brown shimmer with life and warmth.

Raine wasn't nearly as fascinated by her hair as Cord was. She simply combed it, wincing occasionally over knots or when her bruised arm protested being used. There was more impatience than pain in her grimaces. The slippery flyaway mass of her hair crackled with the static electricity of dry, windy air.

"Ruddy hell," she muttered, making another futile pass with the comb.

Her irritation peaked when she finally managed to get one hand around all of her hair at once, then couldn't find the clip to hold everything in place. It must have gone flying when she was knocked to the ground with such stunning force. She glanced around, but couldn't see the clip anywhere.

Maybe Cord had it.

When she turned to him, he was watching her, the rucksack in his lap and the sketch pad forgotten in his hands. He had a be-mused, fully male smile on his face. She had never seen a man look at her quite like that. The realization that he enjoyed watching her comb her hair made her skin hot.

It wasn't embarrassment. Like his smile, the heat was something new to her.

"Well?" Raine asked, arching her left eyebrow. "Did you find the secrets of World War Three in my rucksack?"

"Water bottle, pencils, rawhide thongs, sketch pad, tape recorder, film, an apple, a chocolate bar, an elastic bandage, and a buckle."

"A buckle? Show me."

Cord reached into the knapsack and brought out a buckle no bigger than his thumbnail. Raine let go of her hair and leaned forward to see better. Wind sent strands of her hair over his fingers. It took an effort of will not to wind the silky stuff around his hand and pull her into his lap, into his arms. He wanted her with a force that shook him.

Yet nothing of his raw hunger showed. He made certain of it. If she had seen it, she would have scrambled up and run like hell.

"So that's where it went," she muttered. "I was polishing Dev's tack when Captain Jon called me. I didn't have time to put the buckle where it belonged and I didn't want to lose it, so I put it in a safe place."

"How long ago was that?" Cord asked. Laughter stirred just beneath the surface of his deep voice.

"Five weeks," she admitted. "I'm forever putting things in safe places and then forgetting where I put them. Captain Jon swears I need a keeper."

"Don't you have one?" Though Cord's voice was casual, his eyes were burning, intent. Blue hadn't mentioned a lover, but fathers weren't usually the first to know about such things, even fathers like Chandler-Smith.

"No. And if I did," Raine added in a crisp voice, "I'd lose him, too."

"That would depend on the man," Cord pointed out smoothly, smiling. But there was no laughter in his voice. Instead, there was a mixture of emotions that were too complex to separate or name.

Her eyes widened as she looked at the man who was so close to her, watching her with unnerving intensity. Self-consciously she lifted her right arm to push back the hair that kept wanting to fall across her shoulder — and his hand. The movement made her wince almost invisibly.

But he saw it. His pale eyes saw everything. "You're hurt."

"It's nothing," she said, meaning exactly that.

"Let me see."

"It's probably only a friction bruise."

He waited, his hand out. He radiated the kind of command that owed nothing to superior strength.

Grumbling, she pushed the faded blue sleeve of her shirt as far above her elbow as she could. "See?"

He saw that a red welt marked her fine-grained skin. The welt began a few inches above her elbow and disappeared beneath the bunched blue cloth. The shoulder seam was torn. It sagged downward, revealing the top of the welt. Tiny beads of blood glistened like red mist.

He hooked a finger in the torn seam and yanked quickly, giving her no time to protest. The cloth gave way as though made of smoke. When he saw the strip of scraped flesh, his lips flattened. He pulled a clean handkerchief from his pocket, wet the white square with water from the bottle in the rucksack, and held the cloth gently against her abraded skin.

"Hurt?" he asked, watching her eyes.

She started to speak, swallowed, and shook her head, caught by the guilt she sensed in him.

"It's all right." Lightly she touched his sleeve. The tension and hard muscle beneath the sand-colored cloth was almost shocking. "Cord? I do much worse to myself twice a week."

"But you didn't do this to yourself. I did."

There was nothing she could say to that, so she watched silently while he worked on her arm. The contrast between the masculine power of his shoulders and the exquisite tenderness of his fingers as he cleaned the abrasion sent unfamiliar sensations shivering through her. She looked at his black hair and icy blue eyes, his angular face, and the sensual curve of his mouth, and she wondered how this man could so thoroughly frighten and then so completely reassure her in the space of a few minutes.

Cord glanced up and saw Raine watching him. He let his fingers slide slowly from her inner elbow to the pulse beating beneath the soft skin on the inside of her wrist.

"Forgive me?" he asked.

"Of course," she whispered, knowing it was true, but not knowing why.

"I don't have any antiseptic." He looked at the red abrasion. "I suppose I could use the oldest remedy."

"What's that?"

"Kiss it and make it well." His voice was as deep as the shadows pooling beneath the fragrant trees.

Her lips parted slightly with surprise and an invitation that she wasn't even aware of.

"But," he continued, his voice dark and smooth, flowing over her, sinking into her, "when I kiss you, it won't be like a parent kissing a child. It will be very healing, though. For both of us."

Raine felt her pulse leap beneath Cord's fingertips and knew that he felt it, too. She glanced away quickly, confused by her response to him. She wasn't the type to lose control of herself merely because a good-looking man had touched her wrist and talked about kissing her.

Then she realized that it wasn't his looks that made her pulse leap. It was his unexpected gentleness that unnerved her, the danger and the strength and the yearning in him, a hunger that called to depths in her that she hadn't known existed.

Until now.

He lifted the wet cloth, examined her arm again, and said matter-of-factly, "We'll clean it better tonight. Are you through here?"

She was off-balance, unable to answer, caught between his assumption that he would be with her tonight and his quick question. Wryly she realized that it would be a useful technique for controlling a conversation. Or an interrogation. First you throw in an assumption that might or might not be correct and then you follow it immediately with a totally unrelated question. The person answering the question is caught between protesting the assumption and fielding the question.

So rather than challenge the assumption, Raine answered the question, and then realized she had just accepted that Cord would be with her that night. Just as she had accepted his statement that he would kiss her, and by accepting it, had all but invited him to do just that.

"That's pretty slick," she said, feeling outmaneuvered but not particularly resentful.

"Thank you," he said, smiling. "You're pretty quick yourself."

Her left eyebrow lifted in silent skepticism. "Next to you, I'm real slow. And I'm not through here. There's at least one more hilltop I have to cover."

"That way?" he asked, gesturing toward the empty hills and twisting ravine.

"Not quite. It's a case of look but don't touch, at least until the day before the event. So," she said, pointing toward a hilltop that was not inside the Olympic course markers, "I'll have to settle for that one."

"Will you finish before dark?"

"Yes."

"Pity," he said, his eyes watching her instead of the land. "I'll bet this place is dynamite by moonlight."

Her expression changed as she remembered the brutal uses terrorists had for dynamite.

"Sorry. Bad choice of words," he said. "Let's go."

As he stood, he took her left hand and pulled her easily upright. They spotted her missing hair clip at the same instant. With startling swiftness, he scooped it up before she could do more than reach toward the barrette.

"I'll take care of it," he said, stepping behind her.

He caught her hair in his right hand and clipped the chestnut mass in place with his left. When he was finished, he gently, slowly stroked her gold-shot hair.

Raine froze beneath the caress as every female nerve ending she had came to full alert. She felt the faint humid warmth of Cord's breath on her neck, and a delicate touch that could have been his lips.

"Your hair smells like sunlight," he said,

his voice husky. Then, as though he had said nothing at all, he asked, "Where do we go from here?"

She turned and stared at him, off-balance once more. He had outmaneuvered her again, only this time the assumption was buried in the question. *We.* Where do *we* go from here? Talk about an open-ended, fully loaded question . . .

She was too smart to touch it. The problem was, she wanted to touch Cord. She didn't know why, but she knew how much.

Too much.

Gathering what was left of her concentration, Raine bent over to pick up her rucksack. Cord beat her to it, swinging the sack up easily over one shoulder. He picked her camera and binoculars off the ground and put the straps around her neck. The pad and pencil appeared in his hand again.

"You handle the camera," he said. "I'll take care of the sketches."

"That bad, huh?" she asked, amused. She knew that her sketches were awkward and all but unreadable to anyone but herself. Captain Jon told her frequently.

"Let's just say that you don't threaten Da Vinci."

"Do you?"

"You can tell me tonight, when you look

at my, um, sketches after dinner."

"Mr. Elliot," she began, determination plain in the lines of her face and her tone of voice.

"Aren't you hungry after all your walking around?" he asked, before she could say any more.

"Of course, but —"

"Good," he cut in smoothly. "You drive me to Santa Anita and I'll buy you dinner. Fair trade, don't you think?"

"But —"

"All right, two dinners," he said quickly, smiling down at her. "You drive a hard bargain, lady. And my name is Cord, not Mr. Elliot."

Raine's teeth clicked together in frustration. She hadn't felt so overmatched since the time years before when she took on both her older sisters at once. It had been a learning experience.

"Lead me to your hilltop," Cord said. Subdued laughter made his voice even deeper than it usually was. Then the laughter slid away, leaving only hunger, an intensity burning in him as he watched her. "If you want me to leave, I will. But I'd much rather stay. I'll be good. I promise you."

Slanting light fell across his eyes, making the countless splinters of blue within the ice-pale irises glitter like a fine diamond. Against the angular male planes of his face, his eyes seemed impossibly vivid, fringed in lashes as dense and dark as midnight.

With an effort Raine forced herself to look away from him. She had come out here to learn about the land, not a man. Even one as compelling as Cord Elliot.

Gradually she saw the countryside rather than the man. The hills were empty, the houses few and distant. Twilight was slowly welling up from nameless ravines, shadow pools spreading and joining, forerunners of the darkness to come.

Suddenly she was glad Cord was with her. Intentionally or not, he had yanked her out of her cozy, civilized world of equestrian competition. It had been a harsh reminder that there was another, much larger and colder world out there, a barbarian world where violence rather than safety was the rule.

"What about your work, whatever it may be?" she asked finally. "Don't you have something you have to do?"

"My work is the same as yours."

She spun back toward him, unable to hide her astonishment. "You're a rider?"

"Not in the way you mean, not anymore." The corner of his mouth lifted in a half-smile. He had been a rider once, broncs and mustangs and tough little cowponies, the sort of horses Raine had never ridden and probably never even seen. "But we're both here for the same kind of work today — a quick recon of the cross-country course."

"If you're not a rider, what are you looking for?"

"Places to hide and seek, fields of fire and radio dead spaces, sniper angles and ambush sites."

Cord's casual acceptance of such violence shocked Raine. She watched uneasily while he took a very small walkie-talkie unit out of his hip pocket, extended the telescoping antenna, and spoke quietly.

"Thorne?" he said clearly. "Another hour. Same place." Pause. "Right."

Raine didn't understand the crackling that came from the flat black rectangle, but Cord did. He collapsed the antenna and replaced the unit in his pocket. Then he took her hand and set off toward a nearby hill. Its top overlooked the dry riverbed that wound through the Olympic endurance course.

"What sort of things does a rider look for?" he asked.

She was walking right next to him, but she didn't really hear his question. She was still caught in the moment of stunned understanding when she realized the kind of world he lived in, a place where violence and treachery were expected rather than shocking.

It was the world of her father.

It was a world she hated.

It was a world she had vowed never to enter again.

"Raine?" Cord asked, wondering at the look on her face.

She took a deep breath and began talking, telling him about riding the three-day event. And wondering why she bothered. The routine of her life could hardly have been more alien to him if he had stepped off a flying saucer.

"Today, I'm just trying to get a feel for the country. It's not at all like Virginia," she added wryly, looking at the sunburned hills.

Cord's glance was quick, penetrating, but all he said was, "You don't have a southern accent."

"My father is with the government. I've lived in too many places to have any kind of accent at all."

Exclusive boarding schools also didn't encourage accents, but Raine didn't go into that. Wealth was the least of the things that separated her from the man who could make her pulse stutter with a word, a touch, a glance.

"What kind of thing are you looking for?" he asked. "Maybe I can help."

She hesitated, then shrugged. "I'd know what to expect if twenty horses went over the Virginia hills in front of me, but a dry land is different." She frowned. "I'll probably have to tape Dev's legs more heavily than usual. In some places here the going will be harder than he's used to."

"Watch the water jumps. There's a lot of clay around. Slippery as sin."

She looked at Cord. "Are you sure you aren't a rider?"

"Not professionally, not since I was eighteen."

"You're too big to be a jockey," she said, assessing his six-foot-plus height. "Strong shoulders and legs, steady hands, and great coordination. Did you hunt?"

His lips curved in silent laughter. "Yes, but not the way you mean. I ate what I shot, and when I rode, it was for pay as well as pleasure. Rodeo."

Intrigued, she waited for him to say more about his past. When he didn't, she asked, "Why did you give it up?"

"Vietnam," he said briefly, opening and closing the subject with a single word.

"And then?" she asked, unable to curb her

curiosity about the man walking beside her, holding her hand as though they were on a date.

"More of the same."

She waited, then persisted. "And then?"

"There wasn't any 'and then' for me."

Raine knew she should let it go. It was becoming clear to her that Cord's life might very well be stamped TOP SECRET, DROP DEAD BEFORE SHARING.

Like her father's life.

"So you're still in the Army or Marines or whatever?" she asked, unable to stop herself, hungry for details about Cord's past.

He stopped and swung toward her, his eyes narrow. Silently he looked her over from her hair to her dusty hiking shoes.

She looked back at him with the same mixture of intelligence and challenge, defiance and yearning that had made her childhood difficult for her and for anyone else who got in the way of something she really wanted.

"Funny," he said sardonically, "you don't look like a cat. No furry ears or long tail or whiskers. But you're as curious as any cat I've ever known."

"And you're a man used to asking rather than answering questions." Her voice was neutral and her eyes were as narrow as his.

"Curiosity, and claws, too." For a long moment he looked down at her oval face, at her hazel eyes with their surprising glints of gold and green, at the feminine mouth that was quick to smile but wasn't smiling now. "What do you really want to know, Raine *Smith?*"

Chapter 3

"I . . ." Raine's voice faded into silence. She couldn't answer Cord's question for the simple reason that she didn't know what she wanted to ask him.

She had seen men who moved like him before. Men walking discreetly through embassy halls. Men watching the crowd while the crowd watched a statesman speak. Men whose job it was to guard diplomats and foreign dignitaries and people whose names and titles and true functions were shrouded in files only a few officials were cleared to read. Men whose very lives were state secrets.

Men like her father.

She hadn't thought about such men in years. She had never really been a part of her father's life. He no longer was a part of hers. She loved him, but she didn't know him at all. She rarely saw her parents for more than a few hours at a time. Despite mutual love, their lives just didn't overlap.

"I don't know what question I was trying to ask," she said finally. She shrugged. "It's been a long time since I've been around a man like you."

"A man like me?" Cord smiled, but there was little humor in the hard line of his mouth or the narrow slash of white teeth. "One head, two arms, two hands, two feet, two legs —"

"And one gun in the small of your back," she cut in coolly. "Or do you carry it under your arm?"

There was a flash of surprise before his face lost all expression. He watched her the way he had when he first saw her walking the hills, winter eyes and icy speculation.

Raine tried to smile; she failed. It hurt too much. There was no logic in her pain. It was simply there, a fact as deep as her own heartbeat.

"So I was right," she said, her voice flat, weary. "You're a man like my father, and like the men who guard him."

A man like her father, devoting his body and soul to an uneasy combination of ambition and idealism. A man like her father, who had little time for the wife he loved, and less time for his own children.

"Your father?" Cord asked, his voice ruthlessly neutral. He was too disciplined to reveal anything now, even interest.

She hesitated. Ordinarily she was careful not to mention her family. But there was nothing ordinary about the situation or the man walking beside her. Or her response to him.

It would be better if Cord knew. Better to end the attraction now, retreating behind an armor of old wealth and impeccable, powerful names.

"My father is Justin Chandler-Smith the Fourth," Raine said, her voice soft, empty. "You probably won't have heard his name. He's what they used to call a 'gray eminence,' a man whose life is international politics, international power. When he talks, presidents, kings, and prime ministers listen."

With every word she spoke, she regretted the impulse that had brought the conversation around to her family. But it was too late now. It had been too late since she had discovered that Cord, too, lived a life that put work first and everything else last.

"My father's recommendations make or break countries and cultures," she continued evenly. "He lives and breathes scenarios of human savagery, betrayal, and violence. It's a horrifying way to live, always focused on the worst side of human nature, where men are viciously evil and genocide serves a political purpose."

"Somebody has to live in that world or it would be the only world left for everyone to live in," Cord said evenly.

"Yes." Her voice was distant. "That's what my father says, too."

"You don't believe him?"

She shrugged. "I'm sure he's right. He always is."

Cord waited, but she said nothing more.

Neither did he. Beneath his exterior calm, anger and adrenaline prowled through his veins like tigers through a hot night. With each word Raine spoke, he sensed her pulling back from him, turning away, shutting him out.

He sensed it, but he couldn't stop it. He could only push ahead and find out how much damage had been done, how much he would have to undo before she came willingly to his arms. He knew she was going to end up there. He was as certain of it as he was of his next breath.

Because he needed her as much as he needed his next breath.

"Go on," he said neutrally.

"About what?"

"Whatever it is that's making you look like

you bit into a lemon."

Anger shot through her, the same anger she thought she had outgrown. But she hadn't. She had just outrun it.

"Fine," she snarled, turning on him. "Dad is a stellar citizen and a boon to humanity. But did he have to live with the savages all the time? Wasn't anything else important to him? His wife? His kids? Anything at all?"

"Maybe it's because his family was so very important to him that he gave himself to protecting them," Cord said tightly. "Did you ever think of that?"

"Maybe." Her voice was flat. "And maybe he just likes the world of adrenaline and violence better than he likes the world of family and love."

"Is that the question you wanted to ask me? If I like the world I work in?"

She tilted her chin and met his pale, fierce eyes without flinching. She spoke distinctly, clipping each word. "Yes. I do believe that's the question I had in mind."

For a moment he hesitated, watching the woman who so disliked being associated with her father that she refused even to use Chandler-Smith's full name.

"My work is satisfying in many ways," Cord said finally. "Exciting, at times. Alarms and excursions," he continued, his voice lightly mocking, but the mockery was aimed at himself rather than at her. "Saving civilization from barbarians, winning and losing and fighting again, life and death as close together as bullets in a clip."

His voice faded as he remembered how it had been fifteen years ago, when he was twenty and everything had seemed so clear. Lately it seemed there was much more death than life, far more doubt than certainty, and nothing was black-and-white; and everything was a thousand shades of gray.

In the past fifteen years, he had lost patience with people who believed in simple slogans, easy solutions, and the inevitable victory of civilization over barbarism. He had learned in the hardest possible way that happiness was a rare gift rather than a God-given right, that people had died and would continue to die so that others could live . . . and sometimes in the hours before dawn it seemed that the barbarians were winning because civilization just didn't give a damn.

Cord pulled his mind away from the dark downward spiral of his thoughts. He knew the danger of what he was thinking. He assessed his own emotions as unflinchingly as he assessed a dark street when he was outnumbered five to one. He was getting cold inside. He was feeling darkness without dawn, winter without spring.

Burnout.

Maybe it was time to let someone else take his place in the thin bloody line standing against the barbarians. Someone who found more excitement than disillusionment in the battle. Someone who didn't feel cold all the way to his soul.

Someone who hadn't frightened a woman called Raine.

"Cord?" Her voice was soft, unhappy.

It was an effort for him to banish his bleak thoughts. Lately they came more often, and they took more energy to turn back. The day would come when he didn't have the energy. When he didn't care. Then he would go under and darkness would be all he knew.

Raine sensed the bleak chill beneath his exterior calm. Without thinking about the past or the future, she reached out to him, unable to bear the thought that she had added to the sum of darkness in him, to the cold condensing like winter in his soul.

"I'm sorry," she said huskily. "I don't have any right to attack you or your work. It's not your fault that my father never had enough time for his family."

Her hand moved in a gesture of appeal that was also an apology. Her fingertips touched the silky black hair on his forearm, then settled against his warm skin with a feeling like coming home.

"Despite how I just sounded," she said, smiling unevenly, "I'm not naive or stupid. I know your work is necessary. It's just that I don't like thinking about it. I can't live that way. It would destroy me."

Very gently he lifted her hand from his arm. He looked at the slender fingers with their clean, short nails. Slowly he ran his thumb over the calluses on her palm, legacy of a lifetime of holding reins and lead ropes.

I can't live that way. It would destroy me.

He needed her. The certainty of that need shook him all the way to his soul.

But if he took her, he would destroy her.

Slowly he bent his head and kissed the center of her hand. The caress was as natural and warm as the late-afternoon light. And like the fading light, the touch told of endings rather than beginnings.

"There are times I don't like thinking about my work, either," he said quietly. "So tell me about your work, Raine Smith-only, no Chandler. How did you come to be an Olympic equestrian?"

The weariness and defeat she heard in Cord's voice made her throat tighten with something very like grief. There was a deep

72

current of longing in him that reached out to her, a need more compelling than simple sexual desire. She couldn't help but respond to the hunger and strange gentleness in him, and to his deeply buried, nameless yearning that called out to her as surely as she called out to him.

Yet he was already turning away from her, his face impassive. Had it not been for his fingers laced so deeply with her own, she would have felt . . . lonely.

Without thinking about it, she pressed her palm along his, her fingers holding tightly to him as they walked. After a few minutes she felt as though they had always walked this way, side by side, intimate. And they always would.

She would have smiled at the thought, but it hurt too much. She knew all the way to her soul that they had no future together. Sooner or later there would be a brushfire in some savage little country, the alarm would go out, and Cord would leave her to walk through the gathering darkness alone.

"I started riding when I was five." Raine didn't look at him while she spoke. She was afraid he could read her as clearly as she read him. She didn't want to shatter the fragile peace of the moment by focusing on the bleak certainty of the future. "I was an afterthought. An accident. Eight years younger than my closest sibling."

His grip on her hand tightened gently, encouraging and reassuring her, telling her that he was listening and understanding . . . even though his eyes constantly searched the surrounding land for possible danger.

"I was always smallest and last and worst at everything the family did," she said, her voice a mixture of humor, resentment, and acceptance. "So I found something no one in the family did, and then I did that better than anyone in or out of the family."

"Riding?"

"Yes. Mom and Dad didn't really care about horses, beyond a certain relief that I had found something to do besides turn things upside down at home."

Cord smiled faintly and looked at the deceptively delicate fingers twined with his. "You mean you weren't a perfect little angel?"

"I was a perfect little witch. But I didn't know it at the time, any more than I knew why I was so determined to succeed at riding. I simply went through life hell-bent on being best."

"Just like your father."

"Do you know him?" she asked, startled.

"A lot of people in the trade know of

74

Chandler-Smith," Cord said easily, neither evading nor really answering her question.

This time Raine didn't push the issue. She liked the feel of his palm against hers and the hint of a smile softening his mouth. She liked being close enough to smell the sun and dust and eucalyptus clinging to his skin. It would end soon enough. There was no need to rush toward the future by asking questions that only silence would answer.

After they paused at the top of a small rise, he looked out at the dry riverbed in the distance. "There's not much light left for a lens as big as you're using. Better get shooting."

She reached for her camera, then realized that her hand was still securely held in his. When she looked up, she found herself reflected in his pale, burning blue eyes. He slid his fingers from between hers so slowly that every pressure of his skin moving over hers became a lingering, sensual caress. When he was no longer touching her, she felt strangely lost, as empty as a cloudless sky.

With fingers that trembled just enough for Cord to see, she adjusted the focus ring on the telephoto lens and began taking pictures. He forced himself to look away. He knew if he kept on watching her, he would have a hell of a time keeping his hands off her. So he took her sketch pad and pencil out of the knapsack. Using quick, efficient strokes, he reduced the surrounding landscape to dark slashes across white paper.

He finished more quickly than she did. She was having trouble holding the heavy lens and camera still for the one-second exposures the dying light required.

As Raine had each time before, she took in a deep breath and let it out slowly. When there was no more air in her lungs, she gently triggered the shutter, hoping she wouldn't jar the camera while it was taking the picture. Since she hadn't planned on being out so late, she hadn't brought a tripod to steady the camera.

With a sense of futility, she heard the shutter open and close very slowly. Too slowly. She simply couldn't hold the awkward lens absolutely still.

"Ruddy hell," she said under her breath.

An instant later Cord was kneeling in front of her, but with his back to her. Startled, she looked at the expanse of masculine shoulders and the sleek pelt of black hair that began just above his collar.

"Use my shoulder as a brace," he said.

She hesitated only a moment before she propped the long lens on his shoulder. She bent over, sighed out a breath, adjusted the focus, and shot.

He didn't move. At all.

"A little to the right," she directed.

He shifted his body, then became utterly motionless once more.

"I'll try to be quick," she said. "I know how hard it is to hold that still."

But instead of concentrating on overlapping the shots to form a seamless panorama, she found herself staring at the clean black line of his hair against his neck. She caught a wisp of fragrance and inhaled deeply, savoring the subtle citrus scent of aftershave blended with his pleasing male smell.

Clean skin stretched smoothly over the tendons and muscles of his neck. He was completely motionless but for the almost hidden beat of his pulse. She wondered what it would be like to touch his pulse as he had touched hers, to feel it accelerate beneath her fingertip. What would it be like to —

"Finished?" he asked, his lips barely moving.

"Um." Raine gathered her scattering thoughts. "One more. A little more to the right."

He moved, then turned into a living statue again. She took another picture, and one more for insurance.

"That's it," she said quickly. "And if you ever want to change careers, I'll give you a high recommendation as a tripod. Where did you learn to be so still?"

"Hunting in the jungle." He rose and turned toward her in one fluid motion.

His quickness startled her, and his words. She knew without being told that men like him only did one kind of hunting in the jungle. Other men.

A wisp of her hair lifted on the teasing wind and floated over Cord's mouth like a caress. His nostrils flared as he drank in her scent, taking it deep into his body.

"I could give you a map of the endurance event that is accurate to the last centimeter," he said quietly. "The margins are full of notes on crowd control and sniper scopes, trajectories and hiding places, targets of opportunity and equations for the dispersion of various gases under different conditions of wind and humidity. But you wouldn't want that, would you? Not even if I erased all the ugly notes. You wouldn't want anything that would give you an unfair advantage over the other riders."

Frozen, unable to speak, Raine nodded. *Gas. Sniper. Target.*

She had always viewed a career like her

father's, like Cord's, solely in terms of what it had meant to her as a child: a father who was never there when she wanted him to be.

But now she was seeing that career in other terms. Now, suddenly, she had a gut understanding of the stark physical danger of such work. Life, even Cord's immensely vital life, was vulnerable; and death was always there, watching for the unlucky or the unwary or the unprotected.

At least her father had a wife who waited for him, children, a home, a place of love and warmth to retreat to when the other world began to freeze all that was human in him. Cord had no such haven. He spent his life guarding a gentle world that he had never been lucky enough to live in. He could easily die without ever knowing that warm world.

Sniper. Bombs. Ambush.

Death.

The realization of his vulnerability both chilled and melted Raine, slicing through the defenses she had been building against him. There was something in him that she could neither refuse nor ignore, something that called to her in a wordless, compelling language.

She wondered if he was hearing that same

language, feeling the same deep pull. It would explain why he stood as she did, silently, almost stunned, feeling as though the world had been turned upside down and shaken until she fell out and there was nothing real, only him.

"Cord," she whispered, reaching out.

An electronic beeper shrilled before she touched him. She recognized the sound instantly. Her hands jerked and dropped to her sides. Her fingers started to curl into fists. At that moment she admitted just how much she had been looking forward to driving back to Santa Anita and having dinner with Cord Elliot.

It was a struggle to make her hands relax, but she managed it.

Without glancing away from her, he reached for his belt. Using his thumb, he punched out a code that acknowledged receipt of the summons.

Anger at herself swept through Raine. She was a fool to be fascinated by a man who was like her father, a man so involved in his work that he lived his life at the end of an electronic leash. She had deliberately left that world behind. She would never enter it again, no matter what the lure.

After anger came the quick coiling of resentment. It lasted only a moment. She had had a lifetime to get used to being second, third, and last.

"You better hurry," she said coolly. She took the sketch pad and pencil from him and put them away in the rucksack she slid off his shoulder. "The nearest phone is back at the clubhouse."

"Raine."

He spoke her name so softly that she almost didn't hear. Then his hands came up to her shoulders, holding her in a gentle vise. He looked at her as though he was afraid she would vanish the instant she was no longer reflected in his eyes.

"Come back with me," he said urgently. "Don't stay out here alone. The world is full of men hungry for warmth, men who would kill for a smile from lips like yours. And some of those men would simply take what they wanted, destroying everything."

As she looked up at Cord, she sensed both his power and his yearning, his body trained for death and his eyes hungry for life. Her resentment crumbled, shattered by the same man who had broken apart a safe world she hadn't questioned since she was a child.

Tears gathered in her eyes, blurring his outline, leaving only the crystal intensity of his gaze. Abruptly his hands lifted. He stepped back, releasing her.

"Don't be afraid of me," he said angrily, sadly. "I'm not one of the barbarians. I won't take anything you don't want to give me."

She shook her head, swallowed, and tried to explain past the lump in her throat. "I'm not afraid of you."

"I don't believe you. Why else would you cry?"

"You've risked so much," she whispered. "You've given so much. Yet you've never known the warm world you make possible for others. You could die without knowing that world, like a sentry barred from the very hearth he protects."

He said her name as he lifted his hands to catch the tears at the corner of her eyes.

"And I could die, too," she said huskily. "You made me realize that this afternoon. Life doesn't last forever — it just seems that way."

The rucksack slipped from her fingers as he drew her close. Hands framing her face, he bent down to her, moving slowly, never using his superior strength to hold her captive. If she wanted to avoid the kiss, all she had to do was step away.

She didn't. She tilted her face toward his mouth, as hungry to be close to him as he was to touch her.

In a hushed silence broken only by a whisper of wind, his lips moved over the chestnut arch of her eyebrows, the smooth skin at her temples, the soft hollow beneath her cheekbone, kisses as delicate as a breath.

Trembling, she leaned closer to him, totally off guard. She hadn't expected such tenderness, his male hunger restrained until it showed only in the tension of his arms. Her fingertips traced the life pulsing in his veins from wrist to elbow and back again. The gentle, searching caresses said more about her own female hunger than she knew.

But Cord knew. His fingers tightened, drawing Raine still closer to him. He felt her breath flow warmly over his neck. Slowly, slowly, his mouth traced the line of her jaw with touches that lingered and haunted.

He knew he should stop with those undemanding kisses. He had no right to ask for more, to plead with his lips and eyes and body for everything she had to give. He was taking unfair advantage of her. First he had frightened her, then he had comforted her . . . and now he was making love to her. From first to last he had always been a step ahead of her, a master of unarmed combat keeping a novice off-balance until there was nowhere to fall but straight into his arms.

He should stop. He had no right to hold a woman like her, a woman made for one man's love, not for casual affairs with men whose lives belonged to war. He *would* stop.

But not yet.

Not until he came just a bit closer to her fire, warmed himself just a bit longer, drove out just a bit more of the chill that had crept like an enemy into his soul, ambushing him when he least expected it.

Willingly Raine shared the deepening kiss, opening her lips and inviting Cord into her warmth, inviting him to dream about a place by her fire. When his tongue moved over hers, she made an involuntary sound of pleasure and surprise. Her fingers slid beneath his short sleeves and clung to the bunched muscles of his upper arms as though she had just lost her balance and must hold onto him or fall.

Her response went through him like a shock wave. He fought an almost overpowering surge of hunger. He wanted to take her down to the golden grass and make love to her until nothing else was real, no past or future, no rights or wrongs, nothing but sunset sliding into night, a man and woman alone, two lovers turning and twining and joining, two flames burning as one in a world of crimson silence.

She sensed the hunger in him even before she heard the almost silent groan that came from deep in his chest. His tongue slowly caressed hers, tasting her, wanting her, wanting everything except to end the kiss.

Without meaning to, she clung to him fiercely. She didn't care about anything but the feel of his biceps flexed beneath her hands, the salt-sweet intimacy of him inside her mouth, their hunger bridging all differences, all difficulties. She didn't want the kiss to end, to stand apart from him once more, to send him alone into the descending night.

The supple strength and taut yearning of her body told Cord more than any words could have. He took what she gave to him, what she demanded that he take, drinking her taste and heat and passion until the world dropped away, leaving only Raine, a sweet fire burning in his arms.

Finally Cord forced himself to lift his mouth. If he didn't stop now, immediately, he doubted he could stop at all. It was that simple.

And that shocking.

The hunger gripping him was new, totally unknown. It wasn't simple lust. He had learned long ago to control his own sexuality. But now he felt as though a dam had given way deep inside his soul, releasing torrents of need that were as complex and unexpected as they were powerful, sweeping everything before them.

Eyes closed, he fought to control himself, but the afterimage of Raine's hungry, parted lips burned behind his eyelids.

Do you know what a blazing, beautiful temptation you are, Raine Chandler-Smith? he asked silently, afraid to speak aloud and frighten her again.

When he trusted himself to look at her, he saw himself condensed in wide hazel eyes watching him, admiring him, needing him. Savage hunger turned inside him, emotion as hot and bright and untested as a sword newly brought from the forge.

"You're coming back with me." His voice was soft and very certain. The words weren't a question or even an invitation, but a simple statement of fact.

Raine knew it would be useless to argue. Nor was there any reason to. For one thing, there wasn't enough light left for photography. For another, it would be foolish to keep wandering alone over the unknown land with darkness coming down.

And, she admitted to herself, there was the simple, overwhelming truth that she wasn't ready to leave Cord yet.

"Yes," she said huskily.

He touched her mouth with his fingertips, then forced himself to turn away. He picked up the rucksack, laced his fingers through hers, and began walking back toward the country club, holding her close to his side. Even as he slowed to accommodate her smaller steps, she lengthened her strides to equal his longer ones. They exchanged a look of almost startled recognition, smiled, and continued walking, their steps evenly matched.

Lights from distant houses glowed in the sunset, making the sky overhead a deep, radiant indigo by comparison. Neither Cord nor Raine spoke. Each sensed that it was safer, if not smarter, to let the simple warmth of their interlaced fingers speak for them.

When they reached the clubhouse, there was a helicopter sitting at the far end of the parking lot, well away from the few parked cars. The chopper was small and sleek. It had neither military nor civilian markings. Its rotors turned lazily, waiting.

Before Raine could control her reaction, her footsteps slowed, then stopped completely. She had seen her father climb into similar helicopters and disappear for weeks at a time with neither warning nor parting words. Her fingers tightened for just an instant before she could force herself to release Cord's hand. She had no right to hang onto him, no claim, no need. She was an adult, not a child.

He felt both the tension of her hand and the sudden release. She didn't have to be told that the helicopter was waiting for him. After all, she was Blue's daughter. She knew all about uncertainty and unexpected good-byes.

Knew it, and hated it, her resentment plain in first the tightness and then the quick, final retreat of her fingers.

Silently, deeply, Cord cursed the life he led, running up against its requirements like a mustang coming up against a fence for the first time in its wild life. Other women had found his job romantic, the secrets of his work tantalizing, the danger implicit in the gun he wore erotic.

But not Raine. She knew his work for what it was, a deadly enemy of intimacy.

With a hoarse sound he pulled her into his arms, holding her hard and close, ignoring the clash of binoculars and camera. When he felt the resistance of her closed lips, he simply tightened his arms, demanding what he must have, not really knowing or caring why.

For a long, agonizing moment, she clenched herself against him. In the next heartbeat she softened, unable to deny him what they both wanted. He spoke her name roughly, relief and hunger and apology in a single syllable.

Then he kissed her until she forgot everything but the taste and feel of him. Passion and restraint, strength and yearning, danger and safety, gentleness and ruthlessness, everything that he was and could be poured through the single kiss.

The reality of Cord swept through her like a storm, shaking her safe, predictable world, shattering her defenses and demanding that she make a place next to the civilized, womanly fire that he had guarded for so many years without ever knowing its warmth.

When he finally loosened his arms and stepped back, Raine could hardly stand. She closed her eyes but still she saw him, his thick black hair and icy, burning blue eyes, the lines of his face harsh with need and his mouth shockingly sensual as he looked at her, wanting her.

Needing her.

"Tomorrow night," he said. "Seven o'clock. Dinner."

"No," she answered, her eyes still closed.

"You don't know where you'll be tomorrow night."

"I'll be wherever you are. Seven o'clock. *Look at me, Raine.*"

Shaking her head helplessly, she opened her eyes. The look he gave her was as shattering as his kiss.

"Seven o'clock," she agreed.

But her tone said she didn't believe he would be there.

Before Cord could speak, the helicopter ripped to full life, its rotors spinning rapidly. The body of the aircraft trembled like a beast crouched to spring on its prey. He handed her the rucksack, then turned and walked quickly away, his black hair rippling in the backwash of the great blades slicing through the twilight.

Eyes narrowed against tears and the harsh wind spinning off the black blades, Raine watched him walk away from her.

The chopper leaped into the air, shattering the twilight into a chaos of flashing lights. Hands clenched at her sides, she closed her eyes.

The sound of the helicopter retreated, swallowed by night and distance, leaving only a fading echo in her ears and an afterimage of a blinking red light in her mind.

When she opened her eyes again, she was alone.

CHAPTER 4

Standing in the stall next to Devlin's Waterloo, Raine was dwarfed by the stallion's height and muscle. Totally at ease with his bulk, she groomed her horse's mahogany-red coat with long, sweeping strokes of the brush. In truth, Dev didn't need the grooming any more than he needed her lingering close to him, speaking in soothing tones. She was talking more for her own peace of mind than for the stallion's.

Waiting to compete was the worst kind of work for her. Patience never come gracefully or easily. Sometimes patience simply wasn't possible. She knew her own restless temperament, and allowed for it. Or tried to. The weeks before any three-day event were difficult. She was discovering that the weeks before the Olympic three-day event were impossible.

The syndrome she called "competition madness" had set in around the stables.

There wasn't much left to do in terms of training either horses or riders. The animals were all but exploding with health and vitality. Other than an hour a day of undemanding riding and a few hours of grooming and walking, the horses didn't require anything.

At this point, hard work or long hours in the ring went against the horses, making them stale and flat rather than eager for the coming test. But not working with the horses left a lot of hours for the riders to fill.

The humans, too, were in peak physical condition, impatient for the competition to begin and the suspense to end. Because they were highly trained athletes, event riders knew better than to deaden the talons of stress with alcohol or drugs. Nor could riders work themselves into a blessed state of numbness, for that would sour them as quickly as it would the horses.

Many riders — and other athletes — relieved the stresses of competition madness with an affair. It was a common and quietly accepted practice that provided a delightful means of killing time without jeopardizing competitive fitness.

More than one man had explained this very logically to Raine. Just as logically, she had explained that she preferred long walks and unnecessary grooming of Devlin's Waterloo to empty bedroom games.

Only once had Raine given in to competition madness. She had been nineteen, competing in Europe for the first time with world-class equestrians. She had been out of her depth in more ways than one. On the eve of the event, a French rider had seduced her almost effortlessly.

She had mistaken his Gallic appreciation of women in general for a particular appreciation of Raine Smith. He had been dismayed to discover that she was a virgin, and worse, a Chandler-Smith. Despite that, he was kind in his own way, telling her beautiful lies for several weeks while he eased himself out of her life, taking her innocence with him.

Raine knew all about falling and getting back on the horse again. After a few weeks, she realized it was her pride rather than her heart that had been hurt by the suave Frenchman. When she found herself being pursued by a teammate a few months later, she didn't shy away. She had known the man for several years, and liked him. Marshall was a serious, hard-working rider whose wife had decided she would rather have more fun. End of marriage.

Unfortunately, Raine was too inexperienced to understand the dangers of love on the rebound. Once Marshall had succeeded in talking her into bed, he took her lack of skill and absence of headlong eagerness as a personal insult to his prowess. He returned the insult, with interest.

For several months after the very brief affair had blown up in her face, things were very tense around the stables. After that, she was careful not to date anyone who was associated with her work. Which meant, in effect, no one at all. She enjoyed the men she was constantly around. She joked with them and traded equestrian advice, planned surprise birthday parties, and was a baby-sitter of last resort for the married riders.

Humorous, unflappable, generous, a hell of a rider, a younger sister in residence, a mind like a whip . . . untouchable. All those words had been used to describe her. All were correct, so far as they went. None of those words described the emotions beneath Raine's disciplined surface, the loneliness and yearning she was always careful to conceal.

Until yesterday, when a stranger had knocked her flat and then gently held her, looked at her as though he saw through the surface to the womanly warmth beneath; and then he had kissed her and bathed both of them in sensual fire.

With a whispered curse, Raine threw Dev's brush into the tack box hanging on the wide stall door. She had been thinking a lot about what happened yesterday. Too much. The darkness beneath her eyes showed her lack of sleep. Yet after hours of turning, tossing, muttering, and turning some more, she still didn't understand what had happened to transform her from a cool rider into an eager, even demanding, lover.

The only rational explanation she had come up with was that her response to the man and the indigo twilight was the result of her own precompetition nerves and Cord's high-stress work. She had been literally knocked off-balance, all her normal certainties shattered. He had been on a hair-trigger adrenaline ride, not knowing if she was a terrorist carrying death in a rucksack.

Under those circumstances, normal reserve or ordinary social responses just weren't likely. She shouldn't be surprised that he had kissed her. She shouldn't be astonished at her own unexpected, over-whelmingly sensual response. They were simply human, a man and a woman with more adrenaline than common sense coursing through their blood.

When she looked at it that way, there was

nothing mysterious or even unexpected about what had happened yesterday. It was simply adrenaline, nerves, and the unexpected all coming together at once.

But I deal with those things every day, she thought stubbornly. *Why was yesterday different?*

There was no answer except the old inadequate one. Nerves. That's all. Just nerves. It had to be. It couldn't have been anything else.

It certainly couldn't have been a silent recognition of her other half, a filling of inner hollows that had waited empty and unknown for a lifetime, a joining more complex and . . . dangerous . . . than she could accept.

Nerves, nothing more. Competition madness.

Period.

"Raine?"

Startled, she spun around. "Oh. Hi, Captain Jon. I didn't hear you come up."

Tall, graying, with a competition rider's innate balance and lean strength, Captain Jon waited just outside Dev's stall door. He didn't offer to come inside. He had a very healthy respect for the stallion's heels. Teeth, too.

"Phone call for you," he said.

Automatically Raine glanced at the sturdy watch on her wrist. Five-thirty. A little late for any of her family to be calling her. Or a little early, depending on whether it was her brother in Japan or her mother in Berlin.

Perhaps it was her sister, calling before the latest round of political fund-raisers. Or, even more likely, it was one of the increasing number of reporters who had discovered that Raine Smith, Olympic equestrian, was also Lorraine Todhunter Chandler-Smith, daughter of old wealth and older power.

"It better not be a reporter," she said. "I'm flat out of polite ways to tell them to get stuffed."

Amused, Captain Jon stepped away from the stall door and opened it. "I could remind you that event riding needs all the publicity it can get."

"You could."

"And then you'd tell *me* to get stuffed."

She gave him a genuine smile. "Nope. You're the only man who has guts enough to help me with Dev."

"Doesn't speak highly of my intelligence, does it?"

Still smiling, Raine patted Dev's muscular rump and walked out of the stall, shutting the door behind her. The broad aisle between rows of stalls was clean, sunny, and dusty, despite constant spraying from the hoses coiled in front of every stall. Hot-blooded horses stood quietly in their stalls, coats gleaming with health, heads turning while they watched everything that happened with alert, liquid brown eyes.

As she and the captain walked down the aisle, horses poked their heads over stall doors. Some of the horses whickered softly when they scented her, asking for a word or a touch. She responded almost absently, stroking velvet noses, teasing the lips that nibbled playfully at her fingertips, and through it all she kept walking toward the phone at the end of the long, dusty aisle, wondering who was on the other end of the line.

"I called your name three times before you noticed me," Captain Jon said. "Perhaps I should get you a beeper."

"Like bloody hell."

His white eyebrows lifted. "I didn't think it was that bad an idea."

"I don't like electronic leashes."

"No kidding," he answered, in a too-innocent tone. The American slang sounded odd coming from the Eton-educated Swiss aristocrat.

After giving Captain Jon a narrow glance,

Raine relented with a smile. "Sorry. It comes of being raised with the damn things. Birthdays, Christmas, Thanksgiving, the Pan-American Games — it didn't matter. Somewhere in the world, hell is always breaking loose. Beep-beep and good-bye."

Captain Jon didn't argue. He knew better than anyone that Raine's father had managed to attend only three of the dozens of competitions she had been in over the years. Nor had those three been the crucial ones, the competitions where a smile or a touch or a thumbs-up from your family really mattered.

"Worry about your own piece of the world," the captain advised, rubbing his hand through his thinning gray hair. "Leave the rest of it to the pros."

Men like Cord, she thought, but she said nothing aloud. She simply stroked another velvet muzzle and kept walking.

"Speaking of the rest of the world," Captain Jon said, "we have an amendment to the security regulations. Riders who want to look over the country around Rancho Santa Fe have to use the buddy system."

"Shit," she hissed under her breath.

The captain's eyebrows rose. The word wasn't a normal part of Raine's conversation. Or even an abnormal part. She must be really on edge. Being a wise man, he didn't mention that fact.

Belatedly Raine realized that she hadn't kept her response soft enough so that it wouldn't be heard. That wasn't like her. She must be a lot closer to competition madness than she thought. "Sorry. Again."

"I hear much worse," he said dryly. "It's a way of letting off steam."

"So I'm told."

"Is it working?" he asked.

"Too soon to know."

"If you run out of American and British slang, try the Aussies. They're very inventive."

"I'll keep it in mind." Impatiently she swiped some hair off her face and stuffed it behind her ear. "Buddy system. Hell on the half-shell. That's all I need, to be yoked to another rider every time I leave the stable."

Despite the sharpness of her voice, her hand was gentle when a dark, eager muzzle reached out to be petted.

Captain Jon wasn't surprised by the endless patience Raine had for horses, but he was startled by the tension in her expression and voice. When everyone else was coming apart with nerves, she was — or at least, had seemed to be — a center of calm.

"The buddy system isn't an unreasonable

request," he said mildly. "Ever since Munich, Olympic athletes have been a target."

Raine made a throttled sound that wasn't quite a word. It was just as well. It wasn't the kind of word she used in public.

"I've seen the countryside around the endurance course," he continued. "There's bugger-all out there but hills, obstacles, and what's left of the original golf course."

"I know. I was there yesterday."

"Alone?" Captain Jon asked sharply.

"Most of the time."

Before he could ask any other questions, Raine took two fast steps and picked up the receiver that was dangling over a bale of straw.

"Hello," she said crisply.

"Seven o'clock."

Hearing Cord's voice shocked her. She had already stuffed him into a mental pigeonhole labeled "competition madness." She hadn't really expected to hear from him again. She certainly hadn't expected her heart to lurch and then race while adrenaline poured into her blood as though she had just taken a hard fall.

His midnight-and-black-velvet voice brought yesterday back all too vividly — first the fear, then the safety.

And then the fire.

In the background at Cord's end of the line, other voices floated like colored leaves, oddly pitched voices riding broken waves of sound punctuated by bursts of static.

Automatically he shifted in his seat and adjusted the volume on one of the many radios and scanners that were within his reach. Now he could hear Raine better. The sound of her soft, quickening breaths licked over him like remembered flames.

Yet she said nothing, did nothing, as though she didn't want to remember him at all. She was in full retreat from yesterday.

From him.

"I know you're there," he said, his voice both gritty and intimate. "I can hear you breathing. I just wish I was close enough to feel your breath, too, and kiss the pulse beating in your warm throat."

Raine's breath came in sharply. She felt like she could taste Cord on her tongue, feel him, know the dizzying thrill of his sensuality pouring over her. It both frightened and fascinated her. He was as much in control now as he had been when he had surprised her in the hills.

And she was as much off-balance.

"Don't you ever play fair?" she asked bluntly.

"I'm a hunter. I don't play at all."

"Well, I'm no dumb bunny, Cord Elliot," she said, her voice clipped.

His laugh was rough yet soft, a purr from an animal that was definitely not a domestic cat.

"I know," he said. "I feel rather like Actaeon must have felt when he hunted Diana beneath her own moon. Not a sport for the faint of heart."

A shiver went through Raine.

It wasn't fear.

"Seven o'clock," he said. "Wear whatever you like. Or, like Diana, wear nothing at all."

He hung up before she could say anything.

It was just as well. She couldn't think of anything to say. The masculine promise and anticipation in his voice should have been illegal.

"Everything okay?" Captain Jon looked closely at her face. "First you went pale and now you're flushed."

"Everything's fine," she said, hanging up the receiver. "The person I was talking to is just a bit . . . unnerving."

"Anyone I know?"

"Doubt it."

Frowning, she fingered the plastic-coated ID badge she wore around her neck on a thin steel chain. The photograph was surrounded by color and number codes that identified her as an Olympic competitor with access to all equestrian areas.

"I know a lot of people," Captain Jon said.

"I just met the man yesterday."

"Oh?"

Raine looked down at her hands and arms, dusty from hours of cleaning Dev's stall and brushing his healthy red hide.

Wear anything you like.

The thought made her smile. It was a slashing, competitor's smile. Mr. Always-in-Charge Elliot was going to have *his* wind knocked out for a change.

But first she needed a long, slow perfumed bath.

"I won't be in the mess hall tonight," she said.

Captain Jon shrugged. His athletes were older than most Olympic competitors. He didn't cluck over his riders, unless they had it coming. Then he could mother-hen with a vengeance. But Raine had never given him a bit of trouble, not even when she had fallen for that smooth-talking Frenchman.

Although he had dumped her just before a big meet, she had kept her concentration, proving she was a world-class competitor. In fact, her performance that day had convinced Captain Jon that Raine was

Olympic material. The unhappy affair with another rider had simply confirmed the captain's original estimate: Raine had that indefinable quality known as class. She rose to meet the professional occasion no matter what her private life was like at the moment.

"Found a man, eh?" the captain asked, smiling widely.

She thought of denying it, then shrugged. He would find out. He always did.

"Right," she said. "He knocked me off my feet."

"Isn't that 'swept you off your feet'?"

"Not this one. Knocked me right out of my shoes."

The captain chuckled, assuming it was a joke. "Don't worry about curfew. You can use the break."

Barely a hundred feet from the phone Raine had used, Cord sat in an RV loaded with electronics. Big as a bus — and built with an unusually heavy framework — the bland-looking motor home was really a mobile fort. From it, he could call any place on earth. And any person.

At the moment he was talking to Virginia. He didn't know the man's name; the man didn't know Cord's. It didn't get in the way of their conversation.

"That's the best you can do?" Cord asked impatiently. "Lives depend on this."

"They always do."

"But this time . . ." His voice died.

It wouldn't help to say that this time a woman's life was at risk, a very special woman, the only woman who had ever managed to reach past his defenses and touch the naked yearning beneath.

"Do better," Cord said bluntly.

"Barracuda isn't an easy target."

"Now, there's a bit of hot intelligence."

The man at the other end of the line winced. "Ease up. I've had my ass chewed raw on the subject of Barracuda."

"You looking for sympathy?" Cord asked.

"Yes!"

"You'll find it in the dictionary between 'shit' and 'syphilis.' *I need information.*"

Cord broke the connection and tried another source. Normally he was a patient man, but since Barracuda had disappeared, nothing could be called normal.

"Yeah," a bored female voice said.

"Any hits on that profile I sent you?" he asked.

"No."

"Radio traffic?"

"No."

"Inspiration?"

"No."

"Shit," he muttered. "Try tea leaves."

"I'm thinking of starting a coffee-scum scam. More coffee gets sucked up than tea."

Smiling reluctantly, Cord disconnected and looked around with pale eyes that had seen too much but kept on watching anyway. Somebody had to.

There were no windows in this part of the bus, just television screens showing the outside world in real time, real sound, and full color. Everything appeared to be absolutely normal. The air around the stables shimmered with heat and sun, dust and an unhealthy dose of LA's infamous smog.

There weren't many people hanging around right now. Cord knew the ones who were — a handful of reporters and horse pundits, a dozen equestrian groupies, some competitors walking or exercising or schooling their horses.

Even though the slate of equestrian events had already begun, workers were hammering and building with a frenzy that came from wrestling with deadlines that should have been met weeks ago. But Santa Anita's racing season hadn't ended until June. That hadn't left enough time to convert a flat racing track into a show-jumping ring, dressage ring, practice rings, exercise areas, massive new bleachers on all sides, and the multitude of living quarters required for both men and animals.

Supposedly the workmen had been thoroughly vetted before they were employed. Cord had checked them again anyway. Personally. Putting on dirty clothes and a tool belt was a great way to become instantly invisible. He had done it himself in the past.

So had Barracuda.

Cord went back to the swivel chair that was nearly surrounded by ranks of electronic gear. He picked up the radio mike and punched in Kentucky's code.

"Good afternoon, Mr. Elliot," Thorne drawled. "Right lovely day."

He grunted. "Where is she?"

"Headed toward her motel."

"Anybody new check in?"

"No suh."

"What about her guards?" Cord asked, referring to the agents who were presently camped out in the rooms on either side of Raine's.

"Merryweather is crying about bad cards."

"And cleaning out the unwary," Cord said dryly.

"Yes suh. I only played poker with her once. It was a learning experience."

"Strip poker?"

A deep chuckle was Kentucky's only answer.

It was all Cord needed. He smiled despite the unease digging into him like spurs. "I'm picking up Raine at seven. If I see anyone peeking out of windows, I'll use them to shovel out stalls."

"I'll pass the word, suh."

Cord disconnected and punched in another code. After a few moments he punched in more numbers, waited, and gave yet another code.

"Anything new since oh two hundred?" he asked when a voice answered.

"No."

"Any rumors?"

"No."

"Guesses?"

"No."

"Shit."

"Always plenty of that," the voice agreed. "Consider yourself logged in."

"Wait," Cord said, before the man could disconnect. "Has Bonner logged in?"

"An hour ago."

Soundlessly Cord let out his breath. "Okay. If Bonner misses a contact, inform me immediately."

"Affirmative."

Cord leaned back in the swivel chair and

wished he knew the source of the uneasiness that was raking him. But he didn't. All he had was the cold certainty that something, somewhere, was going to hell.

CHAPTER 5

Raine wasn't quartered at Santa Anita with the rest of the Olympic three-day event team. Her teammates were all male. Rather than take a room at the track by herself — and force other athletes to squeeze more men into the few other available rooms — she had decided to stay at a nearby motel.

The Winner's Circle was more accustomed to high rollers than high jumpers, and was decorated accordingly. Gilt, mirrors, and red velvet were everywhere. Raine privately referred to the decor as "whore's Christmas." But the water was always hot, the sheets were changed every day, and the towels were fresh twice daily. That was all she asked of any lodging, and more than she usually got.

When she opened the motel door, the cool, slightly stale smell peculiar to rented rooms and air conditioning washed over her. The good news was that the room no longer felt like walking into a refrigerator. It had taken two days, but she finally convinced the management she preferred a temperature in the upper seventies to one in the sixties.

Peeling off dirty clothes as she went, she hurried into the bathroom. The water in the black-tiled shower came out in a thick, hard pulsating spray that rapidly reduced her aches and bones to jelly. With a groan of sheer pleasure, she let hot water knead muscles knotted by impatience and nerves.

It would only get worse. The days and hours and minutes before the beginning of the three-day event unrolled before her like eternity.

Stop thinking about it.

The silent command was automatic. So was the response. She turned her thoughts away from the competition to come. The only way she could make time move faster was to distract herself.

Smiling thinly, she decided that Cord qualified as one hell of a distraction. She wasn't in the running for an affair. No matter how much he appealed to her, she knew better than to get involved with a man who lived with an electronic leash. But dinner and the chance to flap the unflappable Mr. Elliot were different. They came under the heading of diversion, and she needed one badly.

She dried her hair and set it in big hot rollers. While heat tamed her hair, or tried to, she rubbed a perfumed cream over her body, put on makeup with a sparing hand, and wandered over to the closet wearing little more than fragrance and a competitor's knife-bright smile.

Without hesitation she bypassed the tailored formality of her dressage clothes — silk hat and starched linen shirt, black coat with tails, clean riding pants with a razor crease — and went directly to the five evening outfits. These were as necessary a part of world-class riding equipment as any dressage uniform.

The Olympic Equestrian Team was supported by private donations. The wealthiest donors often threw stylish parties; riders were urgently "requested" to attend. Raised in an atmosphere of political reality, Raine knew better than to balk at such requests. She had acquired a wardrobe suitable for elegant parties.

After a brief debate with herself, she ignored the floor-length gold-shot bronze dress of Indian silk. She passed over the crimson silk pants and filmy top from Italy. Her fingers settled on the hanger that held a black ankle-length sheath. The clinging cloth was slit to mid-thigh in the front.

Then she remembered Cord's long-legged stride. Even with the long slit, the dress would be like wearing hobbles. Her hand moved on, to a hanger that supported a rustling mass of jade-green watercolor silk. The top of the dress overlapped, making a deep V to her waist. Although the silk rarely revealed more than a hint of her gently curving breasts, the cleverly draped folds always seemed on the point of coming undone. A pleated belt of the same material finished the almost-knee-length dress.

Still humming, Raine pulled on some very sheer, very French pantyhose. The dress's deep neckline made a bra impossible. Not that it really mattered. She wasn't built to overflow any bounds of propriety. She stepped into the dress, closed the invisible side zipper, and arranged the neckline so that it concealed a lot more than it revealed.

Though she didn't notice, the deep, shimmering green of the dress made her skin look like porcelain lit from within by flame. She put on earrings and a long, handmade gold chain that followed the neckline of the dress. The necklace wove light into glimmers of gold that were picked up and repeated in her hazel eyes. Emeralds glowed among the gold links and winked in each earlobe, echoing the green flecks in her eyes.

Balancing on first one foot and then the other, she fastened on a pair of very high evening sandals made of wisps of butter-soft gold leather. She headed for the bathroom, pulling out rollers with both hands, ready to do battle with her hair.

Even after the hot rollers, her hair was as stubborn as any horse she had ever tried to school. She combed out the crackling, silky mass until it was a wild cloud around her shoulders. Then she gathered the slippery chestnut hair in her hands and built a smooth, sophisticated coil on top of her head. As a finishing touch, she pulled free a few curling wisps and let them fall softly around her temples, ears, and the nape of her neck. A few more tendrils escaped on their own, giving a soft contrast to the sleek discipline of the chestnut coils.

When she was finished, she examined the result in the mirror. She wouldn't stop traffic, but at least she didn't look like she had just crawled out of a haystack.

With the ingrained neatness of someone who was used to living out of suitcases, she straightened up the motel room. When she was finished, she looked critically at her fingernails. Short, buffed rather than polished, they looked almost childlike next to the elegance of her dress. With a shrug, she dismissed her nails. They were clean and healthy, which was all she asked. Long, brightly painted fingernails were a nuisance around the stable and uncomfortable inside riding gloves.

Lights flashed in the parking lot. A few moments later there was a brisk knock on her door that fairly shouted of Cord Elliot's male confidence. She glanced at the incredibly thin gold watch that had been her father's gift to her after he had been forced to leave the Pan-American Games before he could see her event.

Seven o'clock.

"Coming," she said.

She took off the chain and opened the door without any further checking to see who was on the other side. There was no point. She already knew.

"Are you always so trusting?" he asked grimly.

She was too busy staring at Cord to answer. If it hadn't been for the pale, brilliant eyes, she wouldn't have recognized him. The rough looking stranger who had ruthlessly knocked her down and searched her yesterday was gone. Tonight Cord was wearing an expensive navy blazer and claret silk tie, white silk shirt, and fine charcoal wool pants. His shoes were sleek leather, Italian, as soft as a baby's cheek. The elegant clothes enhanced his male grace and strength, quietly proving that clothes were only as good as the man who wore them.

With a sinking feeling, she realized that he had done it again. She was knocked off-balance while he stayed in complete control. She told herself that it was accidental, he didn't mean to unnerve her.

She didn't believe it.

Silently Cord looked down into the face of the woman who had troubled his thoughts even more after he had decided that she wasn't a terrorist bent on death. The ripped blue blouse and faded riding pants she had worn yesterday were gone. So was the dusty, tear-streaked face.

Tonight there was only elegance and poise. Gold-shot brown hair, eyes alive with intelligence and humor, the tantalizing curve of neck and shoulder, the feminine swell of breasts beneath silk that teased even as it concealed. She stood before him with unconscious pride. Her wealth, position, and poise were pulled around her like medieval armor.

Princess at work. Touch not.

But he had expected her to wear full social

armor. He had dressed for it. He was an old hand at getting past barriers, at camouflage and passing unseen in every kind of crowd. He had lived with savages and prime ministers, could talk with barbarians and Ph.D.'s.

So he smiled down at her while his senses quickened with her scent. His eyes memorized the chestnut coils and teasing tendrils of her hair, the subdued glint of emerald against the sensuous lobes of her ears, the sheen of smooth silk against smoother skin, feet arched as delicately as a dancer's.

Not a princess . . . a queen. Centuries of wealth and power condensed into a deceptively slender form.

Idly Cord wondered whether Raine had dressed to intimidate him. Probably, but not solely. Her clothes were an automatic defense against the rest of the world. Like a fawn freezing at the first hint of a wolf, she let her polished exterior conceal the heat and life inside.

He smiled at the thought, a slow smile that did nothing to conceal the male intensity of his appraisal. She wasn't beautiful in the usual sense of the word, but she was a woman to tempt any man who had the intelligence to see her and the confidence to pursue what he saw.

Cord had both, in abundance.

He also had a hunger that grew with every breath he took, she took, the heat of their bodies reaching out in silent, sultry invitation.

After a moment Raine smiled at him in return. The tentative curve of her lips was wistful and aloof and so beautiful to him that he couldn't prevent a sudden, silent intake of breath. He held out his fingers, needing to touch her. When she took his hand, he lifted hers to his mouth. His lips found the warm center of her palm.

Both of them felt her fingers curl slightly in sensual response.

"My compliments to your fairy godmother," he said, looking at her with eyes that were hooded, their dark centers wide.

"Cinderella was a scullery maid, not a stable hand," Raine said lightly, dismissing the compliment as she had dismissed so many before, not believing in her own feminine allure.

Yet his response to her changed appearance affected her the same way his lips against her palm did. Frissons of warmth rippled through her, setting off slow fires in the secret places of her body.

She had expected the same combination of surprise and retreat from Cord that she had seen in other men when she dressed with the wealth and elegance that were her heritage. Those other men had been first startled, then uneasy. They had expected a socially awkward rider and instead found themselves with a woman who had graduated from Europe's finest finishing schools and social circuits.

It wasn't a life she had particularly enjoyed, but it had its uses, especially as a deterrent. Until now. Cord had been attracted rather than uneasy.

And she was off-center again, feeling as though she had to cling to him for balance. Again.

"Ready?" he asked.

She didn't know. But she knew she was going to find out. She scooped her purse off the coffee table. "Ready."

He put his hand behind her elbow, guiding her out of the room. He shut the door, checked that it was locked, and ushered her toward a black Pantera that crouched like a big cat in the parking lot. He handed her into the low-slung sports car, fastened her seatbelt, closed her door firmly, and got in the driver's side.

From the corner of her eye, Raine watched while he folded himself into the low seat. He should have looked awkward. He didn't. He slid into place with the easy coordination that marked all his movements.

"Anything you can't eat?" he asked, as he brought the car's engine to life.

"Curry." She sighed. "Unfortunately, I love the taste. It just doesn't love me."

He gave her a sympathetic look and eased the Pantera out into traffic. "How about Asian food?"

"Love it. Chinese, Japanese, Korean."

"Vietnamese?"

"Never tried it," she admitted.

"If you don't like the appetizers, I'll take you somewhere else."

She relaxed into the leather seat as the car accelerated with an eagerness that reminded her of Dev. The engine's sound rose an octave, sending discreet messages of raw power into the passenger compartment. She watched while he controlled the car with small, easy movements of his hands, an economy of motion that spoke of skill and confidence.

"You must have been a good rider," she said, as he downshifted coming into a curve.

He gave her a brief sideways look before returning his attention to the heavy traffic. "Why do you say that?"

"Your hands. Quick. Sure. Calm. Sensitive."

As she spoke, she remembered the feeling

of his hands framing her face. She was glad that the light in the car was too dim to show the pulse beating too rapidly in her throat and the heat climbing her cheeks.

"Legacy of a misspent youth," he said dryly. "And a family tradition. My great-grandfather and grandfather were mustangers — wild-horse hunters. They followed the mustangs on foot, always keeping the horses on the move, never letting them eat more than a few bites of food or drink more than a few cups of water at a time. They would literally walk those mustangs into the ground."

"Why?" she asked, startled.

"Poor man's round-up. No corrals, fences, extra riders, nothing but dogged determination."

"Why didn't the mustangs just run away?"

"They're territorial. They move in a broad circle, keeping to the water holes and grazing lands they know. Two men could work a herd, leapfrogging each other as they cut across the country from water hole to water hole, arriving ahead of the mustangs and stampeding them off toward the next water hole before their thirst was slaked."

"How long did that go on?"

"Until the horses got so hungry and thirsty and sore footed that you could walk right up and put a rope on them. They would follow you anywhere for a hat full of water."

Raine turned toward Cord, caught by the quality of his voice; darkness and textures of emotion, very masculine, oddly soothing. It was the kind of voice she could listen to endlessly, like music.

Unaware of her intent eyes, he kept talking as he drove. It had been a long time since he had thought about the people and places and scents of his childhood. For some reason he found the memories almost unbearably sharp tonight.

"Dad went on the last of the hunts when he was only nine," Cord said quietly. "The good mustangs were gone by then. Nothing was left but slab-sided scrub beasts as mean as the rock desert that men had crowded them into."

"I'll bet they were tough little ponies."

"Hardest hooves in the world. Hardest heads, too."

Memories shot through him. Old photos that were faded and curling, taped to his father's bedroom wall, pictures of mustangs and mustangers long since dead.

"What did your father do when the good mustangs were gone?" she asked.

"Granddad and Dad took to breaking the

rough string, other men's horses that were either too green or too mean to be ridden by most hands. Granddad was a regular shaman. He had a voice that would mesmerize the meanest stud."

She smiled to herself. The grandson had definitely inherited his grandfather's gift. Listening to Cord's voice was like being wrapped in warm, dark velvet.

"What did you do as a kid?" she asked.

"I learned to ride on horses that no one but my dad would touch. I learned to move confidently, cleanly, and never to turn my back. I also learned that even the most savage horse can be gentled, given time, patience, and," he grinned, "enough apples."

He fell silent, suddenly remembering the tickling feel of an apple being lipped off his palm by a horse that had finally learned to trust. A sense of longing shot through him, shocking in its intensity. He didn't know precisely what he missed. He knew only that he missed it.

"Dev could have used a man like you," Raine said.

"Was your horse a hard case?"

"Yes."

"With reason?"

"The best. Or the worst. Dev's owner shouldn't have been allowed to keep flies, much less horses."

Cord's smile was a white slash against the shadowy darkness of his face. "Tell me about your horse."

"The first time I saw Dev, I was eighteen, walking a one-day-event course with my father. We saw Dev go down, throwing his rider."

"It happens."

"All the time," she agreed easily. "But this was different. When we got to the obstacle, Dev was still down. His front legs were tangled in the bars of a fixed jump."

Silently Cord shook his head. He didn't have to be told how dangerous that could be, the near-certainty of permanent injury to the horse and anyone who tried to help.

"Dev's rider was standing next to him," she said, her voice echoing with remembered outrage. "He was cursing and kicking and whipping Dev as hard as he could."

Cord muttered something too low for Raine to hear.

"Dev's eyes were rolling white and wild," she said. "Bloody foam was dripping from his body. Any other horse caught between a whip and a trap like that would have panicked and broken both legs trying to fight free. But not Dev."

He gave her a quick glance. Her eyes were

narrow as she stared through the windshield. It was the past she was seeing, a past that still had the power to make rage slide hotly in her veins and thin her full mouth into a flat line.

"What did you do?" he asked, when she didn't say anything more.

"I grabbed that cruel, brainless bastard and shoved him into my father's arms. Then I stood and talked to Dev until his eyes stopped rolling. When he finally let me touch him without flinching and offering to bite, I went to work getting his legs free of the bars."

Softly Cord whistled through his teeth. He pictured a teenage girl working dangerously close to a stallion that was half out of its mind with pain and fear. "That took a lot of nerve."

"There was no other way to get the job done." Her voice was matter-of-fact. "When I coaxed Dev to his feet, he was bloody and scraped and lathered all over, trembling in every limb. Yet he stood and watched me with his ears up, his eyes calm, the picture of well-mannered attention. I knew I couldn't give a horse like that back to a sadist."

Cord gave her a swift glance, trying to match the elegant woman in the seat next to him with the brutal episode out of her past. If he saw only the silk dress and emerald earrings, what she said was unbelievable. If he remembered the woman who had controlled her panic when she was helpless beneath a stranger's intrusive hands, her words were quite believable.

Yes, Raine was an elegant, vulnerable woman. She was also a woman who didn't flinch from doing what had to be done.

"I asked that obscene son of a bitch what he thought his horse was worth," she continued, unaware of Cord's brief, intense appraisal. "He said, 'A bullet. He's too old to geld and too mean to ride.' " She hesitated, remembering what had happened next. It was the only time in her life when her father had been there when it really counted. "So my father pulled his gun, shucked out a bullet, and flipped it to the man."

"That's one for our side, Blue," Cord said beneath his breath.

She turned with a swiftness that showed she had heard. "That's my father's nickname. You know him, don't you?" There was accusation in her voice.

"I doubt your father knows Cord Elliot," he said with a half-smile, enjoying a joke he couldn't share with her. He had had so many identities that Blue no longer kept track.

After a moment of hesitation, Raine decided that what Cord said could very easily be true. It was quite reasonable that men who were strangers to Justin Chandler-Smith knew his nickname. Her father had worked in many embassies overseas, as well as in the State Department and in the Pentagon in the United States. His titles had varied with the assignment: undersecretary, assistant to the secretary, or the oldest joke of all — chief assistant to the assistant chief.

The titles were meaningless. In the covert world her father inhabited, men without power held impressive titles. Men with true power moved almost anonymously, gray eminences in the marble corridors of state. It was a system used by all world governments, though few carried it as far as the Soviets, who routinely gave their highest KGB men the cover job of chauffeur in Soviet foreign embassies.

"Did you have any trouble with Dev?" Cord asked, driving into a small parking lot and changing the subject in the same neat maneuver.

She thought about it and quickly decided there was no more point in pushing Cord for information than there was in pushing her father. A waste of time all around.

"I had to retrain Dev completely. I turned him out to pasture for three months before I even tried to put a bridle on him. It took more than a year to bring him up to the most basic level of schooled responses."

"You were unusually patient for an eighteen-year-old."

"Dev was worth every minute of it. He was born for eventing. He has more sheer guts than any horse I've ever ridden. Brawn and brains, too." Then she added wryly, "He's saved my butt more than once on a downhill jump."

Cord thought of the course he had gone over yet again today: hellish jumps, dangerous obstacles, blind turns. Next to them Raine seemed frail, overmatched, like a candle burning against overpowering midnight.

"Dev's only drawback is that he won't tolerate strange men handling him," she said.

"Or riding him?"

"Every man who tries ends up on the floor."

A parking attendant trotted over, eager to get his hands on the Pantera. He opened doors, handed over a claim check, and eased into the car.

"What about you?" Cord asked, as his car started off with an unnecessary growl. "Does he try to unload you?"

"Dev has never dumped me intentionally. But I've hit the floor more than once out of my own stupidity."

"Somehow I can't picture you being stupid." He ran his fingertip from the softness of her earlobe to the pulse accelerating in her throat. "Taken by surprise, yes. Next to treachery, surprise is the best way to take a highly fortified position."

Surprised, she stared up at him and felt like a castle whose keys had just been handed over to a strange knight.

Off-balance. Again.

CHAPTER 6

As Raine should have expected, the restaurant Cord chose was a surprise. She had assumed an Oriental restaurant would have the usual mock-Asian decor — red tassels and wall hangings from Taiwan. But the Year of the Rainbow was decorated with Continental restraint and richness: heavy linen and crystal, bone china and sterling silver napkin holders. It took her a moment to realize why the place settings still managed to look odd.

There was no silverware on the table.

The menu was also a surprise. It was printed in ideographs with French translations. At least, she assumed the French was a translation. She couldn't read ideographs. The only price appeared at the very bottom of the menu. The figure assured her that the food was either marvelous or served on solid gold plates.

Perhaps both.

She wondered how Cord managed to afford elegant clothes, transportation, and restaurants. What she had heard of his background didn't suggest inherited wealth. And while people who worked for the government at the highest levels were paid well, they weren't paid *that* well. Most diplomats had to supplement their salaries with personal wealth just to be able to entertain on the scale their jobs required. The United States might be one of the richest countries on earth, but its diplomatic budgets were bare bones.

When Raine looked up from the menu, Cord was watching her openly. His ice-blue eyes were unusually vivid in the candlelight. His thick black hair gleamed with vitality. He was very close to her, because he had chosen to sit at a right angle to her rather than across the table.

"If you like haute cuisine after the French manner," he said, "order from the right side of the menu. If you're feeling adventurous — or would trust me to order for you — go to the left side. And don't worry about the lack of silverware. They'll bring the proper tools to eat whatever you choose."

He watched while she read the French side of the menu with a speed and attention that suggested utter familiarity with the language and cuisine. He would have expected no less from a Chandler-Smith.

Yet in so many ways she continued to surprise him. Open one moment, wary the next, and aware of him every single instant.

Just as he was aware of her. He watched her with a barely leashed intensity, fascinated by the candlelight that shimmered and slid over the chestnut coils of her hair. When a wisp of hair floated forward, tickling the corner of her mouth, he tucked the silky tendril back in place. As he removed his hand, his fingertip traced the rim of her ear.

She gave him a startled look, followed by an almost shy smile that made him wish they were alone in a fortress, the doors locked and bolted against the world outside.

As though she knew what he was thinking, she cleared her throat and turned to the left side of the menu. "I'm feeling adventurous."

"Not trusting?" he asked with a wounded expression on his face and a wicked glint in his eyes.

"Adventurous," she said firmly, refusing him the satisfaction of being trusted.

"There's a lot to be said for adventure." His smile matched the gleam in his eyes.

"Then let's just say I'm hungry enough to eat anything." When she heard her words, she winced and wished she had bitten her tongue.

"An adventurous woman," he agreed blandly. "You came to the right man."

Cord took Raine's menu and set it on top of his own, which he hadn't bothered to open.

The waiter materialized as though summoned by a king.

Cord spoke to him in a sliding, sing-song language. After a discreetly startled reappraisal of his client, the waiter began scribbling ideographs on his pad. When Cord finished, the waiter made a few recommendations. Cord took two and discarded the others.

The wine steward came over. They conferred over the list in two languages, neither of which was English.

Watching, listening, Raine smiled with a mixture of amusement and appreciation. Cord reminded her of her father, a man at home in several tongues and utterly fluent in the oldest language known to man — power.

When Cord was finished with the wine list, Raine saluted him silently.

He gathered her hand into his and watched her expression closely. "No inherited wealth, just the best education Uncle

Sam and experience could provide." He smiled slightly and added, "The steward was polite enough not to wince at my French accent."

"Inherited wealth only means money, not the brains to use it. And there's nothing wrong with your accent," she said, defending him instantly.

"Tell that to a Parisian."

"You can't tell *anything* to a Parisian."

Cord's dark pupils dilated. "The queen is very kind to her soldier," he said softly.

He lifted Raine's hand to his lips. For an instant he savored her sweet-smelling skin with the hidden tip of his tongue. The caress was so casual, yet at the same time so intimate, that she could barely control the shiver that went through her.

"I'm not a queen," she whispered through suddenly dry lips, "and you're hardly a common soldier."

He simply looked at her, making no effort to conceal the hunger in his eyes, a hunger reflected in the slow movement of his thumb over her fingertips. When the wine arrived, he went through the ritual of tasting it almost indifferently, not even releasing her hand.

Yet she was certain that if the wine had been inferior, he would have noticed and sent it back instantly. Cord Elliot wasn't a man to accept second best in anything.

The wine was both delicious and unfamiliar, a Fumé blanc that exactly balanced the exotic meal. There was shrimp paste broiled on narrow strips of sugarcane, tiny crepe-like wrappers containing a miniature leaf and crisp julienne of marinated vegetables, very small meatballs simmered in a piquant sauce, and shrimp that tasted like rainbows and melted in her mouth.

There were other dishes, too, temperatures hot and cold and tepid, tastes sweet and vinegar and salt, flavors and textures and colors combined in endless array, a feast for the eyes as well as the mouth.

The meal arrived with sterling silver chopsticks and a lemon-scented fingerbowl. Raine watched Cord, ate the appropriate foods with her fingers, and used the fingerbowl as she would after any meal. The chopsticks, however, baffled her. The cuisines she was familiar with would have used a tool shaped like a chopstick to skewer and broil chunks of meat, not to eat anything as tiny and elusive as rice.

"Like this." He took her hand and positioned her chopsticks correctly. "Keep them almost parallel to the plate, instead of vertical, as you would a fork. Now, hold the bottom one steady and move the top one. Or vice versa. I'm not a purist. Whatever gets it done."

As the meal progressed, she became more skilled with the slippery sticks, but still lost about one out of three tidbits. It could have been because she kept being distracted by Cord. He used the chopsticks with a dexterity that fascinated her. Divided between admiration and exasperation, she watched him eat. When yet another succulent shrimp escaped her, exasperation won out.

"Ruddy slippery beast," she muttered.

Deftly he picked up the shrimp in his chopsticks and held it near her lips. Without hesitation she opened her mouth and took the morsel. He looked hungrily at the white gleam of her teeth, the pink tip of her tongue, the sensual fullness of her lips as they closed for an instant around his chopsticks.

The memory of a twilight hill and the taste of Raine on his tongue stabbed through Cord and settled deep inside, the potent heaviness and ache of male hunger. With an effort he looked away from her mouth. Tonight he wanted to prove to her that he was a gentleman as well as a man trained in violence. He wanted to seduce her in more than a merely physical way.

He wanted her to trust him.

Everything about Raine told him that Justin Chandler-Smith's youngest daughter was neither worldly nor wild when it came to men.

But she was wise. There was no trust in her.

Anger uncurled in Cord's gut. That kind of bone-deep distrust was learned, usually with pain. He wondered which bastard had hurt her, and why, and how deeply. Deeply enough that she shied from Cord's admiration, his compliments, his touch.

Bleakly he wondered if he had time to gain her trust before the Summer Olympics were over. Then he told himself it shouldn't matter. He had no business touching her, much less wanting her with a force that grew with every breath he took. But he did want her. He ached to be the chopsticks sliding in and out of her mouth.

With a silent inner curse, he forced himself to concentrate on food rather than her tempting, sultry lips.

"Mmmm," she said, neatly cleaning her chopsticks with her lips. "This shrimp sauce is magic. What's in it?"

"You don't want to know."

She blinked. "I don't?"

"Nope."

"What if there's curry in it?"

"There isn't. Trust me."

She smiled. "Pass the shrimp, please."

By the time dinner was over, Raine was thinking of ways to loosen her silk belt without getting caught at it. For the last ten minutes she had been telling herself that she would take just one more bite of crisp vegetable or one more rainbow bite of shrimp. But each bite had demanded another from a complementary dish, foods and flavors blended with such sophistication that the palate always wanted just one more taste.

Finally she groaned and put her chopsticks on their ivory rest. "No more."

Cord smiled. A woman could say polite words and push food around her plate, but only someone who truly enjoyed the flavors would have eaten with Raine's enthusiasm.

"Are you sure?" he asked. "If you're tired of using chopsticks, I can feed you."

Absently she flexed her right hand. Tiny little muscles ached with the unaccustomed strain of holding chopsticks. "You could feed me," she agreed with a crooked smile, "but could you digest it for me?"

Laughing, he shook his head and lifted his right hand slightly. The waiter reappeared and cleared the table with elegance and speed.

"Dessert?" Cord asked, taking Raine's hand again.

"Impossible."

"Coffee? Liqueur?"

"Would you believe a walk to the car? If I don't get moving, I'm going to pop."

Smiling, he spoke to the waiter. A few moments later the man returned with two pieces of hand-dipped chocolate candy wrapped in gold foil. They were perched like gems on a sterling silver tray.

The waiter also had a Styrofoam cup of coffee laced with Armagnac.

She barely managed not to laugh out loud at the odd marriage of plastic and sterling. Laughter and pleasure fizzed through her. Perhaps it was the wine, perhaps it was the food, most likely it was the man who tucked her into the sleek sports car with hard hands and a gentle touch.

When the parking attendant handed Cord the coffee and candy on the expensive tray, Raine gave in to laughter. She barely managed to balance the cup and the candy when he put them in her hands.

"What's the punch line?" Cord asked, as he got in the driver's seat.

"Styrofoam and sterling."

"The waiter tried to talk me into taking one of their china cups, but I held out for the real thing."

Snickering, she balanced the coffee in one hand and the chocolates in the other.

With the skill she was coming to take for granted, Cord drove the Pantera through darkened streets and onto the freeway. While streams of cars flowed around them, she fed him one piece of candy, ate the other, and carefully pried off the plastic lid on the cup. The marvelous aromas of Colombian coffee and French Armagnac expanded to fill the interior of the car. She inhaled deeply, greedily, but didn't take so much as a sip.

He smiled without looking away from traffic. "Go ahead. I got it for both of us."

"You sure? I already passed up my opportunity back at the restaurant."

"I'm sure."

Cautiously she sipped at the hot, heady liquid.

His hand went to the tape deck. There was a soft click, then the haunting strains of Debussy moved through the car like a caress.

After an initial instant of surprise at his taste in music, she sighed and gave herself over to the lyric beauty. When he lifted the coffee cup out of her hand, the sliding warmth of his fingertips over her skin became another kind of music.

The opposite lanes of the freeway slid by in a silver-white dazzle, a racing river of light sixty feet wide and hundreds of miles long. Directly ahead, traffic was a shimmering ruby ribbon with random amber lights winking as invisible cars changed lanes.

When the music finally faded into silence, Raine was all but mesmerized by the beauty of the night and the calm male presence at her side. Saying nothing, she watched the world slide by as Cord turned the car off the freeway. They wound through hills and parked in a lot high on a ridge overlooking the dazzling, light-shot reaches of Los Angeles.

"Where are we?" she asked lazily, not really caring. As she spoke, she stole the cup from Cord and drank the last drops from its fragrant depths.

"Griffith Observatory."

"Lovely view," she said, sighing.

It was, but not nearly as beautiful to Raine as Cord was. His profile was clean and black against the lights, and his eyes were deep and calm. He took the empty cup from her fingers and put it on the floor.

"If I could, I'd give you the moon and the stars so that you would forgive me for

143

frightening you yesterday. But the moon and stars are beyond my reach," he said, unlocking their seatbelts and lifting her across his lap with a fluid motion. "So I'll give you the next best thing. A guided tour of the universe."

While his mouth brushed over her lips, her cheeks, her eyelashes, his fingers smoothed the sensitive nape of her neck. When his lips returned to hers, the tip of his tongue moved tantalizingly over the curves of her mouth. Her lips parted, wanting more of his sensual touch. With melting gentleness, his teeth closed over her lower lip. His tongue caressed the soft, captive flesh.

Raine felt herself losing her balance again . . . and she didn't care. She was surrounded by a warm velvet world, nowhere to fall but Cord's arms and he was holding her as though she was made of moonlight and stardust. With a shiver of pleasure, she relaxed against him. Her hands slid over the soft wool of his coat to the silk shirt beneath. Slowly her fingers searched over the warm, smooth cloth, enjoying the muscular resilience of his body, instinctively wanting more.

Strong arms tightened around her, his answer to the restless seeking of her hands over his chest. He heard her tiny sigh when her fingers tangled in the hair at the nape of his neck. With a final caress, he released her lower lip. He fitted his mouth over hers, searching her darkness and warmth as though she was wholly undiscovered territory. Not one hidden surface, not one warm texture escaped his slow, intimate exploration. Finally he captured her tongue with his own and drank deeply of her sweetness.

A hunger that was both dark and incandescent shot through his veins. His arousal grew with aching swiftness. The slight shift of her hips against his thighs made him groan deep in his chest. He knew that her move wasn't calculated. She wasn't trying to cut the steel ropes of his discipline. She wasn't urging him to strip off her silk panties and take her right here, right now, hot and deep and hard.

But he was very close to doing just that.

The knowledge of how near he was to the brink brought Cord back under control. Reluctantly, feeling as though he was tearing off his own skin, he separated his mouth from Raine's. When he saw her dilated pupils, her flushed cheeks, her quick, shallow breaths, he knew that she was as aroused as he was. It was a bittersweet comfort.

Gently he pressed her head against his

chest and held her close, rocking her very slowly. The depth and recklessness of his hunger for her shocked him. So did her headlong response. Her subtle shifts and hesitations at the beginning of the kiss had told him that she was a sensual rather than an experienced woman.

Yet she had opened to him like an undefended valley, inviting and warm, welcoming the soldier coming down from the frigid heights of a mountain pass.

And he needed that welcome the way fire needed to burn.

Sighing, Raine slid her arms around Cord and snuggled in close. She enjoyed the solid feel of his flesh, his heat, the deep rhythm of his heart against her cheek, the strength and vitality that hummed just beneath his surface. She had never felt quite so safe as she did right now, and so cherished. All the relentless pressures weighing her down had evaporated in his presence.

"You were right," she said softly. "Kissing you is a healing thing."

She felt his breath stop, then resume. Slowly his hand stroked the length of her dress from shoulder to waist to knee. Silk whispered seductively, asking to be stroked again. His finger tilted up her chin. Gentle kisses touched every contour of her face, lingered over the softness of her lips.

"You're very beautiful," he whispered.

When she opened her mouth to protest, his tongue slid between her teeth, silencing her with a slow, penetrating sweetness that made her shiver. It was a long time before he lifted his head and looked down at her with eyes more silver than blue, their centers dark and wide with passion.

"If I don't put you back on the other side of the car," he said huskily, "we'll miss that guided tour of the universe."

Her breath broke at the hunger burning in his eyes, the stark need that vibrated through him. Yet his hands were gentle as they moved over her.

"I thought this was the tour," she admitted, unable to conceal the catch in her voice or the quiver of her response to his long caresses.

He looked at her eyes as though he could see the future reflected in their hazel depths. "Is this a new world for you?"

"Yes," she said simply.

"It's new for me, too."

He bent down to kiss her with a gentleness that made her want to melt and flow over him, into him, until they filled each other and there was nothing in the world but them.

Headlights flashed through the windshield. Another car pulled into the parking lot. Laughter and conversation drifted through the Pantera's open window as people walked toward the observatory's entrance.

With a whispered word that could have been a curse or a prayer, Cord eased Raine back into her seat. Silently he got out and walked around to her side of the car.

She watched his lithe stride, the male grace of his body, and remembered the feel of him, the taste of him, the sheer heat and strength. Unfamiliar sensations raced over nerve endings she hadn't known she had, making her shiver as though with cold. Yet there was a melting heat at her core.

When he reached in to help her out of the car, the simple touch of his hand on hers made muscles tighten deep inside her body. It was the elemental reaction of a woman needing her mate. She stared up at him with an almost dazed look. Being seduced by other men hadn't been nearly as exciting as simply being kissed by Cord Elliot.

The realization dismayed her, making her distrust her own responses. Yet when he smiled and took her hand, she couldn't bring herself to withdraw.

Slowly they walked toward the domed

planetarium, barely noticing the glittering, jeweled carpet of Los Angeles spread from horizon to horizon at their feet. The interior of the building was cool, the ceiling shaped like a hemisphere, the seats oddly slanted so that people looked up rather than forward. Silently, hand in hand, Raine and Cord sat and waited in darkness for the universe to condense across the arched ceiling.

Stars materialized, countless silver shimmers scattered across the featureless black ceiling-sky. The stars moved in graceful swirls, sliding down the sides of artificial night until a single spiral galaxy filled the viewing area.

A polished voice began to speak, pointing out the relationship of the planet Earth to the languidly turning galaxy known as the Milky Way. The tiny sparkle of Earth's sun along one arm of the galaxy increased and the rest of the galaxy expanded until stars blurred and ran in silver streamers down the ceiling to vanish in the black walls. The Solar System grew until individual planets could be seen gliding at the end of invisible leashes around the burning center of the Sun.

The balanced dance of force and counterforce, attraction and retreat, was as seductive as Debussy or the haunting fragrance of Armagnac and coffee. Each planet was featured separately: the ochres and tawny browns of Mercury; the fierce heat beneath Venus's brilliant, seething cloud cover; the fragile silver and blue beauty of Earth; Mars's ruined, red-brown surface; the great Red Spot of Jupiter, set immovably in fluid, multicolored bands of cloud; and Saturn's incredible rings, curves of silence and beauty turning endlessly around their own frozen center.

Raine watched without moving, enthralled by a perspective that was as new to her as the alien landscapes condensing and vanishing in silent counterpoint to the narrator's serene voice. Some of the views were composite photographs taken by space-faring machines. Other views were drawn by artists with rigorous scientific backgrounds.

No matter the source, the pictures reminded her that the Solar System was huge and mysterious, the universe unimaginably vast, the possibilities literally infinite. For all its variety of people and geography, when viewed against the larger universe, Earth was only a wisp of a dream circling an unknown star. And human life was simply a dream within that dream.

Slowly, light seeped back into the auditorium. Raine blinked, still lost within the vastness and beauty of what she had seen. The sense of infinity suspended within eternity was oddly comforting to her. Life was both fragile and fierce, brief and able to embrace eternity.

She sighed with a pleasure that was unlike anything she had felt before. The new sense of being rooted in a vastly larger reality was like being taken out of a cage and set free to soar on endless currents of possibility. She hadn't known that the cage was there until the door was opened.

Now she would never go back.

"That was . . . incredible," she murmured, turning toward Cord. "How did you know I needed that? I didn't even know it myself."

His fingers tightened over hers. "I knew I needed it. I thought you might. It's easy to get so tangled in one small reality that you can't see forest, trees, or even the hand in front of your face."

"It's called focus."

"That kind of concentration is fine. Usually it's the only way to get a job done. But sometimes too much focus ties you in tiny little knots."

"Competition madness," she agreed. "Nothing else seems real but the contest ahead. The world shrinks and shrinks and *shrinks* until it's all you can do to take a deep breath. You have to find something to distract yourself or you suffocate."

"We're more alike than you think we are."

"What do you mean?"

Cord stood and pulled Raine to her feet. "That's the way it is in my job. Too much focus will kill you."

"But losing your concentration is a good way to get hurt, too," she said. "At least it is for me. Especially in the three-day event."

"No argument there. A careless man — or woman — doesn't last long in my business, either. So we walk the tightrope between too much and not enough, and the survivors err on the side of too much." He put his hand on the small of her back as they walked out of the planetarium into the warm darkness. "I guess you could call it a kind of competition madness."

She saw the thin gleam of Cord's teeth, but his smile was more grim than amused. She knew that the stakes he played for were lives rather than medals or ribbons. For an instant she almost asked what, precisely, his job was, but growing up with a father like Chandler-Smith had taught her that asking that kind of question was useless. The answer would always be the same.

Silence.

CHAPTER 7

"Can you walk in those sexy little sandals?" Cord asked.

Raine looked down at the thin straps and outrageously high heels on her feet. "Depends on what you mean by walk. Anything less than a civilized stroll on a sidewalk could be a problem."

"Don't worry. I'll take care of it."

"How? Pave Griffith Park?"

"Nothing that extreme. I'll just carry you."

"Promises, promises," she said under her breath. But she was smiling. Tonight she felt light enough to float away.

He guided her to a paved pathway that wound along the edge of the hills. While they walked, a fitful wind sent shivers of sound through the silence, distant voices and nearby trees whispering to themselves.

The path led to a secluded loop overlooking the valley below. Southern pines grew around the viewpoint. Their black trunks and airy branches made lacy patterns against the golden illumination of city below and silver stars above. Each city light was vivid, distinct, an echo of the vastly larger stars flung in diamond brightness across the sky.

For Raine the night and the man were magic. Everything was magnified — the soft scrape of leather soles on pavement, the rub of needles against branches, the fluid ripple of sprinklers on another hill, the whisper of silk caressing her legs. Warm air flowed over her skin, tugged gently at her hair. The air smelled of pine and summer flowers and freshly watered grass. The city lights below were stitched together with the ruby and silver threads of countless freeways.

Cord's fingers moved caressingly over hers, sending streamers of invisible warmth through both of them. It had been a long time since he had been with a woman who enjoyed silence, who drank the scents of night, who wore silk and jeans with equal ease. He couldn't remember ever enjoying a woman's presence as much as he did Raine's. Being with her was . . . peaceful.

It also aroused him to a point just short of violence.

She drew a deep breath, threaded her fingers more deeply through his, and let herself float on the limitless glittering night. Nothing else was real but this instant. Nothing else mattered but the man whose every touch said how glad he was to be with her.

Because of Cord, she was in a new world tonight, a world where she didn't have to worry about each word, each gesture. She didn't have to wonder what he would think or not think, do or not do in response to her. His presence expanded her personal space rather than limiting it.

And the heady freedom of his company brought each of her senses intensely alive. Everything around her was brighter, better, more vivid and complete than anything in her memory.

Silently thanking Cord for the gift, she raised his hand to her mouth and brushed her lips over his fingers. The gesture was so natural that she didn't realize what she was doing until she had done it.

His thumb moved slowly over her lips, telling her how much he had enjoyed the spontaneous caress.

"Now I know how Dev feels after I wash and groom and polish him and then ride him dancing to the starting gate," she said dreamily. "Everything is ahead, anything is possible."

Cord's thumb traced her cheekbone and

the hollow beneath it before settling on the corner of her mouth. When he tilted her face, her lips parted and her arms moved to circle his waist, silently welcoming the coming embrace.

Even though his breathing thickened with the sudden, urgent demands of his body, he didn't stop thinking. Swiftly, gently, he captured her hands and kissed each palm. Then he put her arms around his neck. He didn't want her to bump into the gun holstered in the small of his back.

At the beginning of the evening, she had been deeply wary of him. He didn't know why, but he knew fear was there. Sensing fear was his business. He had thought about it during the drive to the planetarium. By the time he pulled into the parking lot, he had decided that her fear had as much to do with her past as with his present job.

But he didn't want to remind her of either just now. He wanted Raine the way she was at this instant, warm and supple, hungry and very female in his arms. When her fingers rubbed over his neck and scalp, he made a low sound of pleasure and arched beneath her touch like a great black-haired cat.

His uninhibited response swept through her like fire, taking her breath. She stood on tiptoe, but still she couldn't reach his mouth to kiss him. Her fingers clenched in the rough silk of his hair. Her nails raked not quite gently over his scalp. She wanted him to lower his head and kiss her, and she wanted it *now.*

He laughed and caught her bottom lip between his teeth. His hard tongue teased her while he slowly devoured her soft flesh. A small sound of pleasure and desire rippled out of her. It made him forget that he was going to stop with a single, teasing kiss. His hands went from her face to her shoulders and down her spine to her hips. Then his arms tightened and he molded her to the hungry length of his body.

When he felt her shudder of response, he groaned softly and cupped the resilient warmth of her hips in his hands. She made a startled sound and tried to step back, only to find herself held by the teeth gently gripping her bottom lip. The instant she discovered that she was the prisoner of his sensual vise, he released her.

Off-balance, she clung to the hard support of his upper arms, staring into his ice-blue eyes. Only they weren't icy now, but smoldering with passion, a silver blue hot enough to burn.

And the proof of his hunger was hard

against her belly. When she would have withdrawn, he held her for an instant. Then he released her. Slowly.

"You tempt me," he said in a low voice. "Unbearably."

"I don't mean —"

"I know," he cut in. "God, I *know.*"

Slowly, almost helplessly, he bent his head and licked her lips with tiny catlike strokes.

The primitive caress made liquid fire run and gather deep inside her. Lost in a swirl of sensation, she said his name, a name he stole from her tongue as he claimed the warm territory of her mouth for his own.

In a heartbeat the kiss went from tender to ravenous. They fought to get closer to each other. His hands kneaded down her spine to her hips, touching each feminine curve, holding her against the blunt heat and hard ridge of his erection. His fingers caressed the deep crease between her buttocks, then slid lower, seeking the smooth curve of her inner thighs, rocking her against his rigid flesh.

This time she didn't withdraw at the intimacy of feeling his erection pressed against her, stroking her, making her dizzy with unfamiliar needs. Her arms locked around his neck and she arched into him, rubbing against him in turn, wanting only to be closer and then closer still.

Hungry for more, he sank his fingers into her before he forced himself to slowly release the taut flesh of her hips. Restlessly his hands swept back up to her shoulders and then down her arms to her waist, devouring the feminine curves of her body. Fingers spread wide, heartbeat speeding, he traced the line of her ribs beneath the thin silk.

Though she expected it, the brush of his thumbs over her nipples made her gasp at the stark hunger that leaped inside her. He murmured against her lips, words without meaning except as another kind of caress, the dark velvet of his voice both soothing and inciting her.

Delicately, his teeth closed over her ear. He traced its shape with the hardened tip of his tongue, then thrust into her with slow, deep, thorough strokes that told her exactly what to expect if she opened herself to him, welcoming him into the sultry velvet center of her body.

He knew just how good it would be.

Eyes closed, letting the world fall away, his fingers probed beneath the chestnut coils of her hair until he felt the heat of her scalp. Then he held her close and hard while his tongue claimed her mouth, telling her all over again how thoroughly he would love her. He smoothed one hand over her throat, finding and savoring the wild race of her pulse. It made him want to shout with triumph. Never had a woman responded like this to him, as swift and hot as his own hunger.

And never had his hunger been this great. With hands as hot as his own breath, his own blood, he slid into the deep neckline of her dress, searching beneath silk until her naked breasts pushed against his palms.

Part of Raine knew it was too much, too fast; she should protest, but the only sound she made was a ragged moan of pleasure as Cord's thumbs circled her nipples. Taut, full, aching with a hunger she had never known before, she surrendered herself to the endless sensuality of his touch.

He brushed aside the fold of silk covering one breast and bent down. Even before the coolness of the night air registered against her flushed skin, a searing pleasure shot through her. His teeth and tongue shaped her hungrily, licking and nipping until she was as hard as he was, as hot, as wild. Then he took her into his mouth and suckled her with a fierce restraint that made her cry out, defenseless against the reckless sexuality he could summon from her depths.

wanted to do was take her down to the ground and discover how much he had been missing before he found her.

"Captain Jon told me not to worry. He thinks I work too hard anyway."

"Do you?"

Her shoulders lifted beneath his hands in a shrug. "I love my work. But . . ."

"But?" His fingers kneaded lightly, smoothing away the tension he felt returning to her neck and back.

"But right now," she said, turning her face up to him, "I don't want to go back to that world. Not yet. I've never felt quite like this."

He looked down into her wide hazel eyes and asked the question he had no right to ask, the very question he couldn't keep himself from asking. "How do you feel?"

"New. No past but tonight. No future farther away than the next instant when you'll touch me, teaching me something about myself I never knew."

Her honesty was more devastating and more arousing than an experienced lover's knowing caress. She was an invitation he couldn't refuse and couldn't accept and couldn't ignore.

"Raine," he whispered, his voice thick with restraint and need, "you don't know what you're doing."

"Does it matter?" Her hands lifted to his face, then tugged his head down to her lips. "You know enough for both of us."

"That's the problem," he said roughly.

He saw the instant of realization hit her, the stillness of shock. Embarrassment stained her cheeks. One moment she was pliant in his arms. The next she twisted free with the speed of the highly trained athlete she was.

"I'm sorry," she said in a strained voice. "That was incredibly stupid of me."

She stepped back on legs that felt weak. Silently, she called herself names. Stupid was the least of them. Just because Cord Elliot was the first man in her life who made her ache with hunger, that didn't automatically mean he felt the same way. She had turned down men in the past. It was only logical that one would turn her down.

Especially a man like Cord. An experienced man would want an equally skilled lover. When it came to sex, she just wasn't any good. Her last lover had made that painfully clear.

"Raine, there's —" Cord began

"You're right, of course," she said, cutting across whatever sophisticated, kind, *experienced* explanation he was going to offer.

She didn't want to hear it. She had heard the only words that mattered.

He didn't want her.

"I do have a curfew hanging over me," she said. "But thanks for the guided tour. I'll take a cab back to Santa Anita."

"Cabs are scarce in L.A."

"Then I'll call up a limousine. The place is crawling with them. Good-bye, Cord."

Even before the words were out of her mouth, she turned her back on him. Blindly she began hurrying along the path, knowing only that she had to get away from the man who didn't want her nearly as much as she wanted him. She no longer saw the dazzle of city lights or the shadow dance of black trees and warm wind. She saw nothing but her own humiliation.

Not that he had intended to humiliate her, she admitted bitterly. He had been a gentleman until she had refused to take a hint. If he had been blunt, it was only because there had been no other way to get through to her.

She increased her pace, ignoring the wobble of her high heels. The sandals weren't made for speed or distance, but right now she desperately wanted both. She could hear Cord coming closer, closing the space between them with long, determined strides.

"I'll take you home," he said quietly from behind her.

Like bloody hell you will, Raine thought savagely.

With two quick swipes she tore off her sandals. An instant later she was running flat out down the path, confident that she would quickly leave him behind. Part of her Olympic training involved running distances up to five kilometers. She had never particularly cared for the required exercise, but she appreciated the results.

Especially tonight.

Tonight she welcomed the physical release of running, the freedom of racing away from the man who didn't really want her. Anger and humiliation became adrenaline coursing through her, feeding her desire to run. Part of her realized that she was heading away from the planetarium, into the black recesses of the huge park. She didn't care. It felt too good to run.

When Cord realized that Raine was going to keep on running, he gave chase without even thinking about it. A hunter's adrenaline coursed through him. Frustration goaded him.

He had never wanted her more than he

did right now.

She ran lightly, silently, a green flame racing among the shadows and pools of light along the path, wildfire running free in the night. The coils of hair he had loosened with his fingers had come wholly undone. Hair streamed behind her like a flag. With each flashing stride, jade-green silk flowed in dark caress up her thighs.

She was faster than he had expected. Stronger, too. But her body hadn't been honed in the same life-or-death kind of training that his had.

One instant Raine was running free. In the next, something hard clamped onto her arm, spinning her around until she slammed into a hard wall.

Even as she realized that the wall was Cord, he surrounded her. One of his hands tangled deeply in her hair, chaining her. His arms closed hard around her, crushing any thought of escape. He invaded her mouth, forcing her to accept the intimacy of his tongue thrusting into her softness while he held her immobile, consolidating his victory.

The transition between freedom and capture was so swift, so stunning, that for a time she couldn't have fought even if he had permitted her to. When she finally tried, he easily countered her untrained struggles. Her helplessness would have frightened her if she hadn't sensed that it was hunger rather than a desire to punish her that was driving him.

Whatever she had thought back on the overlook, he wanted her now with an honesty and an intensity that was more shattering than any words, any touch could have been.

Her body changed beneath his hands, softening and flowing over his hard male surfaces, surrendering what he had already taken. Her response mocked the very idea of victory or defeat, flight or capture, invasion or surrender.

She felt the shudder of desire rip through him, felt as much as heard the groan that began deep in his chest, felt and was inflamed by the sinuous movement of his hips as he lifted her. Then he let her slide down his body, silently telling her exactly how much he desired her.

"I thought you didn't want me," she whispered, when he finally freed her mouth.

He laughed once, harshly. "Kiss me." His eyes looked hungrily at her mouth as he lowered his head again. "I want to feel your tongue rubbing over mine. *Kiss me.*"

She opened her lips, inviting the sweetness and heat of his mouth even as she sought his tongue, demanded it. She kissed him the way he had kissed her, nothing held back. Hunger raged through her with each stab of flesh sliding hotly against flesh. She pushed inside his jacket, seeking the hard, coiling male strength of him. Her fingers searched beneath his tie, then slid boldly into the opening between buttons on his shirt. Even as her fingertips found his skin, his hands cupped her breasts beneath the folds of green silk.

Cord drank the broken sound Raine made when he stroked her nipples until they were hard peaks begging to be kissed. His body was rigid, shaking, straining against the leash of clothes. Desperately needing what he shouldn't have and couldn't take, he raked his open mouth down her neck. He had just enough restraint left not to leave loving marks on her, staking out her smooth flesh as his own.

But he wanted to. He wanted to discover and claim every bit of her softness and feminine hunger, to feed and then to possess the heat inside her, to spend the night listening to the cries pouring out of her as she burned alive in her own fire.

With a groan, he kneaded her hips, loving the satin flex and slide of muscle when she moved against him. Beneath his jacket, a rider's strong hands stroked around his body, encircling him, demanding that he come even closer. He lifted her against his heavy arousal, dragging her closer until all that held them apart was a few layers of cloth.

She gave a low, reckless cry and abandoned herself to the fire. Her head fell back as she answered with a swift movement of her hips, then another. He felt the tension and hot need in her, a sultry mirror of his own desire. Her nails raked down his spine until they found the gun nestled in the small of his back.

She went utterly still. Her withdrawal from him couldn't have been more complete if she had turned and run again.

"I wouldn't have expected Blue's daughter to be afraid of a holstered gun," Cord said in a husky voice, "but if it bothers you that much, I'll take it off."

"It's not that." She felt numb and foolish and totally off-balance. But she wouldn't reach for him this time. She would find her balance on her own, because she remembered now. "I'd forgotten what you were."

"What I am is a man."

"Yes." Her voice was distant and sad at the same time.

One of her hands slid beneath his jacket once again. This time she continued down to his waistline until she felt the hard case of the electronic pager fastened to his belt.

"You're a man who has clothes specially tailored to conceal the bulges of beeper and gun," Raine said. "Or is that your spare ammunition clip?"

"No," he said, his voice even. "That's on my right side."

She didn't bother to verify it. There was no need. The knowledge chilled her. She rubbed her hands over her arms, trying to warm herself.

Seeing the gesture, understanding it, Cord swore savagely, caught in the aftershocks of hunger and a frustration that went much deeper than lust. He should have known better than to get involved with a woman like Raine. She was wealthy, successful, gently raised, and burned beyond recovery on the subject of certain types of work.

His type of work.

"I'm more than a gun and a beeper," he said roughly.

"Really? My father isn't."

"Bullshit," Cord snarled. "If you don't believe me, ask your mother. She sure as hell knows what Blue is."

"I'm not my mother. I want more from a

man than money and position."

"Blue loves your mother!"

"Perhaps," Raine said politely.

"You don't think so?"

Her false calm evaporated. "Depends on what you call love," she retorted bitterly. "Being left without warning again and again, never being able to count on the man who 'loves' you for something so simple as a shoulder to sleep on, never knowing if he's coming back, never —"

"He always has," Cord broke in. "Other men might screw around, but Blue never did."

Her laugh was like broken glass, all cutting edges. "I believe you. Only a wife would put up with a man who is ruled by a beeper. A mistress would tell him to go to hell."

"Or a daughter?" he asked sardonically.

"Wife, mistress, or daughter, the beeper means the same thing. You're second place in a two-entry race."

"That's not —"

"The hell it isn't!" she cut in fiercely. "I had all I could take of second-class citizenship as a child. The kind of work my father does is important, addictive, and carnivorous. But then, I'm not telling you anything you don't know, am I?"

"No." The line of his mouth was grim as

172

his voice. "The instant my beeper went off yesterday, I knew how you felt about my work. About me. That's what I meant when I said that you didn't know what you were doing. I knew you didn't want me, even though you thought you did."

She trembled, torn between fiery hunger and the numbing cold of childhood memories. *"I wanted you."*

"Not enough to see past the gun and beeper. Not even for one goddamned night. I suppose I should be grateful. Neither one of us is the one-night-stand type. Sure as hell you would have hated me in the morning." He bent and picked up the purse and sandals she had dropped when he caught her. "Here. Put your shoes on."

She tried to, but couldn't. Her fingers were shaking too much. With an impatient sound, he grabbed the sandals and fastened them on her feet. In silence, they walked back to the car. The silence remained unbroken until he pulled up and parked several doors down from her motel room.

"Give me your key."

She stared at him as though he had lost his mind.

"Don't worry, Baby Raine. I'm not planning to spend the night between your pristine sheets."

"I don't like that name," she said tightly.

"I know." His smile was no more than the biting edge of his teeth. He opened her purse and took out the room key. "Stay here."

After a swift look around, Cord walked to the door of Raine's motel room. No curtains moved in her room or in the rooms on either side. He tested gently to see that the door was still locked. It was.

Just as he lifted the key with his right hand, he caught movement at the corner of his eye. Even before he spun completely around, his left hand had yanked the gun out of its holster in the small of his back.

He recognized Raine before the muzzle cleared his belt.

With a startled gasp, she retreated two steps before her mind took over. Even though Cord didn't look very civilized at the moment, she knew he wouldn't hurt her.

"I told you to stay in the car," he said curtly. He holstered the weapon with a quick, casual motion.

"I didn't want to stay. So what?"

"Just this, Baby Raine. There might be a bomb behind this door, waiting for your key to complete the circuit."

Her hand came up to her mouth in an involuntary gesture of shock. "But then you

— you'd be the one to —"

"That's my job," he broke in impatiently. "Go back to the car."

"But —"

"Relax. I'm more worried about someone waiting in your room than having a bomb going off in my face."

Without another word she spun around and walked back to the car.

Cord opened the motel room and eased inside. He was all but certain that no one could have gotten past the agents who had rented the rooms on either side of Raine. Almost certain, but not quite.

That damned three percent.

Holding his breath, he listened for a minute. Nothing moved, nothing breathed. He flipped on the light, searched the places big enough to hide a person, and found exactly what the odds said he should. Nothing.

He went back to the car and walked Raine to her door. For a moment he stood there, very close to her, watching her with eyes that were as clear and empty as ice.

"You live in a beautiful castle, with a fire burning in every hearth," he said finally. "I wish to hell there was a place by all that fire for me."

He gave her a fierce, yearning kiss. Then

he turned and went to his car, leaving her standing with his taste on her lips and her nails digging into her own palms.

He didn't look back.

CHAPTER 8

Raine pushed a wheelbarrow of feed up the dusty stable row. Southern California's dry heat sucked up water almost as quickly as it came out of the sprinklers that worked to keep the dust under control. When she reached Dev's stall, he wasn't waiting as he usually did, with his neck stretched over the door and a soft nicker quivering through him.

"Good morning, Devlin's Waterloo," she said clearly. "I'm early, but not that early. Wakey-wakey, sleepyhead."

No mahogany head poked over the stall door.

Alarm stabbed through Raine. She abandoned the wheelbarrow and rushed to look into the stall. The stallion was inside, moving easily, totally alert . . . and edgy as hell. He snorted at her as though he didn't quite recognize his own rider.

"Hey, boy. It's all right. Nobody here but me."

The horse eyed her warily.

"What is it, Dev? Is the wind spooking you?"

Usually Dev came right to her and all but shoved her into the wheelbarrow in his eagerness to say hello. But today he was being coy, mincing around his stall and snorting at her as though she had a frog in her pocket and was waiting to spring it on him.

"Easy, boy," she murmured.

She propped her elbows on the bottom half of the Dutch door and talked softly to the stallion. Behind her a desert wind stirred among the fragile leaves of pepper trees, making lacy shadows shiver and run over the ground. The early morning breeze lifted her unbound hair, blowing it over her face.

Ears pricked, Dev minced forward to investigate the flying strands. Nostrils quivering, breathing deeply and then snorting to clear his senses, the stallion drank in Raine's scent as though uncertain of who she was.

"What is it, boy?" she asked softly, holding out her hand. "What's wrong? You aren't the type for nerves this early in the waiting game."

With consuming interest, Dev sniffed her outstretched hand, then her arm, then her neck.

"Hey," she said, backing away from the relentless inspection. "I know I didn't shower this this morning — I'm mucking out your stall, not going to a cocktail party. I smell a lot worse after a workout and you don't give me the vacuum treatment."

Dev snorted a long comment, then resumed snuffling over every inch of Raine. He reserved his most intense interest for her hair, face, neck, and hands.

Baffled, she simply stood quietly and let the stallion get whatever it was out of his system. The last time Dev had showed such a persistent interest in her, she had been wearing a new cologne. But whatever artificial scent she had on now was left over from last night, and it was the same cologne she had worn for years. Nothing new. Nothing different. Nothing had changed.

Except that last night she had let a man's hands and mouth move over her as though he owned her.

A flush of embarrassment heated her skin as she realized that Dev was fascinated by her scent because it *was* different. Cord Elliot lingered on her skin, in her hair, behind her ears, in the hollow of her throat, between her fingers where she had rubbed them through his hair. Invisible traces to her, but not to the stallion's acute senses.

Cord's male scent was all over her, blended with her own.

Gritting her teeth, she waited for Dev to get used to the new scent. The horse's ability to find each place Cord had touched her was unnerving and more than a little embarrassing. She only tolerated the ruthless inspection because it was easier than driving back to the motel and taking a very thorough shower.

After a final long snort, Dev turned away and lipped casually at the straw on the stall floor.

"Finished?" she asked cuttingly. "You're sure, now? I'd hate to have you mistake me for someone else."

Except for the flick of a black-tipped ear, Dev ignored her.

She turned back to the wheelbarrow and pried off a few thick flakes of hay. The feed had been shipped in from Virginia so that Dev wouldn't have his digestive system upset by new food. Later in the morning he would get a special round of corn and oats and vitamins. For now he would get the bulky food.

Tucking the hay under one arm, she went into the stall and closed the lower half of the door behind her. Suddenly there was no room for her to move. It was all taken up by the muscular expanse of Dev's butt. She slapped a gleaming mahogany haunch.

"Move it, pal, or no breakfast."

Good-naturedly, the stallion shifted aside while she dumped the hay in the manger. Even before the slab of hay hit the metal trough, Dev's teeth were tearing apart the inches-thick hunk of fragrant, cured alfalfa.

While the stallion ate, she raked manure and old straw out his stall. There was no lack of stable help to muck out Dev's quarters, including girls who would have little to fear from his heels. Despite that, Raine preferred to care for her horse herself. Watching how Dev ate, how he moved, even how he breathed, all added up to her own version of a daily checkup of the stallion's health. If anything was wrong with Dev, no matter how subtle, she would notice.

Humming quietly, she went to work cleaning Dev's hooves with a blunt steel pick. In order to do the job, she had to hold each hoof braced between her bent legs like a blacksmith. If the stallion hadn't been cooperative, the job would have been impossible.

But for her, Dev was a gentleman down to his polished black hooves. All she had to do was touch a fetlock and that hoof was presented politely for her inspection.

When each hoof was clean, and she had satisfied herself that each shoe was on securely, she brought in fresh straw for the stall. She made several trips, scattering straw lavishly. Naturally, by the time she came back with a last armful, Dev had produced more for her to clean up.

"Never fails," she muttered, grabbing the manure rake and taking care of the problem. "Feed one end and the other goes to work."

Dev stuck his muzzle deeper into the manger and ignored her grumbling.

Still humming softly, letting the stallion know where she was at all times, she reached into the box that held Dev's personal grooming tools. She went to work on him with a soft oval brush, bringing his already gleaming hide up to a high red gloss.

From the yard came the sound of voices. They were too distant for her to make out individual words, but the subtle shifts of tone told her that Captain Jon was one of the people talking. With half of her attention, she listened as his voice come closer.

"None of the animals I've pointed out so far would give your men any problem," Captain Jon said in his clear tenor. "This next one, however, is different. Devlin's Waterloo should never be handled by anyone but his owner, Miss Smith. In a pinch, the stallion will tolerate being handled by me, but I'm bloody careful about making sudden moves. Not that the horse is naturally vicious, mind you. Dev was badly abused by a man and has never forgotten it."

There was silence broken by the subtle whisper of a soft brush over Dev's softer hide. Finished with breakfast, the horse stood three-legged, his head hanging, his eyes closed, the picture of equine serenity. He groaned his pleasure each time Raine's careful grooming scratched all the places he couldn't scratch himself.

"Are you telling me *that* is the terror of stable twelve?" asked a deep, amused voice from just outside the stall door.

She almost dropped the brush when she recognized Cord's voice. Ignoring the sudden wild beating of her heart, she finished a long stroke down Dev's haunch. She hadn't expected to see Cord again. Ever. She certainly wasn't prepared for it so soon.

When Cord came and stood close to the stall door, the stallion turned, head up, ears pricked forward. Raine saw the flare of Dev's nostrils when he scented Cord. As though comparing scents, Dev nosed his rider. Then the horse turned and began a thorough vacuuming of Cord Elliot.

Motionless, Cord watched the stallion's ears while his black muzzle traveled from the man's fingertips to his arm and then to his ear. The horse seemed particularly fond of his neck.

"Hello, Devlin's Waterloo," he said calmly, unafraid of the huge horse's attention. "Are you trying to tell me I should have taken a shower before rather than after my rounds of the stable?"

Raine flushed and looked away, hoping no one had noticed. She also prayed that she would be the only one to figure out why Dev was so interested in Cord's scent. And so unafraid of a man who was a stranger.

"Bloody fascinating," Captain Jon muttered. Like Cord, he was watching Dev's ears, the early-warning system of any horse's temper. The stallion's ears were up. He was interested but not nervous. "Dev isn't afraid of you." He gave Cord an appraising look. "And you aren't afraid of him."

"I was raised around horses," Cord said quietly. Very slowly, watching the stallion's ears, he lifted his hand.

Dev snorted, then sniffed the man's fingers with renewed interest.

"I'd scratch your ears for you," he murmured, "but I don't think you're ready for that, are you?"

The horse whuffled a soft answer, blowing warm air over the man's neck.

"You're a beauty," Cord said, his voice velvet and deep, as mesmerizing as a moonlit river flowing through darkness. "You're big as a mountain, but so well made that you seem more like fifteen than seventeen hands. Healthy, too. Look at those muscles slide when you move. Graceful as a woman and strong as a god. My great-granddaddy would have killed to get his hands on a stud like you. Red hide and black socks, mane and tail like slices of midnight. The devil's own colors. But you aren't a devil, are you? You're an angel dressed to go sightseeing in hell."

Dev stood and listened, bewitched by a shaman's voice, forgetting even to sniff the oddly familiar scent of the man who stood so quietly before him.

"Raine," he said, not shifting the tone of his voice at all, "come over and stand in front of me."

It took her a moment to realize that the velvet words were directed at her. She moved slowly, pulled by an invisible leash.

Cord neither looked away from Dev nor moved as she came and stood in front of the stall door, facing him. His voice never paused, words and nonsense syllables blending into a soothing river that lapped dreamily at consciousness, draining tension into a boneless contentment.

"Turn around and face Dev," he said.

Again, it took Raine a moment to respond to the warm velvet voice. Slowly she turned and faced her horse.

"Don't be startled," he murmured. "I'm going to put my arm next to yours."

Cord followed his words with action, slowly bringing his arm forward until it lay along hers. His voice continued all the time, sound flowing soothingly.

"Raise your hand and pet Dev," he murmured. "Slowly, love . . . slowly . . . that's it . . . perfect . . ."

She obeyed, almost as mesmerized as her horse by the spoken music of a shaman's voice. As she moved, so did Cord, their arms lifting as one.

Dev didn't flinch when her hand, with the man's covering it, scratched the sensitive areas behind the stallion's ears. Cord continued speaking, a murmurous, hypnotic flow of sound, a voice that was also a soothing lullaby.

"Slowly, gently, ease your hand down to your side," he said.

Moving with a dreamlike lack of urgency, Raine's hand retreated to her side.

Dev didn't seem to notice the instant when his rider's familiar hand was gone and he was standing as placid as a cow while a strange man scratched itchy places with unerring skill.

"Move away from me in slow motion," Cord murmured, "along the stall door. Very, very slowly. That's the way. Good."

She obeyed, fascinated by what was happening.

It took a few moments for Dev to realize that his mistress was gone and in her place was a man who was neither wholly familiar nor wholly strange. By the time Dev was aware of what had happened, it was too late for panic or anger. The contact had been made.

Dev's ears wavered, then settled at a relaxed half-mast position. Sighing, the stallion nudged Cord's skilled fingers, not only accepting his touch but asking for more.

For a time he stroked and praised Dev lavishly, using his voice and touch to reward the stallion's acceptance. When he removed his hand and stopped talking, Dev looked vaguely surprised. He snorted once, resoundingly, gave Cord a bemused look, and turned his attention back to Raine.

"Bloody incredible," Captain Jon said, looking from Dev to Cord. "I don't care

what your job is, Elliot. If you aren't training horses, you're wasting yourself."

"I had an edge," he said in his usual voice.
Smiling thinly, he looked directly at Raine.

At that instant she knew he understood
exactly why Dev had been so interested in
his scent. Cord smelled of her, just as she
smelled of him.

In his own way, Cord had knocked the
stallion off-balance just as much as he had
her.

"An edge!" Captain Jon snorted. "You had
the whole bloody campaign in the palm of
your hand and you knew it. That's a rare
gift, Elliot. Use it." Then, as an afterthought,
the captain said, "If the rest of your men
are a tenth the horseman you are, they can
be underfoot all you like. I'll withdraw my
complaints immediately."

"Your men?" Raine asked, really looking
at Cord for the first time.

He was dressed in blue jeans, work shirt,
and a faded denim jacket. There was nothing to distinguish him from other stable
hands except the aura of power that he wore
as naturally as he wore the casual clothes
and the gun that was no doubt concealed
beneath his jacket.

"Sorry," Captain Jon said to her. "I haven't
introduced you. Miss Raine Smith, Mr.

Cord Elliot. Mr. Elliot is with Olympic security."

Cord held out his hand. Years of ingrained politeness made her take it.

"Hello, Raine." His voice was suddenly velvet and darkness again, beguiling.

"Don't use that shaman's voice on me," she said coolly. But she couldn't help the warmth that raced through her when his hand closed over hers. "I'm not as good-natured as my horse."

"I know," he said. His voice was flat now, emotionless. He turned back to Captain Jon, who was looking both puzzled and more than a little curious at the undercurrents flowing between the two of them. "I met Raine a few days ago, but we've never been properly introduced. In fact, she's the reason I amended the security regulations to include taking a buddy along for any inspections of the endurance course."

"Then you're the chap who swept her off her feet," Captain Jon said with a sly, sideways look at her.

"Is that what she said?" Cord's voice was bland, but the center of his eyes expanded blackly against the pale blue irises.

"Not quite," she retorted, looking at him. "*Knocked* me off my feet was how I put it. More accurate, don't you think?"

He smiled crookedly. "You think I'm more truth than poetry, is that it?"

She started to agree, then remembered how it felt to be with him, how she had changed as he touched her . . . a new world opening before her.

And then the cold steel gun, the old world she had escaped coming back to claim her all over again.

"That's the way life is." Her voice was sad and bittersweet. "More truth than poetry." She turned to talk to Captain Jon, only to discover that he had withdrawn.

"The guy who took your picture should be shot," Cord said calmly.

"What?" she asked, off-balance again, turning toward him.

"Your picture." He touched the laminated ID badge clipped to Raine's collar. "Is that the best the photographer could do?"

She shrugged. The picture had been taken just after she'd arrived in California. She was jet-lagged and exhausted, having spent the previous forty-eight hours without sleep, her head in the toilet while food poisoning ravaged her until she devoutly wished to die. When she showed up for the required ID photo, her normally clear skin was thick and sallow, her eyes looked like a raccoon's, and her hair hung in wet strings around her face. When the photographer said "Smile!" her lips had thinned into a pale, humorless line.

"I'd been sick," she said.

"I believe it." He shook his head. "I might not have jumped you if your ID had looked more like the real you."

Her eyes narrowed.

"But then, it probably wouldn't have mattered," he admitted. "Photographs are dicey. You can get burned to the bone by depending on them. When you started to reach into your knapsack, I had no choice but to take you down."

She opened her mouth to disagree hotly. Then she remembered last night, when he had taken the key out of her purse and opened the door to her room. To a man who spent his life knowing that every key turning in a lock could trigger a bomb, the idea that she might have a weapon in her rucksack would be inevitable, not incredible.

Her glance went to Cord's badge. It had his name and the word "Security," followed by a code number that assured access to every nook and cranny of any Olympic site.

Beneath the laminated plastic, the face in the picture was hard and unyielding, older than he looked now. The flash had highlighted the narrow sprinkling of gray that would one day become a solid forelock of silver, pure and vivid against the black thickness of his hair. In the picture, his eyes were as hard and transparent as glacier ice, almost no blue showing, and the line of his jaw was grim. He looked like what he was, a man who wore a gun and knew how to use it.

"Your picture looks more like you than you do," she said without thinking.

Cord's expression changed subtly, like a mask slipping into place. He looked more like his picture now. Cold. "I was angry when that picture was taken. I had just been pulled off a matter I'd been working on for a long time."

"And reassigned to Olympic security?" she guessed.

He hesitated.

The pause was familiar to her. It was her father's response when she asked questions and didn't have enough security clearance to hear the answers.

But, unlike Chandler-Smith, Cord answered. "Yes."

"Will you go back to the, er, *matter* when the Summer Games are over?" she asked quickly, knowing she shouldn't. Nor should she be holding her breath to hear his answer.

For a timeless moment Cord looked at

her, letting her see him, all barriers down. He had spent a lot of time thinking since he had left her and walked away. He wanted her. Even more, he needed her in a way so deep he couldn't fight it, only explore it.

And resent it.

He really didn't welcome the understanding of just how close he was to burning out. He hadn't known how cold he had become until he felt her warmth reaching deep into him, touching him.

But he knew now. After that, the rest was just a matter of timing and luck. Of surviving long enough to use his new knowledge of himself.

"I don't know if I'll go back," he said evenly. "The matter may be concluded by then. If it isn't, I'll see it through to conclusion." He hesitated, then added, "I owe them that much."

The blend of harshness and yearning in his voice sent emotions twisting through Raine — anger and sympathy, resentment and a yearning that was too much like his.

"You don't owe me any explanations or answers," she said tightly. "I know how the game is played."

"Do you?"

"I grew up with it. Have you forgotten who I am?"

"Not for a second," he said. Then his voice caressed her while he looked at her with eyes that remembered everything. "You're the woman I kissed until you melted and ran over me like molten silk. So much heat . . . and all of it locked away from men like me. Who are you waiting for, Raine *Chandler*-Smith? A well-trained lapdog who always shows up for his meals on time?"

The cutting assessment made her furious. It was too close to the truth. "Yes. That's exactly what I'm waiting for."

"Bullshit."

"You don't know what you're talking about," she snarled.

"Don't I?" His voice was calm, relentless. "You're surrounded by well-trained lapdogs. You have been since you were old enough to have a period. But not one of those polite, soothing men has touched the fire inside you."

"How do you know? I might have had a string of lovers as long as Dev's tail!"

"You might have, but you don't."

"You've read my file," she said coldly, outraged at the invasion of her private life.

"No. I read *you*. And everything I see tells me I'm right. If you liked lapdogs, you would be riding a lapdog. You would be cool and regal on top of an impeccably mannered dressage horse. If you liked lapdogs, you sure as hell wouldn't be riding a blood-bay stud as big and mean as a falling mountain."

"Dev isn't mean. Not with me, anyway."

"No, not with you." Cord's voice changed, smoky velvet and yearning, bittersweet darkness. "You can reach inside the hardest creature and hold its heart beating in your hand."

Raine felt herself falling again, off-balance, as unprepared as Dev for Cord's ability to slide through defenses that had turned away every man. Except one.

She shook her head, unable to speak, refusing to believe his words. She couldn't have touched him that deeply, that finally.

The way he had touched her.

Dev nudged her hard, all but knocking her off her feet. Automatically she reached for the stallion's halter rope, which was hanging high on the wall nearby. She clipped the rope onto Dev's halter.

"It's time for his walk," she said in a strained voice.

Cord looked at the loose halter. If the stallion decided to bolt, the halter wouldn't give her enough leverage against the horse's huge strength.

"That's it?" he asked. "Just a regular halter?"

She looked at the halter, muttered under her breath, and went to the tack box. She came back with a different halter. It was almost a hackamore — a bridle without a bit. As long as Dev behaved, the special halter would remain loose around his muzzle. If he acted up, a pull on the lead rope would tighten the strap across his nose and cut off the flow of air. In terms of control, the halter was as effective as a big steel bit, but gave Dev greater freedom to eat and drink in the stall.

"Good enough?" she asked coolly.

Cord nodded. "Leave it on him all the time. That's a request, but I can make it official."

"Dev is a gentleman."

"With you, yes. With the rest of the world, he's hell on four black hooves."

"Not with you," she said almost resentfully as she led Dev out into the yard.

"That's because I smelled like you," he said, his voice deep, caressing. "I noticed it this morning, like the scent of spring on the wind. But it isn't spring, is it? With you, it's winter all year round."

"That's not —" she began.

"Fair?" he cut in sardonically. "Not much

is, or haven't you noticed? Open your eyes, Baby Raine. There's a world out there you haven't seen."

"I've seen it." Her hazel eyes were defiant as she turned on him, her voice was as cold as his. "It didn't impress me as a good place to live in. A fine place for dying, though. Or hadn't *you* noticed?"

"Is that what you're afraid of? Dying?"

She tilted her head to one side and considered the question.

He waited, angry and impatient, but he couldn't say with what or whom. He did know that he wanted to reach out and shake Raine's perfect, safe world until everything shifted around enough to make room for him.

Patience, he told himself. *You can't divide your attention right now. You have one very deadly man to catch. Afterward there will be time.*

If there is an afterward.

It wasn't the first time Cord had confronted the dangerous nature of his work. But it was the first time the thought of dying had truly bothered him.

"No," she said finally, "I'm not afraid of death. I'm afraid of living like my mother, waiting for the man she loves to be assassinated. Waiting alone, because he's too busy saving the world to live with her. That's what I'm afraid of, Mr. Cord Elliot. Loving the wrong man."

"So you haven't loved any man."

"My choice."

"A lonely choice. More lonely than your mother's. She at least has someone to wait for."

"The choice was forced on her. Dad was just a lawyer when they married."

Cord's patience frayed, slipped. Snapped. He moved closer in a single, predatory stride.

"If you ever find the tame *gentle*man of your dreams, Baby Raine, what will you do when he takes one look at you and your rogue stallion and runs like hell?"

She wanted to look away from Cord. She couldn't. The intensity in him was like a net suddenly thrown over her, chaining her in place.

"What do you mean?" she managed finally.

"Look at yourself. Rich. Graceful. Pedigreed back to the Dark Ages. Smart and strong and elegant, a rapier turned on a master smith's forge. A *gentle*man could probably get past all those fences, but what about the rest?"

"What do you mean?"

"What about the wildness burning inside you?" he asked softly, harshly. "The risk-taking part of you that saw seventeen hands of savage horse and said, *'This is mine.'*"

"What about it?" she retorted.

"Simple. There's part of you that loves danger. Like your father. Like me."

"That's not true!"

Cord's laugh was harsh and humorless. "Like bloody hell it isn't."

The words were as relentless as his icy blue eyes. His voice was a knife cutting away her certainties, her world, leaving her no place to hide. She wanted to run, but there was no place to go, no safe place where his words wouldn't reach her, threatening years of hard-won certainties about herself and the world.

"You complain that my job or your father's is risky," Cord said sardonically. "What the hell do you call taking Dev over blind downhill jumps when he's so tired you can hear the breath groaning through him?"

"All right," she snapped. "The three-day event can be dangerous. It tests horse and rider to the breaking point. Some riders are attracted to the danger. I'm not. It's a way of testing myself, of proving that I'm good at something more than being born rich."

Her words pulled at something deep

within Cord. He, too, was drawn more to the testing of himself than to the adrenaline of danger.

"Whatever you call it," he said evenly, "the first time your tame dream *gentle*man sees you bruised and bloody after a three-day event, he'll turn pale and go looking for a nice, safe, sedate dream *gentle*woman to marry. It won't be you, Baby Raine."

Her nails dug into the lead rope she was holding. Unconsciously she shook her head, denying the truth in his words. "I'll find what I want," she said, her voice husky and certain. "When I do, I won't need adrenaline and tests to give meaning to my life."

Cord's voice changed, velvet again as he bent over her, so close that he could sense the warmth of her, taste her very breath. "What do you want, Raine?"

Suddenly her eyes were brilliant with unshed tears, tears that would never be shed because she had learned that crying didn't make any difference in the world her father inhabited. "I want a man who loves me enough to live with me."

The loneliness and yearning beneath her words slid through Cord's anger, making him hurt as much as she did. He closed his eyes at the twisting, unexpected pain. "You wouldn't recognize your man if he stood in front of you. You're afraid of loving."

"And you're an expert on love?" she challenged, her voice hard and dry.

"No. I'm an expert on dying. On not loving. On being lonely. On looking at castles from the outside. On finally finding a woman worth having and then watching her bar the gate against me because I'm just a soldier, not a king."

Slowly Raine shook her head, defenseless against the emotions flowing beneath Cord's words, a hunger as deep and painful as her own.

"That's not why," she said. "It has nothing to do with my background or yours."

He didn't answer. He simply watched her with eyes that didn't believe her. He was no *gentle*man, and he knew it much better than she did.

Raine looked at the man who stood so close to her, quiet and yet dangerous, hungry and yet aloof, as powerful and yet as vulnerable as Dev had been the day she found him fallen, tangled helplessly in his own strength. If she hadn't run to the stallion, helped him, healed him . . . Dev would have died.

The thought made her throat ache against a cry of pain and protest. *Cord isn't Dev,* she told herself quickly, savagely. *Dev had no choice about who owned him. Cord does. And he chooses to be owned by the dark side of humanity.*

Yet he wanted her as no man ever had. She wanted him in the same agonizing way.

And there was nothing to be done for it.

So Raine did what she always had when she ran up against something that couldn't be changed, couldn't be healed, and hurt like hell on fire. She put it all out of her mind and concentrated on the one thing she *could* do.

"Come on, Dev. Let's stretch those long legs."

CHAPTER 9

Motionless, Cord watched Raine walk quickly away. It wasn't the first time that had happened to him, or the only woman. He had looked over a lot of castle walls, shrugged, and gone on, caring only for the next mountain range, the next skirmish beyond the valley, the next battle in a war older than he was.

But somewhere between all those valleys, the mountains had become higher and the battles had become colder, chilling him so slowly, so deeply, that he hadn't even noticed until a very special woman gave him a few moments next to her fire. She had showed him the possibilities of life and warmed him all the way to his cold soul.

Then she had talked of gentlemen and kings and turned away from him, leaving him with mountains all around, their icy reaches waiting as they always had waited for men like him.

Now, for the first time, Cord realized that he didn't want the mountains anymore. He had heard all the variations of their siren call, height and distance, victory and exhilaration, loss and despair. He had taken mountain ranges and passes one by one, held or lost them until the battle moved on to a different range. Then he had walked down through green valleys on the way to the next mountain, the next pass, the next battle.

When he left, he hadn't missed or mourned the soft, warm valleys. There were always more mountains and passes singing to him, rank upon rank of heights, eternity stretching before him, a battle without end. And he had walked forward eagerly.

Behind him lay a lifetime of skirmishes, of men who fought and men who died, memories and years sliding away into ice. He could barely remember what it felt like not to climb, not to be cold, not to fight. All the years were slowly congealing inside him, freezing him to his core.

Some day he would no longer know the difference between valley and pass, warmth and ice. Or he wouldn't care. He had seen men like that. Cinder cases.

Burned out.

Like other men, Cord had always sworn it

would never happen to him. Like other men, he had assumed he would die before he burned out.

Like other men, he had been wrong.

Now it was time to assess the damage, to see if there was anything left to save. Anything *worth* saving.

The beeper at Cord's belt pulsed rhythmically. As though it was coming down a long, long tunnel, he heard the summons. Years of reflexes took over. He stopped thinking about himself and punched in the required code.

Then he walked quickly toward the huge motor home that was parked just inside the stable fence. He didn't really see the containers of flowers lining the paths between stables and yards. He didn't see the golden cataracts of sunlight pouring around him or feel the breeze or hear the vibrant murmur of bees settling delicately between fragrant petals. He saw nothing but bleak mountain peaks, felt nothing but ice, knew nothing but the battle that had yet to be fought.

The dust-colored motor home was connected to Santa Anita's power supply by several wires. Only one of them carried electricity. The others were secure phone lines disguised by the presence of more ordinary lines. Except for an unusual number of antennae, there was nothing noteworthy about the motor home. Many people associated with the Olympics found it easier to bring their sleeping quarters with them than to commute through the tangled traffic of the Los Angeles Basin.

A man whose name was temporarily Thorne waited in a lawn chair out in front of the motor home. He was a man who apparently had nothing better to do than sit and dream in the sun. For all his outward relaxation, however, his glance was shrewd and alert.

"Morning, Mr. Elliot," Thorne said, his soft southern drawl as misleading as his lazy sprawl.

"Morning, Thorne," Cord said, automatically using Kentucky's latest identity, just as Kentucky used his. "Any visitors?"

"No suh. Not even any rubberneckers."

"Good."

Cord unlocked the combination key-and-pressure lock on the motor home's side door and went inside his mobile command station.

An air conditioner hummed discreetly. The decor was a tawny mixture of gold and buff and chestnut with refreshing jade-green highlights. A couch that made into a queen-size bed occupied the wall opposite the door, facing a game table large enough to seat four. Television, stereo, a few books and maps, nothing at all odd to a casual glance.

It would take an unusually perceptive or suspicious person to notice that the walls were too thick and the storage compartments and cupboards were constructed to keep out all but the most skillful thieves.

The interior door to the back of the motor home was open. On either side of the narrow hallway lay a bathroom, a kitchen, and a bedroom. All were done in shades of buff and jade. The last third of the motor home could be entered only through another interior door. It was locked in ways both subtle and obvious, electrical and mechanical.

Cord was the only person on the West Coast who knew the combinations. He unlocked the door, opened it, and relocked it behind him.

The room was surprisingly large. Part of the furnishings were utterly commonplace, consisting of a bed, a bedside table, and a reading lamp. The other walls looked more like the cockpit of a fighter plane or a modern recording studio than the master bedroom suite of a luxury motor home. Electronic equipment bristled from every available nook and cranny. A separate air conditioner worked tirelessly, keeping the room at the ideal temperature for the most sensitive of the equipment.

A computer terminal waited in the corner, screen blank. Cord pulled a swivel chair away from the radio and sat down in front of the keyboard. He entered a long, intricate code sequence and waited. Within seconds the screen lit up.

BLUE MOON CONTACT BLUE HERRING

Adrenaline flicked over his nerves. For this operation, Bonner was Blue Herring. And Bonner was hunting Barracuda.

Cord punched in the acknowledgment, swiveled to a radio telephone that was fitted with a scrambler, punched out another series of code numbers, hung up, and waited.

After a few minutes, the phone rang.

He picked up the receiver. Even though the conversation would be scrambled, he and Bonner would stick to code. You never knew who might have slipped a bug in somewhere along the line.

"How's the fishing?" Cord asked.

"They're rising, buddy." The voice floated up from the speaker on a soft wave of static that lapped at the silence of the room.

Cord smiled grimly at the excitement he sensed beneath the radio-flattened voice of "Blue Herring." Bonner was a man who still lived solely for the next range of mountains, the next freezing pass, the next battle.

"That so?" Cord asked. "What kind of fish are biting today?"

"Barracuda."

He went utterly still. "You're sure?"

"Eighty-six percent certain. Department of Fish and Game confirmed sighting on basis of file photo taken at extreme range. I know how you feel about photos, buddy, but I thought I'd pass on the nibble."

"Where did he surface." Cord's voice was flat. It was a demand, not a request.

"LAX. Last night."

He thought quickly. The assassin known only as Barracuda had been spotted at Los Angeles International Airport by immigration officials. Or, to be precise, a man who resembled the only known photograph of Barracuda had been spotted. If the match was correct, it would be a giant step toward catching the terrorist. Permanently.

Cord was one of the few people who had seen Barracuda close up and lived to tell about it. But Cord wasn't comfortable with photo IDs, particularly when it came to Barracuda. The one photo they had of him was taken from very long range. Worse, it was a profile shot. It didn't show the terrorist's most outstanding feature — a narrowness between the eyes that had made Cord dub the man Barracuda.

"Who ID'd him?" Cord asked.

"Good old Eagle Eye."

Absently Cord traced the line of his chin with one knuckle while he digested the information and played with possibilities. His eyes were narrow, intent, focused on a different world, a place that was darker, colder, a place where dusty sunshine and warm breezes never came.

If Mitchell — Eagle Eye — was the one to ID Barracuda, Cord couldn't afford to ignore the sighting. Mitchell had an uncanny knack for matching grainy two-dimensional photos to moving three-dimensional faces. That was why Mitchell had been assigned to Customs and Immigration at LAX for the duration of the Olympics, when foreign nationals of all kinds would pour into L.A.

Including terrorists.

"Probable target," Cord said curtly.

Bonner's laugh was as thin as a razor. "You, if he sees you."

"Of course." His voice was impatient. Barracuda had wanted to kill him for a long time. An assassin's success depended on anonymity as much as skill or nerve. "But does he know I'm here?"

There was a soft, static-filled pause. "Doubtful. The boys upstairs figure that Old Blue is the target. Backup target is Baby Blue."

Cord's breath came in with a harsh sound. *Raine. Raine was an assassin's target.*

He swore viciously beneath his breath. It was well known how proud Chandler-Smith was of his youngest daughter. At least, everyone but the daughter in question seemed to know. Blue had vowed he would see his daughter ride in the Olympic three-day event if it was the last thing he did.

It just might be.

Anything that made Chandler-Smith's actions predictable to an assassin was dangerous. A father's desire to see his daughter perform in the Olympics was as predictable as sunrise. That was why Cord had been yanked out of his normal position as a covert anti-terrorist operative and assigned as liaison to Olympic security.

Blue's boss had wanted the best available protection for Chandler-Smith, and as President of the United States, Blue's boss was in a position to demand it.

"You're sure about the primary and secondary target," Cord said in a clipped voice.

"There's no substitute for good bait when you're going fishing. We've got a nice, juicy night crawler on the hook."

"So a worm finally turned." Cord wondered which member of Barracuda's terrorist group had gotten scared and run for cover in the enemy's arms.

"Believe it, buddy. He's wriggling and oozing all over the place. Ugly little bastard, but he's *our* ugly little bastard now. Blue's going to have someone's butt when he finds out that Baby Blue is on the menu."

"Blue will have to get in line."

Cord's voice was bleak, colorless. Memories turned in him like knives, the softness and grace and surprising fire that was Raine Chandler-Smith. He had spent his life protecting people he didn't know.

He knew Raine.

She had made it clear that he couldn't have her. Before Bonner's call he had been ready to argue the point. But not now. Now there was only the old, familiar shadow world closing around him in icy embrace.

He couldn't have Raine, but he could make certain that she survived to look for her safe and gentle dream.

"Tell Blue there's only one way Barracuda

will get to Baby," he said. "That's through Cord Elliot."

"But Blue doesn't know anyone called Cord Elliot," Bonner said, laughing.

"Neither do you. Just pass the message along."

"It's on its way." Then, quietly, almost casually, Bonner asked, "Still play chess, buddy?"

"As often as you do, *compadre.*"

Soft laughter faded into static, then silence.

Cord replaced the receiver. For a long time he was motionless, looking at nothing, feeling nothing, thinking about too many things. So many deadly possibilities. So many grainy photos and sullen lives. So many angles of attack. So many weapons. So many ways to die.

So few ways to live.

When he focused once more on the here and now, he discovered that he had taken a worn gold coin from his pocket. While he thought about assassins and Raine, the high price of life and the terrible cost of death, castle and fire, mountain and ice, he had rubbed the smooth, warm gold between his fingers like a talisman.

"So it's that bad, is it?" he asked softly. He flipped the good luck piece over. A woman's face looked at him through slant-ing eyes. "Are you listening, Lady Luck, Lady Death? Or am I the one who should be listening to you?"

The woman said nothing, merely watched him through a lattice of ideographs. Behind her rose an alien city where roofs turned up to the sky in silent prayers to unknown gods. Different culture, different reality, different lives.

Same world.

It was all part of the huge, interlocking puzzle of languages and cultures, people and desires that was humanity. A haunting, ever-changing mixture of experience and memories and dreams . . . the smell of piñon and campfires, the eight-limbed elegance of a dancing god, flooded rice pad-dies the color of tears, muffled gunfire, a woman's sidelong glance through a shad-owed window, the terrible green silence of a jungle when guerrillas were on the prowl.

And a gold piece given to Cord by a man he had carried on his back out of the jungle. But not in time.

Green silence and death.

He looked at the alien coin and wondered who would be next to fall. The golden face had no answer for him except the one he already knew.

He would die before he let Barracuda get to Raine.

For the rest of the day, Raine avoided any possibility of seeing Cord. Her dreams weren't as kind to her — he haunted them. She slept very little, just enough to slide into vague nightmares that were a mixture of yearning and fear, of running from and running to, of having a destination and never getting there because something — everything — got in the way before she reached her goal, whatever that goal might have been.

That was the worst part of the nightmare. Not knowing where she was going, but knowing that she wasn't getting there.

Seeing a car in her rearview mirror all the way from the motel to the racetrack didn't settle her nerves a bit. At first she thought it was Cord, but when both cars stopped at a traffic light, she saw that it was a woman.

Raine's relief at not having to confront Cord lasted as long as it took her to park her car near the stables. She was so early that there were few other people stirring. Yet no sooner had she gotten out and shut the car door than she was aware of being watched. An instant later the door to a big nearby motor home opened and Cord

215

stepped into the cool, dusty pre-dawn of Santa Anita.

Even as she told herself that she was wrong, there wasn't enough light to identify a man she had seen only twice, she knew it was Cord. Nobody else moved with that combination of strength and male grace. With rising anger she waited for him to walk up to her.

He didn't even look her way.

Relieved, disappointed, and thoroughly irritated, she stalked to Dev's stall. She didn't understand the warring impulses in herself. Her mind was certain that Cord was the wrong man for her. Her instincts were just as certain that he was the right one.

The day went downhill from the instant she spotted Cord. Dev was on a hair trigger and stubborn as a concrete slab. More than once she felt like screaming at the big stallion. She didn't. She simply settled deeper into the slim little English saddle and rode him for all she was worth.

It didn't help that Cord was never more than a hundred feet away. Whether she was alone or with another member of the team, listening to instructions from Captain Jon or leading Dev lazily through the linked yards, Cord was nearby. Always. If she went to one of the practice rings, he was already there. Watching her. If she went to the stables, so did he. If she went to the restroom, he did everything but hand her toilet paper.

But not once did he talk to her. He simply circulated through the area like a rumor, always present and impossible to pin down.

By late afternoon her nerves were frayed and she was furious. One moment she was leading a freshly groomed Dev down the stable row. The next instant she vaulted on and rode the stallion bareback right up to Cord. He didn't turn around at the sound of hoofbeats. It was as though he hadn't even noticed her.

"Who do you think you're kidding?" she began hotly. "You've been following . . ."

Her voice died when he turned and looked at her. That was all. Just a look. His eyes were pale, impersonal.

"May I help you, Miss Chandler-Smith?"

She tried to speak. Nothing came out, not even a dry rasp. Cord couldn't have been more distant from her if he had been on the far side of winter.

And that was how he looked. Cold.

After a moment he nodded politely and went back to watching the activity around the stable yard. His assessing eyes missed nothing, not even the smallest shift of wind-ruffled pepper trees.

He didn't look toward Raine again. There wasn't any point. No matter how long he had stared at the alien coin that morning, he hadn't found a way to follow both his desire and his duty. After Barracuda was caught, it would be different. Then Cord would be free. If he survived. Until then, Raine was the queen and he was the soldier hired to protect her.

Period.

Motionless, Raine sat on Dev, unable to believe that Cord had looked at her with such utter lack of feeling, then turned away as though she didn't exist at all. She should do the same. Turn away. Now.

But she couldn't.

When he had spoken his brief, polite greeting to her, she saw the flash of white teeth and the sensual gleam of tongue. Suddenly it was the night before, when he gave her a guided tour of the universe and offered her the dazzling lure of real passion. The clean, masculine lines of his mouth brought back memories of being kissed until there was nothing in her universe but him.

She felt again the sensual vise of his teeth holding her lower lip while his tongue teased and soothed, incited and pleasured. Then came searing memories of being held by the man who was so close to her now, the man who was ignoring her as though his hands had never explored her naked breasts, as though he had never dragged her over his aroused flesh, making her moan with sheer desire.

When Cord shifted position to watch a different part of the yard, the flex and play of muscles beneath his faded work shirt drew her eyes. She wanted to bend down and bury her fingers in his thick black hair, to touch him again, to run her hands over his hard body until she was so close to him that she could feel him groan with pleasure and hunger. Then she wanted to peel away his shirt, his jeans, her own clothes, everything that stood between her and the feel of Cord's silk and steel body.

Heat and a heady kind of weakness coursed through her. Suddenly she understood why people gave in to competition madness. Anything would be better than the violent, twisting need inside her when she looked at him.

She took a slow breath and tried to bring herself under control. Coming this close to him again had been a mistake. A big one. She wasn't sophisticated enough to play the kiss-and-forget game. Being dismissed by him the morning after a simple necking session made her feel young and stupid, hot and cold, furious and sad enough to wail.

How much worse it would be if they had been lovers.

The breeze stirred, dust glittered, bees rocketed from flower to flower. And Raine watched Cord helplessly, caught in the coils of a kind of passion she hadn't even known was possible.

Without warning he turned back to her. His pupils dilated when he saw the hunger in her wide, haunted eyes and soft mouth. Sexual heat poured through him, hardening him in a single savage instant. His uncontrollable response made him furious.

"I'm still wearing a gun."

His words were a whip of ice cutting across Raine's hot, unguarded emotions. She wheeled Dev and set off with a speed that sent dirt spattering over Cord's feet.

But she couldn't leave the truth behind.

You're surrounded by well-trained lapdogs. You have been since you were old enough to have a period. But not one of those polite, soothing men has touched the fire inside you.

Cord had.

And he was the wrong man.

Raine tested Dev's cinch, checked her watch, and led the stallion to the mounting block. The U.S. team's turn in the practice jumping ring would begin in half an hour. Time in the various rings was carefully divided among the competing countries. She didn't want to waste a minute by being late. By the stroke of nine, she should have Dev warmed up and ready for the jumps.

While she settled into the smooth, nearly flat English saddle, she took a quick, furtive look around the yard. Cord was there, leaning against one of the green stable walls, watching everyone who came and went among the tree-shaded rows of stalls. Though he never spoke to her after that one time, for the past several days he had been nearby whenever she moved from stall to practice ring, parking lot to stable, or wherever else her mood or duties took her.

Hastily she looked away from him. She didn't want to be caught watching him. She didn't want to feel the slicing, irrational pain that came each time he treated her like he had never held her, never kissed her, never tasted her hunger.

He didn't want her.

She shouldn't want him.

I'm still wearing a gun.

The words had echoed in her head for days, warning her, haunting her. She couldn't forget Cord's sensuality, her own unexpected response, the heady spiral of passion wrapping around them in a kind of kiss she hadn't even dreamed existed. But worse than that, worse than the passion and the pain, was the terrible feeling that she had stumbled over the other half of herself.

And then she had thrown it away.

Competition madness, she told herself bleakly. *That's all. Just competition madness.*

She wanted to believe it. Needed to. Even more, she needed to look over her shoulder and catch Cord watching her right now. She was certain he was. She felt his attention as surely as she felt the heat rising out of the stable yard.

Yet she knew that no matter how suddenly she turned, she wouldn't catch him looking at her.

He's too quick. Too damned quick. I'm always off balance with him, always searching for a center point that keeps sliding away, out of my reach. Like him.

Taking a deep breath, she tried to shake the uncanny feeling of always being the center of his focus, a permanent reflection in his ice-blue eyes. If he wanted her, he would approach her.

He hadn't.

Yet still she looked for him, sensed him, remembered the heat and hunger of his kiss.

"It's just competition madness, you little fool," she muttered to herself. "Get over it."

Dev's left ear flicked back, then forward.

"Competition madness," she said firmly.

She repeated those two words all the way to the jump ring. It was her own private litany designed to exorcise the man who wore a gun and spoke with a shaman's midnight-and-silver voice.

As Dev strode forward, bees in the potted flowers along the paths and fences hummed in counterpoint to Raine's whispered words. *Competition madness.* The stallion's ears flicked occasionally as he registered the erratic flight of insects or a shift in the tone of his rider's voice.

She took off her riding helmet, wiped her forehead, and replaced the hard hat, checking that the chin strap was secure. Today her hair was ruthlessly jammed beneath the tough plastic hat. Only a few wisps had escaped to tickle her hot cheeks.

It was barely eight-thirty A.M., but the temperature was almost eighty degrees. The rising heat of the day was reflected back on Santa Anita by acres of blacktop parking lots and the massive, stony rise of the San Gabriel Mountains just beyond the track. Despite constant attention from water trucks, the grounds were dry. Dust hung in the air, bright gold in the morning sun.

She held Dev's reins loosely, letting the stallion pick his own pace. He shambled along with deceptive laziness, as calm as a rental nag. He barely flicked his ears at the background noise of voices calling and horses whinnying across the parallel stable yards. Men came and went around them, hauling in feed and hauling out yesterday's straw. Laughter and jokes and stablegirls giggling around the tack house hid the fierce tension that coiled just beneath the serenity.

Competition madness reigned.

Dev had been at Santa Anita long enough for the background noises to become familiar. And the climate. The dry heat barely raised a sheen of sweat beneath his gleaming leather tack.

Raine noted the stallion's calm acceptance of his surroundings and smiled with satisfaction. It had been worth coming out to California early so that Dev could get accustomed to Santa Anita before the Summer Games began. Some of the other horses she saw being led around were still snorting and shying at shadows, anxious in the midst of unfamiliar scents and sounds.

As she approached the practice rings, she collected Dev beneath her, tightening her contact with him until he was up on the bit and looking around alertly. Though he had never showed a tendency to be combative with other horses, Devlin's Waterloo was nonetheless a stallion. When he was close to the other animals, Raine was never careless.

"First one, as usual," Captain Jon said, walking slowly toward the stallion.

Dev's ears came fully forward. He watched the man with dark, somewhat wary eyes.

"Never let up, do you, old boy?" murmured the captain. His hand came up slowly, firmly. He gripped the reins just below the bit.

Dev snorted, then stood quietly.

"Nothing fancy today," Captain Jon said, looking up at Raine. "Give him fifteen minutes of light dressage. Concentrate on the counter-canter for the last five. If he's not behaving, keep after it. I'll start Mason in the other ring and leave you here if Dev isn't working well."

She didn't object, even though she knew it would be more of a workout for her than the stallion. Dev didn't like the counter-canter, but it was a necessary skill for dressage, endurance, and show jumping. He had to be ready to switch leads instantly on his rider's cue. In the show ring it made for pretty jumping. On the endurance course, it could be the difference between a clean jump and a dangerous crash.

"I'm not setting up any jumps higher than a meter in the ring," the captain continued. "Watch that triple combination. I've placed it so that you have a full stride, a half stride, then four and a half strides."

She sighed. Diabolical, as usual. A jump approach of four and a half strides was just long enough to allow you to lose control of the horse, particularly if you were on an animal that liked rushing fences. Fortunately, Dev usually didn't.

But today might not be usual. She was on edge. He was humming with health. Beneath his shambling act lurked a great, powerful stallion eager to fly over miles of hills and rivers and tricky jumps. In six days he would get to do just that. Until then she would have to stay deep in the saddle and firm on the reins or he would be scattering bars from show jumps like straws in the wind.

With an expressionless face and sure hands, she rode Dev into the first practice ring. Other horses worked around the big ring, polishing whatever skills needed attention. Some practiced the absolutely immobile standing required by dressage. Others practiced changing leads at all paces. Still others flowed across the ring in the elegant diagonals of dressage.

Keeping to the outer circumference of the ring, Raine positioned Dev to begin the workout. Unlike most riders, she rode without a whip of any kind. Dev wouldn't tolerate one. Whatever displeasure she felt with her mount's performance would be expressed with her heels and voice.

She worked quietly, talking to Dev through lips that didn't move, using a voice that went no further than the stallion's sensitive ears. He worked willingly for her. Too willingly. The least shift of her weight was greeted with an eager bunching of muscles that fairly screamed the horse's desire for fifteen miles of violent exercise.

Dev had been carefully, thoroughly trained for galloping over rough country and rougher obstacles. He loved it with a fervor that made him a great event horse. It also made him temperamentally unsuited for the mincing niceties of dressage.

"Listen to me, you great red ox," Raine muttered through clenched teeth as Dev tugged hard on the bit and danced sideways. "You'll get all the run you want in a few days. Until then, *settle down.*"

Gradually the stallion accepted his rider's unyielding demand for a restrained walk, trot, extended trot, and all the rest of the highly controlled dressage movements. The counter-canter was different. He flatly refused Raine's first instruction. After a brief, almost invisible struggle between rider and mount, Dev gave in. At least the counter-canter's pace was more to his liking, though still far too slow.

When she gave the command for walking again, Dev fought it. She locked her wrists and knees and bore down. When the stallion accepted the walk, she asked for him to stop and stand. Motionless. He did, finally, chewing on the bit in frustration.

From the corner of her eye Raine saw Cord walk up to the fence. Adrenaline surged through her, a helpless response to her own emotions.

Sensing the sudden change in his rider, Dev danced in place.

Cursing silently, she brought the stallion back under full control with pressure from her hands and legs.

Cord's deep voice carried easily above the muffled hoofbeats of horses working in the ring. "There's a call for you."

"Later," she said curtly.

"It's your father."

CHAPTER 10

"Dad?" Raine asked Cord in disbelief. "He called me?"

"He's waiting on the phone right now."

She stared, still not quite believing. Her father hadn't called her in . . . she couldn't remember the last time.

Dev sensed his rider's divided attention. He went sideways in a single catlike leap. Swearing as much at herself as at him, she fought a brief, sharp skirmish over control of the bit. She won.

"He's full of vinegar," Cord said, half smiling, admiration clear in his eyes as he watched the blood-bay stallion dance. Then his voice shifted, velvet and moonlight and a silver river flowing. "Aren't much for dressage, are you? I don't blame you, boy. Don't blame you one bit. Dressage is for people who like fences and rules."

Firmly Raine held Dev where he was — ten feet away from the fence. He resisted, dancing in place, wanting to get closer to the fascinating voice. Smoothly, relentlessly, she guided him toward the exit to the ring.

Cord followed along the outside of the fence, talking to the stallion every step of the way. Ears pricked forward until they almost touched at the tips, Dev minced closer to the shaman's voice.

"Bet you're one hell of a ride," Cord murmured. "Go the distance without whimpering, take a mouthful of water, and turn around and do it all again. Will your mistress ever let you sire blood-bay colts, or is she going to keep you on a tight rein all your life?"

As soon as Dev came through the gate, Cord grasped the reins just below the bit. The stallion stood motionless, his velvet nostrils flaring as he drank the man's scent and watched him with liquid brown eyes.

"Ask for Operator eleven," Cord murmured. "I'll take care of the Prince of Darkness for you."

If it had been any other man, she would have refused. But if it had been any other man, Dev wouldn't have been standing around with a bemused look on his handsome face.

"You're as bad as I am," she muttered to Dev. "Idiot."

"What?" Cord asked.

"Nothing."

She slid off the huge horse and landed lightly on the ground beside Cord.

"If you've bitten off more horse than you can chew," she said irritably, "you have only yourself to blame."

He ignored her. Talking soothingly the whole way, he led Dev toward the stables.

For a few seconds she stared at her well-behaved stallion. Then she shook off the spell of Cord's voice and sprinted for the nearest phone, wondering what had gone wrong with her family. She grabbed the phone and asked for Operator eleven. By the time she was connected with her father, she had imagined every possible calamity that could have happened to her family.

"Daddy," she said urgently as soon as she heard his voice, thinned by distance and static but still unmistakably Justin Chandler-Smith. "What's wrong?"

"Nothing. I just wanted to be the one to tell you that I'll be out with your mother and your sibs for the Olympics."

"You will?" Raine asked doubtfully, years of hope and disappointment mingling in her voice. "You'll try to be here?"

"I *will* be there, Baby Raine."

She laughed almost sadly and shook her

head. "I'm not a baby anymore."

"You never were," he said ruefully. "Not really. Comes of being the fifth child, I suppose. You were going to be as old as your brothers and sisters or know the reason why."

"Speaking of siblings, are you sure everything is all right?"

"Positive. All six of us will be there."

"Impossible," she said dryly. "The six of you haven't been in the same place at once since William was old enough to drive."

"The six of us never had a seventh competing in the Olympics. I'm not going to miss this one, Raine. I mean it."

She swallowed, trying to keep emotion from closing her throat. Before now, her father always had hedged his promises with the phrase *if I can.*

"You don't have to," she said quietly, meaning it. "If not this time, there's always another."

"Not for you, baby. I've got a cast-iron hunch that you're through with wanderlust and adrenaline. If I don't see you ride in a world-class competition this time, there won't be another chance."

Her hand tightened on the phone as her father's calm words swept through her, telling her what she was still discovering about herself. She was tired of living on the road, tired of the relentless demands of training and competition and pressure, the excitement that was a little bit less each time, diminishing so slowly that its loss could only be measured over the years.

She still looked forward to the Olympics, still wanted very badly to compete and win. But her father was right. This would be the last time she hungered for world-class competition.

"How did you know?" she whispered. "I just found out myself."

"You're a lot like me. Except you're smarter. A whole lot smarter. It took me a long time to figure out what I was missing. Well, I'm not going to miss it anymore. Look for me, Baby Raine. I love you."

She was too surprised to answer. By the time she whispered, "I love you, too," her father had already hung up.

She replaced the receiver and stood staring across the yard, seeing nothing at all.

"Bad news?" Cord asked.

She blinked and turned slowly toward the man who was holding Dev's reins as easily as she would have. And Dev was just as calm. It was more than the shaman's voice. It was the man himself.

"Raine?" he asked, his voice very gentle.

"Is everything all right?"

"Daddy says he's coming to the games." Her voice was clear and almost childlike. "Always before he said he would *try.* This time he promised. He's never promised before."

Cord's mouth flattened into a grim line. "Don't tell anyone else. If anyone asks you about it, lie. And then tell me who was asking you questions about your father."

The change in Cord from gentle to harsh was like a slap. She flinched and stepped back, off-balance again.

"Why?" she asked.

"Why?" His voice rose in disbelief. Then it went as cold as the ice color of his eyes. "Grow up, Baby Raine. There are people in this world who would murder your father if they could find him. But they can't. That's the reason his schedule is always unpredictable. It's called survival. If you were an assassin and you knew your target had a daughter competing in the Summer Games, what would you do?"

She closed her eyes on a wave of sickening fear. "No," she whispered, shaking her head quickly, not wanting to believe.

"Yes," he snarled. "Why in hell do you suppose Blue has missed all your important competitions? Why in hell do you suppose he never came to his children's graduations? Why in hell do you think he missed every Broadway opening night your sister ever had? Why in hell —"

"I didn't know," Raine broke in, her voice tight as she tried to stop the relentless words.

"You didn't want to know."

Her hands clenched. "Daddy never told me."

"He didn't want you to know. If he knew I was telling you now, he'd have my butt for punting practice."

"Then why are you telling me?"

"Maybe I don't believe a father should have to be a sitting duck for an assassin just to convince his daughter that he loves her."

"I never asked for that!" Her voice shook. "I just wanted to feel like part of the family instead of a fifth wheel. I wanted to feel like I belonged! Is that so much to ask?"

The anger went out of Cord as he saw the trembling of her pale lips, the tears that she refused to shed, the corded lines of her throat as she fought to control her voice. He wanted to gather her into his arms, to stroke and soothe her until her eyes weren't haunted and her face wasn't pale.

He might as well wish for the moon while he was at it.

"No," he said, "it's not so much to ask. Just everything. Just the whole world in your palm, spinning like a bright blue ball."

"But —"

"Some of us aren't meant to belong," he said simply, relentlessly. "Some of us have to turn the world upside down and shake the hell out of it until we make our own place in it."

"Is that what you did?"

"Yes. Once." He watched her with eyes that were suddenly measuring. "And that's just what I'm going to do again."

"What do you mean?"

He shrugged as though it didn't matter, yet it mattered very much. He was going to shake her beautiful world until there was a place in it for him. But not today. Not even tomorrow. Someday.

First he had to take care of Barracuda. Permanently. Cord was damned if he would go through the rest of his life looking over his shoulder for the assassin who had vowed to kill him.

Saying nothing, Cord handed over Dev's reins and turned to go.

"Wait," Raine said urgently, putting her hand on his arm.

She didn't see the sudden tension in his expression or the hungry way he watched her fingers resting on his sleeve. Then he looked at her hazel eyes, more brown than green now, almost as beautiful as the tempting curves of her mouth.

"I'm waiting," he said, keeping his voice neutral with an effort.

"What if I called Dad and asked him not to come?"

Cord hesitated, wanting to take her hand, to run his thumb over her fingertips and touch the center of her palm with his tongue. But he couldn't do that, either.

And he couldn't stop wanting to.

"If it would make you feel better," he said evenly, "go ahead. But it won't change anything. Sometime in the last few months, Blue discovered that he missed getting to know quite a woman. The fact that she's his daughter just makes it worse. He's coming, Raine. Hell or high water, he's coming."

She remembered her father's words, the absolute certainty in his voice, and knew that Cord was right. Justin Chandler-Smith was coming to see his daughter's Olympic ride.

Her fingers closed with surprising strength over Cord's wrist. "I don't want to make it easier for someone to kill him!" Her voice broke. "Cord, *please,* what can I do to make Dad believe that?"

"He already knows how you feel."

"But —"

"Why do you think he worked so hard to protect you from knowing that he's a target? Only Lorraine knows how dangerous his work is, and even she doesn't know precisely what his work involves. Not because he doesn't trust her, but because it's another way of protecting her. What she doesn't know, no one can force her to talk about."

Raine's face went white. The thought that her mother could be a target had never occurred to her. "What can I do to protect him — *them?*"

Cord would have laughed, but the intensity of her emotion wasn't anything to smile about. "There are a lot of well-trained, very competent people protecting your father and his family."

She looked at Cord with hazel eyes that were dark, shadowed by emotion. "Are you one of them?"

"I have several spots picked out for Blue on the endurance course," he said, neither admitting nor denying her conclusion. "Great views of the action, and only exposed on one side."

"Is that what you were doing when you jumped me, looking for a safe place for Dad to watch me ride?"

This time a corner of Cord's mouth turned up in a wry smile. "Still pissed about that, aren't you?"

She waved away a bee that had mistaken her bright red riding helmet for an oversized flower. "No. Not anymore. If you're supposed to be protecting my father, you didn't really have much choice but to assume the worst when you saw me out there. You had no way of knowing who I was. And in your world everyone, *everyone,* is a potential assassin."

"It's your world, too."

She bit her lip and said, "Yes, I know. Now. If Dad dies because of me . . ." She couldn't finish.

"I'm good at my work," Cord said calmly.

Wanly, she smiled. "If you're one of Dad's men, you're a lot better than good. You're the best."

"Raine!" Captain Jon called. "You're up!"

"Coming."

Cord laced his fingers together to make a flesh-and-bone stirrup for her. Automatically she accepted the aid in mounting her tall stallion. She was in the saddle before she had a chance to feel more than an instant of his smooth strength boosting her into place.

"Take care of her, boy," he murmured in

239

a voice that went no further than Dev's black-tipped ears, "or I'll have your red hide for a wall hanging."

She settled firmly into the saddle, collected Dev, and headed toward the practice area at a smart trot. She wished she could collect her mind as easily. She felt as though someone had taken her carefully mapped-out world, turned it upside down, and shaken it until she was forced to look at old realities in entirely new ways. Her picture of her father had shifted subtly, irrevocably.

She couldn't remake the past, but she could look at its pieces arranged in a new way, a different pattern, different truths. Her father did love her. At some level she had always known that, but she hadn't always admitted it. It was easier to be angry with him than to try to understand the choices he had made.

Yet even that understanding wasn't enough. She couldn't accept a life lived as her father had lived his. Not for herself. Not for the children she someday hoped to have.

Loving a man like Cord Elliot would destroy her.

Yet she wanted him as she had never wanted anything in her life. The depth of her need was frightening.

". . . listening?" Captain Jon snapped.

Quickly she searched her mind for the words she must have heard while she was thinking about Cord instead of Captain Jon's instructions.

"I take the triple jump once clockwise, once counterclockwise," she said, repeating the captain's instructions. "Then I go through again, changing leads twice, getting Dev to take the jumps unexpectedly, on the wrong lead."

"Right. He must understand that when you say jump, he bloody well jumps whether or not he's on the right lead. Now, on the second round, that last jump is set at a right angle into the ring fence. Watch that Dev doesn't run out along the unfenced side just because he's on the wrong lead."

Banishing Cord from her mind, Raine rode into the ring. Dev went through the first series of jumps like a perfect gentleman. While he slowly cantered around to approach from the opposite side, a group of equestrians walked by just outside the ring. The riders talked among themselves as they watched the muscular stallion's progress over the low, tricky jumps.

Suddenly one of the horses screamed, shied violently, and bolted straight into one of the American riders who was sitting on his patient mount, waiting for a turn in the ring. The American horse went down. His rider slammed into the fence with a sickening crack. The horse that was out of control burst through the fence and hurtled blindly toward Dev.

Toward Raine.

Cord was already racing toward the ring, knowing it was too late, refusing to accept it. In a rage of adrenaline, the world slowed, then stopped, letting him see everything with terrible clarity. The American rider was down, tangled in the fence. His horse was scrambling up, favoring its foreleg. Another horse had bolted through the fence and across the ring, the rider barely hanging on, scrambling desperately to control his mount. Heading toward Raine like a runaway truck.

Too late.

The berserk horse slammed into Dev with a force that staggered the big stallion and sent Raine flying out of the saddle.

No! Cord screamed, but it was all in silence, in his mind, because he had breath only for the terrible needs of this instant, when Raine was hurtling beneath the plunging horse, dusty ground rushing to meet her, no time to duck, no time to roll out of the way of steel-shod hooves, no time even to throw up her hands to protect her head.

She hit the ground and lay without moving.

He put his hands on the top rail of the fence and vaulted into the ring.

With a stallion's chilling scream, Dev attacked the strange horse, biting cruelly into living flesh. The horse squealed frantically, then twisted away in a lunge that finally unseated its rider. He hit the dirt, pulled himself to his feet, and staggered in Raine's direction, not even knowing she was there.

Ears flattened to his skull, bared teeth gleaming, eyes rolling white, Dev reared and screamed in primitive rage. He came down straddling Raine. His neck moved with a deadly, snakelike motion, warning the rider to stay away.

The man was too dazed to realize what was happening. He kept weaving toward Raine.

Cord hit him with a flying tackle that carried them away from the raging stallion. He rolled to his feet with the grace of a highly trained fighter. "Get out of here," he snarled to the rider in low voice.

When the man didn't react quickly enough, Cord picked him up and physically threw him over the fence. Then he spun and looked at Raine.

She hadn't moved.

He wanted to run over and throw himself down by her, to find her pulse, feel it, know that she was still alive. But he couldn't. Right now the blood-bay stallion was a wholly primitive creature, as savage as any mustang ever born beyond the reach of man. He stood over his fallen mistress like a huge guard dog, responding to her unnatural stillness with a stallion's protective instinct.

Dev would kill anyone who tried to touch her.

Slowly, slowly, Cord eased across the ring toward Raine. Every breath he took was a soothing murmur of sound, a shaman's voice curling caressingly around the quivering stallion.

"Easy . . . easy, boy. I'm not going to hurt your mistress. Remember me? I'm the one who smells like her."

He extended his right forearm, the arm that Raine had held only moments before, when Cord had believed that there was time to wait before he took down her castle gate and began to live with warmth instead of ice.

But now there was no more time, only Raine lying facedown in the ring.

"Easy, Dev. Easy. Put those ears up, boy. Smell me . . . remember me . . ."

His voice poured over the stallion like a warm, darkly gleaming river, ceaseless, peaceful, bewitching with hints of moonlight sliding among deep currents.

Dev's ears lifted just a fraction from his skull. He watched Cord, but not with feral rage.

"That's it, boy. I'm not a wolf or a lion after a foal. I won't hurt you or Raine. That's it . . . that's it . . . easy, boy."

Quietly he praised each subtle shift in the stallion's attention, each tiny quiver of the horse's ears lifting from his skull.

"Smell me, boy. I smell like her . . ."

Behind Cord, shouts and startled cries sank into a spreading pool of silence. Everyone's attention was riveted on the ring and the fallen rider, the soft-talking man and the huge horse quivering on the breakpoint of rage and fear, a stallion's savage instincts battling with a shaman's voice for control of Dev's deadly body.

Voices called out offering advice and warnings. With each new male voice, Dev shuddered as though a whip had fallen on his sweat-blackened hide.

Cord wanted to shout at the men to shut up, but if he raised his voice, Dev would explode.

Fucking idiots, he thought viciously. *Can't*

they see they're making things worse?

Suddenly, clearly, Captain Jon's calm tones cut across the rumble of male advice. "I will personally horsewhip the next person who speaks. If anyone can get close to that stallion now, it's the man in the ring."

"But —" began one rider.

"Shut it."

Though Captain Jon didn't raise his voice, there was an immediate and total silence.

Cord's mesmerizing words continued without pause, the sounds of peace, of safety, of grassy fields and sweet water forever flowing.

Dev's ears shifted nervously as he stretched his head down toward Raine. Velvet nostrils expanded and quivered as the stallion's muzzle moved over his rider's motionless body. Her stillness was puzzling, unnerving.

With almost invisible movements, Cord glided closer. Words and nonsense mixed into a gentle murmur of sound that calmed Dev's uncertainty and fear.

"Let me look at her," he said. "I won't hurt her, boy. I just want to touch her, help her. That's what you want, too. You want your beautiful rider back on her feet and grooming you and cussing you out for being such a spring-loaded knothead. She can

246

cuss me out, too. I was as big a knothead as you. I thought we had all the time in the world . . ."

Ears not quite flattened, Dev stretched his powerful neck toward Cord. Black nostrils expanded, quivered, scenting again the mixture of Cord and Raine on the man's sleeve. With a long breath that was almost a groan, Dev's ears came up. He nosed Cord, then Raine, as though asking if the man knew why she was so still.

He praised the stallion even as his strong fingers closed around the reins. Dev shuddered, tried to toss his head, then accepted Cord's mastery.

Despite the urgency shrieking inside him, Cord was careful to move very slowly as he knelt next to Raine. She was facedown, arms flung out as though to deflect a blow. Delicately his fingertips found the soft skin of her neck. He held his breath and sought for the least sign of her life.

He felt nothing.

Jaw clenched, he let his breath out, slowing his own heartbeats so that he could feel hers no matter how faint or far apart they were.

After a wrenching moment, he felt the beat of Raine's life flowing just beneath his fingertips. Relief swept through him with a force that left him weak.

"Alive," he said, in a voice that was still dark magic.

"Do you want me to take Dev?" Captain Jon asked.

At the sound of the captain's voice, skin rippled nervously along the stallion's sweaty body.

"Not yet," Cord said soothingly. "Dev won't tolerate it."

With a low groan, fighting for the breath that had been knocked out of her, Raine tried to get up.

"Lie still. You had a bad fall." The quiet order was enforced with a hand between her shoulder blades. "Dev's all right," Cord added swiftly, knowing that Raine's first concern would be for her horse. "Do you hurt anywhere?"

The world whirled around her when she tried to lift her head. She let it sink back into the loose dirt of the ring. When everything settled down again, she opened her eyes. "Just dizzy. Breath knocked out."

"Tell me if I hurt you."

Holding Dev's reins in one hand, Cord ran the other over her, beginning at her neck and working down, probing for broken bones with surprising skill and gentleness. When he was finished, he looked a silent question at her.

"I'm okay," she repeated. Her voice was already stronger.

"You didn't look okay," he said bleakly. "You were facedown in the dirt, out cold."

Warily she moved her head. Muscles complained. She winced, knowing she would be stiff later.

"Can you sit up?" he asked.

"Sure."

But it wasn't as easy as it sounded. Her head hurt and her stomach thought she was on a merry-go-round. When he put his arm around her, bracing her, she leaned into him.

"You sure you're ready for this?" he asked.

"I've been sitting up for years. What happened?"

"One of the horses went crazy. Bee sting, probably. He shied into another horse, broke through the fence, and then hit Dev like a runaway train. You were knocked off right into the middle of it. Dev drove away the other horse and then stood over you like a one-ton attack dog."

She smiled weakly. "Sounds like Dev. He gets a little protective of me when I fall."

Cord's black eyebrows lifted at her understatement.

Abruptly she remembered seeing one of

her teammates thrown into the fence. She turned toward the fence so quickly that she startled Dev.

"Jameson," she said urgently. "Is Jameson all right?"

Captain Jon was standing next to the American rider. Jameson turned toward the ring. His face was pale and sweaty. The way he held himself suggested that his shoulder was either fractured or dislocated, or both.

"Shoulder," the captain said, watching Dev warily.

"What about Show Me?" Raine asked.

"Right foreleg probably is strained. Nothing serious," the captain added. "But Jameson won't be riding for a while."

She exchanged a long look with Captain Jon. The United States had to field a minimum number of three contestants in the three-day event. Four was the maximum permitted for a team. Four was also the preferred number, because it gave some margin for accident after the beginning of the event.

With Jameson out, one of the alternate riders would move up to take his place. There would still be four riders competing, but they wouldn't be the four who Captain Jon thought had the best chance of winning.

Grimly she started to get to her feet.

"What do you think you're doing?" Cord demanded, holding her down.

"I'm getting up," she said in a clipped voice. "Either help me or get the hell out of my way."

He looked at her for a long moment. Then he pulled her to her feet with startling ease. She hesitated a moment, letting dizziness pass, before she reached for Dev's reins.

Cord didn't release them.

Raine turned on him, furious because a man and a horse had been hurt, undercutting the hopes and dreams and years of hard work by the whole U.S. Equestrian Team. "Give me the damned reins," she snarled.

"I can lead Dev back to the stable," he said reasonably.

"Not yet. First he has to go over the jump."

"What happened wasn't Dev's fault."

"I know. But if he doesn't go over that jump now, there could be merry hell to pay later."

"She's right, you know," Captain Jon said, looking shrewdly from Cord to Raine. "It's a matter of the horse's confidence."

"What about the rider's neck." Cord's voice was uninflected, professional, and very cold.

"Event riders rather routinely finish the

course with concussions, broken teeth, and bashed ribs," the captain said. "Comes with the territory."

"Shit."

Without warning Cord bent, turned, straightened, and all but threw Raine up into the saddle. Then he let go of the reins and stepped out of the way. His pale eyes never left her face as she guided Dev back around the ring. He saw her fight dizziness, conquer it, and line up Dev for the jump.

You're Blue's daughter, all right. Stubborn to the bone. Brave, too. You don't think of it that way, do you? You just see what has to be done and then you do it.

How can anything as sweet and soft as you be so stubborn? But then, I never did like things easy. You've met your match, Baby Blue.

Problem is, so have I.

Dev flew over the jumps like the black-maned devil he was. When he landed after the third jump, Raine slumped against the muscular arch of his neck. Before she could fall, Cord was there. He lifted her off the blood-bay stallion and into his arms.

"I'm . . . a little . . . dizzy," she managed.

She fainted before she heard Cord's blistering response.

CHAPTER 11

"You're certain it was an accident?" Chandler-Smith demanded.

Cord looked down the hospital corridor into the waiting room. No one was close enough to the public telephone to overhear. "Ninety-seven percent."

Chandler-Smith grunted and ran his fingers through his thick salt-and-pepper hair. With Robert Johnstone, ninety-seven percent was as good as it got. "A god-damned bee. Who would have thought it?"

"If I had, there wouldn't have been a bee left alive within a five-mile radius of her."

"Tell me again that she's all right," Chandler-Smith said wearily.

Lights on every phone on his desk blinked, demanding his attention. He ignored them. Several computer screens beeped, cheeped, rasped, and in general made annoying noises so that he would respond. He ignored them, too.

"She's your daughter," Cord said dryly. "She'll be fine. Her skull is every bit as thick as yours."

"Ah, you've discovered that she's stubborn."

"Stubborn? Hell, she makes a Missouri mule look wishy-washy. She got on that damned stud and took him over the rest of the jumps as soon as she could stand up. Sooner, if you want the truth. Only after the jumps did she do the sensible thing."

"And that was . . . ?"

"She fainted," he said succinctly. "Or maybe she just didn't want to hear what I thought of her getting back on Dev for a round of jumping before she got her thick skull X-rayed."

Chandler-Smith cleared his throat, but a snicker still escaped. He rubbed the back of his neck, rotated his head, and rubbed some more. It had been a long night. It would be a longer day. "I wish I'd been there."

Cord closed his eyes and thought of the endless terrible moments when Raine had been facedown in the dirt and he hadn't known if she was alive or dead. But he didn't want to talk to Blue about that. The man was far too shrewd. He would suspect that Cord's concern was more than professional; it was intensely personal.

He breathed in, trying to control the tension gripping him. The aroma of the hospital clogged his nose, ammonia and desperation in equal parts.

"It's probably better that you weren't here," he said neutrally. "You would have ripped bloody strips off everything in reach. And she would have torn a few off you."

"Baby Raine?" Chandler-Smith laughed outright even as he curtly waved off his personal assistant, who had stuck his head into the lion's den to find out why all the lights were still blinking. "She's a pussycat. Never a hard word for anybody."

"Tell me that after you get between her and something she wants to do."

"Not me. I plan to live long enough to collect Social Security."

Cord smiled. "If you want updates on her condition, have someone contact the motor home. I won't call you unless things go from sugar to shit."

"Does the doctor expect that?" Chandler-Smith asked sharply.

"No," Cord said, but his tone said that he was used to planning for worst-case scenarios. "I'm not taking her back to her motel room. I'm keeping her in the spare room at the command center so that I can check on her every half hour."

Chandler-Smith's eyebrows rose. "Hire a nurse."

"There's not enough time to vet anyone. Right now, there's only one person I trust without reservation. Me."

"What about Kentucky?"

"Ninety-seven percent."

"You're a hard son of a bitch."

"You're my role model in all ways but one," Cord retorted.

"Should I ask?"

"I'm getting out."

Cord didn't say anything more. He didn't have to. Both men understood that when a man in their line of work started talking about getting out, it was just a matter of time. Short time, usually.

"You could have had a desk job anytime in the last five years," Chandler-Smith said.

"All the way out."

Silently Chandler-Smith looked at his polished shoes. Robert Johnstone was the best agent he had ever worked with. He didn't want to lose him.

And he liked him far too much to make him stay.

"When?" Chandler-Smith said simply.

"After Barracuda's funeral."

"That could be a long time."

Cord looked at the palm of his hand. The

gold coin gleamed back at him. Lady Luck. Lady Death. "I don't think so. As soon as you've seen Raine ride, I'm going under. I won't come out until he's dead. If that's too much heat for you, fire me . . . but don't change the codes."

"Done," Chandler-Smith said simply.

"I can walk," Raine snapped. When she heard her own tone, she winced. She had the kind of headache that made morphine look attractive. "Sorry. I didn't mean to take your head off. But you can have mine, if you want. Please."

"I'll pass, thanks. I've had concussions before." Cord put her on her feet and shut the car door behind her. "This way."

When she started walking, he put his arm around her waist, ready to grab her if her knees gave way. He expected her to snap at him for that, too, but she didn't. She just sighed and held one hand between her face and the sun, shading her eyes.

"Afternoon, Thorne," Cord said when they reached the motor home. "Anything for me?"

"No, suh. Things have been real quiet."

"Raine, this is Thorne. Thorne, Miss Chandler-Smith."

Her headache didn't keep her from seeing

the slight narrowing of Thorne's eyes, or the instant reassessment of her rumpled, dirty clothes. She smiled wryly, knowing that she looked exactly like what she was — a woman who had gone facedown off a tall horse and then spent several hours in a hospital emergency room being probed, X-rayed, and questioned while Cord watched with pale eyes and a mouth that had forgotten how to smile.

"Call me Raine Smith," she said. "Everyone else does."

Thorne nodded. "Miss Smith, I'm pleased to meet you."

"Raine," she said, stressing her first name.

Cord hid his smile. Her informality wouldn't make a dent in Kentucky's southern sense of propriety. After three years, he still called Cord "Mister." Cord had given up trying to change it; Kentucky was intelligent, close-mouthed, and deadly with any weapon that came to hand. For those qualities, Cord could live with a few social formalities.

"See if you can find a recliner for Raine," Cord said. "You two can sit together under the pepper tree."

"I have to see Dev," she objected.

"You can see him right here."

"Who's going to bring him?"

"I am."

She started to object, but didn't. The pepper tree's lacy shade was calling to her. "If you have trouble with him, come get me."

Cord turned to Thorne. "While I get Dev, send someone to check Raine out of her motel."

"What?" she said, turning back to him swiftly, then wincing. Sudden movements did bad things to her headache.

"Yes, suh," Thorne said, turning toward the motor home.

"I thought you would want your luggage," Cord said to her. "But if you don't mind sleeping in one of my T-shirts, that's fine."

"What are you talking about?"

"My job."

She opened her mouth, saw the bleak certainty in Cord's eyes, remembered their conversation about her father and assassins, and shut up. If necessary, she'd argue with Cord later, after she had checked Dev over. Right now it was enough just to be standing up. A battle was beyond her.

Especially with someone as smart and tough as Cord Elliot.

Feeling headachy and tired, she followed Thorne to the pepper tree, waited while he set up the lounge, and then stretched out in the shade with a sigh of relief. She got slowly to her feet when Cord appeared, a bucket of grooming tools in one hand and Dev's lead rope in the other. The stallion was edgy, but not hard to handle. His walk was springy, muscular, completely sound.

Ignoring her pounding head, she went over Dev with eyes and hands, paying particular attention to the long tendons in his legs. While she fussed over him, the stallion lipped at her loose hair and nuzzled her neck, made whuffling noises at her cheeks, and sniffed hopefully for carrots in her hip pockets.

"Back off, brat," she muttered.

Dev returned to lipping her hair.

Cord watched, simultaneously worried about the pallor of Raine's skin and amused by the big stallion's efforts to tease his mistress.

Warily, Thorne watched, too. He made certain to stay in the shade of the pepper tree, well away from the big stud.

For the third time, she went over Dev's legs. If there was any soreness or swelling, she couldn't find it. Other than dried sweat dulling his normally glossy hide, the stallion looked perfectly normal.

"That should do it," Cord said, when she straightened slowly. "Go back and lie down on the lounge."

"Not yet. He needs a good grooming."

"I'll take care of it."

She hesitated, gave in without an argument, and headed for the shade. "If Dev puts up with it, fine. Otherwise I'll do it myself."

Talking calmly, caressing the big stud with his voice, Cord selected a currycomb from the bucket of tools and went to work on the dried sweat.

Dev glanced around at the unfamiliar touch, sniffed Cord's hand and the currycomb, and went back to searching for something edible in the dusty yard. He didn't find anything. With a massive sigh at life's injustice, the stallion shifted to a three-legged stance and dozed.

"It's that damned shaman's voice," she said beneath her breath, listening to the mesmerizing music of Cord's words as he worked over her horse. "It's even getting to me."

"Ma'am?" Thorne asked politely.

"Nothing." She sighed and settled back into the lounge to enjoy the unheard-of pleasure of watching a man groom Dev without the aid of cross ties and hobbles.

The murmur of Cord's voice mingled with the warm breeze, draining away her tension.

A deep weariness stole over her, a reaction to the stunning fall and all the restless nights since she had shut Cord out of her castle and barred the gates.

Without even knowing it, she fell asleep.

"Mr. Elliot," Thorne said quietly.

Cord put down the currycomb and walked quickly to Raine's side. As gently as butterfly wings, his fingertips found her pulse. Slow, steady, deep, like her breathing. Skin neither clammy nor dry, cold nor hot. He nodded to Thorne, then returned to grooming Dev. Talking softly, ceaselessly, he worked over the big stallion.

After the first ten minutes, he no longer watched Dev's ears every second. After twenty minutes, he decided that it was time for the final test. He pulled a hoof pick from his hip pocket and touched the fetlock on Dev's left front leg. Without really waking up, the stallion shifted his weight and presented the left front hoof to be cleaned.

Thorne slid one hand beneath his jacket and watched the stallion as though he was a rattlesnake coiled to strike.

Cord looked up at the motion and said quietly, "It's all right."

Thorne nodded, but he didn't remove his hand. He watched each hoof in turn get cleaned. When Cord traded the hoof pick for a soft brush, Thorne let out a silent sigh of relief.

Dev stood with his head down, his weight on three legs, his ears utterly relaxed. From time to time he sent his long black tail swishing over his body, flicking away the flies. Sometimes he snorted and rubbed his head against his foreleg or Cord's chest to get rid of the persistent insects.

Eyes narrow, dark, Thorne watched the stallion. His hand was never far from the gun he wore in a shoulder harness beneath a light cotton jacket.

"Word around the stables is that horse is a killer," Thorne said after a long time.

"He could be."

Cord swept a soft cloth down Dev's hard-muscled haunch. The strokes were strong, rhythmic. The stallion groaned in a contentment that was almost comical.

"You don't think he's a killer?" Thorne asked softly.

"Never with Raine. Probably not with me, so long as I'm careful. Given enough time," he added, smoothing his palm over Dev's satiny coat, "he would come to trust me completely."

Stepping back, he admired the result of his work. There wasn't a trace of dried sweat or dust anywhere on Dev's powerful body.

The stallion's thick mane and tail shimmered like coarse black silk, emphasizing the blood red of his coat.

When Cord lifted his hand to brush a fly away from his face, the unique, pungent scent of horse lifted off his fingers, bringing back a rush of memories from his childhood. He hadn't known how much he missed horses. He hadn't even suspected.

"Damn, but it's good to work with a horse again," he said softly, surprised by the intensity of the feeling. "Especially a horse like this one."

Thorne looked from the huge stallion to Cord. "I'm a city boy, myself. I'll take your word for it."

"There's nothing like it," Cord murmured, remembering the long rides over rough country, the smell of horses and piñon trees, the feel of the Nevada sun hot on his back and a horse running cleanly between his knees. "Nothing in the world," he added, discovery and surprise rippling like music in his voice.

Dev snorted and stamped his front foot, dislodging a fly.

Cord looked over at Thorne, then at Raine sleeping in the filtered shade of the pepper tree. "How long?"

Thorne checked his watch. "Almost half

an hour."

Cord went to the chaise and sat on his heels beside it like the range rider he once had been. He checked her pulse and breathing. Still deep, still even. Slowly he stroked her face, waking her as gently as he could.

"Cord?" she murmured.

"Right here."

Not truly awake, she turned her lips into his hand, kissing him sleepily. His other hand came up in a slow caress, smoothing her hair away from her face. She sighed and gave herself back to sleep, knowing she was safe.

"Raine," he whispered, his throat aching at the evidence of her trust. "Look at me, honey."

She stirred again, nuzzling his hand. His breath caught. He wanted to brush his lips over her cheek, to breathe her scent in all the way to his soul.

"Open your eyes," he said softly.

One of her hands came up in silent protest at being awakened. When she discovered Cord's fingers touching her cheek, she murmured in pleasure and pressed her hand against his. Cradling his hand between her cheek and her palm, she slid toward sleep once again.

Bending close, he put his cheek alongside

hers for a moment and breathed her name too softly for her to hear. Then, reluctantly, he straightened.

"Wake up, Raine," he said in a low voice. "I have to check your beautiful eyes." The caressing pressure of his fingers on her cheek increased. "Wake up, honey. Look at me."

Long, dark brown lashes stirred and slowly lifted. Hazel eyes looked out at him, dazed by sleep. Her pupils were dilated, but they contracted quickly in the light. Quickly and evenly.

Thank God. Cord let out a breath he hadn't been aware of holding. "Go back to sleep." His voice was soothing, velvety, urging her back down into the sleep she needed. "Everything is all right. Go to sleep."

"Cord . . . ?" she whispered.

"Go to sleep, little queen. Your soldier is here."

Before her breath sighed out, she was asleep.

And even asleep, she clung to his hand.

For several minutes he didn't move. He simply looked at the silky half circles of her eyelashes, the shimmering wealth of her chestnut hair tumbling over the lounge's pale cushion, the pink curve of her lips, and the skin stretched smoothly over her cheek-bones. When he could take no more of the gentle torment, he bent and kissed the hollow of her cheek. Softly, reluctantly, he eased his hand out of hers.

When he glanced up, Thorne was pointedly looking somewhere else. Nor did Thorne say any of the sensible things about getting involved with the woman you were supposed to guard, a woman whose father was one of the most powerful men in the government.

Thorne kept silent even when Cord carried Raine into the communications room of the motor home, put her in his own bed, and locked the door. She stirred fitfully, but calmed as soon as he bent and murmured a few words against her cheek.

As soon as she was fully asleep, he went to the swivel chair in front of the computer, punched in his code, and began updating himself on all that had happened in the last half day.

Next to him a radio scanner worked ceaselessly, hunting among all local, state, and federal law-enforcement frequencies. When the scanner found a channel that was in use, it stopped to listen in on the transmission. Unless Cord intervened, the scanner would soon move on, surfing the frequencies, picking up disembodied voices.

For the most part, he ignored the transmissions, halting the scanner only if he heard certain codes used. Occasionally he would reach for the two-way radio set that was nearby. Like the scanner, the radio was capable of reaching all law-enforcement frequencies. He also had a top-secret satellite phone that he could use when absolute security was required.

One way or another, he had at his fingertips all of the various civil and military agencies whose responsibility it was to protect Olympic athletes, VIPs, and spectators against everything from pick-pockets to a full-scale terrorist attack.

Working quietly, Cord sifted through intelligence reports graded according to their reliability. He read them, then made assessments and reports of his own.

Every half hour he checked on Raine. Each time he did, she reached for him as she came out of sleep, holding his hand against her and curling around it like a lover. Each time, it was harder for him to pull away.

He wanted to lie down beside her, let her burrow against him and sigh with contentment while he held her. He would settle for that. Just holding her. He was lucky to get even that much.

She could have died this morning, and she had a dented riding helmet to prove it.

For a time he sat on his bed next to her, watching her. Her color was normal now, not even a hint of paleness beneath her smooth, translucent skin. She was neither hot nor cold, and still vaguely dusty from her fall in the ring. Her breathing and pulse were normal.

Slowly he caressed her cheek with the back of his fingers. "Wake up, honey. It's Cord."

She awakened as before, her hand reaching up to curl around his. When her lips touched his palm, he felt a wave of heat all the way to his knees.

"Open your eyes," he murmured. Carefully, thoroughly, he rubbed his fingers over her scalp. There were no lumps, no swellings, barely even a tender spot to make her flinch. "That was one hell of a good riding helmet, lady."

Her eyes flew open, wide awake and startled. Both pupils were evenly dilated. Both responded with equal quickness to the light level in the room.

The tension in him eased a few more percentage points.

"Cord?" she asked, her voice husky with

sleep. She looked past him, seeing the room for the first time. "Where am I?"

"In the motor home."

"What time is it?"

"Almost five. Hungry?"

"Starved. Whatever happened to lunch?"

"You turned it down in favor of sleep."

"Do I get a second chance?"

"Anytime," he said, caressing her cheek with his captive fingers.

Abruptly Raine realized that she was holding Cord's hand against her cheek. Color bloomed beneath her skin. She let go of his fingers as though she had been burned and sat up hurriedly.

"Dizzy?" he asked.

"No."

"Headache?"

"A little," she admitted.

"How does your stomach feel now?"

"Predatory."

Smiling, he stood up. "If you can still tell me that when you're on your feet, I'll fix an omelet for you."

Immediately she stood up. His ice-blue eyes noted every hesitation, every wince.

"Nauseated?" he asked after a minute.

"No. Just hungry. And — does this place come equipped with a bathroom?"

"First door on the left."

He unlocked the door and walked out of the room. Though he seemed not to notice whether she followed, he was listening very carefully, ready to turn around and grab her if he heard her stumble or hesitate at all. She didn't. Like her stallion, she was very steady on her feet. Utterly normal.

"Holler if you need me," he said. "I'll be in the galley."

Raine took one look at herself in the bathroom mirror and shuddered. "Put a hold on that omelet," she called out. "I'm taking a shower first."

Very quickly Cord appeared in the doorway. "Sure you're up to it?"

"Positive."

He hesitated. The shower had a bench and a long-necked flexible wand so that she didn't have to stand up. But he didn't like the thought of her falling when he wasn't around to catch her.

"Don't wash your hair," he said finally.

"Don't be ridiculous. It will crawl right off my head if I don't."

He smiled. "Then I'll wash it." He waited long enough for her expression to get indignant, before he added, "In the sink."

"What?"

"I'll wash your hair in the sink. That way,

if you get dizzy, I'll be right there to catch you."

"It's not necessary. I'm fine. Hardly even a headache."

"That's nice. In the sink or not at all." When she opened her mouth to protest, he spoke first. "Want me to sweep you off your feet again?"

Muttering beneath her breath, she walked two steps to the sink. His razor, toothbrush, and aftershave were laid out on the narrow counter. Next to his things, lined up in a neat row, were a squeeze bottle of her shampoo, her toothbrush, toothpaste, hairbrush, and the colorful packet of birth control pills that made certain her period wouldn't come in the middle of a world-class competition.

"What's going on?" she asked tightly. It was an effort to keep her voice level.

"You refused to stay in the hospital."

"Of course I —"

"You have to have someone wake you every hour or so during the night," he continued ruthlessly. "Otherwise you could slip into a coma with nobody the wiser. You didn't have a roommate who could check on you, so you'll stay here, where I can keep an eye on you."

Her mouth flattened. "Like bloody hell I will."

CHAPTER 12

Cord watched with lazy interest while color and anger changed Raine's face. "There's more than one bed in this place," he said calmly. "Just one bathroom, though. Don't worry about it. I may wear a gun, but I'm quite civilized about closed doors."

She felt like a fool. Again. An ungrateful fool at that.

"Do you want your blouse on or off while I wash your hair?" he asked as he walked to the sink.

Her eyes widened. Silvery heat prickled over her breasts and shot straight down to her thighs at the thought of Cord undressing her. She swallowed quickly. "On."

"Okay," he said, reaching for her blouse.

Before she could protest, he had the first two buttons undone and was folding her collar underneath. She jerked back, entirely too conscious of his fingers brushing over her neck and the hollow of her throat.

"What do you think you're doing?" she asked, startled.

"Getting your collar out of the way. Or did you want the blouse washed, too? If so, it would be easier if you took it off. Not nearly as interesting, though. All in all, I like your idea better. Wash the blouse with you still in it."

His voice was so bland, the implication of his words so outrageous, that he had her head in the sink and was running warm water over her hair before she realized precisely what he had said.

"Cord Elliot," she told the bottom of the sink, "whoever taught you how to talk should have been shot!"

His only answer was a chuckle that could have been the sound of water flowing.

She muttered some words she usually reserved for Dev at his worst, then gave in to the luxury of having her hair washed by strong, gentle fingers. The only problem was that water — and soap — kept trying to run into her eyes and nose.

The third time she had to come up for air, Cord reached for a towel. He mopped off her face.

"You're right," he said. "This isn't working. Let's try your idea."

"Mffph?" was all she could get past the

275

towel drying her chin.

"Washing everything at once." He smiled slowly, wickedly, knowing she couldn't see. Then he kicked off his shoes and pulled her into the shower.

"Sit." Gently he pushed her down onto the bench and pulled the towel away from her face. "Tip your head back so soap won't run in your eyes."

Raine sat, head tilted slightly back, off-balance again. Ruefully she admitted that he had a definite talent for keeping people that way, teetering on the edge, unsure, a step behind and not very damn likely to catch up.

At least, he had that effect on her. The smooth, bland voice coupled with outrageous words. The gentleness and humor that made her forget the lethal knowledge implicit in the gun he wore. The heat and hunger of his hands contrasting with the icy assessment she had seen in his eyes.

Cord stepped out of the shower. With easy, familiar motions he unfastened his holster, ammunition clip, and beeper, and set them aside. He came back to the shower and stood in front of her, legs braced.

"I should object," she said.

"Why? I won't drown you."

She gave him a bittersweet smile. She was

already drowning, and he didn't even know it.

Wrong man, wrong time, wrong place.
Wrong.

Yet her body was humming and she ached for his kiss, a kiss that was both claim and plea, victory and submission, blissful heaven shot through with a bright, sweet streak of hell that brought every nerve alive.

Cord picked up the shower wand, turned on the water, and waited until it was just the right temperature. He certainly was. Or wasn't. Something about having his hands deep in Raine's wet, slippery hair was viciously arousing. He told himself that he was grateful she still had her blouse on.

He lied.

He wanted to peel her blouse off, unhook her bra, slide his fingers under the silky weight of her breasts. He knew just how her nipples would feel, velvet and hard at once, pouting for his mouth, demanding the caresses that were their due. He could see them, feel them, taste them . . . and they were just the beginning of her female riches. There was a heat in her that made his whole body heavy with desire.

Maybe I should turn the water on cold and stuff the wand in my jeans, he told himself sardonically. *Better yet, I should let her wash her own hair and watch from a safe distance.*

A mile might be about enough.

But he doubted it.

"Cord?" she asked, looking at his grim face. "Is something wrong?"

"Just adjusting the temperature. The water heater is sulky."

Smiling, she waited while he fiddled with the wand. He had rolled up his sleeves before he tried to wash her hair in the sink, but he should have taken off his shirt, too. Water had splashed over him, turning the light blue cloth into a rich autumn sky color that clung to the lines of his chest and arms. Black hair curled over his tanned skin like a satin shadow. When he adjusted the faucets, muscles slid and coiled with casual strength.

She watched with admiring eyes, fascinated by his masculine grace, remembering the moments when she had kissed him and her fingertips had traced the full, thick veins just beneath his skin.

With a muttered word, Cord nudged the faucets again. They didn't need fussing, but he did. He wasn't going to turn back toward her until his arousal was under control. Or semi-control. That seemed to be as good as it got when he was close to her.

"Tilt your head back and close your eyes," he said, turning around finally.

Even as he spoke, he tilted her head back for her. The thought of having her mouth level with the bottom button on his jeans was making him get hard all over again.

She stared at the wet shirt that concealed nothing of Cord's strength, at the very male lines of his chest and shoulders, sinew and muscle; and the pale, wild blaze of his eyes in a face that belonged to a dark angel.

Heat and dizziness swept over her, a reaction that had nothing to do with her fall. She closed her eyes, but still she saw him standing only inches away, another memory to haunt her nights. When his fingers eased into her hair, she couldn't entirely conceal the delicious shiver of response that raced through her body.

"Cold?" he asked, concern clear in his voice.

Numbly she shook her head, not trusting her own voice. Another picture had flashed behind her eyes: a headlong fall beneath a berserk horse, steel-shod hooves flailing near her face, just missing her eyes, then the dark dirt of the ring exploding around her.

She had always known that there was a possibility of serious injury, even death, in the strenuous demands of the three-day event. She thought she had accepted the danger as simply part of the life she had chosen. But twice within a few days her world had been stood on end and shaken until she fell out, slamming face first into a new reality.

Tomorrow was a matter of faith, not a guarantee. The only guarantee was here and now.

Understanding that all the way to her soul was subtly rearranging her thoughts, her expectations, her self-assurance. Questions she had never asked before were turning in the depths of her mind, demanding answers that were neither easy nor comfortable.

Who am I to smile and blithely plan for life-ever-after with some imaginary man I can't even see in my dreams?

Who am I to play cold, uncaring queen to the battle-worn soldier who defends my life with his own?

Who am I to disdain competition madness when it's an ache and a burning in my own body?

There was no answer but the one that stood before her. She shivered again, accepting it. Accepting herself.

Accepting him.

Warm water poured through her hair. His strong, lean fingers worked gently over her head. With each stroke of his hands, scented liquid soap became mounds of slippery lather. He massaged her scalp with slow, powerful strokes while lather slipped and ran through his fingers.

Head tilted back, eyes closed, Raine lived only in the moment. With every cell of her body she absorbed the sensations of water and warmth, of Cord standing so close that she could feel the occasional brush of his shirt against her face and breathe in his oddly familiar scent. The smell of him haunted her like a half-remembered song. When she realized why his scent was so familiar, she laughed softly.

"Ticklish?" His voice was very deep, almost raspy.

"No." She opened her eyes and looked into his, smiling. "You smell like Dev."

His lips shifted into an off-center smile. "Is that a polite way of saying I need a shower?"

Her long eyelashes swept down, concealing the laughter and light in her eyes. "Not at all. On you, essence of Devlin's Waterloo smells . . . sexy."

His hands paused, then resumed their slow, deep massage. His heart was beating too hard and deep. The purring sound of relaxation and pleasure she made didn't help cool the heat in his blood. Her head tilted forward, all but brushing his jeans.

He was glad her eyes were closed. If she opened them, she would have plenty to look at. He wondered if she would be shocked or . . . interested.

You're a damned fool, Cord told himself bitterly. *Even if she wanted me, I'm not the kind of predator who would take her the way she is now, off-balance, still in shock from nearly dying.*

He shouldn't even be this close to her, enjoying her, letting the heat and scent of her sink into him like sunlight after endless winter. He shouldn't be, but he was. Her hair was a thousand silken strands holding him. So was the knowledge that he was giving her pleasure. The certainty of it had no weight, no substance, and was stronger than any chains ever forged.

With another shiver, Raine sighed and rested her head against the hard muscles of Cord's torso.

He moved quickly, surely, keeping lather from sliding into her eyes. Without shifting her away, he tilted her head back again, keeping her close, not caring that his jeans were getting soaked. Warm water slid over her again, rinsing white ribbons of lather from her hair. Warm water ran over her shoulders, between her breasts, over her stomach and thighs.

She let out a long breath and smiled dreamily. The sensation of being bathed in liquid warmth while fully clothed was both odd and exquisite.

"Once more," he said. His voice was deep, husky in its intimacy. He didn't care. It was all he could do to stand up against the waves of heat and heaviness beating between his legs.

Soap came out of the squeeze bottle in fragrant pulses that sank into her dark hair. His hands moved in slow motion, creating pleasure and iridescent bubbles. The changing pressure of his fingers encouraged her to put her cheek against his waist.

She didn't resist. She didn't even hesitate. She simply leaned into his tough warmth and smiled.

The motion of his hands shifted subtly, caressing her scalp as much as washing her hair. Eyes closed, savoring the moment, he stood and rocked her very slowly against his body.

For a long time there was no sound but warm water flowing from the wand Cord had braced between his knee and the shower bench. Finally, reluctantly, he picked up the wand again.

"Not yet," Raine said, putting her arms

around his hips as unselfconsciously as she had rested against him. "It's so good just to be held by you."

He whispered her name as he cradled her again. Tenderness and restraint coursed through him as much as passion. She was so vulnerable now. Too vulnerable. He knew enough about the physical and mental aftereffects of trauma to understand that she wasn't completely responsible for her actions right now. She was at the mercy of instincts she didn't understand.

But he understood. When confronted by death, life reverted to a basic biological strategy: reproduction.

He had seen it happen too many times, to too many people, choices made in heat and regretted in confusion and pain, just one more danger in an already dangerous profession.

He would no more take advantage of her vulnerability at this moment than he would deliberately get her drunk and then haul her into his bed and overwhelm whatever reservations alcohol hadn't already drowned.

She pressed her cheek closer to him, savoring the warmth radiating through his soaked clothing. "You're all wet,"

He laughed oddly, wondering if she had

been reading his mind. Without being conscious of it, he let his hands slide down to her neck, her shoulders. The pink of her shirt was dark with water, almost cherry colored. Streamers of lather wound over and between her breasts. Her nipples stood out clearly, defined by water and clinging cloth.

Unable to stop himself, he looked, memorizing and remembering at the same time. She had felt so good in his mouth, hard and soft, salty and sweet, giving and demanding, utterly feminine. The soft cries he had dragged from deep in her throat had echoed through his sleepless nights.

With a soundless curse and a stifled groan, he bent and picked up the shower wand. He rinsed her hair carefully, ignoring the siren call of her cheek pressed against his abdomen, the warm water flowing over her, sliding over him, warm water joining them in an intimacy that was fast eroding his control.

He was losing it. He had to stop.

Now.

With quick, hard movements he turned off the faucets. Yet his hands were gentle as he squeezed water from her hair. And he was very gentle when he loosened her arms from around his hips.

"All done," he said, his voice neutral.

He turned away quickly, before she could open her eyes. He knew that his arousal wasn't at all concealed by the wet jeans plastered against him.

Dreamily she began to open her eyes.

"I'll wait out here while you finish your shower," he said. "Holler if you need anything."

When the shower door closed firmly behind him, she blinked and rubbed her eyes as though waking from a deep sleep. Confused, she looked at the opaque rectangle of glass and the man silhouetted just beyond. She knew that he had enjoyed touching and holding her as much as she had enjoyed it. What she didn't know was why he had stopped.

"Cord?"

Instantly the shower door opened. Eyes that were oddly smoky and brilliantly blue looked out at her from an expressionless face.

"I feel a little dizzy," she whispered.

It wasn't a lie. When he looked at her like that, she felt weak and dizzy, hot and cold, hungry to taste and feel the male textures of him.

He moved with startling speed, scooping her off the bench and holding her tightly. "I never should have let you out of bed."

Soft, laughing agreement was breathed into his ear as her arms wound around his neck like a lover. He stood very still for an instant, fighting for control. When it came, he set her carefully on her feet and tilted her chin up until she met his eyes.

"Nearly being killed is the most potent aphrodisiac known to man," he said, with a casualness that went no deeper than the expressionless mask of his face. "Don't trust your reactions until tomorrow."

When Raine understood what Cord was saying — and what he *wasn't* saying — she felt as though she had been dropped into ice water. Flushing red in one instant and then going pale in the next, she jerked her arms away from him. But when she would have turned and walked off, she discovered she couldn't. His arms were still around her.

"You don't need to hold me." Her voice was as pale as her skin. She didn't meet his eyes. "I'm fine now. Not the least bit dizzy."

"Raine . . ."

She refused to look at him.

He turned her chin until she had no choice. The sensible words he had been going to say caught in his throat. He hadn't meant to hurt her. He hadn't really even believed he could, not like this, her eyes narrowed, her lips pale.

"Let go of me," she said quietly, keeping herself together with the same discipline and nerve that had made her a world-class rider. "I've taken enough falls for one day, don't you think?"

Abruptly he pulled her close and hard, pressing her against the entire length of his hungry body. He didn't care anymore if she knew just how savagely aroused he was.

"If it was tomorrow," he said roughly, "I'd be in that shower with you right now, pulling off your clothes and licking water off every bit of your skin. Call my name like that again tomorrow and see what happens."

He couldn't help the slow, blazing surge of his hips against her body, but he could let go of her. And he did.

She closed her eyes, wondering how she had so badly misread herself, him, everything.

Off-balance. Again.

She resented the feeling, and the man who caused it. "Maybe, maybe not." Her voice was a cool echo of his when he had told her about death and aphrodisiacs. "Competition madness is unpredictable. Besides," she added distinctly, "tomorrow might never come."

"I used to believe that."

"You should. You're the one who taught me."

"I don't believe it anymore. Tomorrow will come for us. When it does, I want it to be right. I want to know that I didn't take you off-balance and more than a little afraid. I'm good at taking people that way. Too good. It's part of my job. But not you." His voice shifted, deepened, a river running through moonlight and darkness down to a warm sea. "I want you in a very special way. I can wait one more day for that. I've already waited a lifetime."

She looked away, unable to meet the hunger and certainty in his eyes. Maybe he was right. Maybe she shouldn't trust her own instincts now.

Maybe she shouldn't trust herself at all when she was around him.

"I'll make your omelet while you shower," he said, his voice matter-of-fact again as he turned away.

This time when the door shut behind Cord, she didn't call his name.

After a silent dinner, Cord took Raine back to the radio room. He saw her looking around with the kind of curiosity that said her mind was alert and in full working order again.

"This is a hallucination," he said.

"What is?"

"This room. It doesn't exist. The equipment doesn't exist. The motor home itself is only an unfounded rumor. Therefore, the fact that you don't have the security clearance to be here doesn't matter."

"Oh. I see."

"I thought you would, being Blue's daughter and all."

"You're sure you don't know my father?"

"I can guarantee he doesn't know my name. Lie down on the bed. If you feel like reading, Thorne brought the books from your motel room. They're on the bedside table."

She stretched out on the bed, surprised that it felt so good to be off her feet. One way or another, she had done little for the past eight hours except lie down. A neat stack of mysteries beckoned. She had bought them at Dulles Airport before she got on the plane to California. She picked up the first book and opened it.

Sixty-two pages later she closed the book and picked up a second mystery, hoping that it would hold her wandering attention. After five chapters she chucked the second mystery on the floor and reached for a third.

Only a few feet away, Cord worked quietly.

The computer keyboard made tiny hollow sounds beneath his fingertips. The scanner cast fragments of scratchy dialogue into the room. Sometimes poignant, sometimes urgent, most often simply bored, the voices had an eerie unreality that nagged at Raine's attention as much as the big man who sat and watched the computer with an intensity that hummed with intelligence.

"Delta/Blue Light, do you copy?"

From the corner of her eye, she saw his hand flash out to the scanner and hit the hold button. She realized that each time she had heard those words, Cord had reacted in the same way. Other words, other codes overheard by the scanner seemed to have no interest for him.

She tried to make out the meaning of the transmission, but couldn't. Both men and women spoke in a staccato shorthand that might as well have been another language.

Curiosity gnawed at Raine. Her assumption that Cord was some sort of glorified bodyguard for her father had shattered against the high-tech, high-tension reality of the motorhome. Whatever Cord did, it was more far-reaching and less obvious than guarding VIPs.

Doggedly she dragged her thoughts back to the second chapter of the third mystery for the fourth time, but its clues and red herrings were less tantalizing than the fragments of conversation pulled out of the night by the scanner. When the words "Delta/Blue Light" came again, and Cord stopped the scanner to listen, she put down her book with an impatient gesture. As soon as the transmission ended, she looked at him directly for the first time since her shower.

"What is 'Delta/Blue Light'?"

He swiveled his chair to face her and said nothing.

"If the equipment doesn't exist, and the room doesn't exist, then I don't exist," she said reasonably. "You can't break any security rules by telling me about Delta/Blue Light, because I'm not really here at all, am I?"

His lips turned up in the shadow of a smile. "You should have been a lawyer." For a moment longer he hesitated, then he shrugged. "Delta/Blue Light is a big secret, badly kept. The newspapers have been hinting about it for eighteen months."

She waited, knowing that he would tell her what he thought he should, and no more. She also knew that it was his way of protecting her, as her father had protected her mother. But even knowing that, she chafed at ignorance in a way she never had before.

She wanted to know more about Cord Elliot, about what he was, about what he did, about his thoughts and memories and dreams. Yet his life was a closed file kept in a locked cabinet in a guarded room, with access only on a strict need-to-know basis.

Well, I need to know. I'll keep asking until I do know, damn it. It isn't smart and I shouldn't care, but I do.

"The Pentagon," Cord continued, watching Raine with eyes that were almost colorless, like his voice, "has set aside fifty million dollars for backup in case of another terrorist attack like Munich. Our hole card is Delta/Blue Light, a group of hand-picked commandos waiting around outside Las Vegas, Nevada. If they have to, they'll come down on L.A. like a hard rain, using all the nasty tricks we've learned from some of the world's nastiest people. Terrorists."

She was utterly still for a second, caught as much by the violence implicit in his words as by the words themselves. Not a bodyguard, not a simple soldier, not like any man she had ever met before. Not even like her father.

"Who are you?" she whispered.

She saw the subtle, devastating change

that swept over Cord at her words. Suddenly he was poised, deadly, waiting for a signal only he would recognize. Fear roughened the skin on her arms.

He was looking at her the way he had the first time, when he hadn't known who she was. He was looking at her as though his pale, uncanny eyes could peel away her soft skin and see whatever might be hidden beneath.

And if he didn't like what he found . . .

CHAPTER 13

The hard-edged smile Cord gave Raine was no more comforting than his eyes. "I'm Cord Elliot, remember?"

"That's not what I meant," she said quickly, words tumbling out of her as she tried to explain, to banish the deadly stranger who was looking at her through Cord Elliot's eyes. "Are you local police or federal or military or . . . something else?"

His eyes closed for an instant. When they opened, the stranger was gone. "I'm on your side, Raine. Isn't that enough?"

He turned away before she could answer.

There was a finality to his movement that told her more clearly than words that the subject of Cord Elliot was closed. With hands that wanted to tremble, she picked up the mystery and began the second chapter for the fifth time.

This time she was more successful, if success could be measured by the number of pages turning beneath her determined fingers as the darkness outside deepened toward midnight. But the words she read were meaningless, the silence and the static cries of the scanner oddly hypnotic.

Cord was right. This equipment, this room, she herself didn't exist. Nothing did but darkness and ghostly voices and the man with pale eyes who sat at the center of everything, listening, waiting.

"— Ontario. Two-eleven in progress. All cars in vicinity respond code three. Repeat. Two-eleven in progress on corner of —"

Static and silence and the hollow clicking of a computer keyboard. She held her breath unconsciously while the scanner searched unknown frequencies.

"— Subject turning right on Sunset. Are you on him, Jake? Can you —"

Silence and clicking, scanner searching.

"— And they're at it again. Flip you for it, Martinez. Last time I got between her and her pimp she damn near cut off my —"

Static and silence, the faint hiss of voices coming over frequencies layered like cards in a deck, waiting for a dealer to pick them out and give them meaning.

"— repeat. Anyone monitoring this frequency speak Chinese? At least, I think it's Chinese, but I —"

Cord snapped on the hold and waited, listening.

"— *can't be sure because I'm no linguist. She looks about six years old, and scared to death in the bargain. This is Kate on Nine. Over.*"

He waited, but no one answered. He picked up the radio, adjusted the frequency, and spoke.

"Kate on Nine," he said, leaving out his own identification. "Is the girl able to hear me? Over."

"Yes. Over."

Raine listened in fascination as sliding, singsong syllables poured out of Cord. When he ended with, "Does she understand? Over," the English words were almost jarring.

"Thank God. Yes, she understands you. Over." The woman's relief was evident even through the static.

He talked for a while longer, his voice soothing even in the odd tones and minor-key phrasing of the language he used. A girl's voice came back to him, high and thin and strangely musical. The exchange continued for a few minutes before Cord addressed the woman called Kate.

"The girl's name is Mei. She's Vietnamese, ten years old, and has been here only a few weeks. Do you live near Anaheim Stadium? Over."

"A few blocks north. Over."

"Call stadium security. She was at an Angels game and she got separated from her parents in the closing crush. Her folks are probably frantic by now, though they won't show it until they have her back. Over."

"What about the police? Shouldn't I call them? Over."

"Only as a last resort. The sight of a uniform might panic Mei. Where she came from, uniforms were worn by enemies. Over."

"Okay. Thanks. What's your name and call number? Over."

"I'll monitor this band for a while. If you need me, just ask for Mei's friend. Over and out."

He set the radio aside, released the scanner, and went back to sifting through electronic reports.

Raine picked up her mystery again. For a long time she lay there, staring at pages she didn't see, wondering about the man called Cord Elliot. A man who could badly frighten her with a single look and the next instant speak gently to a lost child in her own language, an alien language thousands

298

of miles removed from the reality of the Summer Games. Fear and gentleness flowed from him so easily, so naturally. As did hunger and passion and an elemental male sensuality that was like nothing she had ever known.

After a long time, the mystery novel slipped from her fingers. She drifted in and out of sleep, listening to fragments caught by the restless scanner, voices crying in the cosmopolitan wilderness telling of drunk drivers and armed robbers, lost children and freeway accidents, drug deals and domestic disputes, murder and rape, loneliness and violence, and a chill seeping into her soul.

Woven through it all like a glittering black thread came the clipped, almost brutal humor of the men who spent their lives patrolling civilization's long nights. Men just beyond the castle, walking cold perimeters while fire danced behind the locked gates they guarded, warmth always alluring, always beyond reach.

Half-asleep, half-awake, suspended between dream and reality, she turned restlessly, seeking peace. But the voices were still there, scratchy static whispers describing life beyond the castle walls, life besieged by violence and unhappiness, life that knew the pain of lonely men and of children crying for lost mothers.

And one man calling to Raine in a dark shaman's voice, telling her to unlock the gate, to come to him and make a new world where fire would drive away the chill . . .

Holding to his voice, she let herself slide slowly into sleep.

From the corner of his eyes, Cord had watched Raine's restless twisting and turning, her fussing with pages, reading and rereading them, then simply staring at the print without seeing it. When the book finally slid from her fingers and her breathing changed, signaling sleep, he punched a code into his computer.

BLUE MOON CALLING BLUE HERRING

Within minutes, the special radio phone buzzed. He activated it quickly so that it wouldn't wake her and spoke quietly into the microphone. "Blue Moon."

"Blue Herring, buddy." The words floated up from a desktop speaker like smoke, softly filling the room. "You took your time getting back to me. Hot date?"

Cord's lips turned in a sardonic curve as he thought of Chandler-Smith's daughter sleeping on his bed only an arm's length away. "You wouldn't believe me if I told you. What's doing, *compadre?*"

Silently Raine awakened. Motionless, she tried to orient herself. Memories came — the fall, the motor home, the shower, the bed. Cord's bed. As understanding came, so did the soft, smoky-rough words that had pulled her from sleep.

"The usual," Bonner said. "Blue is using field boots on everyone in sight. He's worried about Baby."

"Tell Blue that Baby is literally within my reach when her one-ton guard dog isn't on the job," Cord said.

"Her what?"

Cord laughed softly. "Just tell him. He'll know."

"He's worried about whether she'll cooperate with you. Says she's damn near as stubborn as he is."

"She is," Cord said succinctly. "But she'll cooperate, one way or another."

"Well, at least you won't have to chase Baby through a lot of bedrooms. The book on her is that she likes horses a helluva lot better than men."

Raine winced and then went utterly still, listening with increasing anger. She knew who Blue was. She suspected that "Baby" referred to her.

"Can't say as I blame her," Cord said.

"Cynic."

"Realist. Did your worm say anything else about Barracuda and friends?"

"No. He couldn't even positively ID the picture Mitchell managed to take at LAX."

"You don't suppose your worm's turning again?" Cord asked.

"Doubt it. He barely got out alive. His ex-friends don't have any sense of humor. Barracuda personally executed the last three who tried to leave without permission."

Chill crept through Raine. Cord's back was to her. It was just as well. She didn't want to see what his eyes were like now — ice around the kind of darkness that sane men and women avoided.

"Sometimes they kill their own just for window dressing," Cord pointed out.

"Yeah, but this time they dressed the wrong window. The worm's girlfriend was five months pregnant when Barracuda scragged her."

Cord heard Raine's gasp. He spun quickly, watching her but saying nothing.

"Believe me, our worm can't wriggle enough for us." The smoky words continued softly, relentlessly, crowding the room. "He wants revenge so bad he sweats thinking about it."

"Anything else?" Cord asked.

"Nothing new, except . . ." Static, soft and scratchy.

"What is it?"

"Bad vibes, buddy. If I were running this show, I'd put a lock on Blue and Baby that an A-bomb couldn't blow. Moving targets are one thing. Sitting ducks are another. Watch your ass, okay? You're the only one I can beat at chess."

"I don't play chess."

"No kidding."

"Neither do you," added Cord, ending the prearranged code that established that each man wasn't acting under coercion of any kind.

"That's a state secret. Hasta la bye-bye, buddy."

"Hasta luego, compadre," Cord said, giving back correct, liquid Spanish for the mangled border Spanglish version of good-bye that Bonner had used.

Biting her lip, trying to control the emotions seething inside her, Raine watched Cord disconnect. She wished she could believe that she wasn't the "Baby" that the scratchy voice had referred to. She didn't want to be another target, another pawn, like the poor woman who was five months pregnant when she was murdered trying to get away from someone or something called Barracuda. Then there was the woman's husband or lover, another pawn, the worm who was turning and twisting under pressures too great for anyone to bear.

And there was Cord, wearing his gun again . . . Cord in the center of all that violence, watching it with eyes the color of ice, colder with every moment, and a darkness in the center that admitted no light.

Even at second hand, Raine couldn't survive the kind of life he lived. Yet the hunger and need in him called to her in a language older than castles or civilization. He was a winter night and she was a fire burning. He needed her in ways she couldn't explain. She needed him in the same ways.

Slowly, never looking away from her, he stood up. With quick, casual motions he unclipped the holster from his belt and put the gun on the chair he had just abandoned. The pager and ammunition clip followed, making an almost musical sound as metal met metal over the leather cushion.

She closed her eyes, unable to bear the intensity of his look any longer.

Hard, gentle hands closed around her face. Her eyes opened dark and almost wild. He was very close, his eyes intent as he tilted her head toward the bedside light.

"What — what are you doing?" she demanded.

"I'm looking at your eyes," he answered matter-of-factly, but his lips curved up in a smile that made his eyes look more like blue diamonds than ice.

Like the man, the smile took her breath away. "W-why?"

"I'm checking that both your pupils are evenly dilated." His voice was patient and very deep.

"Oh. Of course."

She bit her lip, caught between the aching pleasure of his touch and the knowledge that he was the wrong man for her, he led the wrong life, he would destroy her and never mean to. Yet his hands were very sure, very gentle, and his fingers curved to fit her face perfectly. His eyes were clear, intent, and so beautiful that her heart turned over.

"Are they?" she managed.

"Are they what?" he asked absently. His thumbs traced the sleek brown curve of her eyebrows. It was like stroking a silky kind of fire. It burned him in the sweetest, deepest way. He wondered how something so normal as eyebrows could be so sexy.

"Evenly dilated," she said. "Are they?"

"Flecks of gold and depths of green, dark

amber shadows . . . do you know what time it is?"

She could only shake her head mutely, caught between his hands and his unexpected question, off-balance again, falling toward him so quickly that she didn't even feel the pressure of her teeth scoring her lower lip.

"It's tomorrow," he said simply.

Then he bent over her until he filled her world. Gently, coaxingly, he kissed the corners of her mouth. When the tip of his tongue traced the teeth pressed into her lower lip, she couldn't control the tiny ice-tipped shiver that went through her.

She was afraid, but not of him. It was his world that frightened her, a world where violence came as surely as midnight. She couldn't be a part of that world.

"Cord," she whispered achingly, "it won't work. We're too differ—"

His tongue slid between her lips, her teeth. The tender invasion of her mouth made speech impossible. He savored her slowly, stealing her words. Stealing her. The velvet texture of his tongue stroked her, exploring her with a deliberate thoroughness that asked everything of her and concealed nothing of himself.

All of his hunger and gentleness and

strength were condensed into a single kiss.

"Give it a chance to work," he said, his voice as caressing as his tongue. "I need you, Raine. I'm cold without you."

His honesty overwhelmed what few defenses she had against him. A wave of longing swept over her, drowning and lifting her up in the same rushing instant.

She couldn't live in Cord's world.

She couldn't deny her world to him any longer.

And it didn't matter. Not really. It was only for a few days, a week, until the Summer Games ended and sanity returned. She could live in his world that long, and he in hers. For that long, he would not have to live in cold and darkness.

She tried to say his name, but the only sound she made came from deep in her throat, a cry of surrender and victory and passionate surprise. Hungry to feel the rough silk of his hair parting between her fingers, she lifted her hands to his head. She heard her name whispered against her lips. He took her mouth again before she could say anything at all, even his name.

The kiss was different this time, a possession that drank her response, filled her, seduced her with slow movements that spoke eloquently of male hunger and the moment when he would hold the center of her body as deeply and surely as he held her mouth.

A strange trembling took her. Deep inside herself, muscles tightened around a melting heat. She knew nothing beyond his taste, felt nothing but the flames spreading through her, burning her, burning him. She gave herself to the fire. To him.

He drank her shivering response as he had her kiss. He felt the heat spreading beneath her skin, the sweet fire he had hungered for since he had first sensed its presence. With a smooth, powerful movement he lowered himself to the bed and lay beside her, pulling her against the ache and need of his body.

Willingly she came to him, fitting herself perfectly against him as though for the thousandth time rather than the first. He held her, surrounding her, needing her with a force that shook him. He lifted his mouth from hers, measuring the depth of his need in the slicing pain of simply ending a kiss.

"Raine, listen to me," he said, his voice deep, a shaman casting spells before a shimmering midnight fire. He kissed her between each word, unable to deny himself the taste of her for more than a few seconds. "I can stop if I have to. Now, but not later. Not even a few minutes from now. Do you understand?"

He captured her lips again, let his tongue move deeply over hers. Then he felt the liquid movement of her hips against his as she silently answered his question.

She understood.

"Tell me in words." His voice was urgent. His hands kneaded down her back, pressing her close to the pulsing ache of his arousal. "I have to hear you say that you want me. Do you understand? I don't trust myself to guess, because if I guess wrong I don't know if I can stop."

Before she could answer, he took her soft mouth again with a controlled passion that made her moan.

"I won't hurt you," he promised, velvet voice and tongue touching her. "Don't be afraid of me."

Her slender fingers combed through his hair, pulling his head back until she could see his eyes. Shards of blue burning within a silver that was smoky, molten. Black, thick eyebrows drawn in waiting. Black lashes motionless, waiting. Muscles tight over the male planes of his face, waiting, and his whole powerful body like a coiled spring against her.

Waiting.

"I'm not afraid," she whispered, brushing the back of her fingers over his lips. "Not the way you mean." She hesitated, not wanting to talk about her past but knowing she had to match his honesty. "It's just that I'm not very good at . . . this."

Still he waited, watching her with eyes that burned.

She closed her eyes, unable to look at him. She didn't want him to see the need in her, and the raw fear of not being able to please him.

"I'm not very experienced," she whispered, her voice so soft he could barely hear the words. "I don't want to disappoint you. I couldn't bear that."

"I had already guessed that you weren't experienced," he said, smoothing hair away from her face with a gentle hand.

She wrenched her head aside as though he had struck her. Shame swept through her that her inadequacy as a woman should be so obvious to him after only a few kisses. When his hands tightened, turning her face back toward his, she struggled against him.

It was futile. He was far stronger, far more experienced in using his superior strength.

"Your hesitations told me you weren't experienced," he said. "Do you know how sweet it is, how hot, when you hesitate and then open to me? To feel your surprise . . . and then to feel you come to me, kissing me the way I kissed you, the way I've always wanted to be kissed by a woman."

The shaman's voice tugged at Raine, unraveling her. She couldn't conceal the quiver that went through her at Cord's words, at the memories blazing in his eyes and the hunger of his sharply defined lips poised so close to hers.

"The kind of 'experience' you're talking about doesn't interest me," he said softly, distinctly. "A thousand women could give it to me. I don't want it. I want you. I want your hesitations and surprise and fire. I want to hear the sexy cries you make when I touch you. I want to feel your body change when I make love to you."

He shifted with the same smooth power he had used to hold her motionless. She felt a premonition of warmth, his breath flowing over her. Then his teeth raked lightly over her breast, capturing the nipple, pulling it into the heat of his mouth.

Her thin blouse and bra offered no real barrier to his caress. She cried out in surprise and passion as her nipple tightened starkly beneath his probing tongue. An instant later she was caught and held with loving finesse between his teeth. Fire shot through her, tightening every muscle in her body. She wanted more of it. Of him.

He laughed softly and arched like a cat against the unconscious demand of her nails raking down his back, wanting him closer, all of him.

"Yes," he whispered, biting her with fierce restraint, savoring the husky sounds of passion he drew from her. "Cry for me. Want me."

When her nails scored down his spine again, he rolled her onto her back swiftly and settled between her legs, opening them, making room for himself at her fire. His teeth closed again over her breast as his hips moved deliberately, caressing her and telling her the full measure of his hunger.

For an instant she hesitated, shocked by the sensations sweeping up through her. Then she moaned and her hips moved helplessly, caressing him as he had caressed her, soothing her need and doubling it at the same time.

He arched above her, inciting her, letting her cries sink into him until he could bear no more and consumed her mouth in a powerful kiss. When he finally tore his mouth away from hers, his breathing was ragged.

"Experience comes in all kinds," he said,

biting and licking her lips between each word. "Did you feel like this before?"

"No," she said, then repeated the word again and again, shivering and burning with each shift of his weight between her legs.

"Neither have I," he said thickly. "Do you want me?"

He didn't want to release her but knew that if he held her, he wouldn't be able to let go if her answer was no. With a struggle that tightened his whole body, he forced himself to move, to lift his hungry weight from her hips so that she was free of him.

She made a sound of protest and reached for him even as he freed her. She buried her fingers in his thick hair and tried to pull his mouth back to hers.

"Tell me," he said. "Don't torture me, Raine."

"Is this torturing you?" She lifted herself until she could move her mouth slowly over his, tracing the line of his lips with the moist tip of her tongue.

"You know damn well it is," he said roughly.

"Now that you've told me, I know." She caught his lower lip between her teeth, holding him immobile as he had held her the first time he kissed her. While she slowly,

slowly released him, she whispered, "Yes, Cord. Yes and yes and yes."

CHAPTER 14

The shudder that went through Cord's powerful body surprised Raine. It told her how much he wanted her, and how afraid he had been that she would not want him enough. She heard the catch of his breath, the husky murmur of her name and his need.

His hands came up to her face, surrounding her with his warmth, his strength. He lowered his head and kissed her with a tenderness that made tears gather behind her eyelashes. As he kissed her, he cradled her against his body carefully, completely, savoring each new point of contact, each new warmth.

She put her arms around his waist and smoothed her palms over the long muscles of his back. He arched his body into her caress, responding with an honesty that made her breath catch, then shatter. Impatiently she pulled his shirt, yanking it free of his jeans. When she felt the sensual heat of his naked skin beneath her fingers, she made a throaty, purring sound of pleasure.

He laughed and rubbed against her hands, his muscles twisting and shifting beneath her touch. She tested him with her nails, caressed him with her palms, and all the while husky little sounds rippled out of her.

"Do you like petting me?" he murmured into her ear, then his tongue followed his words in a hot, caressing stroke.

She shivered in response. "Can't you tell?"

"Can't you tell me?"

"You feel wonderful, all hard and sleek and strong." Humor glinted in her hazel-brown eyes. "Like Dev's rump."

Chuckling, Cord nuzzled Raine's neck. "I've never been called a horse's butt so nicely."

Her laughter turned to a gasp as he seduced her ear with a few quick, deep strokes of his tongue. Then his teeth closed in a hot and loving bite that sent fire spearing through her center. Blindly her hands sought him. Her fingertips found and traced his spine as far as she could beneath the shirt that stretched tightly across his muscular back. She pushed against the cloth, then made a sound of frustration when all she did was imprison her own hands.

"Unbutton my shirt," he said. He bit her neck with exquisite restraint, leaving no marks but the spreading flush of passion beneath her skin.

She hesitated. She had wanted to run her hands over his bare chest since the instant her fingertips had slipped between the buttons of his dress shirt in Griffith Park. The silky feel of him had haunted her dreams. But the first — and last — time she had tried to unbutton a man's shirt, he had laughed at her inexperienced, fumbling fingers.

"I'm not very good at undressing men," she said unhappily.

Cord felt the change in her, hunger draining into uncertainty. Once he had wondered what had soured her on men so thoroughly that she allowed none into her life. Now he knew. Silently he cursed the bastard who had made Raine feel less than the sexy, sensual woman she was.

"Practice on me. Undress me." Cord lifted his head and smiled down at her. It was a warrior's kind of smile, challenging and barely civilized. "I promise I'll do the same for you. And more."

Before she could answer, his head dipped swiftly and he buried his tongue in her sweet, soft mouth. She tasted of everything he had ever wanted and never had.

Swiftly he rolled over onto his back, releasing her while he still could. "See?" he said huskily. "I'm making it easy for you to get to the buttons."

She slid off him and leaned awkwardly across his body. Her fingers worked over the first, stubborn button of his shirt.

"Surely an Olympic equestrian can think of a better way to keep her balance," he teased, his voice velvet and rough at the same time.

She gave him a startled look, then accepted the challenge. With a fluid movement, she settled onto him as though he was Dev waiting patiently by the mounting block. Perfectly balanced, she bent over the buttons again. It was much easier now.

"I do believe," she said, her smile as uncivilized as his, "that I finally have you at my mercy."

"You like that, don't you?" he said, watching her with eyes that were a smoldering band of silver around dark, dilated pupils.

"Considering that I've been off-balance since the first instant I met you, *yes*."

Smiling to herself, she unbuttoned until she could push aside his shirt entirely. Her eyelids lowered as she slowly stroked the crisp black hair on his chest with the back of her fingers. When she brushed over his dark male nipples, his breath caught. She paused, then returned, circling him with delicate, curious fingertips.

He watched her dreamy, absorbed expression with a concentration as intense as hers. His body tightened, his breath wedged, and he shuddered in pleasure as she teased his flat nipples into nailheads of sensation. She bent down, licked each nipple as delicately as a cat, then caught him between her teeth with the tender ferocity he had taught her.

Hunger ripped through him, a hot, bittersweet pain raking him with claws that were neither kind nor wholly cruel. His hands clenched at his sides. He knew that if he touched her in that searing instant, he would tear off her clothes and bury himself in her fire.

But she was worth every bit of patience he could find, worth each passionate agony and savage pleasure she innocently gave him while she explored him, becoming as hungry for him as he was for her. At least he hoped she was seducing herself, because she had him on an exquisite rack of desire that tightened with every caress. He had felt nothing like it before, known no one like her before.

With her, the world was clean and new.

And so was he.

When she lifted her head and looked down at him, he was smiling. His fingers searched through her clean, soft hair as he pulled her mouth down to his for a kiss that promised a hot, seamless mating of their bodies. Soon. She shivered uncontrollably when his hands cupped her breasts through the thin white shirt she wore.

Before the kiss ended, her blouse and bra were open and his hands were caressing her bare breasts. She tried not to cry out when he gently devoured her, pulling her deeply into his mouth, making fire burst deep inside her. But in the end she couldn't help herself, husky cries pouring from her lips with each movement of his tongue over her breasts.

The room swung dizzily as he shifted without warning, taking her down beneath him on the bed. From mouth to thighs, his body covered her in raging demand. It wasn't enough. He needed to be closer, utterly naked, buried inside her.

With a hoarse sound he rolled aside and stripped off his clothes. His eyes never left her while he kicked his jeans and underwear aside. Passion gave her a beauty that made him lightheaded. Her eyes were brilliant, her skin flushed, her nipples dark rose, still taut from his hungry mouth.

She was watching him with a heart-stopping combination of hunger and wariness and hope.

"I know I should wait," he said almost roughly, "but I have to see you. All of you. Will you let me?"

She shivered. "Of course."

He peeled off her blouse and bra and tossed them aside. His hands swept over her jeans, unsnapping them, pulling them off her. Her silky underwear soon slid down the length of her legs and followed her jeans onto the floor.

"Let me touch you," he said hoarsely.

"You have."

"Everywhere, Raine. *Everywhere.*"

She looked at him as he stood beside her, naked as the desire he had for her. Need twisted through her, shaking her. She had to touch him, to have him lie beside her and hold her, fit himself to her, fill her.

"Cord —" Her voice broke on a rush of passion. She shook her head, impatient at her inability even to speak.

All he saw was the negative movement of her head and the flat line of her mouth. He brought himself back under control with an effort that left him shaken.

"Don't be frightened, little queen," he said

finally, turning away. "It's all right. I know you don't want me. Not really. Not enough."

At first she was too shocked to speak. Then the words tumbled out. "You're wrong. I want you so much that I — I can't think, can't speak, can't do anything right. I don't know what to do. Please, don't turn away. *I need you.*"

Before the last words were out, he came down on the bed beside her, naked, close, not touching her.

"I need you the same way. Too much. I don't trust myself." He made a sound that wasn't quite laughter, wasn't quite pain. "That's a first. It scares the hell out of me."

"What I feel scares me, too. But it doesn't stop the wanting."

"I'm beginning to wonder if anything will."

Slowly, hungrily, his hands stroked up her body from her ankles to her temples, then back down again. He lingered over her breasts, teased the shadowed hollow of her navel, then slid down until his fingers tangled in her dark, springy hair. At the same moment, his mouth caught her breast again, tugging swiftly at its already hard peak.

The twin assaults made her cry out and hold his head fiercely against her breast.

She felt his fingers ease down to her thighs, her knees, then stroke slowly upward, pressing, asking, wanting. Instinctively she shifted, opening herself to his touch.

He whispered her name against her mouth as his fingertips touched the liquid heat of her. She was everything he had hoped for, hotter than his dreams. Words could lie or try to please, but not this. This slick fire came only from passion. His head swam as her heat licked over his fingers, promising everything he needed, promising things he hadn't even known he must have to live.

With a hoarse sound he caressed her deeply, only to withdraw with slow pressures that tormented her. He returned again, and then again, exploring her sleek center as thoroughly as his tongue explored her mouth.

She arched and twisted into the deep caress. She had never been touched like this before, never savored and lingered over while her lover's body shook with hunger that he held in check for her. Just for her. The contrast between Cord's stark passion and tender restraint turned her bones and her flesh to honey. Currents of sheer pleasure pulsed through her.

Her hips moved sensually, increasing the pressure of his fingers within her. When she arched up against his hand, his voice came to her in shades of darkness, shaman's words murmuring over her, asking that she give herself to him, telling her that she was everything he desired, more than any man had a right to hope for.

Tiny shudders rippled, quickened, passion growing with each shared movement, each redoubled caress. Moaning without knowing it, she melted in waves, flowing over him like hot honey.

Shock froze her as she felt her own heat spilling out. Fragmentary words tumbled from her lips, pleasure and confusion and apology all at once. He kissed away her words, cupped his hand around her heat, and pressed lovingly. He savored the hot lick of her pleasure and the knowledge that it was shockingly new to her.

"That's what I want," he murmured against her lips, stopping her stumbling apologies.

"But —"

"I came to you for your fire. Then you came to me. It's just beginning, Raine. Just beginning."

He moved slowly over her, caressing her with his hands until she shuddered and clung to him, melting, and he knew her pleasure again. Only then did he take her fully, burying himself in her hot, sleek body. Her eyes opened as she felt the extent of his possession.

He saw her surprise and smiled down at her through lips drawn back with a need that was too consuming to be called either pain or pleasure. His hips moved and her breath came out in a moan. He moved again, joined with her in an intimacy greater than he had ever known, for her heat was inside him as deeply as he was inside her. He felt her shudder, felt her molten response spreading between their bodies.

"Yes," he said roughly, triumph and passion thickening his voice. "Give me more. Take more."

She barely heard. What had begun as pleasure had become something more, something different. It consumed her, biting deep, wringing hoarse cries from her, cries she never even heard. Her body coiled tighter and then tighter still, pulsing, poised for a leap into the burning unknown. She would have been frightened if she hadn't trusted him all the way to her soul. But she couldn't even tell him that. She could only push and twist against him, asking and demanding in a hot, primitive language that had no words.

Clenched over her, breathing as though

he had just finished a long run, Cord held back as long as he could. He wanted to infuse himself with the searing, silky, pulses of her climax. He wanted to absorb her heat so that he would never be cold again.

Her hips lifted hard against him once, twice, and she shattered. He was so deep that he felt each of her shivers and pulses and cries as though they were his own.

And then they were. He was lost, burning with her. His eyelids trembled down and he began moving hard within her, deep, answering her need with his own body.

The shivering, shimmering tension that had just spent itself in her body speared through her again. Her body tightened, coiled, clenched until she would have screamed but for his mouth over hers. Her nails raked down to his thighs and she rode his powerful body with all her strength. He answered by driving into her until her world shook apart, exploding into an ecstasy so intense she couldn't breathe, only feel the elemental release throbbing through her.

It was no different for him, the shattering pleasure, the pulsing surrender as he gave himself to the fire he had called from her. Blinding heat consumed them until there was nothing left but ragged sounds of ecstasy.

Through it all Cord held Raine, sharing the tremors that swept through her as the world reformed around her, around him. He stroked her hair and kissed her cheek, cradling her. She sighed and nuzzled against him, smoothing her cheek against his furry chest.

"You're . . . beautiful," she murmured.

He laughed softly against hair. "You have strange ideas of beauty. I'm about as pretty as a rock slide."

"I'm not talking about pretty." Her eyes followed her hand down his body. "Beautiful. The way mountains are beautiful. The way Dev is beautiful when he takes an impossible jump — rippling with fierce pleasure and power and purpose."

"Like I said," he murmured huskily, "a strange idea of beauty. I have a more conventional idea of beauty. You."

"How did you get this scar?" she asked, looking away from his clear, intense eyes.

"Why do you tighten every time I say you're beautiful?"

"Because I'm not, and I know it."

"Crap."

She turned back to him, startled by the certainty beneath the lazy sensuality of his voice. "You've never seen my sisters. They're beautiful. Particularly Alicia. Men quite literally stop and stare when she walks by."

A shrug sent a ripple through Cord's muscular body. "That's one kind of beauty."

"It's the only kind."

"No. It's the least important kind. There's another kind of beauty, one that only special women have. A fire burning, hot and soft and incredible."

Wanting to believe, not wanting to be flattered, Raine turned her head aside. His hard palm came up and turned her face toward him while his shaman's voice flowed over her.

"It's the kind of beauty that sinks into a man's bones until he can't breathe without remembering how his woman's breath felt on his skin, can't lick his lips without tasting her, can't move without remembering the soft weight of her sliding over him, can't feel anything but her burning around him, can't hear anything but her cries of pleasure. That kind of beauty can make a blind man weep. It's the only kind of beauty that matters, Raine. It's your beauty."

She blinked back sudden tears. She had known him such a short time, yet he had slipped by all her defenses. He had made her laugh and he had made her cry. He had frightened her and he had protected her. He was dangerous and kind, hard and gentle, aloof and sensual, self-sufficient and needing her more than anyone ever had.

He was the wrong man for her.

And he had become as much a part of her as the passion he could draw from her with a look, a touch.

"Do you believe me?" he asked softly.

She nodded. She believed that she was beautiful to him.

He pushed damp tendrils of hair away from her face. "What's wrong, honey? Why the tears?"

She lowered her eyes and whispered, "I thought I knew myself."

"Don't you?" he asked, shifting until he could see her face.

"Not when you touch me."

"It's the same for me. A new world and a new man experiencing it." Despite her subtle resistance, he shifted her close enough to brush his lips over hers. "Don't pull back, sweet rider. Is it so terrible when I touch you?"

"No . . ." The word came out as a shiver and a sigh.

"Tell me," he murmured, shaman's voice coiling around her like an invisible warm river. "Whatever it is, I'll take care of it. Tell me."

"You're the wrong man for me," she said

helplessly.

The hurt was all the more intense for being so unexpected. Cord closed his eyes and wished he could close his heart as easily. But he couldn't. All he could do was be reminded of what he already knew — whatever feelings she had for him weren't enough to overcome the obstacle of his profession.

"No," Raine said quickly, hating to see the satisfaction and peace in Cord's face turn to distance and ice. "That's not true. There's nothing wrong with you. It's me. I'm the wrong woman for you."

He swore, a single vicious word. Then he moved abruptly, pinning her beneath him. His kiss was harsh, overwhelming, for he expected her to fight.

She locked her arms around him and returned the kiss as fiercely as he gave it. His hands clenched in her hair, then gentled even as his mouth softened. The kiss ended very slowly, tender as a wistful sigh.

Feeling as though she was being torn apart, she held on to him, simply held on with every bit of her rider's strength. She couldn't live in his world. But having met him, having found a man who called to her heart and body and soul, she didn't know if she could bear to live alone in her own world anymore.

Yet she must.

She owed it to too many people, including herself. Riding in the Summer Games was the culmination of a lifetime of dreams and sheer hard work. She didn't know how she could rise to the demands of the three-day event when her world was being shaken apart. Yet she couldn't give less than her best to the Olympics and face herself afterward.

Wrong man. Wrong time. *Wrong.*

And so agonizingly right.

The tension in her body locked against his owed nothing to sensuality. Cord knew it as surely as he knew his own body, his own reactions.

"Talk to me," he said with a calm he didn't feel. "Together, we can find —"

She put her fingers over his mouth, cutting off his words. "I can't," she said simply.

He kissed her fingers and pulled them down to his chest. "Can't what?"

"I can't handle everything at once."

"Does that mean you're walking away from me — from us?"

"I can't do that, either," she said tightly. "Can't win, can't break even, can't get out of the game. It's tearing me apart. And I can't let it."

He wanted to argue, to make her agree

right now that there was a future for them, to hear her admit once and for all that he had a place by her fire. Yet the cool tactician who lived within the warrior knew that he would lose her if he pushed. Worse, he would hurt her.

So he said nothing, simply watched her eyes, hazel and shadows and unexpected brightness of gold. Pain. Tension. The edginess of a trapped animal.

"After the three-day event, we'll talk about . . ." Raine's voice died.

She didn't know what good talking would do. He was what he was. She was what she was.

They never should have met each other.

"Maybe it will be clearer then. God, I hope so. It can't be any muddier." She laughed, but it sounded more like a sob. "Until then, just be with me when you can, and I'll be with you when I can."

Tactician and warrior struggled for control of Cord. He sensed her need of him, her fear of his world, and her searing pain. He had deliberately shaken her world to make a place for himself in it. Now she was suffering the aftershocks, unable to realize or admit the extent of the changes he had made.

"Promise you won't run from me." His

voice was deep and gritty with emotions barely held in check. His hand brushed her cheek with aching tenderness. "I never wanted to frighten you."

She closed her eyes against the tears welling up, another kind of fire scalding her. Helplessly she shook her head. She knew he was the wrong man and she was the wrong woman, and she wanted him anyway, wanted him until she was weak with a need that only grew more overwhelming with each word, each look, each touch.

"I can't run, either. What have you done to me?" she whispered. "Last month I didn't know you. Now I can't imagine living without you. Or with you."

"Don't cry." He kissed the tears that gathered and glittered on her lashes before sliding down her cheeks. "After the Summer Games you'll see that you don't have to worry about your world or mine. Things will look different then. I promise you. Look at me, love. Believe in me."

Raine opened her eyes and saw the certainty in Cord's. She didn't want to question it, to make him as bitterly unhappy as she was. Better to let go of the cruel future, to live only in the present. She had spent her life pursuing tomorrow in one form or another, one world-class competition after another.

Tomorrow, beautiful tomorrow. It had always been brighter than today, more vivid and more real, a vision forever dancing just beyond her reach. But it danced no longer, and it was dark instead of bright.

With lips that trembled, Raine smiled at her lover and hoped for the first time in her life that tomorrow wouldn't come.

CHAPTER 15

Raine and Cord ate breakfast in an easy silence punctuated by smiles and undemanding touches — his fingertip stroking the back of her hand as she poured him coffee, the delicate pressure of her hand on his cheek as she gave him a steaming mug of coffee, the brush of his lips over her palm. He understood the acceptance and intimacy implied by the small caresses.

He doubted that she did, or she would have bolted.

"What's your schedule?" he asked quietly, reluctant to end the warm silence.

"Dev, Dev, and more Dev."

"Never thought I'd be jealous of a horse."

Cord's off-center smile went into her like a knife turning. She didn't know how he had become so important to her. She only knew that he had.

And she couldn't afford to think about it until the Summer Games were over.

"Dev doesn't really need that much attention," she admitted. "It's more for me than for him."

"What do you mean?"

"Competition madness." She stood and began gathering up dirty plates. "Time hanging and clanking around your neck like six iron horseshoes."

"I'd think you would be too busy to fret."

"Wrong." Unbreakable dishes clattered into the stainless steel sink. "It's all done now but the waiting."

One eyebrow raised, he watched her quick movements around the galley. "I don't understand."

"Simple. If you work your horse too much, he'll go stale. If you work yourself too much, you'll lose your edge. So you wait until you're all edges and angles and time moves like it's nailed to the floor."

And a lot of people have affairs while they wait, she added silently. *Like me.*

Yet this didn't feel like an affair to her. It didn't feel like something brief and mildly distracting, a pleasant way to kill time until the main event started. Summer games until the Summer Games began.

Affairs just weren't her style. She wished they were. She wished she could learn to give a little and always hold a lot in reserve, to walk carefully instead of running head-long over life's obstacle courses. She wished she could approach life like a dressage rider, always serene, always utterly in control. But she never had.

Cord was right. It was no accident that she had chosen to rescue and tame a half-wild blood-bay stallion called Devlin's Waterloo. It was no accident that she had found the risk and adrenaline and challenge of the three-day event irresistible. She gave all to everything she did or she gave nothing at all.

There was no safe, easy, comfortable in-between for her. She had taken some hard falls in her life. She would take more. That was the nature of the world she had chosen. Ride tight or fall hard, victory or defeat, all or nothing at all.

"I feel like the invisible man," Cord said.

She blinked. Without realizing it, she had been staring at him while she tried to put the pieces of her world back into place. "Just planning what to do next."

"And?" His eyes were pale and intent, sensing that there was more than one level of meaning to her words.

"Usually, I'd run a few miles."

"But today isn't usual?" he asked softly.

"I'm a bit late," she said, glancing at her

watch. "And besides, I'm not exactly over-flowing with nervous energy at the moment. I woke up feeling lovely and . . . lazy."

He smiled slowly. "I know just what you mean."

She gave him a sideways look, remembering the reason for her delicious feeling of relaxation. They had reached for each other many times during the night. Each time it had been better. And now the look in Cord's eyes told her he was remembering it, too, the primitive fire when he entered her, filled her, and her voice was a husky demand enforced by her teeth.

He enjoyed the bright color staining her cheeks. He enjoyed even more remembering a few other ways to spread fire beneath her smooth skin. A kiss, a darting lick, a gentle closing of the teeth on taut, pouting flesh . . . yes, there were a lot of ways. The best way of all was to open her thighs and push into her slick, clenched heat until molten honey spilled.

And if he kept thinking about it, he wouldn't be able to stand up straight.

"Since you aren't going to run," he said in a husky voice, "what comes next?"

"Clean out Dev's stall. Feed him. Groom him. Walk him a bit. Take him to the ring. Work him. Groom him again. Polish tack.

Fret about the endurance course that I can't see for four days. I've a lot of that yet to do — fretting."

Frowning, Cord looked at his hands. They were tight with the effort not to turn into fists. He hated thinking about her on that course. He had seen the plans, knew the dimensions of each obstacle to the last millimeter. The thought of an exhausted Raine pounding over that course on the back of a big, equally exhausted stallion made ice condense in his soul.

"The course is worth fretting about," he said distinctly, spacing each word. "It is one brutal son of a bitch."

She looked at his eyes, cold blue and very intent. She knew suddenly that he was worried about her. No, that was too pale a word. He was *afraid* for her.

The idea that a man like Cord would be intimidated by the endurance course startled Raine. Seeing her chosen work through his eyes somehow made it seem more . . . dangerous. She opened her mouth to explain that it really wasn't that risky, not if she was careful and Dev was healthy. Then her mouth closed.

There was little she could tell Cord Elliot about skill, danger, risk, and safety.

"I'm a good rider," she said quietly, walking over to stand close to him, "and Dev is one of the ten best event horses in the world."

He said nothing, merely pressed his mouth against her abdomen as though to absorb her into his soul. He tried not to see her as she so recently had been, sprawled unconscious in the dirt while seventeen hands of savage stallion stood over her. His mind knew that the bee had been an unpredictable accident. A lightning strike of bad luck that wouldn't happen again.

Yet he couldn't forget that she had nearly died.

"I'm not doubting your skill or Dev's worth," Cord said finally, rubbing his lips against her as he spoke. "There's such a thing as luck, though."

His expression changed as he remembered the gold coin in his pocket. Lady Luck. Lady Death. Same coin, different faces . . . and such a terribly thin margin separating them.

"Let's go take care of Dev," he said abruptly, pushing back from the table. He swept the rest of the dishes into the sink and turned toward Raine, who hadn't moved. "Well?"

She tilted her head to the side, studying him. "Don't you have to work?"

"I will be working."

He turned to pull a denim jacket off a hook. Despite the warmth of the day, he would wear a jacket. He always did, because he always wore a gun.

As he turned to lift the denim, Raine caught the blue-steel gleam of the gun holstered in the small of his back. She hadn't noticed the gun, hadn't even seen him put it on. The jacket settled into place. Blue denim concealed gun and holster, beeper and ammunition clip.

"Do you need that just to watch me groom Dev?" she asked tightly.

Temper flared in Cord, surprising him with its speed and bite. He paused before he turned to face her. He hadn't had to struggle like this against himself for a long, long time. It was unnerving to know how quickly, how deeply, she could get past the control that was so necessary for his job.

"Anyone who can face that damned endurance course without flinching can face a few other things, too," he said curtly.

"Such as?"

"I was dragged out of crucial project and dumped into the middle of Olympic security for two reasons — to protect your father, and to protect you."

Her eyes widened. They looked dark

against her suddenly pale face. "Me?"

"You're a tempting target, Raine *Chandler-*Smith. Your father is very powerful. Your mother is the only heir to one of America's great fortunes. You're a favorite news item on the society and sports pages. Reporters swarm around you because of your family connections and the fact that you're a woman competing at the highest level in a sport formerly reserved for men only, and military men at that."

No words came to her. She made an oddly helpless gesture with one hand. She never thought of herself like that, an object of envy or greed or revenge. She was just a woman who had a certain skill with horses, a skill she had worked all her life to hone.

Outside the motor home, a man called and was answered by one of the stable girls. Another voice joined in, laughing. To Raine, they seemed far away, the other side of another world.

"If that's not enough," Cord continued, his voice as flat and cool as his eyes, "there's the fact that if certain people can't get through my men to kill your father, they can always grab you and come in the back door."

She listened and knew her world was being shaken again, forcing her to accept the very things she had ducked for years. She didn't like it. She didn't want to see reality this way, feel it like a cold lump in her stomach. Fear.

Cord wouldn't lie to her about something like this.

"Is that what the man on the radio told you?" she asked, her voice tight.

"Which man?"

"Hasta la bye-bye," she said sardonically.

Her tone told Cord that she resented the unknown man, resented the other, harsher reality that had been intruding on her world since she was old enough to recognize and name it. Most of all, right now she resented the messenger bringing bad news: Cord Elliot.

His smile was brief. When he spoke, his voice was as clipped as his smile had been. "Good old *hasta la bye-bye.* Yes, he told me. But I already knew. I just didn't know which killer was going to be looking through a sniper scope at the prize. Not knowing which enemy is at play makes it hard to do a good job of protecting people."

Suddenly chilled, Raine rubbed her hands over her arms. "You made sure I was cooperative, didn't you?"

"What do that mean?"

"The only bedroom you had to chase me

through was *yours,*" she retorted, remembering the words she had overheard.

"I caught you, too."

She looked away, unable to meet his piercing ice-blue eyes. Instead of apologizing to her for seducing her to make his own job easier, he was pushing her as hard as she was pushing him. It made her angry. She let anger take her, preferring a hot argument to the cold tactics of a colder war.

"Was that why you installed me in your motor home?" she asked furiously. "A simple exercise in tactical economy? Killing two birds with one bullet, as it were?"

Something flared in his eyes, something hot. Without warning, he reached for her and pulled her against him. His arms wrapped hard around her, as though he expected her to fight. Though her body was stiff, she didn't struggle.

"That's not why I made love to you," he said, his lips against hers. "Being your lover makes my job harder, not easier. When you're out of my sight I worry about you. And when you're in my sight I want you."

His mouth fastened over hers in a kiss that left no doubt about his hunger. Neither did the hard length of his erection pressing against her.

After a moment's hesitation, she put her

arms around his waist and kissed him hungrily in return, ignoring the deadly gun her fingers stumbled over in the small of his back. It was only for a few days, so few . . . she could live in his world that long.

As though sensing her decision, Cord lifted his head just enough to speak. "If I don't stop right now, the only riding that gets done today will be done right here."

He saw the centers of her eyes expand, felt her shiver, sensed the sudden, lush heaviness of her hips seeking him. She wanted him.

"You're tempting me," he said thickly.

"Good."

"After last night, I was afraid you'd be sore." He had reached for her during the night, and she had come to him each time with new eagerness, new skill. Just thinking about it made his pulse quicken.

She gave him a look from beneath dark, thick lashes. "So was I."

"Are you sore?"

"Nope." She laughed and ran her hand down his chest to his waist. She didn't have to go an inch farther to feel the thick arousal beneath his jeans. She slid her fingers between the steel snaps and tested him. "Mmmmm, lovely. It's a good thing I'm an endurance rider."

He was too busy trying to breathe to answer.

Cord opened the outside door of the motor home. Sunlight streamed in, bringing with it the smell of dust and horses, and sprinklers working valiantly against the normal southern California summer drought. Faint voices drifted into the silence, people too far away to be clearly heard. A car horn honked and somebody shouted a greeting.

Utterly normal.

He went down steps. Raine followed him, admiring the strength implicit in his wide, muscular shoulders and the coordination that showed in the easy movements of his body.

Thorne was in his customary spot near the motor home's door. With his straw cowboy hat pulled low and his legs stretched out in front of him, crossed at the ankles, he looked as lazy as a lizard sleeping in the sun. Yet his eyes were alert and wide open in the shadow of the hat brim. Despite the heat of the sun, he wore a lightweight jacket.

"Morning, Mr. Elliot."

"Morning, Thorne. I'll be with the U.S. Equestrian Team today."

"Yes suh." Thorne's glance switched to Raine. "Good morning, Miss Smith. Cap-

tain Jon said to tell you that you're sched-
uled for an hour later than usual."

"Er, thank you." She knew she was blush-
ing, but was helpless to stop it. Women her
age spent the night with men all the time
and no one blushed over it.

But it was new to her, and it showed.

"You going to bring that red devil out here
for another combing?" Thorne asked.

She smiled despite her embarrassment.
"Red devil, huh? No, I'll groom him in his
stall."

"Now, that's a shame," Thorne drawled,
letting the languid southern syllables roll off
his tongue. "I was looking forward to seeing
Mr. Elliot get bit by something meaner than
he is."

Laughing, she shook her head. "He's not
that mean."

"Me or Dev?" Cord asked, smiling.

"I'd recommend the Fifth Amendment for
that question, Miss Smith," Thorne said
smoothly.

"Sold." She smiled widely at Thorne, her
embarrassment forgotten.

Cord stepped to her left side, put his hand
at her elbow, and began walking toward the
stables. After a few steps he dropped behind
her, turned, and said casually, "Thorne?"

Raine turned around, too. She watched

both men, caught by something hidden just beneath the calm surface of Cord's voice.

"Yes suh?"

Cord's thumb gestured carelessly at the cloudless sky. "Have you noticed? It's a blue day today."

Thorne changed subtly, coming fully alert without shifting his position in the least. "I hear you, suh."

Just as she started to ask Cord if he meant Delta Blue, she noticed two people coming out of the shadows between the rows of stalls. The couple was close enough to have overheard everything that she, Cord, and Thorne had said. She waited until the people had passed beyond the range of her voice before she turned back to Cord. He was watching her with narrow, knowing eyes.

"You're Blue's daughter, all right," he said approvingly. "Nobody needs to tell you when to talk and when to shut up."

"Would that be Delta Blue you're referring to?" she asked sweetly. "As in the color of the sky today?"

He smiled, but it wasn't a comforting gesture. Once again he stepped around her, moving to her left side. They set off for the stables again. While they walked, she gave him curious sideways glances. From the first time she had encountered Cord in the hills outside Rancho Santa Fe, he preferred to walk at her left side.

Always.

"Is there something wrong with my right side?" she asked.

He looked blankly at her.

"You keep moving to my left side," she pointed out.

"I'm left-handed."

"So?"

"So my holster is positioned for a left-hand draw."

"Oh," she said numbly, wishing she hadn't asked. "My God. How can you stand it?"

"Being left-handed?" he asked, deliberately misunderstanding her question.

"Living like you do. Always having to remember to look around before you say anything, making sure that you can't be overheard. Always having to plan your movements so that your left hand is free to grab the gun you always wear."

"Do you have to remember each one of the hundred little things that help you to keep your seat on Dev?"

"If I did, I'd spend all of my time in the dirt. By now, keeping my seat is a reflex."

"Precisely." His voice was neutral despite the bleak blaze of anger in his eyes. "Not

349

thought. Reflex."

She knew him well enough to sense the anger coiled just beneath his control. She didn't want to pry at it; there was no reason to spoil what little time they had together. She had regretted her question the moment it was out of her mouth.

"I'm sorry. I have no right to judge your choices."

He gave her a sideways look. She had every right, but not now. Not when it was his job to protect her.

While they walked toward Dev's stable row, Raine was careful to keep the conversation away from anything related to Cord's work. She talked about tack and Dev's leg bandages, oat hay versus alfalfa hay, the benefits and drawbacks of certain kinds of horseshoes for jumping versus speed. He asked questions with a depth of understanding that surprised her. He was truly listening to what she said.

Yet despite his very real attention to her words, his eyes were never still. He was always measuring the people lounging against stable walls or carrying feed up the row, the people who walked horses or groomed them or simply stood with them in the dappled shade of trees. He looked at roof lines and deep shadows, and knew instantly if someone was coming up behind him.

And he did it all while exchanging greetings with other people and carrying on a conversation with her. No fuss. No dramatics. Just years of reflexes sharpened in the cold world beyond the castle walls.

A door banged open across the yard, startling Raine. Before she could do anything more than register the fact of an unexpected noise, Cord was between her and the sound.

Even as his left hand swept beneath his jacket and closed over the butt of his gun, he recognized that the source of the sound was harmless, a stall door banging in the wind. He stepped back into place at her side as though nothing had happened. And to him, nothing had.

She shivered, feeling the lethal cold of that other world blowing across her neck. For a horrible instant she hadn't known whether the sound was harmless or deadly, whether to freeze or run, scream or stay silent.

But Cord had known.

His fingers laced between her. "Don't worry, love," he said softly. "I'm as good at my job as you are at yours."

Her fingers tightened in his. She was very glad to know that he was close by. The thought of being a target had settled in her like winter. She suddenly had a gut understanding of why people built high castles and higher walls and barred all gates against the icy darkness beyond.

The cold was so great.

The fire was so fragile.

And it was so unfair to ask a man like Cord to live out there alone until he froze, never having known warmth.

The radiophone squealed chillingly, an electronic scream in the deep three A.M. silence. Even as Raine sat upright, heart pounding, Cord shot out of bed. In two strides he was on the phone. Soft static and harsh words filled the room.

"Bomb threat at the stables. Smoke spotted. They're moving horses now."

She leaped for her clothes before the last word faded into Cord's vicious curse. He turned, reaching for his jeans, and saw her dressing hurriedly.

"Stay here," he snapped. "Thorne will guard you."

She ignored him and grabbed the first shirt she could find. His. She threw it toward him and found her own.

He let the shirt sail right past him. His fingers locked around her wrist. "You're staying here."

She spun to face him. "No," she said curtly, buttoning her blouse one-handed. "With all the commotion, Dev will be an inch away from going ballistic. If anyone but me tries to lead him out of his stall, there will be bloody hell to pay."

Cord didn't like it, but he knew it was true. He dropped her wrist. Ignoring his shirt, he scooped up his holster, pulled out the gun, checked its load with a few practiced motions, and secured the gun in the holster. He clipped it to his belt at the small of his back. The whole process took no more than five seconds.

He was reaching for his boots in the darkness when a stallion's savage scream ripped through the night.

"Dev," Raine cried, leaping for the door.

As fast as she moved, Cord was faster. He grabbed her and held her struggling against his hip while he searched the television screens that showed the area around the trailer. Some of the cameras on the trailer were immune to darkness. They showed nothing but shadow and the heat signature of distant streetlights. No radiation from a warm body as big as a man.

Fingers locked around Raine's upper arm, Cord headed for the outside door. Standing to the side, forcing her to do so as well, he opened the door. With a single sweeping glance, he checked the moonlight, shadows, and occasional pools of yellow lamplight for anything that shouldn't be there. All he saw was Thorne running toward him. No one else moved or crouched in ambush.

"Let's go," Cord said curtly.

He leaped to the ground and landed running. She was a half step behind him.

Dev screamed again, shrill and wild, a sound of feral rage.

Driven by adrenaline and fear, Raine ran flat out, her bare feet pale blurs against the darker ground. She had to get to Dev before he went crazy with a horse's instinctive fear of fire. If he couldn't be kept calm, he might injure himself.

Or kill someone. It was there in his scream, fear and fury united in a mindless savagery.

Praying silently, she ran as fast as she could. She wasn't even aware of Cord running beside her, his eyes as feral as the stallion's cry. She ran without feeling the hard ground or the stones that bruised her feet. She ran without hearing herself call Dev's name with each breath in a litany of hope and fear.

Smoke darkened lamplight into Halloween orange. Other horses were neighing now, frightened by the scent of smoke. Instincts at red alert, they kicked against their stalls and whinnied constantly, wanting to flee their oldest enemy — fire.

Raine sprinted heedlessly through the night, dodging the men and horses that were streaming out of the stable rows. All around her, men cursed and horses shied violently, their eyes rolling white, sensitive as horses always are to equine and human emotion. Especially fear.

Dev's scream was a black wildfire raging through the stables, igniting panic despite everyone's efforts to stay calm. It was important to move swiftly but without fright, to speak softly to the nervous animals as they were led out of familiar stalls into the unfamiliar, threatening darkness.

Thick, oily smoke billowed blackly toward the moon. As Cord and Raine hurtled around the corner leading to Dev's stable row, the stallion's chilling scream sounded again. Captain Jon's slight figure darted through smoke to open Dev's stall door.

The stallion reared and plunged violently, lashing out with deadly front feet. His mouth was wide open, screaming rage, and his ears lay flat on his skull. Captain Jon managed to hold onto the lead rope for one lunge, two; then the rope whipped through his gloved hands and Dev exploded out of the smoky stall like a devil coming out of hell.

Blind with rage and fear, wholly out of control, the stallion thundered straight for Raine and Cord.

CHAPTER 16

Raine's first thought was to grab a double handful of mane and swing up on the stallion's back as he raced by. She discarded the idea as fast as it came. Dev was already in full stride. He would yank her arms right out of their sockets if she tried to mount him from a standing start.

Her only hope was the wildly whipping lead rope. If she could grab it and hang on long enough to slow Dev, she could mount and prevent him from injuring himself or someone else in his panicked flight. Smoothly she pivoted, preparing to run alongside Dev as she held onto the lead rope.

Cord saw it all as though in slow motion. Smoke. Captain Jon. Lead rope. Blood-bay stallion rearing. Dev raging free into the night with the white rope snapping alongside, ready to tangle in the stallion's pounding feet and bring him down in a pile of mangled legs and agony. Raine nearby, reaching out, ready to grab the deadly rope when Dev hurtled by. Thorne running up behind them.

Cord's hands flashed out. Before Raine knew what had happened, she was thrown into Thorne's arms.

"Get her out of here," Cord said flatly.

In a heartbeat she turned into a raging, clawing fury that Thorne simply, efficiently overwhelmed. When she knew she couldn't get away, she stopped struggling and watched her stallion, closer with every long stride he took.

"Dev!" she cried futilely.

"Easy, ma'am. Mr. Elliot will take care of that damned red devil."

And if he didn't, Thorne would. He yanked his gun out of his holster and waited.

Cord didn't even glance away from the stallion charging toward him. He had no doubt about the outcome of any physical contest between Thorne and a woman who knew nothing about unarmed combat.

He also had no doubt that Thorne had drawn his gun. If Cord was lucky and strong enough, the gun wouldn't have to be fired. If he wasn't . . .

It was Cord's predatory stillness that warned Raine of what he was going to do. A terrible new fear exploded in her, crowding out the old. "Cord, no! *Dev will kill you!*"

He never looked away from the shadow barreling toward him. Adrenaline flooded him, wiping out everything but the stallion racing out of the darkness straight at him. As always in combat, time slowed for Cord until each heartbeat seemed to take a minute. Ice-pale eyes measured distance and velocity.

Dev was in full flight, steel-shod hooves pounding out a drumroll of fear, muscles bunching and sliding, ears flattened.

Thirty feet away. Twenty.

Ten.

Muscles flexed, body poised, Cord waited.

Five.

Now.

His fingers sank into the long mane. He sprang off the ground like a cougar just before the stallion's momentum would have ripped his hands from the flying mane. A rider's powerful legs clamped around Dev's barrel. Cord crouched low over the stallion's neck, fishing for the lead rope that whipped dangerously around the horse's feet.

The stallion ran like unleashed hell, too caught up in fear and sudden freedom to register the presence of an unfamiliar weight on his back. Cord grabbed the lead rope and settled deeply into the stallion's stride, letting reflexes ingrained by years on horseback take over.

Automatically he coiled the long rope to keep it away from Dev's legs. Then Cord tightened his legs around the horse's muscular barrel and began pulling on the rope. The special halter closed over Dev's flaring nostrils, cutting down the flow of air.

Unable to get enough oxygen to meet the demands of a headlong gallop, the stallion was forced to slow down. He fought it. His neck arched in a rigid bow. His hindquarters stiffened with resentment. His gallop became choppy, brutally hard on his rider.

Cord kept pulling on the lead rope. As he did, he wondered what would happen when Dev calmed down enough to figure out that it wasn't Raine on his back.

He found out a few seconds later. The stallion screamed once, raw fear and fury, and then he came apart. His black nose plunged down between his front legs. He bucked and twisted and swapped ends, trying with all his huge strength to shake off the hated weight of a man.

Cord's legs locked down like thick steel bands. He hauled back on the lead rope, trying to bring Dev's head up so that the stallion couldn't put his full strength into bucking. Dev didn't seem to notice. He just kept trying to turn inside out.

Raine and Thorne came running around the stable row and stopped as though they had slammed into a wall. Both of them realized the same thing at the same time: there was nothing they could do but stay out of the way.

Shirtless, barefoot, Cord rode the screaming blood-bay whirlwind. The man's muscles bunched and shifted and gleamed in the bright moonlight. So did the stallion's. They were two powerful, supremely conditioned males fighting for dominance.

For the space of several breaths Raine stood motionless, barely breathing, riveted by the primitive battle in front of her. Finally she took a deep gulping breath and prayed that somehow, some way, neither man nor horse would be hurt.

Inch by straining inch Cord dragged up the stallion's head. His arms knotted with the effort of the fight, but his body remained supple. A nearly still center in the raging equine storm, he balanced against of the stallion's wrenching, twisting bucks with deceptive ease. And slowly, relentlessly, he forced Dev's head up. The stallion's neck became an arch of arrogant rebellion that made each muscle and vein stand out. The horse lashed out futilely with his heels, shredding shadows and moonlight, screaming in frustration.

Elbows tight against his sides, Cord held the lead rope in both hands and pulled until Dev's nose was nearly at his boot. All the stallion could do to vent his fury was to spin in tight little circles.

Then Cord began to talk to Dev, his shaman's voice filling the darkness, a murmurous warm river of sound curling around the horse, washing away fear. Gradually Dev's circles became fewer and less frantic, his body less bunched with fear, his ears less flat against his skull.

Finally the stallion stopped, stood, and snorted. His blood-red hide rippled uneasily. He made a last stiff-legged circle before he paused and sniffed his rider's leg. Nostrils flared as widely as the special halter allowed, Dev drank Cord's scent.

He murmured and stroked the stallion's neck with a gentle hand. "That's it. Go ahead and smell me. You know me, Dev. I've been grooming you for five days, and for five nights your mistress has slept in my arms. I smell like Raine and like me and a little like you after that wild ride you put me through. See? I smell just like the three of us. Nothing to be afraid of, you blood-bay idiot. Just me."

The voice continued, dark velvet reassurance, words and nonsense, praising and petting. Slowly, slowly, Cord eased the pressure on the lead rope, giving Dev back his freedom an inch at a time.

The stallion pranced and snorted, his ears swiveling every which way in their own nervous release. The man's arms gave a few more inches, allowing Dev to release the tension of a neck bowed too tightly. The horse stretched gratefully.

After a few moments a black muzzle came back to sniff Cord's foot tentatively. Nostrils flared widely, fluttered, and blew out a warm stream of air, only to flare again, drinking the mixed scent of Cord and Raine and dust from the stable yard.

The shaman's voice continued to cast its spell, winding around Dev like a gossamer net, holding him in thrall. The stallion snorted hugely and moved jerkily. He was uneasy with his strange burden, but no longer wild with fear and rage. There was a man on his back, yet no whips or spurs or savage bits cut into tender flesh. There was only a hand stroking his neck and a shaman's voice flowing caressingly around him.

When Cord gathered the lead rope and turned Dev toward Raine, the stallion's ears came up. As though walking on eggs, he minced diagonally toward her, dancing through moonlight to the rippling music of a shaman's voice.

She walked forward a few steps, then stood motionless, entranced by the sight of a shaman riding bareback on a dancing stallion. Moments later Dev's black velvet muzzle searched lightly over her face, drinking her scent. Automatically her hand came up in a familiar caress, rubbing Dev's ears.

But her eyes were only for the man who rode her dangerous stallion. She touched Cord's leg as though she couldn't quite believe he was real.

Only then did she admit to herself how terrified she had been that her lover would be killed by Dev's unruly rage. With a shuddering sigh she put her cheek against Cord's thigh. Dev lipped at Raine's hair and minced sideways, trying to see her.

Cord's hand tightened on the rope, stilling the horse's restive movements.

"Come up here with me," he said. His voice was still low and reassuring, still velvet magic. He held out his left hand and locked his left foot into a rigid platform for her to use to mount. "When you're barefoot around this blood-bay lummox, the best place for your toes to be is out of reach."

Raine took Cord's hand and used his foot like a stirrup. He swung her easily into place behind him. Dev pranced a little at the strange weight, but settled down quickly when he smelled Raine's familiar scent and heard her voice floating down from his back. He snorted, flicked his ears, and danced in place, waiting for a command from his riders.

With a rush of emotion that was too complex to sort out, Raine put her arms around Cord's waist and pressed her lips against his naked back. Even sitting behind him, holding him, she couldn't believe that Cord had ridden Dev, was riding him now. And both man and horse were alive, unhurt, radiating the heat of their brief battle into her.

Startled by the sound of the walkie-talkie that Thorne carried, Dev shied suddenly. Both she and Cord kept their seat as though they were a part of the stallion. A brief mutter of voices came from the walkie-talkie.

Thorne listened, then called out to Cord in a calm, low voice. "It was a smoke bomb. Some bastard's idea of a giggle. He's probably out there somewhere, busting a gut laughing."

The steel buried in Thorne's voice told anyone who was listening that he would enjoy getting his hands on the man who had set off the smoke bomb, then called in a bomb threat just to watch the fun that followed.

"We'll keep Dev out here until all the stables are checked and everyone is out of the yard," Cord said. "I don't want anything to spook him again."

"Did you see Captain Jon?" Raine asked. "Is he all right?"

"My hands are sore," Captain Jon said, walking up behind Thorne, "but otherwise I'm intact."

"You should have waited for me," she said bluntly. "Dev could have killed you."

"I didn't know if Cord would let you come to the stable." Captain Jon's voice was matter-of-fact. "It would be a fine snare, you running in all upset and all of us dashing around turning loose horses. Then the smoke started. I assumed that fire wasn't far behind. I decided it was better to try to lead Dev out than to leave him in his stall to roast like a Christmas goose."

Raine didn't say a word. She was still absorbing the fact that Captain Jon knew she was a target and Cord was her keeper. She started to ask how long the captain had known. Before she could frame the question, he was talking again, walking toward them slowly.

"Bloody amazing," Captain Jon said, looking at Cord sitting easily on Dev's back. "Bloody, *bloody* amazing."

Dev shied and turned effortlessly, making sure that he always faced the captain. The stallion's riders stuck with him like his own red hide.

"I used to ride a lot," Cord offered dryly.

Captain Jon said something beneath his breath.

"Bloody rodeo king" was all that Raine caught. She laughed softly, remembering what Cord had told her about his childhood.

"I shipped out before I won the silver buckle for bareback bronc riding," he admitted, smiling slightly. "The old reflexes are still there, but I'm going to be stiff and whining like a pup tomorrow."

Captain Jon laughed shortly, shook his head, and strode back to the stables. He would be lucky to sleep again tonight. There were too many things to check before the equestrian team went into the dressage ring tomorrow.

Wind breathed softly over the stables. The last of the smoke thinned and lifted into the starry sky. With a long sigh, Raine stirred enough to loosen her arms from their tight grip around Cord's body. But she didn't let go of him. She couldn't. She kept thinking about what would have happened if he hadn't been strong enough, skilled enough, and patient enough to ride out her horse's panic.

"We should walk Dev to make sure he doesn't stiffen up," she said. "He has to be supple for the dressage test tomorrow."

Her voice broke as the realization hit her. The culmination of a lifetime effort was thundering toward her like a runaway horse.

Within twelve hours, she would be riding in the Olympics.

Unconsciously her arms tightened around Cord. Tension swept over her like another kind of night. She didn't know if she was ready, if she was good enough, if —

Dev shied at nothing, distracting her.

"Think about something besides tomorrow," Cord murmured to Raine. "Dev reads you real well."

Her curt laugh said a lot about the tension coiling inside her. She pressed her cheek against Cord's naked back and tried to think about something else besides the Olympics. Anything else. The moment that Cord would slide into bed, into her arms, into her, seemed like a good start.

Cord's head turned toward Thorne, who

had stepped back until he was little more than a tall shadow beneath the eaves of a nearby stable. "We're going to walk Dev around the yard."

"Yes suh."

That was all either man said, but Raine knew that Thorne would follow them, a shadow watching shadows for movement that shouldn't be there.

Cord turned Dev toward a deserted part of the stable yard. The path he chose avoided the men and horses who were returning to the area they had so recently abandoned. There was no point in testing Dev's good nature by mixing with horses that were still neighing and kicking and shying nervously.

"Do you think that the smoke bomb was more than a sick prank?" she asked after a few minutes.

"It could have been, but I doubt it."

"Why?"

"Too dicey with so many people running around. If someone just wanted to kill you, the smoke bomb might have worked. But what they really want is to use you to get to your father. For that, you have to be alive."

She flinched at the blunt assessment but didn't argue the point. "What about the rest of my family?"

"They're well guarded against kidnapping."

What he didn't say, what he had no intention of saying, was that there was no foolproof way to guard against assassination. Anybody could be killed, as long as the assassin didn't mind dying, too.

So far, Barracuda had been more interested in surviving to strut on the international stage than in dying a martyr to a blood-drenched cause. Barracuda had had a long, violent run as a terrorist.

But it would be over. Soon.

In the quiet hours while Raine had slept in his arms, Cord had planned how he would fish Barracuda out of troubled international waters. It would be his parting gift to Justin Chandler-Smith. Blue was one of the few men on earth Cord truly respected.

It would also be Cord's gift from the cold violence of the past to a newer, warmer future. He didn't want to spend the rest of his life looking over his shoulder, watching for a nameless man who was narrow between the eyes.

Watching for the assassin who would kill Cord's wife, his children, his soul.

"Don't worry about your family," he said quietly, bringing one of Raine's hands up from his waist to his lips. "I'll take care of it."

"How?" she whispered.

He didn't answer.

She didn't ask again.

Together they rode Dev until he was cool and calm, ears pricked alertly, nostrils sniffing the night air. All the other horses were back in their stalls. Except for a few curious people — the ones who couldn't believe that a man had ridden Devlin's Waterloo bareback and lived to tell about it — Cord hadn't seen anyone in half an hour. He knew Kentucky was still out there, watching, but he was invisible. Cord smiled in cool satisfaction. Kentucky was a good man. One of the best.

With a growing feeling of contentment, Cord absorbed the feel of a fine horse between his knees and Raine's soft, trusting weight lying warmly against his back.

"Back to the stall," she said finally, reluctantly stirring against him.

"Afraid that carrying my weight will wear him out?"

She snickered. "He could carry two of you for five miles at a hard run."

"I like this better. Slow and lazy." But he could feel the tension returning to her. "Back to the stables it is."

The soft sound of hoofbeats going down the deserted stable aisle brought a few curious whickers from other horses. Otherwise it was quiet. The smell of hay and dust and horses was slowly overcoming the bitter aftermath of the smoke bomb.

Together Cord and Raine groomed the big stallion. Dev ignored both of them, except for a nudge with his muzzle from time to time if he felt someone wasn't working hard enough.

"You're so spoiled it's a wonder you don't rot where you stand," Cord said, stroking the black muzzle.

Dev blew softly against the man's chest, utterly content. Peace slid through the stable like a special kind of moonlight. Cord petted the stallion for a little while longer, but he was watching Raine. He could see the tension in her.

It was still there as they walked back to the motor home. Her movements were quick, restless. Her eyes were wide and clear. She wasn't ready to go back to sleep.

He pulled out an odd-looking key and opened the motor home door. "Worried about Dev?"

"No."

He drew her into the motor home and locked the door behind her. "Competition

372

nerves?"

"Yes," she admitted, following him to the bedroom. "Being awakened like we were didn't help."

"Puts the adrenaline count right over the moon," he agreed.

He braced his hands against the wall and stretched his back and legs thoroughly, easing muscles that were complaining of recent abuse. A lot of his body wanted to knot up and stay knotted. Dev was a hell of a powerful horse.

Raine watched Cord, remembering the violent ride and its unexpectedly gentle ending. "I can't groom Dev, which is what I usually do when I get edgy like this. So," she said slowly, "I'm going to groom you."

His black eyebrows arched in amusement. He pushed away from the wall.

"I'll bet the brush will tickle like hell," he said, unclipping his holster and spare magazine and putting it aside. "As for the currycomb," he added, slipping out of his jeans and standing naked, hands on lean hips, "forget it. My hide just isn't that tough."

"Wrong color, too." Her words were soft. She was enjoying his honey colored, smooth skin, and the shadow patterns of body hair gleaming in the subdued light.

"I'm getting a better idea," he said, watching her approving glance move over his body. Blood beat thickly, quickly, arousal surging.

"I can see that," she retorted. "Facedown on the bed, Mr. Elliot. It's your turn for a rubdown."

"I wondered why you brought that liniment from the stable."

"It's the least I can do in return for saving my knot-headed horse."

Cord could think of a few other things she might do — quite a few — but she had a determined look on her face and liniment on her hands. Besides, a rubdown beat the hell out of being worked over by a currycomb.

The pungent odor of liniment filled the room. Oily, sharp, clean, oddly soothing, the smell brought back a rush of memories from Cord's childhood. He lay across the bed on his stomach and remembered horses and men and campfires, the scents and laughter of another world. Silently he asked himself why he had ever left that world.

There was no answer.

Raine's strong hands kneaded his back and arms and hips, loosening tense muscles. He made a long, low sound of pleasure and contentment.

"I love your hands, sweet rider. Strong and

competent and . . . womanly."

"Comes of working with my knot-headed stallion."

His back moved in silent laughter. "Comes of grooming the red devil, too."

Smiling, she leaned into her work, using all of her strength to loosen the long, powerful muscles of Cord's body.

"Wait until you see me work over Dev after the endurance run," she said. "I'll spend most of the night kneading him like a great pile of dough. Otherwise he would be too stiff to canter the next day, much less to jump anything."

Cord's only answer was a purring groan of pleasure as liniment and knowing hands turned his muscles into putty.

Smiling, she leaned harder into her work, probing and kneading until his muscles became supple beneath her hands. Then she slid down and concentrated on his legs and hips. She knew just which muscles he had used during the wild minutes when Dev acted like a rodeo stud.

For a long time the only sounds were the slide of her hands over Cord's legs, his occasional rumble of contentment, and the erratic mutter of the scanner. She didn't notice the scanner. She no longer even heard the mutter of electronics or saw the flicker of television screens. They had become like chairs or desk or bed, just a part of the room.

At last she sighed and sat up, flexing her hands. Cord didn't move. His head was turned away from her and he was breathing evenly, deeply, utterly relaxed. Asleep. Smiling, she very gently brushed a kiss between his shoulder blades. She wanted more — she ached for it — but she wasn't going to wake him up. She knew that he had slept even less than she had in the last few days.

Careful not to disturb him, she slid off the bed. Maybe one of the mysteries she had kicked under the table could hold her interest this time.

Before she could take a step, a muscular arm snaked around her knees.

"Still restless?" he asked, turning his head so that he could see her.

"A little," she admitted.

His hand slid up between her legs. When he discovered the wet, ready heat of her, he forgot to breathe. "What do you do after you've groomed Dev and groomed him again and you're still on edge?" he asked huskily.

"I usually get on bareback and take a slow, lazy ride."

He rolled over and pulled her down astride

376

him, sliding into her hard and deep. "I thought you'd never ask."

CHAPTER 17

The sound of his beeper going off brought Cord instantly awake. He grabbed it from the bedside table, read the numbers in the lighted window, and got quietly out of bed.

Raine made a sleepy sound and started to sit up.

Despite the adrenaline licking in Cord's veins, his hands were gentle as he urged her back down. "Sleep, honey. You don't have to get up for almost two hours."

She hesitated, sighed, and settled back into the warm nest she and Cord had made. He brushed a kiss over her lips, touched her cheek with his palm, and smiled when she snuggled against his hand like a kitten. With a gentle caress, he tucked the covers under her chin.

There was nothing gentle about him when he went to the special phone, punched in numbers, and said, "Blue Moon here. Where's Blue Herring?"

A few moments of hissing static, then the answer came. "Hello, buddy. How's fishing?"

Bonner's voice was calm, but Cord knew him well enough to hear the anticipation surging beneath.

"The way I like it," Cord said. "Lazy and calm."

"Well, they're rising just outside your quiet little bay."

Even though Cord had expected it, his mouth flattened. "Anything worth getting up early over?"

"How about a Barracuda?"

"Just one? They usually hunt in groups."

"Not this time."

For a moment Cord was quiet. Either something had gone wrong with the inner cell of terrorists or Barracuda figured he had a better chance of success this time if he went in alone. If so, Barracuda was right. It was always harder to spot one man than a crowd.

"When?" Cord asked, knowing Bonner would understand.

"Not today."

"Positive?"

"As close as I ever am. Timing is wrong. The fish would have to swim like hell just to get to your bay."

"Tomorrow?" Cord pressed.

"The guessing here is divided."

"What's your guess?"

"After the whole event is run, when everyone is relaxed and passing out medals."

"Next best guess?"

"During one of the Baby contests, when everyone is in one place, watching all the contestants do their tricks."

Cord's smile was thin, cold. If Barracuda thought Chandler-Smith was going to be quietly watching from a ringside seat — or from any single location — the terrorist was in for a real disappointment.

"Sure hope Blue has kept in shape," Cord said. "The last thing he'll be doing is sitting in my boat watching the waves go by."

Raine awoke to the alarm and the smell of liniment. She rolled over beneath the covers, expecting to find and curl up against Cord's solid presence for a few quiet moments.

He wasn't there.

She sat up suddenly, heart pounding, eyes searching the room. Television screens and electronics flickered restlessly, but no man sat in the chair, monitoring them. She listened, but didn't hear the sound of the shower in the small bathroom nearby.

"Cord?"

There was no answer.

Vaguely she remembered hearing his beeper go off earlier, remembered him kissing her and urging her to go back to sleep. Amazingly, she had.

At the moment, sleep was the last thing on her mind. In less than six hours she would ride in the Olympics. There was a lot to do between now and then.

Keeping one eye on the clock, she shot out of bed, dressed, and ate in a rush of coordinated movements. She only had a few hours to polish tack, groom Dev, and groom herself to the elegant standards required by Olympic dressage.

Mentally she composed a list of what had to be done before she was ready to ride Dev in front of the three expressionless judges who would decide whether she was a credit or a burden to the U.S. Equestrian Team. Everything, right down to the quality of the crease in her black jodhpurs, would be judged.

For someone like Raine, who preferred the adrenaline and physical demands of the endurance run, the dressage ring was an exquisitely balanced, beautifully subtle, absolutely necessary, nitpicking torture.

She was still juggling chores in her mind

when she let herself out of the motor home. Thorne was in his usual position, a man who apparently had nothing better to do than sit and watch the world go by.

"Morning, Miss Smith."

"Good morning, Thorne. Is Cord around?"

Thorne glanced around the immediate area. "I don't see him, ma'am."

She smiled slightly. It had become a game with them. If Cord wasn't around, she would ask about him. Thorne would reply politely and very vaguely, saying nothing at all about the movements of his boss.

"If you see Cord, say hello for me," she said.

"I'll do that, ma'am." Thorne smiled. "Count on it."

Morning ritual completed, she started toward the stables.

Thorne stood up with a lithe speed that belied his outward laziness. He spoke briefly into his walkie-talkie and then caught up with her.

Surprised, she looked aside at him. This wasn't part of their usual morning game.

Thorne said nothing. He simply walked beside her as if he did it every day. Unlike Cord, Thorne walked on her right side. She understood the implication — the gun he

382

wore was positioned for a right-hand draw — but she didn't dwell on it. There were too many other things that demanded her attention right now.

"Going to watch me comb the red devil?" she asked dryly.

"Yes, ma'am, I'm going to do just that."

"I didn't know you liked horses."

"I'm easing up to it," Thorne said in a resigned voice.

He stayed with her the rest of the golden, sun-struck morning. He was never out of sight and rarely out of reach, following her everywhere but into the restroom. And even there he made her wait until the place was empty. Before she went in, he did, making certain that all the stalls were indeed unoccupied.

Other than that, he was remarkably discreet. Like Cord, Thorne made radio checks at random intervals and petted the cats that haunted the stable yards. He faded into shadows when other members of the equestrian team came to talk to her. If he didn't recognize the people walking toward her, he put himself in front of her and quietly, firmly, told them that whatever it was would have to wait until after she had performed in the dressage ring.

To Raine, the presence of a quiet, muscular shadow had become normal. If it weren't for the fact that she kept looking up at odd moments, hoping to see Cord, she wouldn't have noticed Thorne at all.

No matter how hard she looked, she didn't see Cord. Finally she knew that she couldn't delay the finishing touches on Dev's preparation any longer. The appearance of her horse would be as minutely scrutinized as her own. The three-day event had begun as a military contest; spit and polish were as important as speed and courage.

Cord had promised to help her put a high gloss on the stallion, but obviously the electronic leash had led him elsewhere.

Damn.

At that moment she realized how much she enjoyed the long, peaceful hours she and Cord had spent grooming the big stallion or polishing tack until it gleamed like mirror.

"Don't be an idiot," she muttered as she began Dev's final intricate grooming. "I know how to do this better than anyone else."

She had done it all herself before, when Dev simply wouldn't tolerate another handler in the tense hours before a competition began. But the stallion had come to trust Cord.

And so had she.

"Fool," she said under her breath as she picked up a curry comb. "You knew he wore a beeper."

Despite that, she really had let herself believe that he would be there to help her prepare for her Olympic test. Though the disappointment was like a knife turning in her, she didn't blame her pain on Cord. The fault was hers. Definitely.

"Foolish little baby," she muttered. "You knew better than to trust a man on a leash. He'll do the best he can, but you'll always be second place in a two-entry race. As in *last* place."

"Ma'am?" Thorne asked, hearing only the murmur of words, not their meaning.

She glanced up, reminded that no matter how lonely she felt at the moment, she wasn't alone. "Er, nothing. I always talk to myself when I work with Dev. It lets him know where I am."

"Smart. That red devil could kick you into next year."

"He's too well mannered for that."

Thorne's smile told her that he didn't believe a word of it. Last night he had seen Dev with the veneer of training stripped away by raw fear. It wasn't something Thorne would forget soon. If ever.

Without intending to, Raine went to the stall door and looked into the yard. No man was walking toward her with the coordinated ease of a cougar. No light-eyed shadow was watching from beneath the eaves.

"Stop it," she said under her breath. "He'll come if he can. And if he can't . . . well, it would hardly be the first time, would it?"

Yet in one very important way, it would be the first. Her father had disappointed her too many times to count. Cord never had.

Then again, I haven't known him very long, have I?

But it felt like forever. The world before she had known his strength and passion and laughter was like an old, old movie — no color, no sound, no life. The world since she had known him was like the Olympic Games themselves, color and pageantry and pulse-pounding excitement.

Her eyes searched the stable yard one more time before she forced herself to look away. Cord would come to her when and if he could. Hanging over the stall door wouldn't bring him here any faster.

Deliberately she turned her back and

began weaving Dev's thick, sweeping mane into an intricate French braid. When she finished there would be nothing but a smooth, textured surface running the length of Dev's heavily muscled neck. There would be no wild black fall of mane or bright, beribboned pigtails to distract from the stallion's performance in the Olympic dressage ring.

After she completed Dev's mane, she brushed his long tail until it was a black waterfall rippling and shimmering nearly to the floor. She polished each hoof until it was dark and gleaming.

Suddenly Dev's head came up, telling her that someone was walking up to the stall. She looked up hopefully, only to be disappointed.

It wasn't Cord.

Captain Jon leaned on the stall door and glanced critically at the stallion. "Should I send over one of the girls to help you?"

"I've got it under control. How are we doing in the dressage ring so far?"

"Better than I'd hoped. The French are having the same trouble we are. Their bloody beasts are damned near jumping out of their skins with health. Their fault scores are still only fifteen to twenty, though. They take to discipline better than you Yanks."

She smiled at Captain Jon's familiar —
and mostly joking — complaint. Yet the
thought of having to hold her edgy, violently
healthy stallion to a mere twenty faults was
troubling.

Dressage wasn't like jumping, where
whatever faults horse and rider made were
obvious to anyone with twenty-twenty vision. A perfect jump was one in which horse
and rider approached from the proper direction, cleared the obstacle without touching
it, and landed right side up. The style of
horse and rider were irrelevant.

In dressage, style was all important. Each
dressage exercise could theoretically be
performed to perfection. But as in any art,
what constituted perfect style was very
much a matter of taste and individual preju-
dice.

Dev usually got high positive marks in
dressage simply because he was beautifully
built and had a commanding presence. Her
own deceptive appearance of fragility also
added to their positive marks; obviously,
she wasn't controlling the stallion through
sheer brawn. The point of dressage was for
the rider to appear to be merely a well-
dressed passenger rather than the one who
was giving orders — "aids" — to tell the
horse what was expected of him.

Unfortunately, Dev often made it clear that his rider was, indeed, having to work to control him. That was why he received relatively high negative, or fault, marks for obedience. He made up for that on the grueling endurance portion of the three-day event. There his great vitality, courage, and trust in his rider brought even seasoned competitors to their feet, cheering.

Captain Jon cleared his throat, paused, and decided he couldn't avoid it any longer. "Raine?"

She realized she was staring past him, looking for Cord. She turned to face the captain, caught by the unusual hesitation in his voice. "Yes?"

"If you like, I'll short-list you. You don't have to go out there and be a bloody target."

She froze. *Short-listed.* Taken off the American Olympic Equestrian Team and replaced by one of the other American riders who had also trained strenuously for four years, hoping to make the Olympic cut.

Yes, Captain Jon could short-list her. It was his right. But he had to do it now, before she entered the first competition of the Olympic three-day event. Once she competed, if she was disqualified for any reason, the Americans would simply have to go on under the handicap of having only three riders on the team rather than four.

In a competition that counted the best three out of four team members' scores, having a team member disqualified during the event was a crippling blow to any hope of winning.

"Are you giving me a choice?" Raine's voice was careful, as colorless as her face.

"Of course."

"I want to compete."

Captain Jon rubbed his cheek thoughtfully. "Even as a target?"

Her chin came up and she met his eyes. "If you're worried about the team, short-list me. If you're worried about me, don't. I'm a candidate for kidnap, not assassination. Ask Cord."

"I did."

Her eyes narrowed. "And?"

"He said he would greatly prefer that you didn't risk your neck on the endurance run. However, he made it clear his position was a personal preference, rather than a professional recommendation. As he put it, he's being paid to protect you from outside attack, not from the dangers inherent in being an Olympic equestrian."

She closed her eyes, silently thanking Cord for not taking advantage of his position. She knew that he was very worried about the obstacles on the endurance course. He could have used his professional status to ground her. He hadn't.

"Mr. Elliot is an unusual man," the captain added. "Honor isn't just a word to him, it is the core of the man. In addition, he has a great deal of respect for your skill and for you yourself."

"Yes," she said softly, "I know."

Automatically she looked past the captain, searching for Cord's lithe male figure. He wasn't anywhere in sight.

Was he going to miss seeing her ride in the dressage competition?

Captain Jon cleared his throat again, accurately guessing where her attention was. Guiltily she focused on him.

"Go ahead and enjoy Elliot," the captain said crisply. "God knows it's about time you let a man get close to you. But don't let him distract you from your major purpose — the Olympic Games."

She flushed, but she met his level glance with one of her own. "I won't let the team down, Captain Jon."

He nodded once, abruptly. "If I thought you might, you would be short-listed right now instead of polishing that bloody great stallion. Give him your best ride, Raine."

"I will."

He smiled. He had expected no less. "Don't worry," he added, gripping her shoulder. "I don't expect miracles from you. Devlin's Waterloo was born to run, not to make pretty patterns in the sand of a dressage ring."

Raine stepped out of the motor home, as polished and ready for the ring as her horse. The door automatically locked behind her. If she wanted to go back inside, she would have to get the key from Thorne. No problem, there. He was never out of sight.

Unlike Cord.

She squared her shoulders and looked around, hands on hips. Instead of dusty shirt, jeans, and old boots, she was wearing the formal riding attire of the dressage ring. Black hat and brilliantly polished English boots, white blouse and carefully tied stock, jodhpurs, and a dark, severely tailored riding coat. White gloves were carefully rolled into a jacket pocket. She wouldn't put them on until just before she went into the ring.

"Only the military would insist on wearing white gloves around the stables," she muttered. "Ruddy nuisance."

She made a small adjustment to her hat, which was also a protective helmet. Her hair was twisted up beneath the hard plastic. There would be no flying locks to detract from the calm, measured elegance required by Olympic dressage.

The clock ticking inside her head told her that she couldn't stall any longer, hoping Cord would appear. With quick strides, she set off across the stable yard.

Instantly Thorne appeared and walked at her right elbow. She didn't ask him if he had seen Cord. She didn't trust herself to play the small ritual game lightly. It seemed that she had spent a lifetime looking forward to someone coming to see her perform, only to be disappointed at the last minute.

Setting her teeth, she took a deep breath and put aside this disappointment as she had learned to put aside others in the past. She was about to enter the first event of an Olympic competition. She had worked all her life toward this moment. She would give the games what they demanded and deserved.

Her best.

When she turned the corner at Dev's stable row, she found the stallion bridled and saddled, standing quietly, black muzzle nibbling at Cord's collar. Suddenly she felt lighter, younger, triumphant, as though she had won the dressage event before she even went into the ring. Her step quickened, lengthened, and she truly smiled for the first time since she awakened and found herself alone.

Dev scented her, lifted his head, and nickered, tugging at the reins. Cord turned and held out his hand to her. He didn't say where he had been, or why.

She didn't ask. She knew that she didn't have the security clearance to hear the details of his professional life.

"You look very cool and elegant." His eyes went over her slender figure from her hat to her boots. "Will you be disqualified if I hug you?"

Instead of answering, she put her arms around him and hugged him hard. His arms came around her just as quickly, just as hungrily. Then, in a voice too low to be overheard, he said, "Blue and the rest are watching through binoculars from a safe place."

She nodded and held tighter. "I'm glad you'll see me ride in the Olympics," she whispered, and felt his arms tighten even more. She tilted her head back so that she could see his brilliant, intense eyes. "Thank you."

"My pleasure, love. But it won't always be my choice to make."

"I understand."

And she did.

When Cord lifted her up into the saddle, she smiled down at him and put her hand along his cheek, savoring the roughness of beard lying just beneath tanned skin. "And thank you for saddling Dev."

"For a smile like that, I'd saddle the devil himself." He kissed her palm and stepped back.

He walked alongside Dev to a practice area where dressage contestants "rode in" their horses, carefully warming up the animals so that their muscles would be supple for the intricate demands of dressage.

Quietly, watching the people milling around, Cord waited while Raine took Dev into the ring, collected him, and began working him. Despite the stallion's impatience to leap and run, she schooled him relentlessly until Dev's weight was poised over his hocks and his neck was a smooth, impressive arch balanced lightly against the bit.

It was a far cry from the kind of riding Cord had been raised with, but he didn't underestimate the skill and discipline that dressage demanded from both rider and horse. Especially now, when Dev was fully rested and his rider's adrenaline was pumping with the knowledge that soon she would enter the ring for the first time as an Olympic rider.

When Raine's name was called as the next competitor, she pulled on white gloves, turned Dev, and rode him out of the practice area toward the competition ring.

Saying nothing, Cord watched her go. He could have called out, wishing her luck or some such trivial thing, but he didn't. He understood that she had to be focused entirely on the Olympic test ahead.

With a quick, almost invisible signal to Thorne, Cord withdrew to a place that would allow him to see the waiting competitors, the show ring itself, and the spectators. He unzipped his jacket partway. He wore a different jacket today, darker, looser. Its folds concealed the small, lethal submachine gun he carried in addition to the customary pistol in the small of his back.

An hour ago, Blue Herring had sent another warning. Barracuda was on the move. Supposedly he was headed south, toward San Diego, where an exclusive golf course had been torn up to create an obstacle course that would test the courage of riders and horses alike.

Cord should have been relieved by the

news that Barracuda wasn't headed for Anaheim and the dressage ring, but he wasn't reassured one bit. It would be like Barracuda to turn around and strike where he was least expected.

Raine waited behind the bleachers while the previous rider's scores were flashed on the lighted board. A round of mild applause came, telling her that the Swiss rider had performed adequately but not well.

Nervousness turned over coldly in her stomach. She concentrated on the flags of the participating countries flying behind the bleachers, along with the flag bearing the Olympic symbol of five interlocking circles. The bleachers were brimming with an excited, attentive crowd. Three judges sat alone beneath an awning at one end of the freshly raked, sandy rectangle that was the competition ring.

Raine heard her name and country announced over the public address system. At Captain Jon's signal, she took a slow, deep breath, collected Dev, and rode her horse into the first test of the Olympic three-day event.

With the contest finally begun, her tension fell away. Focused, determined to do well, she entered the smooth-surfaced, rectangular performance area. At a pre-arranged place she stopped Dev neatly in front of the judges, saluted, turned her horse, and immediately started the required pattern of dressage exercises which every Olympic competitor performed.

For the next seven minutes and thirty seconds, the judges would scrutinize both horse and rider. What they were looking for was a harmony between man and beast that would be expressed in serene, elegant, yet powerful movements over the freshly raked sand. While Dev changed paces and leads, directions and diagonals, Raine was supposed to sit gracefully and not in any way show that she was the one giving the horse its cues.

With horses that were trained and bred only for dressage, there was a gentleness of spirit that greatly aided the rider's appearance of being merely a well-dressed passenger. Event horses, however, were competitors bred and trained for aggressive health and the kind of spirit that wouldn't quit no matter what the obstacle ahead or the exhaustion of the moment.

As a result, Dev didn't want to confine his bursting energies to seven and a half minutes of restrained, civilized patterns of walk and slow trot, slow canter and fast walk, switch leads and working trot, stand immobile and wait for an invisible signal to move, and so on. The stallion's spirited displeasure at being curtailed showed in his tossing head, his champing at the bit, his constant testing for a weakness in his rider's grip on the reins.

For seven and a half minutes, Raine and Devlin's Waterloo fought a fierce covert battle for control of the bit.

For her it was like trying to control a swift river with her hands cuffed together at the wrists. The minutes stretched on and on, as though the clock in her head was caught in a continuous loop of seconds without end. She didn't hear the crowd or feel the breeze that kept the flags snapping colorfully. She didn't feel the moisture sliding down her spine. It wasn't nerves that made her sweat, it was the sheer strength it took to keep her stallion in line.

Dev never broke loose or refused a signal from his rider, but there were moments when he didn't display the calm, submissive style that dressage judges favored. At those times, he required "aids" of a strength that were hardly invisible.

On the other hand, the stallion's impressively powerful hindquarters and muscular, arched neck made him appear to be more collected beneath Raine's hands than he often was. In addition, her slender, long-legged grace showed to particular advantage against Dev's huge, coiled body. The obvious contrast in strength between rider and horse added to the impression that Dev was willing rather than mulish.

With a serene expression and a steel grip on the reins, Raine signaled the last lead change as she turned Dev back toward the judges. She halted the stallion and held him immobile beneath her, using the combined pressure of the bit and her legs. Then she saluted to the Olympic judges and ended the longest seven and a half minutes of her life.

Outwardly unruffled, she waited until her scores were flashed on the board. She looked only at the faults recorded by each judge: 33; 40; 23.

With no change of expression, she turned and rode out of the ring. Considering that the average three-day event horse compiled fifty faults per judge, Dev's and her performance was better than adequate. Considering the French team so far, she could hardly crow about her appearance in the dressage ring.

The audience had no such problem. The spectators had loved Dev's sheer beauty and muscularity. They cheered the big stallion as though he had put in a flawless round. Dev minced out of the ring, pulling eagerly at the bit. He had pleased the audience, if not the judges, and he knew it. Now Dev wanted nothing more than a good hard run.

"You'll get it, you red devil," Raine muttered. She turned Dev toward an open area set aside for exercising horses. "Not as much as you want, though. Just enough to clean out your pipes before we ship you to Rancho Santa Fe for the cross-country. There you'll get all the run you want and then some."

Shying, prancing, cakewalking, Dev did everything but crawl out of his skin to free himself from the restrictions of the bit and his rider's gentle, implacable hands. Nervous lather formed on his shoulders and flanks by the time he danced to the area where he would be allowed to run.

Cord was waiting at the gate. He swung it open, allowing the eager stallion inside. "That was a world-class piece of riding," he said simply. "Dev's a hell of a lot of horse to keep the lid on."

"He's going to get his reward now," Raine said rather grimly.

She settled deeper into the flat saddle as Dev leaped sideways, trying to unsettle her enough to get control of the bit. She let out the reins slightly.

Dev went from a standing start to a full gallop, fighting for control of the bit every inch of the way.

Cord watched with an expression on his face that was admiring and harsh at the same time. Raine rode with a joy and skill that almost made him forget how big Dev was, how fiery, and how powerful. But no matter how great her expertise on a horse, Cord couldn't forgot how completely her life depended on the trust between herself and the volatile blood-bay stallion.

The thought of the cross-country made ice condense in Cord's veins.

But there was nothing he could do about that. Nothing he *would* do. Raine had made her choice long ago. He respected that, as he respected her. In a few hours he would drive her down to Rancho Santa Fe, where he had first seen her walking alone amid tawny hills and towering eucalyptus trees. There — away from the heat and smog that Prince Philip had rightly decreed weren't suitable for the cross-country part of the Olympic three-day event — were the obstacles designed to test the courage of horse and rider.

And there Barracuda waited.

CHAPTER 18

Rancho Santa Fe's dry winds combed restlessly through the tawny grass and silver-green eucalyptus leaves. The cloudless sky was blue-white, radiant with heat and light. Despite the beautiful day, Raine barely noticed her surroundings as she sat on a hilltop, writing quickly in a steno notebook. Its pages contained the condensed wisdom of Captain Jon, herself, and her teammates on the subject of the endurance course of the three day event.

The course was divided into four segments: (A) roads and trails; (B) steeplechase; (C) roads and trails; (D) cross-country. Together, A and C equaled about fifteen miles. Those fifteen miles must be covered at the average speed of a canter. The rider could choose a combination of walk, canter, and gallop. Or the rider might simply try to canter the whole fifteen miles.

The judges didn't care. What mattered

was that the horse took the course and obstacles in the assigned order without using up more than the allotted time for any segment. Pacing was crucial in order to get good marks. No points were given for going faster than the required times on the roads-and-trails segments, but points were deducted for taking too long.

A steady canter would be the ideal pace, easy on both horse and rider. The course was cleverly laid out so that it rarely allowed an easy canter.

The rider's job was to balance the terrain's demands, the time requirements, and the horse's own reserves of strength. If the rider was too careful of his horse, the pace would be too slow and time faults would be deducted from the score. Too fast a run would take too much out of the horse, making the final cross-country segment of the course impossible rather than merely very difficult.

Any errors at all on roads and trails segments would reduce the team's chance for an Olympic medal. There simply was no excuse for not pacing the horse properly or taking any of the course out of its assigned order.

As Raine flipped through her pages of notes, she glanced occasionally at the map each contestant had been given when the game officials walked the riders over the course. She figured that part B, the steeplechase, would require the horse to move at a fast gallop for about two and a half miles, with jumps placed on the average of every thousand feet.

These were solidly fixed jumps, not showring jumps that fell over if the horse misjudged. In the steeplechase, if you hit a fence, *you* went down, not the fence. Unlike the roads and trails segments, if you went faster than required over the steeplechase course, you could make up points. If you went too slow, you lost points. If you took twice the required time to complete the steeplechase, you were disqualified. Period.

There was no way to spare your horse on the steeplechase and still stay in the event. Refusals or falls at the jumps counted heavily against a competitor. In order to have a chance at the gold, horse and rider had to put in a perfect round. The steeplechase was a test of nerve and speed and judgment.

But it was part D, the cross-country, that was designed to separate the merely fit and skilled horse-and-rider teams from the superbly fit and consummately skilled. A fall within the penalty area around each obstacle — and falls were common — cost sixty points. A team might survive one such fall by one rider and still place in the medals. A fall by two different riders would likely end a team's hope of finishing in the medals.

There were many opportunities to fall. The cross-country was five miles of trails that went up and down hills and over obstacles designed to force a horse to trust its rider's judgment. No trust, no jump. The first refusal of an obstacle cost twenty penalty points. The second refusal of the same obstacle cost forty. The third disqualified you.

The obstacles averaged one every eight hundred feet. Thirty obstacles. Five miles.

Although none of the obstacles required more than a six-and-a-half-foot drop from the takeoff point, some of the obstacles were diabolically placed in the middle of ponds or just beneath the crest of a hill, on the downhill side. On those jumps, the horse must literally jump blind on a signal from its rider, who knew the course. Other obstacles came at the end of a long uphill run, testing the will of the horse to continue.

The cross-country course was exactly what it had been designed to be — five brutal miles of run, scramble, and jump. It came on the heels of nearly eighteen miles of hard work for both horse and rider, including the breakneck steeplechase. Except for a fifteen-minute break just before the cross-country segment — when a veterinarian examined the horse to see that it was fit enough to finish the course — horse and rider were tested relentlessly.

As Captain Jon had put it, the endurance event was a "right bastard."

"You aren't supposed to be out here alone."

Cord's voice came from behind Raine, startling her. She looked up from her notes and realized that everyone else had scattered over various parts of the course, measuring yet again what would be required of horse and rider.

She glanced back at Cord. He was sitting on his heels and looking over her shoulder at her notebook. His eyes were shards of silver and blue, so beautiful that her breath caught.

"I'm not alone," she said huskily. "You're here."

Smiling, she brushed her lips over his. His hand rested against her cheek, savoring the smoothness and heat of her skin. She was so warm, so soft, so *alive.*

And Barracuda's world was so damned cold.

Reluctantly Cord released Raine and stood up, pulling her with him. She wondered what had put the grim lines back around his mouth, but she didn't ask. She glanced at her watch. Barely an hour had passed since the beeper had called him away.

"That didn't take long," she said.

One of his hands slid into her hair. He pulled her close and kissed her hungrily, deeply, as though it had been months rather an hour since he left her side.

"Promise you won't go anywhere alone. *Anywhere*." His voice was rough, almost harsh.

She glanced up at his ice-blue eyes and felt the tension in his muscular shoulders. "Is it Dad?" she asked tautly.

Cord looked at her. He could have told her that the guard around her father had been tripled. So had her own guard. The rest of her family had flown back to the East Coast; they would watch her ride on television.

Barracuda had eluded Bonner and his men.

But telling Raine wouldn't make her any safer, and it could distract her at a time when she needed every bit of her focus to get Dev over the man-eating obstacles on the endurance course.

"Promise me," he said, his voice gritty and intense.

"I have to walk parts of the course again."

He laced his right hand through hers. "Let's go."

"Cord . . ." She hesitated, knowing that he wasn't going to like what she had to say. "If your beeper goes off again and you have to leave, I still have walk the course. I can't take Dev over obstacles that I haven't had a chance to study."

His face settled into harsh lines. "We'll burn that bridge when we get to it."

She wanted to ask what had happened in the past hour to make him so wary, so hard, so savagely angry. But she didn't say anything. There was no point. He wouldn't tell her any more than he already had.

He most definitely did *not* want her to be alone.

"Where to?" he asked.

"Steeplechase. I want to look at the water jump again, as well as the bigger fences."

They walked quickly, saying little as she studied the steeplechase part of the course. From time to time she wrote in the notebook, tested the quality of the dirt, noted the angle of the sun at the obstacles, and mentally paced Dev through the course.

Though Cord knew that his men were all over the course like a rash, watching through binoculars, he didn't let down his guard. Silently he concentrated on everything but the jumps. It was easier not to look at them. He was a rider raised in rough country on rougher horses, but the steeplechase was enough to make him sweat.

He wished to hell that Raine had taken up ballet or needlepoint or pure dressage — anything but the three-day event.

The water jump involved a stout fence followed by a small artificial pond. The whole jump was thirteen feet wide. It would take a powerful, well-balanced leap to clear everything. The other obstacles were no easier. There were mounds of logs nailed together, solid as a house. There were brush and water jumps. Jumps into shadow and then into sunlight and leap up again half-blind. Twist and turn and jump repeatedly, two and a half miles at a hard gallop.

Just as dressage had its roots in war, as a way to instill the obedience and agility required by an officer of his horse in battle, the endurance and steeplechase part of the three-day event were meant to reproduce the kind of obstacles a mounted messenger might face while racing overland carrying battle orders.

All they left out was the gunfire, Cord thought grimly.

His job was to see that it stayed that way.

Stretching fingers cramped from writing, Raine closed the notebook. "On to the cross-country."

"All five miles of it?"

"I'll walk fast."

"I'll starve."

She reached back and patted her rucksack. "Food."

"Mind if I rummage?"

"Didn't we meet this way, with you so eager to rummage in my rucksack that you knocked me off my feet?"

His lips relaxed into a smile. Slowly, caressingly, the pad of his thumb moved over her high, slanting cheekbone.

"If I knew then what I know now," he said huskily, "I'd have taken off your clothes and made love to you right there. Maybe I should do that now, undress you and pull you down into the grass, love you until you shiver and burn and cry out my name."

Her breath caught at the desire in his eyes. She swayed toward him and he kissed her until she shivered and burned against him. The sound of voices floated up the riverbed, reminding him that they weren't alone. Not really.

He groaned and tore his mouth away from hers. "Too damn many people."

She laughed shakily. "A while ago you were complaining about it being too lonely out here."

"Then I was thinking like a bodyguard. Now . . ." Pale, burning blue eyes looked at her lips, reddened from the force of his kiss. "Now I'm thinking like a lover. *I want you.*"

"Don't tempt me." Sensual hunger raced through her. "I happen to know of a perfect little hideaway. It's too heavily wired for my taste, and the background music leaves a lot to be desired, but the locks are the best that money and ingenuity can provide."

"Background music?"

"The scanner."

Laughing, he folded her against his body, cradling her, rocking her, comforting himself. "After this morning, I didn't think anything could make me laugh. You're so good for me, sweet rider."

He brushed his open mouth over her neck, tasted her heat, touched the beat of her life with the tip of his tongue. She arched her neck to give him more freedom. He gave her a slow, tender bite and forced himself to release her.

"I like you in one piece," he said, "so let's see the rest of what this 'right bastard' course has in store."

"You've been talking to Captain Jon."

Cord shrugged. He had walked the course before the riders were ever allowed on it, but he hadn't been looking at the obstacles themselves. Barracuda's style was hit, run, and brag. If he had hidden inside the course itself, he could have hit whatever he wanted, but he wouldn't have been able to run afterward.

Dead men don't brag, either.

If Barracuda got past the redoubled security, he would be heading for one of the many positions Cord had already noted — hilltops where a sniper would have a good view of the crowd. And the contestants.

"Even after seeing the specs for myself," he said, "I couldn't believe the cross-country segment was as bad as Captain Jon made it sound. He's done professional events all his life, and he says this is the toughest course he's ever seen."

Raine's chin came up. The tone of Cord's voice told her that he wanted her out of the competition. "The course is what it's supposed to be. A test."

He said nothing, but his mouth was a thin, hard line as he rummaged in the rucksack she was wearing. After a few moments he asked, "Ham-and-Swiss or Italian?"

"Italian."

Eating as they walked, Raine and Cord cut across the course to the last segment, the cross-country. Between bites of Italian sandwich, she answered his questions. All of his queries had one thing in common: a blunt concern for her safety.

The more obstacles he saw up close, the more he worried. Taken by themselves, many of the obstacles were hair-raising, even for a man brought up racing mustangs through broken country. But these obstacles weren't taken alone by a fresh horse. They were taken at the end of nearly eighteen miles of running and jumping.

Taken that way, the obstacles were appalling. They were conceived in hell and dedicated to the principle that any horse-and-rider unit could be broken into its component parts.

And left that way.

There was one obstacle called the Coffin. It had a sharp downhill approach, a pair of rails planted on each side of an eight-foot-wide stream, and an uphill landing. If horse or rider misjudged at any point, a vicious fall was inevitable.

Then there were the Steps, a gigantic

staircase with each step just wide enough for a horse to land on and not one bit more. There was no space for a stride before the next step loomed up ahead. Without perfect timing, willingness and coordination, the horse could break a leg and the rider a neck.

The water jumps weren't any easier. Water was softer than logs, but mud made for nasty footing. One of the jumps was styled after the type of obstacle any nineteenth-century military rider might have encountered — a stream sunk between banks that were almost four feet high. The stream was too wide to jump across from bank to bank. The horse was forced to jump down into water and then *back* up and out, jumping onto the far bank without knowing what kind of footing was there.

Another obstacle involved jumping blindly into water. There was a wall of logs that dropped into water on the far side. The horse had to take two strides in knee-high water and then leap over a chest-high fence in the middle of the pond. Jumping the fence required a wet, uncertain takeoff and a worse landing.

The more Cord saw of the course, the less he liked it. He measured another nasty test, which was a rough uphill run separating two obstacles. There was a jump at the base of the hill, a jump onto the crest, and another rugged jump hidden just below the crest on the far side.

"What if you fall between obstacles?" he asked.

Raine swallowed a final bite of her sandwich, savoring the crunchy mild pepper. "No penalty points. There are officials at each obstacle to make sure you take the obstacle in the right direction and land right side up. If you fall within the penalty area, you lose sixty points."

"Not to mention teeth, among other things," he muttered. The wood rails were solid and as thick as his arm.

She smiled, showing two unbroken rows of white teeth. "So far, so good. I still have the ones I was born with."

"Broken bones?"

She shrugged. "Sure. It comes with —"

"— the territory," he cut in, his voice hard.

"Yes. Like the scar across your left hip that you won't tell me about. And the other one on your right side. And the third one buried beneath your hair at the back of your head."

His right hand clenched in his pocket around the solid-gold coin. She was right. He of all people should know just how much abuse the human body could take and still survive. Yet a sense of disaster had been riding him since he had talked to Bonner that morning.

Cord had felt like this five times before in his life; three times people had died. Silently he cursed the Scots grandmother who had passed on her fey premonitions to him but had not passed on the means to prevent the disasters. He could only sense them through veils of coldness and unease.

He would give anything he had, everything he had ever hoped for, if only Raine wouldn't ride tomorrow.

"Even if it wasn't my job," he said quietly, "I'd still want to protect you. You're so beautiful, so alive, like a fire burning in a winter world."

Tears magnified her eyes. She didn't know what to say. She put her hand on his arm, and was shocked by the tension vibrating beneath his control.

Cord closed his eyes for an instant. Then he chose his words as though his life depended on them. He had never wanted anything so much — or been so helpless to get it.

"I know what it is to live out on the edge," he said finally, "to test yourself and find out just what you're made of, to test and test again until you can live freely, sure of your own abilities."

She stared at him, seeing herself reflected in his eyes, his words.

"But there comes a time," he said slowly, "when the old tests don't teach you anything new. Do you understand what I'm saying?" His eyes changed, focusing on her, silently asking what he wouldn't say aloud.

She touched his cheek. "I have to ride tomorrow."

He didn't move, yet it was as though he had. He held himself like a man expecting a blow.

"If it was only me, I might hesitate," she said. "For you, Cord. Only for you. But it isn't just you or just me."

He closed his eyes, accepting what he couldn't change. Very gently he kissed the center of her palm. "I know. God help us both, I know."

And he did, for he was caught in his own responsibilities, a steel net that was drawing tighter, harder, pulling him away from everything he had ever wanted.

Raine.

Sighing, she sat back in the motor home's small dinette. She sipped at the half glass of white Burgundy that was all she had permitted herself to have tonight. Using her fingers, she picked at the few remaining greens on her salad plate, ate a crunchy leaf, and neatly licked her fingertips.

"That's the best thing about this restaurant," she said.

"What is?" Cord asked.

"I can eat with my fingers and no one cares."

He smiled and held his hand out to her across the table. "Let me do that."

"Do what?" she asked lazily.

"Lick your fingers."

The fire that was never far beneath her surface when she was with him licked through her. "Why do I suddenly feel like dessert?"

"Do you?" he asked, his voice velvet and dark. His finger traced the line of her neck and throat and the valley between her breasts. "You don't look like a strawberry waiting to be dipped in chocolate. You're too rich and smooth. More like a vanilla sundae. Only much better . . . much warmer. I wonder how you'd look with chocolate running all over your creamy skin."

Her breath rushed out as she tightened deep inside. Her nipples hardened against the soft navy T-shirt she wore.

He saw, and fought a sharp struggle for self-control. He wanted to slide out of the chair and kneel in front of her, to undress her and cherish every bit of her sweetness until she melted in his hands, bathing him in her fire.

"We've checked Dev and eaten a meal to warm a nutritionist's heart," he said. "Do you have to follow any other rules for the night before the competition?"

"Such as?"

"Sleeping alone."

She smiled slowly. "Not a chance."

"Thank God." Cord's voice was gritty with restraint. "I don't think I could keep my hands off you tonight. Especially knowing that you want me as much as I want you."

For a moment he simply looked at her, his eyes pale and intense. The thought of her hurtling over that brutal course tomorrow was riding him mercilessly. Two nightmare visions kept turning in his mind like sides of a slowly spinning coin. The first was Raine, lying crushed at the bottom of a jump that had proved to be one obstacle too many for even Dev's great strength. The second was an assassin's bullet taking out the secondary target because the primary target was unavailable . . . Raine lying motionless, a casualty in an undeclared war, blood and silence and death.

Cord's grim expression sent a cool trickle down Raine's spine. "I'm not the only nervous one," she whispered. "Is it getting very blue outside, Delta Blue?"

His smile was so brief she almost missed it. "Don't worry about it. You have enough on your mind."

"Why don't I just tell Dad not to come to the course?"

"It's too late. It's been too late since Blue decided he was going to see his Baby Blue ride. Not that I blame him. If you were mine, I'd see you ride tomorrow if I had to take on hell with a garden hose."

She whispered Cord's name as her hands came up to frame his hard face. His eyes were like ice, but his mouth was warm, gentle, and very seductive against hers, nibbling, licking, touching, tasting, promising wild, sweet oblivion. When he reluctantly lifted his lips from hers, she sighed his name again.

"Shower first," he said firmly, picking a piece of straw out of her hair. "I have a call to make."

"You'll pay for that," she said in a husky voice.

"What?" he asked innocently.

"Teasing me and then telling me to take a cold shower."

"Try the handle on the left. The one marked H."

She muttered something succinct and unladylike. Then she walked toward the shower, shedding clothes with each step.

Cord watched until the bare curve of her shoulder emerged from her blouse as she shrugged aside the cloth. The elegant, deeply feminine movement went into him like a knife, making a floodtide of fierce, aching heat rise in him. With a curse, he turned away to make his call.

Still muttering, Raine tucked her hair into a green terrycloth shower turban. She went into the shower stall, turned on the water, and grabbed the soap. Before she had worked up a decent lather, the shower door opened and Cord stepped in, filling the small enclosure with his male presence.

He was fully naked, fully aroused.

She stood with soap forgotten in one hand, warm water running over her skin, desire spiking hotly through her. His eyes were silver-blue, smoky. The tension of passion showed in every muscular line of his body.

"What about your call?" Her voice was throaty, aching with need for him.

"He was out fishing."

CHAPTER 19

Smiling, Cord slid his hands slickly over Raine's neck and shoulders, down her back, around her waist. He lingered over her hips, leaving heat and lather wherever he touched. When his fingers slid up and circled her breasts, she groaned softly. He watched her change at his touch, felt the silky resilience of her breasts and the tempting hardness of her nipples pouting against his palms.

"I've been wanting to do this since I washed your hair," he said in a low voice. "Why the hell did I wait so long?"

Need blossomed inside her, a long, pulsing rush of liquid heat. "I'll play your silly game. Why did you wait so long?"

"Stupidity." He turned her toward the pouring water and watched iridescent lather slide down every feminine curve of her body. "Sheer criminal stupidity."

She laughed, then made a throaty sound of surprise and desire when he bent and licked the smooth warmth of her neck. His lips and teeth and tongue caressed her, gently cherishing her while he fought to banish the fey nightmare . . . Raine hurt, dying, and he was too far away to help her.

With a groan, he spread his hands wide and held her against his hungry body, trying to touch all of her at once, know all of her, hold all of her *now,* because tomorrow would come too soon, bringing with it blood and silence and death.

His mouth moved to her breasts, licking and love biting, ravishing her tenderly while warm water poured over him, over her. Slowly he slid down her body until he was kneeling in front of her. His tongue traced her navel while his hands cupped her hips, tilting her toward his caresses. His teeth closed lightly on the inner curve of one thigh.

Her breath came in sharply. When she looked down, she saw his hair black against her pale skin, his teeth white and gleaming, the hard tip of his tongue teasing her inner thigh. And then his head turned, seeking her greatest heat, finding it, cherishing it with an intimate caress that made the breath stop in her throat.

"Cord —" Surprise and savage desire jolted through her, loosening her knees.

"It's all right, sweet rider." He turned his head away from the sleek flesh that called to him and laid his beard-roughened cheek against her thigh. "Everything is all right."

He came to his feet in a single coordinated rush. As though he had never touched her, he shut off the water, stepped out of the shower, and reappeared carrying a soft towel. He rubbed the cloth slowly over her skin, drying her with gentle movements of his hands.

She watched him with hungry eyes, wishing that she was more sophisticated, that she could tell him that he had surprised her, not horrified her.

"Cord . . ." Her voice was husky, shattered.

He quieted her with a brush of his thumb over her lips.

When he pulled off her turban, she closed her eyes and leaned her forehead against his chest. Her fingertips tangled in the black mat of hair that was both coarse and oddly silky to her touch. Her nails scraped lightly over his nipples.

For an instant he went completely still. Then he shuddered and resumed drying her. When he was finished, he carried her to the bed and set her down, pushing her shoulders lightly until she was stretched out on the covers.

"Roll over," he said. "I'll rub the tightness out of your shoulders."

"I didn't mean . . ." she said in a soft voice. "You just surprised me."

"I know. I'm sorry."

He bent over her, wanting her until he ached and afraid that he would shock her again.

Raine looked up at him. Water glistened all over his skin. He hadn't bothered to dry himself, only her. Restlessly she combed her fingers through his wet hair, seeking the warmth of his scalp, trying to pull his head down to her. With gentle motions he disentangled her fingers and rolled her onto her stomach.

A clean fragrance filled the air as he poured lotion into his palm. For long, silent minutes, hands that were both gentle and very strong kneaded her back from her waist to her shoulders. When her body was utterly relaxed, his hands changed, caressing where they had been almost impersonal. He spoke softly, his shaman's voice another kind of caress.

"You don't know how beautiful you are to me," he said simply.

His thumbs smoothed down the muscles on either side of her spine. His hands shaped her buttocks, savoring the resilience and warmth of her flesh. Slowly his fingers moved on, learning each womanly curve of thigh and calf before sliding inevitably back up her legs toward the aching warmth of her.

"Poets always talk about flower petals and cream and peaches," Cord said, his voice dark magic. "Nice enough things, I suppose . . . but it makes me wonder if a poet ever touched a woman like you, felt the strength and silk and fire. Soft?" His long fingers traced the shadow cleft of her buttocks until he found the warmth of her. "God, yes, you're soft," he murmured, sliding deeply into her, "but it's a living softness with strength beneath, the strength to hold a man forever."

Raine's breath came out in a ragged sound of desire. She would have rolled over, but Cord allowed her to turn only as far as her side. He fitted her back against his chest, her hips against his, his leg between hers, his hand caressing her with slow movements that melted her.

"You're no fragile petal to be bruised at a touch." His voice was deep, mesmerizing. "You're no peach to be picked once, eaten, and forgotten."

His breath was hot as he lovingly bit her

neck, her shoulder, her arm. Even as his tongue smoothed out the faint marks of his teeth, he felt the fire sweep through her again, felt her body clinging to his touch, wanting him. He moved his hips against her slowly, letting her know his own hunger, savoring the intensity of her response.

When she turned toward him again, he shifted until he was over her. He spoke softly, voice and hands and mouth caressing her, drinking her moans and tiny meltings. He found her breasts and ravished them tenderly with his mouth until she cried out in passion, knowing nothing but the fire and the man who called it from her.

"You're no bowl of milk, white and bland and still." His tongue found her navel. "You're hot and sweet and seething. I love the taste of you, Raine. I . . . need it." The shaman's voice curled around her as his mouth slid down her body. "Don't refuse me."

At that moment, she couldn't have refused him anything, least of all herself. When his mouth nuzzled her, easing her legs apart, she didn't stiffen or withdraw. Then she felt again the hot, secret lap of his tongue. Her breath rushed out, his name torn from her by the force of her response.

His answer was a murmur of encouragement, love words that both soothed and incited her. Putting his hands beneath her hips, he held her while he learned every bit of her.

Breathing brokenly, as though in agony, she twisted against his mouth, lost in the sensual instant. Heat surged up, a savage, beautiful fire consuming her even as he did. She shuddered and arched against him, calling his name. He answered with a hungry, searching intimacy that undid her.

She gave herself to him blindly, wholly, accepting everything, holding back nothing of herself. Waves of ecstasy swept through her, shaking her until she cried out with each broken breath she took.

He held her tightly, tasted lightly, and savored every bit of the fire he had called from her. When her shudders finally, slowly passed, his hands moved hungrily over her smooth skin.

Her eyes opened. They were dark and still half-wild. With a last, loving caress that made her shudder all over again, he slid up her body. He buried the fierce ache of his hunger in her, needing her as he had never needed anything in his life.

With a husky sound of pleasure, she took him into her arms, into her body, and held him with all her rider's strength. He moved once, slowly, measuring the depth of their joining.

And then he moved more quickly, pushing harder, lifting her hips to go deeper still. She melted over him, sharing her heat and ecstasy. He heard her cries as she burned again in his arms, and he felt fire swelling and building in him until it burst. He shuddered with a pleasure so intense that control wasn't possible. He could only hold onto her, giving himself to her until he was utterly spent. And even then, echoes of ecstasy shuddered through him with each breath.

Raine slowly came back to herself, to the room, and to the weight of the man lying in her arms. As she smoothed her hands sleepily over Cord's back, an idea condensed out of the silence and intimacy, an idea that had been growing as inevitably in her as love itself. She would make a home for him by the fire he had guarded so long and so well. She would give him the very warmth that he had spent a lifetime protecting without ever having for his own.

"Cord . . ."

He rolled onto his side, pulling her with him. "Go to sleep, sweet rider," he murmured. He kissed her slowly, gently. "Tomorrow will be a hard day for you."

She started to tell him about his place by

her fire, but all that came out of her mouth was a yawn that sounded like his name. He was right; she needed to sleep. Tomorrow, after she rode, she would tell him.

"Tomorrow," she agreed.

She curled against him and fell asleep even as he tucked her head against his shoulder and cradled her against his body.

Tomorrow.

He lay awake, listening to her deep, even breathing. He didn't want to sleep, to lose even a moment of time with her. He didn't want to close his eyes and see the nightmare of death and destruction, Raine hurt, dying, and all his skill wasn't enough to make a difference.

For a time he wished that she had pursued figure skating or target shooting or swimming or pure dressage riding — anything but the dangerous, demanding sport she had chosen. Yet he admired her courage and skill, her grace and dedication. He wouldn't have changed her if he could.

Nor had she asked him to change, though he knew his work lay between them like a winter night, long and black and cold. It haunted her eyes. It haunted the silence that came when his beeper went off.

It haunted him.

He wanted to tell her that it was all right,

that he had decided to get out, all the way out. But first . . . first there was the matter of Barracuda. Cord didn't know how long it would take to fish the terrorist out of troubled international waters. He only knew that it must be done.

He also knew that there was nothing he could do to change any of it now, this instant, this night. Her choices were made. So were his.

So Cord did the only thing he could. He held Raine, kissed her very gently, and prayed that once, just this once, tomorrow would never come.

It did, of course. Tomorrow always comes.

The day was hot enough to raise a sweat and dry enough to take the moisture from Raine's skin before she even felt sweat condense. Dev moved restlessly as she stood beside him. Cord held the reins while the stallion tugged and snorted and chewed on the bit.

Dev sensed that he was finally going to be allowed to run.

"You're next." Captain Jon's voice was clipped, yet calm.

She turned toward Cord, suddenly wanting to feel his arms around her once more. He pulled her close, kissed her with fierce tenderness, and pressed a gold coin into her hand. She looked at the alien writing and the graceful, equally alien woman on the face of the coin.

"Lady Luck." He folded Raine's fingers firmly over the gold. "She's brought me out of a few tight places. Let her ride with you."

"Mount up," Captain Jon said.

Raine shoved the coin deep into her pocket. Cord helped her mount and then held the dancing stallion. She gathered the reins, checked the watch taped to her wrist outside her riding glove, and waited for the official to call her. Each rider rode the course alone, running against the clock rather than other horses.

"Ready," she said.

Concealing her nervousness behind a calm expression, she waited for her turn. She didn't see the crowd seething around the starting point or the masses of people clustered at various places along the course. She simply concentrated on gathering herself for the coming trial.

Cord stood very still, looking at Raine as though memorizing her. Suddenly she turned and looked the same way at him. He touched her hand and stepped back.

"Gate," Captain Jon said tersely.

She went to the starting posts, held the

fidgeting stallion, and waited for the endurance event to begin. The instant the Olympic timekeeper signaled her, she punched in her own stopwatch and let Dev out into a canter.

As always, her nerves evaporated once the contest began. The stallion's didn't. For the first few miles, Dev fought against the bit, demanding a faster pace with every hard muscle in his body. She held Dev to a canter, pacing him through the twists and turns and inviting open spaces of roads and trails, part A.

"Easy, Dev," she murmured, talking to him constantly. She checked her watch to see that she was within the time allowed. "Don't fight me, boy. You'll wear both of us out before the work really begins."

After the first four miles, Dev accepted the easy cantering pace with more civility. Hill and shadow, twist and turn, dirt road and narrow trail — Dev took them all with equal ease despite the lead weights he carried to bring his load up to the required 165 pounds for tack and rider.

Dev flashed through the timing gate at the end of section A. Thirty seconds under the mark. Score 0, no faults.

Raine reset her stopwatch even as she increased Dev's speed. He was warmed up, moving loosely, ready for whatever came next. And what came next was the steeplechase, two and a half miles of gallop and jump, jump and gallop. The crowds would be thick around the jumps, for it was there that the most spectacular action took place. Solid jumps and solid horses. Jump clean or fall hard.

She checked her watch, loosened the reins slightly, and leaned forward. In a single stride Dev went from a canter to a gallop. When he spotted the first jump, his ears came up. He tongued the bit, testing his rider's control, then accepting it without a fuss.

"All right, boy. Let's go flying!"

Ears pricked, hooves digging great clods out of the earth, Dev went over the first fence with a power that brought a low sound of admiration from the crowd.

Raine didn't hear anything but the clock ticking in her head. A tiny corner of her attention noted the presence of Olympic officials and medics off to the side of the jump, but it was only an instant of awareness. She shut out the crowd, the officials, everything but Dev and the course. Alert for the upcoming jumps, she rode almost without moving. Her weight was poised over Dev, letting him gallop freely beneath her.

Captain Jon had warned her about one jump in particular. Despite its innocent appearance, the obstacle had brought down several riders already. It was a very tricky combination, a brush-and-water jump. The horses weren't meant to leap entirely over the wall of shrubs, but rather to jump *through* the last few feet brush. If the horse tried to clear all the brush, the jump ended up being too high and too short. That forced an awkward landing in the water on the other side. Or a fall. An off-balance landing in mud was a risky maneuver.

Dev had no way of knowing what was ahead. Raine did. The brush-and-water jump was a test of the horse's trust in the rider. Dev must accept his rider's judgment and jump on command, for only the rider knew about the water on the far side of the shrubs. If Dev did it his own way — jumping too soon in order to clear the brush cleanly — they would be lucky to land right side up.

As they approached the jump, Raine gathered herself, sending Dev the multitude of tiny signals that warned she was in control. She could feel his readiness to jump, but it was too soon.

"My way, Dev," she said, holding the stallion to a rapid gallop. "Not yet, not yet, not yet — *now!*"

Dev sprang like a great red tiger for the top of the brush, but it was too high to clear completely since he hadn't been allowed to jump as soon as he wanted. Tiny branches whipped past his broad chest and straining haunches. Water rushed below his belly. He landed cleanly on the far side, well clear of the water, and galloped off without a break in stride.

The crowd cheered wildly.

Raine checked her watch, deaf and blind to all but the requirements of the course.

"That was a beauty," she said, praising Dev even as she calculated what remained to be done and the time it would take.

One ear flicked back to listen to her. The other stayed forward. Dev was running easily, breathing deeply, head up, ears pricked, looking for the next jump. Another fence loomed, then vanished as the stallion sprang over it and landed like a cat.

"You were born for this, weren't you?" Raine asked, grinning fiercely.

The rhythmic driving power of the horse beneath her was all the answer she needed. She laughed without knowing it. Excitement raced through her as Dev cleared another obstacle, then another.

The remainder of the jumps flew beneath

Dev's black hooves. When he went through the timing posts at the end of the steeplechase, sweat had darkened his coat and he was breathing hard. The score flashed out: 0 faults; 20 positive points for coming in under the required time limit.

Raine felt a single thrill of elation before she forced herself to concentrate on sparing Dev through the second round of roads and trails. Despite having just finished a steeplechase, the stallion fought against being slowed to a canter. She didn't give a quarter inch of rein to him. She intended to take every second of the allotted time for part C.

Before two miles were up, Dev caught his second wind. He cantered easily, rhythmically, giving the impression that he could do this all day and well into the night. His rider knew that wasn't true. The course had already demanded a lot of the stallion's strength. She checked her stopwatch regularly, giving Dev every break that the course, careful riding, and time allowed.

Even so, when Dev approached the timing posts at the end of part C, he was breathing heavily. Lather gathered whitely down the slope of his shoulders and flanks. Yet his rhythm was still good, and his breathing was deep rather than gasping. He was tired, but not exhausted.

Not yet. That would come somewhere during the last segment, the cross-country. Raine knew it even if her stallion didn't.

She dismounted the instant the time-keeper signaled her arrival at the end of part C. Captain Jon and Cord walked forward quickly. Cord stripped off tack and held Dev while Captain Jon and Raine worked rapidly, washing down the stallion.

Normally a stable crew would have worked over the horse while the rider rested and Captain Jon described the state of the course ahead — what was muddy from the passage of horses, what was dry, which obstacle had fooled the most riders. But with Dev, handling was never normal. So Cord held the restless, adrenaline-loaded stallion while Captain Jon talked and worked and Raine listened and worked.

"The French have four refusals and a fall so far on the cross-country," the captain said tersely. "No pattern. One obstacle is just as bloody awful as the next. We have two refusals."

"Dev never refuses," she said. She sponged out the stallion's mouth. That was as close to a drink as Dev would get until the endurance event was over and he was cool again.

Captain Jon grunted. "A refusal is cheaper than a fall."

She bit her lip. She knew better than anyone how hard it was to come out of Dev's more spectacular jumps still in the saddle. The stallion's greatest virtue as an event horse was that he would try to jump anything he saw. It was also his greatest vice. A well-timed refusal was better than a bone-breaking fall.

The veterinarian came over, watched Dev move, listened to his breathing, and checked for swelling or injuries to his legs. Cord and Raine held the stallion firmly, her words mingling with the shaman's murmur of Cord's voice. Dev's ears flattened when the vet's hands probed his legs, but the stallion tolerated it. Barely.

"Hell of a horse," was the vet's comment as he stepped out of reach. "Steel tendons and a temper to match." He nodded to Raine. "You're in, young lady. Saddle up."

Cord lifted the weight-laden tack to Dev's back and cinched the saddle in place.

"One minute," the captain said, looking at his own watch.

Cord boosted her onto the tall stallion's back. Dev was still breathing deeply, but wasn't laboring for air. Not the way he would be in a few miles, as each obstacle demanded more from the stallion's diminishing reserves of stamina and will. The cross-country segment of the course was five miles long.

Five very long, brutal miles.

"Jump straight and clean, you tough red bastard," Cord said, smoothing Dev's hot neck.

The stallion bumped his nuzzle against Cord's chest and breathed out twin streams of hot breath.

Raine checked her watch, then looked at Cord, wishing there had been time just to touch him. He watched her as though he knew her thoughts. She saw his lips move, but the meaning was drowned in the roar of the crowd greeting a new horse and rider. She could see that he spoke only three words. They could have been, *Good luck, Raine.*

Or they could have been, *I love you.*

She turned to ask him which, but it was too late.

"To the posts," Captain Jon snapped.

Automatically she obeyed.

Even as Cord stepped back, his beeper squealed in a series of coded staccato pulses that made adrenaline pour into his blood.

Blue all the way to the moon.

Delta Blue.

Quickly, ruthlessly, Cord pushed his way through the crowd and ran toward the command center.

Just as Raine positioned Dev at the starting posts, she had heard the faint, familiar electronic squeal of Cord's beeper. She wanted to look over her shoulder, but it was too late; her own electronic leash had shortened.

The timer clicked over, the course waited, and she must take Dev over it.

She brought the stallion out of the posts in a steady canter, a pace she would try to hold for the next five miles. The obstacles would make that impossible. It was what they had been designed for — to test horse and rider mercilessly.

Blind jumps tempted a horse to refuse. Blind landings rattled a horse's confidence and tested the rider's ability to stay in the saddle. Two falls were permitted, though heavily penalized. The third fall disqualified horse and rider.

Raine didn't see the Olympic officials or the crowds around the obstacles. She focused solely on the harsh requirements of the cross-country. The course unrolled in her mind even as it unrolled beneath Dev's feet.

Downhill and turn left, jump up onto a bank, two strides, ditch and rail, turn right, long downhill with the Coffin at the bottom

— *fly, Dev!* — now uphill uphill uphill and over the top sliding into a blind downhill jump — *easy boy, easy, No!* — and the terrible shock of a bad landing, Dev nearly pulling her arms off as she fought to keep his head up, to keep him on his feet and herself in the saddle.

She didn't hear the cries of the crowd as she rode with every bit of her strength and skill and leverage, hauling Dev's head up so that he could gather himself. The force required to put him right left her back and arms and legs aching.

But that was nothing new. She had been aching since the first miles of the event, time blurring into eternity. When you rode to spare your horse, you suffered for it.

After the bone-rattling landing, Raine collected Dev and talked to him, praising his courage, letting him feel her confidence despite the miscalculation. The stallion's ears came up again. He settled into a rhythmic canter, eager for the next obstacle.

She checked her watch. Still on schedule. Dev's long-legged strides ate up distance. She reached up to wipe sweat from her eyes and saw blood on the riding glove. Somewhere in those wild seconds of nearly falling and then recovering she had cut herself, probably on the buckle at the top of Dev's bridle.

If she was lucky, it would be the worst that happened to her today.

Talking to Dev, riding to spare him and not herself, she took the stallion over obstacle after obstacle, enduring as he endured, knowing that the landings would be harder for him each time, for each time he would have less strength to call on. It would be the same for her, each time less strength.

The pond was a nightmare, a blind leap into water above Dev's knees, mud slick and sucking at his hooves. He slid, wrenched free, and cleared the center jump on sheer guts and determination, landing blind again, cantering out of the pond, spraying sheets of water and mud.

Dev was breathing very hard now, the air groaning in and out of his body, lather running in white ribbons down his shoulders and flanks. Yet he cantered with his head up, ears pricked forward, game for whatever lay ahead. He was a stallion in his prime, born for the grueling test. He needed no whip but his own love of extending himself, no goad but his own desire to please the soft-voiced rider on his back.

Though her breath was coming as harshly

as Dev's, Raine praised him lavishly, continuously. Sweat ran from beneath her helmet into her eyes, mingling with blood until she wiped impatiently with her already reddened glove. She saw the next obstacle, chose her approach, and settled in for the final two miles. She rode lightly even though her muscles ached to sit back and let Dev do the work.

The end of the course was almost a shock. The last obstacle, the time posts, the cheering crowd. Two scores were posted. The first score was 0, no penalties, a perfect cross-country run. The second score was +20, the total of penalties and plus points for the endurance event.

Dev had redeemed his indifferent performance in the dressage ring.

She reined the stallion down to a walk, praising him constantly with a voice that had gone hoarse. When the official signaled that she could dismount, she slid off Dev and leaned against him, letting her shaking legs absorb her weight.

After a few moments she undid the cinch and slowly led Dev to the weighing stand. Staggering slightly under the burden of lead and leather, she stepped on the scales. The official read the weight aloud and approved it.

For Raine and Dev, the endurance event was over. All that remained to test them was stadium jumping. But that was for another day.

Tomorrow.

As she led the stallion away, her eyes searched the people around her. She didn't bother to look for her father or the rest of her family. She knew they wouldn't be allowed within shouting distance of her. But she looked for Cord. At that moment she wanted nothing more than to feel his arms around her and see the relief in his eyes. Dev had performed brilliantly. She had finished the brutal course with no more than a cut to show for it.

Abruptly she remembered hearing Cord's beeper. Her shoulders sagged and her feet slowed. He wouldn't be here.

Beep beep and good-bye.

She fought down irrational tears, knowing that they were the aftermath of adrenaline and exhaustion as much as disappointment. She would see Cord later, when he had finished whatever business had called him away. Until then, she had plenty to keep her busy.

"Come on, boy." She tugged gently on Dev's reins. "We've got a lot of work to do on you if you're going to be in any shape to jump again tomorrow."

Neither Dev nor his rider noticed when people made way for the exhausted stallion and the slender woman with blood welling down the side of her face. Slowly, very slowly, they walked through the dust and heat back to the stables.

Three helicopters were parked on rough desert ground that had never known the weight of a machine. The unmarked, matte-black choppers looked frankly menacing against the wide, empty land at the edge of the Mojave. The setting sun called long black fingers of shadow out of every ravine, every crease.

Cord lay in one of those shadows. He no longer looked like a stable hand. He was covered head-to-toe in black. The weapons he carried were equally black. Nothing on him would reflect light, telling an enemy where he was, providing a target.

He prayed for darkness the way a sinner prays for salvation. In the dark, more things were possible. Deadly things.

No one knew how Barracuda had sensed the trap closing around him in Rancho Santa Fe. They only knew that he had. The assassin had abandoned the field, stolen a car, and fled east, over the dry mountains.

447

Followed by Bonner, Barracuda had driven into the vast uninhabited desert.

Cord spoke softly into a headset that was very much a part of his fighting equipment. "Blue Herring?"

The answer was long in coming. Too long.

"No change." The voice was weak, hoarse, the sound of a man who had lost too much blood. "Still . . . there."

Bonner had taken a bullet trying to get close enough to Barracuda to kill him. Now the agent was up in the rocks bleeding and waiting, bait staked out by a Barracuda. From time to time the assassin would call out taunts. He had offered to exchange the agent's life for safe passage to Libya. Bonner had said he would kill himself first.

Cord believed him.

"Nobody shoot until I order otherwise," he said grimly. "I'm getting our man out. I need two volunteers."

He had twenty.

"The two closest to me," Cord said tersely. "When we're clear, the rest of you move in. If he won't surrender, leave enough of the bastard for me to make a positive ID."

A muted assent filtered through Cord's delicate headphone. The various invisible warriors hugging the contours of the land would wait for his signal before trying to move in. Without a sound, he began gliding from shadow to shadow, working his way up the dry ravine.

Cord was fifteen feet from Bonner when he caught a motion from the corner of his eye. Even as his brain registered the silhouette of a man — head, shoulders, and sniper scope — bullets exploded in a deadly line that started at Bonner and ended up with Cord. Metal thudded into flesh.

Cord staggered and went down. Even as he fell, he turned toward the rocks where the shots had come. Then he waited, fighting off waves of pain and darkness, clenching his teeth against making an animal noise of agony.

Five minutes later, Barracuda looked over the rocks to check on his kill.

Cord managed two shots before darkness broke over in him in a long, howling wave.

A medic slithered forward, clinging to shadows. It didn't take long to assess the damage. He spoke into his headphone. "All clear. Two gone. One more will be if we don't move our asses."

Before he finished talking, the bloody gully was swarming with black-clothed men.

CHAPTER 20

Raine climbed down the motor home's steps without her usual grace. She was stiff from yesterday's endurance run, but not as stiff as Dev would be. She was also restless and deeply uneasy. She hadn't seen Cord since he had boosted her up onto Dev's back for the last part of the course.

Thorne was in his usual place, doing his usual good job of looking lazy while being very alert.

"Have you seen Cord?" She wasn't able to keep her voice light. Asking about him was no longer a joke. She needed to know where he was.

Without even making a pretense of looking around the area for Cord, Thorne shook his head. He appeared older today, harder, and when he spoke, his voice sounded harsh despite his southern accent. "No, ma'am, I haven't."

She bit her lip against a protest. *Where is he?*

It had been Captain Jon, not Cord, who helped her care for Dev last night. It had been Thorne, not Cord, who drove the motor home from Rancho Santa Fe back to Santa Anita, where the final part of the Olympic three-day event would be held. It had been Thorne, not Cord, who discreetly guarded her when she checked on Dev late at night.

And it had been Raine alone who listened to the scanner's erratic mutter. It had taken her a long time to achieve even a troubled sleep.

Maybe Cord came back while I showered and dressed, she told herself. *Maybe he's at the stable right now, saddling Dev for the last competition.*

The thought that Cord might be waiting sent her running through the lacy shadows of pepper trees and down the green rows of stables. Her heart quickened when she saw Dev standing in front of his stall, all groomed and saddled.

He's here!

Before she could call Cord's name, Captain Jon walked out of the shadows to greet her. Disappointment turned in her like a dagger.

"Did you get Dev ready?" she asked.

"Yes. You need your strength for riding. Besides, he was too tired to do more than flatten his ears at me."

She schooled her expression as ruthlessly as she would soon be schooling Dev. "Thank you."

"How is your eye?"

"Just a cut."

"Bled like a stuck pig," Captain Jon said bluntly.

She shrugged and fiddled restlessly with the saddle blanket. There were no weights put into the pockets yet. They would be added just before Dev went into the ring.

Where is Cord?

"Raine."

She gathered herself and turned toward Captain Jon. "Yes?"

"You didn't let that French rider throw you," the captain said bluntly. "Whether or not Elliot is here, you have an event to ride. You owe it to yourself, to your horse, and to us."

Numbly she nodded her head. Then she took a deep breath and let it out slowly. "Don't worry, Captain Jon." She stepped onto the mounting block, then turned quickly back toward him. "Are we still in the medals?"

He smiled widely. "That's my rider! Yes, we're right up there. The French and Brits have knocked down some rails. If your bloody great beast can refrain from knocking down any jumps, you'll have a bloody great medal to show your grandchildren."

It was an effort, but Raine managed not to groan as she settled into the saddle. She had only eighty minutes before she was due in the competition ring. She would need every one of them to get Dev loose enough to jump.

The way the stallion walked to the practice area told her that he would just as soon have stayed in his stall, thank you very much. She patted and praised him with a voice that was still a bit hoarse. Once in the practice area, she worked Dev carefully, using simple dressage exercises designed to ease the stiffness in his huge body. By the time they were called out of the practice area and weights were added on, the stallion was willing if not eager to face the jumps.

For once Dev stood quietly in the opening between the bleachers as he waited to be called into the jump ring. The flags and crowds were as colorful as they had been for the dressage event, but the ring was neither empty nor freshly raked. Instead, the area was filled with brightly painted jumps set in combinations that would force horse and rider to adjust stride and approach for each individual jump.

No fence was fixed or high. The horses and riders had already proved their ability to jump yesterday in the steeplechase and on the brutal obstacle course. Today's event was simply to prove that horse and rider were willing — and able — to take to the field again.

There was a small round of applause for the rider who preceded Raine. His horse had refused once, costing ten penalty points, knocked down a rail for five points, and gone too slowly. Total, eighteen penalty points. Barely adequate.

Zero was the only score worth having.

Yet Dev was sluggish beneath her, and her own body lacked the strength and flexibility that had helped Dev yesterday. But the skill was still there, and so was the determination to do well.

Raine's name and country were announced. As she brought Dev into the ring at a slow canter, doubts and nervousness dropped away. The stallion's ears came forward when he spotted all the jumps. His gait was a bit ragged and difficult to ride, but otherwise he was willing.

Cantering slowly, she waited for the

buzzer that would signal the beginning of the timed event. When it came, she turned Dev toward the first jump. He took it easily, not pulling at the bit or fighting for a faster pace, leaving everything to her.

In some ways Dev's laissez-faire attitude made the ride much easier on Raine. Her arms were simply too sore and tired for a tug-of-war with the powerful stallion. Unfortunately, he was just a bit *too* easygoing about the jumps. He ticked a bar with his back left hoof on the third jump.

The crowd groaned, but Raine wasn't able to see whether the bar had fallen. She wouldn't know until she saw her score at the end of the event.

A triple jump provided another heart-stopping instant. Dev's hoof clattered against wood and the crowd groaned. Again, she couldn't tell whether or not the bar had fallen.

"All right, boy. You've had your fun. Now let's do it right."

She collected Dev and turned him toward the last jumps. He finished with a clean show of agility and strength that brought an approving round of applause. Instantly, she turned to look at the scoreboard.

Zero. No penalty points. Dev had rattled the bars but he hadn't knocked any down.

Smiling triumphantly, Raine threw her arms around Dev's muscular neck and poured praise into his ears.

"Good show!" Captain Jon said as she rode Dev out of the ring.

She sighed and stretched her aching back. "He felt about as lively as a balloon full of water," she said, worried.

The captain smiled and shook his head. "Ease up. It's over, now. Home free, as you Yanks say."

The words came as a shock.

Over. A lifetime of training, work, hope.

Over.

"Smile, Raine. You took us to the gold!"

Dazed, she looked at the caption while conflicting emotions swept through her, shaking her. It was an incredible feeling to win gold, to know that a lifetime of training had paid off so richly. Triumph exploded in her, but in its wake came the emptiness of knowing that something extraordinary had ended — all the sweat, all the fears, all the injuries, all the exhilaration of training and riding one of the best horses in the world to Olympic gold.

Triumph and emptiness and then triumph again, a starburst of conflicting feelings consuming her.

As though seeing them for the first time,

Raine looked around slowly at the crowd and the horses and the rippling Olympic flags. Strangers cheering and laughing, applauding Dev's achievement and her own. She smiled and waved back, sharing the moment of triumph with the crowd.

When another rider took to the ring, Captain Jon led Dev away. Emptiness surged up in Raine again. She looked at each face, each shadow, searching for . . . something.

Cord.

He wasn't there.

Dev stumbled tiredly, jarring her. The sound of cheering had faded. No one was near except Captain Jon, and soon he would have to return to the ring. She would be alone.

Over.

The word echoed in her mind like her heartbeat. Her work was finished.

And so was Cord's.

Is that why he left? Competition madness, lovers' games until the Summer Games were over. And then . . .

Nothing.

Over.

The last of Raine's strength leached out of her. She slumped in the saddle.

"Raine? I say, are you all right?"

She pulled the last shreds of her determination together. "I'm fine," she said, her voice flat. "Just tired."

Raine was still tired when she sat on a newly washed, curried, and polished stallion and received her gold medal alongside her teammates. The feeling of exhaustion vanished when she felt the crowd's triumphant cry, people shouting and cheering until the ground trembled.

By the time the national anthem ended, tears were streaming down her cheeks. She didn't notice. She smiled and waved to the cheering crowd, transported for the moment by the outpouring of emotion from people she would never know, people who had shared the intense emotions of the American Equestrian Team's ride to gold.

Finally she and her teammates rode from the ring, leaving the thousands of well-wishers behind. The other members of her team were soon engulfed in the noisy, exuberant congratulations of family and friends and reporters.

Raine didn't look around for her own family. She knew without being told that Cord wouldn't allow them in such a public melee.

With the ease of long experience — and some discreet shouldering by Thorne and his men — she evaded the press. She hugged

Captain Jon tightly.

"Thank you," she said, smiling at him. "We never would have gotten past the first obstacle without you."

Captain Jon cleared his throat and returned her hug with a huge smile, his Swiss reserve forgotten for the instant.

She released the captain into the bearhugs of her teammates. Then she stood on tiptoe, searching for a man with black hair and ice blue eyes, a man who moved like a cat gliding through dusk, silence and strength combined.

She saw no one like him.

Still searching for Cord, she eased through the knots of friends and families. Absently she responded to invitations to victory celebrations with a wave and a smile. Soon she was at the edge of the crowd, where he had often waited for her.

There was no one standing patiently back in the shadows.

For an instant she stood absolutely still, feeling as though she was being torn in half. Part of her still thrilled to the triumph of Olympic gold.

And part of her simply wanted to walk away, to keep on walking until there was nothing around her but silence and space. For the first time she realized how tired she was, tired clear through flesh and bone to her soul.

The feeling wasn't entirely new. It came to her after every competition, win or lose. Endings, not beginnings. Yet this time was also different. She had no desire to begin again, for there was nothing *to* begin. The ultimate Game was won, the highest goal achieved: Olympic gold.

And now it was over. Nothing to fight for, to work for, to train for, to risk for. Nothing and no one waiting for her.

She felt like a balloon released by a careless child, free floating high into the blue, higher and higher until cold shriveled the fragile envelope and it fluttered back to earth as a ruined shell.

Slowly she walked back to the motor home. Thorne was in his usual place, but the motor home itself was gone.

"Where's Cord?" she demanded.

Her voice trembled despite her attempts to keep it level. She had so hoped that he would be here to see her wearing Olympic gold. She could hardly accept that she was alone, no one to share her triumph with, no one to understand why she suddenly felt empty.

"Ma'am —"

"Where is Cord?"

"I'm sorry, Miss Chandler-Smith. I no longer know a man called Cord Elliot."

Raine called her father that evening, only to find out that he was already on his way to see her. He met her in her motel room, accompanied by two men who moved like Cord, calm and alert and strong. They searched the motel room thoroughly before fading back into the red velvet shadows like the accomplished bodyguards they were.

"Tell them to wait outside," she said tightly.

Justin Chandler-Smith was weaker, thinner, and older than the men with him, but a single look was all it took to rout them. They left as quietly as they had come.

Her father walked over and hugged Raine hard. "They wouldn't let me or any of the family near you during the games. Your mother and sibs watched on television. Said it was too great a risk. I stayed, but they still wouldn't —"

"I'm used to it," she said, not waiting for him to finish. "No apology needed."

Chandler-Smith looked down into his daughter's face. She looked older than she had when he watched her through binoculars on the endurance course. She should look elated, triumphant, relaxed. She didn't.

She looked like she was hanging onto control by a very fine thread.

He didn't know what was wrong. He only knew that something was. He started to ask, then decided against it. She would tell him the same way she did everything else — in her own time, in her own way.

"That was a hell of a ride you made," he said simply. "Half of me was proud. The rest of me was nearly too scared to watch. I had a good view, too. The man who scouted the land for me knew what he was doing."

"Cord Elliot," she said curtly.

"What?"

"Cord Elliot scouted the land for you."

"Tell him thanks for me."

"You tell him. He's one of yours."

Chandler-Smith held his daughter at arm's length. "What is it, baby? What's going on?"

She looked at him with hazel eyes that were nearly opaque. "Have I ever asked you for anything?"

"Not since you were ten and I missed your birthday party," he said sadly. "You never asked me for anything after that."

"I'm asking now. Cord Elliot. I want to know where he is, or at least to say goodbye." *Just to see him again. Just to hear his voice.* "But everyone I ask about him, even the men who worked with him, say, 'Cord who? Never heard of him.' "

Now Chandler-Smith recognized the change in his daughter. Pain and loneliness were etched into her face, her body, her voice. "You love him, baby?"

She closed her eyes. She had asked herself that question a hundred times a day. A hundred times a day the answer came back. Yes. Win or lose, *yes*.

And she was a thousand times a fool for loving him.

She had wanted to give him a permanent place near her fire, to save him from the freezing cold and night of the other world. But it was a world that he wanted more than he wanted anything else, including a life with her.

He could have left his work at any time in the past. He hadn't. She had been a fool to misunderstand what he was offering, to give far more of herself than was required by their private summer games. But that was the way she was. All or nothing at all.

With cold fingers, she reached into her pocket and drew out the gold coin Cord had given her. The irony of two gold medals for two different kinds of games made her lips flatten and turn down at the corners. She wondered if Cord had meant to be so cold. Maybe he simply had been trying to tell her that their lovers' games, though over, had been world-class.

"Find him," Raine said, looking at her father with eyes as blind as the gold coin gleaming on her outstretched palm. "Give this to him. He needs it more than I do." She turned away, hiding her tears. "When you're finished, I'll be here."

Chandler-Smith made two telephone calls from his car. The first told him that Johnstone's cover name for the Olympics had been Cord Elliot.

The second call was to the woman who was technically Robert Johnstone's boss.

"Where is Johnstone?" he asked.

"According to our records, he's dead."

An icy weariness settled over Chandler-Smith. He closed his eyes and bit back a futile protest. "Tell me."

"Are you on a secure line?"

"Yes."

"Okay. Barracuda cut and ran toward the desert. Bonner followed. So did the Delta boys. Johnstone, only he was called Cord Elliot for this operation, caught a ride with them. Bonner went after Barracuda and got shot. Johnstone waited almost until dark and went in to pull Bonner out. Barracuda killed Bonner, only we're calling him Johnstone now, and then Johnstone killed Barracuda, but —"

"Wait," Chandler-Smith interrupted curtly. "Who died?"

"Barracuda killed Bonner. Johnstone killed Barracuda. But he damn near died doing it."

"Is Johnstone alive?"

"Didn't I just say so?"

"You told me he was dead!"

"No, I said our *records* indicated that Johnstone is dead. You asked me to find a graceful exit from government service for Johnstone if and when he succeeded in taking out Barracuda. Bonner had no family. We tagged his body bag with Johnstone's ID. Good-bye, Robert Johnstone. Rest in Peace, and all that."

"Christ," Chandler-Smith muttered, breathing out a hard sigh. "You took a decade off my life. Where is Johnstone?"

"Air-lifted to the San Diego Naval hospital."

"What's his status?"

"Fucking lucky to be alive, sir. A medic kept his thumb on the femoral artery all the way to the hospital. Took three hours, but the surgeons got everything sewed back together again."

"I have to see him. What name is he under?"

"None. Brought in unconscious, no ID. They call him Patient X."

The hospital smelled like hospitals always do: disinfectant, bad coffee, and fear. Accompanied by a harried doctor, Chandler-Smith strode toward the end of the corridor where Patient X lay semiconscious.

"We have to drug him to keep him down," she said irritably. Being forced to permit a visitor to a patient in the ICU made her angry. On the other hand, in addition to being a doctor she was a naval officer. She understood all about rank and privileges. Chandler-Smith had both, in abundance. "He won't make much sense if you're planning on questioning him. Ninety seconds, sir. No more. And you shouldn't have even that."

Patient X was barely conscious. Tubes sprouted from him like fungus. Beneath the tan his skin had a shocking pallor. Slowly his eyes focused.

"Blue?" The voice was hoarse.

"Yeah. Helluva mess you got yourself into."

"Raine . . ." But the effort to talk defeated him.

Chandler-Smith took one of Johnstone's hot, restless hands and pressed the gold coin into it. "Here. Raine said you need this more than she does."

The texture and weight and shape of the coin was as familiar as Johnstone's own skin. Lady Luck. Lady Death. His fingers closed around the gold in a grip that even drugs couldn't ease. He tried to asked why Raine hadn't come herself. He needed her as much as life. More than life.

"She . . . here?"

"No."

Disappointment was another kind of pain breaking over him, giving him back to the darkness and the drugs. He never heard Blue leave.

Raine waited, hardly noticing the hours heaping silently around her. The darkness of night finally gave way to another perfect Southern California dawn.

The knock on her door sent her heart racing. When she heard her father's voice, she opened it. The same two men came in first, searched the room, and then stood aside until Chandler-Smith entered. A single gesture sent the men outside, leaving Raine alone with her father and the dizzying feeling that minutes rather than hours had passed.

"Tell me about Cord Elliot," her father said the instant the door closed behind his men.

Raine thought of the ways to explain — bodyguard and escort, horseman and companion — but there was only one truth that mattered. "He's my lover."

Chandler-Smith held out his hand to her. "Baby Raine, when did you grow up on me?"

"Years ago, Daddy. Long years."

"I hope so," he said beneath his breath. She would need every bit of her poise and nerve.

"Did you find him?" she asked tightly.

"The man you call Cord Elliot is one of my best men. One of the best, period, if that means anything to you. Officially he works for the Defense Intelligence Agency. He's assigned to a part of the agency that has no name, no budget, and no forwarding address."

"You didn't find him?"

"I didn't find a man called Cord Elliot."

She noted the evasion and understood that was all she would get from her father. He had broken more rules for her in the past night than he had in a lifetime. He would break no more.

"I understand," she said. Her voice was so controlled that it sounded like a stranger's. "Thank you." She held out her hand. "I'd like the good-luck piece back."

Her father's eyes narrowed into hazel slits. "I don't have it. I gave it to Robert Johnstone. Didn't Cord mention him?"

Numbly she shook her head. "He was like you, Daddy. No names, no facts, nothing . . ."

Her voice trailed off as the implication sank in: her father had been in touch with someone who knew not only *who* Cord really was, but *where* he was. The good-luck piece had been returned to Cord, but there was no message for her.

Or perhaps there was. Silence is more effective than good-bye, and less awkward.

Had those been the three syllables Cord had said? Not *Good luck, Raine,* or *I love you,* but *Good-bye, Raine?* And then had he faded back into the crowd, going on to another job, another challenge, another danger . . . another chance to die?

"Baby." Chandler-Smith held his daughter and stroked her hair. "Don't look like that. Sometimes things aren't what they seem."

She laughed, but there was nothing happy in the sound. "No, things aren't always as bad as they seem. Sometimes they're worse." She gave her father a quick, hard hug and stepped away. "Forgive me. I wasn't thinking very well. I never should have sent you chasing my former lover through Most Secret files."

Chandler-Smith started to speak, but years of ingrained silence won out. If Johnstone had wanted her to know his true identity, he would have told her. Caught between duty and a father's desire to ease his daughter's pain, Chandler-Smith watched Raine begin throwing her few things into a suitcase.

"Where are you going?" he asked finally.

She shrugged. "I'm taking a vacation. I've earned one."

"But where?"

"I'll think of somewhere," she said indifferently.

She swept up the contents of the bathroom shelf and dumped everything into her suitcase.

"Where will you be two weeks from now?" her father asked.

"Somewhere."

"How about in three weeks, or four?"

"Somewhere else." She shut the suitcase with a snap.

"Baby? Why don't you come home?"

"No." Her voice was soft, final. "I have a life to make for myself. It's time I grew up and quit playing games."

"What about Dev?"

With two quick motions she locked the suitcase. "Captain Jon will make arrangements to have him trailered home."

"Who will take care of Dev if you're not there?"

Her hands clenched. She didn't want to go home again. She couldn't. The past would reach up and smother her.

"Hire a groom," she said curtly, then remembered that Dev's temperament would make it impossible. "Damn it!"

"A man I know has a ranch in Arizona," Chandler-Smith said. "He's been overseas so much that he's thinking of selling it. I could arrange for you to trailer Dev there. It's a new place, Raine. All new. Up in the mountains. Clean water and grass and pine trees."

She blinked back sudden tears. She had never cried when her father had let her down, so why did she want to cry simply because he understood her need to put something new between herself and the past?

"Thanks." She hugged her father quickly.

"And don't worry. I will never ask you to break the rules again."

CHAPTER 21

Raine stood in the doorway of the guest cabin and watched the granite peaks massed against Arizona's cobalt sky. The air was cool, sweet with the scents of pine and water and grass bending gracefully beneath the wind.

In the five weeks she had stayed there, she had felt a sense of homecoming that blended strangely with the desolation of losing a man called Cord Elliot. Each day the loss was new, agonizing, for she woke up with his name on her lips and his dream-presence warm around her.

And each day she rose alone to put the past behind her as she stood in the cabin doorway and looked out over the huge fenced meadow where Devlin's Waterloo reigned supreme.

After a last sip of coffee, she set the thick mug aside and walked down the short dusty path to the meadow. The cabin had come

473

equipped with all the creature comforts, including a surprisingly modern kitchen and bathroom. It also had the one thing she required: privacy.

The main ranch house had the only phone on the ranch. The house was a half mile away, across the pasture. The retired couple who took care of the ranch in the owner's absence were careful not to interrupt Raine's solitude, though they had made it clear that she was welcome anytime she wanted to visit them.

The meadow's split-rail fence was new enough not to have been bleached by summer heat. Though it was only a few hours after dawn, sunlight had already warmed the air and the land. Dry heat seeped through the short-sleeved cotton sweater she wore. The sweater's deep jade color caught and held sunlight. Her riding pants were the same black as Dev's mane. Her hair fell in soft disarray around her shoulders and tickled her where the pullover's deep V revealed her neck and the gentle swell of her breasts.

Dev's head came up as he scented Raine. He cantered toward the fence, nickering a welcome. She watched closely while he swept across the pasture, coat gleaming like fire, muscles rippling with power. He had come back from the three-day event stronger than ever. She would have to begin riding him soon, working him, jumping him. Not for any goal or competition, but simply because they both enjoyed it.

Like her, the stallion had settled into the mountains as though born there. Getting him to go back to stalls and barns would be a problem. But there was no rush. Her father had assured her that the ranch's owner was engaged elsewhere. She and Dev could stay as long as they liked.

But the longer she stayed, the less she could bear to think about leaving.

A velvet muzzle pushed impatiently at her shoulder.

"You're after a carrot, aren't you?" she muttered, pushing back.

Dev snorted and waited, ears pricked, every inch of him vibrating with health.

"You win." She reached into her back pocket. "You always do, you red beggar."

While Dev ate the carrot, she stroked his neck and enjoyed the sleek, solid feel of him.

"Would you like to live here, Devlin's Waterloo?" she asked. "I've never touched the money G'mom gave me when I turned twenty-three. I could buy this lovely mountain meadow for you, and some lively, leggy mares to go with it. I could spend my life here, raising blood-bay hellions and training them to fly over fences and streams."

Raine didn't realize she was crying until she felt the tears sliding down her cheeks. It was Cord who had talked about putting Dev out to stud and raising red hellions. She had laughed then, not believing in tomorrow.

Tomorrow had come. It was here. Now.

And it was lonely.

She forced her grief back down beneath her consciousness. Tears had done no good. Getting on with life might. Just because tomorrow had come without Cord was no reason to abandon all of the dream. She could breed and train event horses in Arizona as well as in Virginia. Better. She would be more at peace here. With her reputation and Dev's foals, people would come to the remote mountains to look and to buy.

Someday, maybe even Cord would come. Maybe he'll remember summer as deeply as I do.

The thought made it all too fresh, too new, as if it had just happened. Silently she raged at the stubborn, merciless hope she couldn't kill.

Each time she believed that she finally had accepted the fact that she loved a man who didn't love her, her mind would turn on her with claws of hope and memory, ripping apart her fragile peace. Then she had to begin over again, rebuilding herself one second at a time, one minute, one hour.

Raine heard the helicopter long before she spotted it flying low, sunlight flashing off its white body. No numbers, no name. The kind of helicopter her father always used. With a fury of sound and wind, the machine landed.

She squinted against the sun. Though the helicopter was only a few hundred feet away, she couldn't see the passenger through the blinding glare of sunlight. Trying not to think of all the bad news that her father could be bringing with him, she slipped between fence rails and ran toward the machine.

"Dad, what are you —" The words shattered into silence when she recognized the man silhouetted against the burning sun. *"Cord."*

She stared, frozen, hardly able to believe that what she saw wasn't one more cruel dream she would awaken from alone.

But this couldn't be a dream. Cord was standing not twenty feet away from her, city slacks and no tie, white shirt open at the throat, his slate-gray suitcoat tossed carelessly over his shoulder. He looked thinner, drawn hard and tight, and the sprinkling of silver in his forelock had become a solid slash against his black hair.

The helicopter took off in a whirl of dust and noise. When it was gone, there was only silence and sunlight and Cord standing there, looking at Raine with eyes the color of ice.

Then he started walking toward her, and she saw the cane in his right hand.

She ran to him, forgetting her anger and pain and questions, forgetting everything except him. She threw her arms around him, unable to say anything more than his name. He held her with a strength that made her ache, his left arm a steel bar across her back, his right arm braced on the cane.

Then he kissed her as though she was fire and he was a man chilled all the way to his soul.

Before the kiss ended, she knew that it didn't matter if he had hurt her by leaving her without warning, without even a word. It didn't matter that he was a man perfectly suited for the dangerous life he had chosen. It didn't matter that his world could include her for only a few days, a few hours, a single kiss. It didn't matter that he was the wrong man for her.

She loved him. There could be no going back from that simple overwhelming fact.

"That answers one of my questions," he said almost roughly.

"Which one?" Her fingers roved over his face and hair, reassuring herself that he was real.

"If you missed me as much as I missed you."

She laughed brokenly. Tears blurred her vision. Impatiently she wiped away the tears, not wanting to miss a single instant of looking at Cord.

"I missed you more," she said.

"That isn't possible."

She looked at his ice-blue eyes, saw shadows of longing and pain. "Where were —"

Abruptly she remembered. She didn't have the security clearance to know the details of his life. *He's here now. Let yesterday and tomorrow go. Love him now, while you can.*

"Come to the cabin," she said huskily, and with every word she kissed him, butterfly touches that were as breathless as her voice.

He wanted to stay there, holding her, kissing her, letting her sink all the way into his cold soul. But he couldn't ignore the demands of his body any longer. Even with the cane, his damned leg was threatening to buckle under him. The doctor had been right; it was too soon for him to be wedged into airplanes, helicopters, or cars.

Cord didn't care. He needed to see Raine.

Slowly, touching him lightly, she walked beside him. She could see that his leg bothered him. Words ached in her throat, all the questions she wanted to ask. She ignored them.

She opened the cabin door and waited for him to climb the few steps up onto the porch. She wanted to help him but knew that he wouldn't want to be helped.

"You look like you've missed a few meals." She kept her voice light, though it required an effort of will that made her nails bite into her palms.

"Food was lousy."

Raine shut the door behind Cord and watched as he crossed the room. He settled on the bed by the fireplace, propping up his leg in obvious relief. Despite his injury, he still radiated the power and grace that had haunted her dreams.

Yet he watched her as though uncertain of what to say, what to do.

And he was. The need to see her had driven him from the hospital before they wanted him to go. But now that he was here, all he could remember was the fact that she hadn't come to him. Not once in five long weeks. All he had had of her was the enigmatic gold coin and her words, equally enigmatic. *Give it to him. He needs it more than I do.*

"Are you hungry? Thirsty? Sleepy?" she asked. They were the only questions she would permit herself to say aloud. "I don't know which time zone you've been in, so I don't know what you need."

"You." He held out his hand to her. "I need you."

In a few quick strides Raine crossed the room and lay down on the bed beside Cord. He held her gently at first, kissing away the tears that fell no matter how hard she willed them not to. Then his kiss changed, hungry and searching, possessing her with a power that drove every emotion out of her but the yearning for him that had made her nights a torment and her days a nightmare.

"I've dreamed of this for thirty-nine days," he said. He tasted her with tiny bites and licks, his hunger tangible in the hard lines and deep tremors of his body. "Even when they knocked me out, I dreamed of you."

Closing her eyes, she shivered beneath the sensual assault. Blindly she sought the warmth and hard male flesh beneath his shirt. The cloth kept getting in the way. With quick, almost savage motions she unbuttoned the shirt. She needed the naked resilience of his flesh against her palms the way a starving man needs food. Fingers spread wide, she rubbed her hands slowly across Cord's chest, savoring the physical reality of the man she had never expected to see again outside her dreams.

As he watched her expression, his pale eyes narrowed with raw hunger. Her face was taut yet strangely languid. Her lips smiled even as they parted and lifted, wanting his kiss. His hands kneaded down her back, pushing her close to the hard ache of his arousal.

Her hips shifted. She fitted herself against him intimately, perfectly. Need clawed through him until he groaned. His hands pushed beneath her sweater. He pulled the soft jade knit off her in a swift motion. There was nothing underneath but the smooth, fragrant skin that had haunted him since the first time he had touched her.

"I've dreamed of this, too," he said, his voice as hard as his need.

He bent over her breasts, feeding on them with violent restraint, nipping at their peaks until she trembled and cried out softly.

"Yes," he said hoarsely, hearing his name repeated again and again. "I dreamed of that, too. I'd wake up yelling for you and the doctors would knock me out again. But I could still hear you crying for me, and it nearly killed me because I couldn't go to you, couldn't do anything but listen to you cry."

She thought his words were a lover's sweet lies. Yet it reassured her to know that he hadn't left her easily, that he had missed her to the point of pain. The way she had missed him, pain in her very soul.

He heard her moan, felt her body tremble in response, and he stopped thinking at all. He had to be inside her now, to know that she was his again. His arms tightened as he began to roll over onto her. Then he froze, chained for an instant by the white-hot agony in his leg. He hissed a curse through his clenched teeth.

"Let me," she whispered.

Gently she pushed him onto his back. She got off the bed long enough to strip away her own clothes. The hungry, smoky blaze of his eyes watching her made her knees weak. She knelt on the bed and pulled his shirt free of his body. While her hands worked over his slacks, she slowly, neatly licked the midnight line of hair that descended to his lean waist and below.

His breath hissed again, but it was a

lightning stroke of pleasure rather than pain. Her mouth was hot, possessive, and it promised him things he hadn't dared to dream.

"I love the way you taste," she said dreamily.

"Come here, sweet rider. Let me give you what you've been asking for."

Smiling like a cat, she turned her back on him and went to work on his shoes.

His fingertips traced the elegant length of her spine from nape to buttocks.

She shivered and his shoes dropped to the floor.

His hand slid lower, tracing the smooth shadow cleft until he found the hidden fire.

She sipped at breath, made a broken sound as desire shook her. Her fingers clenched on his socks, but she didn't even know it. His touch was sweet agony. She forgot what she was doing, forgot even to breathe; she lived only in the heated darkness where he touched her.

Cord made a sound deep in his throat as he felt the hot, silky rain of her response. "I dreamed of this, too. It was cold, everything was cold, winter coming down and fire calling to me, but I couldn't move, couldn't even scream. And I wanted to. I wanted to tear down all the castle walls, grind them to dust. But there were straps cinching me to a bed as white and cold as snow, winter freezing me. So I dreamed of you, of fire bathing me."

Shuddering, helpless, she surrendered to the passion coursing through her, liquid heat like heartbeats swelling until she moaned. His voice caressed her, midnight and velvet, asking for her fire, telling her how the silky pulses pleasured him. She swayed, shaken by passion, and he smiled, watching his dream.

"I'll never get you undressed," she managed finally. The words were as ragged as her breathing. "I want to see you, to touch you, to feel all of you naked against me. Inside me."

With a reluctance that nearly undid her all over again, he released her soft, slick flesh. Her hands were trembling as she pushed his slacks down. She felt clumsy next to the masculine power of his legs. Then her hand brushed a new knot of scar tissue on his thigh, and she froze.

"Go on," he said. "It's all right."

He helped her ease the pants past the recent wound. When she saw the raw slash of barely healed flesh, she went pale.

"My God. What happened?" she asked starkly.

"Later." He twisted out of his remaining clothes with a speed that mocked even the idea of injury. "It doesn't hurt nearly as much as wanting you does."

He rolled toward her, but she saw the instant of hesitation as his wounded leg rebelled. She wanted him, but not at the cost of the pain she had seen on his face for one terrible instant.

"Does it bother you when you lie on your back?" she asked.

Cord smiled crookedly. "Come to me, sweet rider."

But despite the smile, his voice and hands were urgent as he lifted her onto him.

Raine settled over him lightly, completely, moving slowly until he groaned with pleasure and stark need. She shuddered deep inside her body and saw by the narrowing of his eyes that he had felt it. His smile was utterly male, as was the sudden tightening of his body as he took complete possession of her fire.

With an open, hungry mouth, she kissed his lips, his neck, his chest, consuming him with teeth and tongue as he had once consumed her, spreading fire wherever she touched him. His breathing shifted, quickened, like his flesh inside her. She deepened her caresses as shivering forerunners of ecstasy rippled through her.

He encouraged her with dark words and sensual hands gripping her, stroking with an intimacy that burned. Her hips moved slowly, rhythmically, riding him until his eyes were smoky, all but closed, his body tight with anticipation and need.

She didn't hear the whimpers that came with each of her breaths. She didn't know that her mouth on his was as demanding as her rhythm was slow. She felt nothing but him as their bodies fused together, flesh on flesh, tongue on tongue, heat swelling, ecstasy raking until they surrendered to it, consuming and renewing each other in the same endless, pulsing fire.

Boneless, utterly spent, Raine lay across Cord's chest and tried to remember how to breathe. It was a long time before she stirred and lifted her head enough to look at him.

He read her satisfaction in her dazed eyes and slow, very female smile. Relief uncurled inside him.

"That answers my second question," he said quietly. "It's as good for you as it is for me. Which leaves only one question. Why didn't you come to me?"

She blinked. "Come to you? How? Where?"

"In the hospital. The same way the good-luck piece did. You did send it, didn't you?"

"Yes, but —"

"And you said, 'Give it to him, he needs it more than I do.' "

"Yes, but —" Her words ended in a harsh sound of frustration. "How could I come to you? I didn't know where you were!"

His eyes narrowed. "Then how did you know I was dying and needed all the luck I could get to pull through?"

She went pale and flinched as though he had struck her. All her worst fears congealed in her soul, crushing her — ice and violence and raw scar tissue scored across the body of the man she loved. He hadn't been telling a lover's sweet fiction about missing her. He had been describing a brutal truth. He had awakened yelling for her and the doctors had knocked him out again and strapped him to the bed.

Her body shook repeatedly, helplessly. She had come so close to losing Cord and never even knowing that he had died. He had called for her, needed her, *and she hadn't been there for him.*

The thought was agony to her, a pain greater than any she had known before. Lightly, blindly, her trembling fingertips traced his features while tears slid down her cheeks. She tried to tell him how much she loved him, that she would have moved heaven and earth to be with him if she had known; but no words could get past the tears filling her throat.

He caught her tears with his lips, kissing her again and again. "You didn't know, did you?" he asked.

Numbly, she shook her head.

"Then why did you send back the good-luck piece?" His voice was coaxing, gentle. He kissed her tenderly, stealing each tear as it fell.

She shuddered as the rest of the truth congealed in her soul; Cord wasn't hers, not really. He belonged to tomorrow, and sooner or later, tomorrow always came. The reality of it was a dry, cold wind that froze her tears.

"The coin wasn't mine to keep, any more than you were." Her voice was flat, lifeless.

He sensed Raine retreating from him, from any emotion at all, shutting down before his eyes, a castle with all gates closing, all bars being drawn. Fear echoed through him, returning as anger. His hands were suddenly hard around her face.

"What are you saying?" he demanded.

"You'll come and go as you always did. No warning, no words, nothing."

"I hadn't planned on getting shot."

She flinched and slid off him before he could protest. Very gently, her hand sought the new scar. "A bullet?"

"Yes."

"Will you . . . heal?" she asked, remembering his pain.

He stared intently at her, his eyes hard and remote. "What did Blue tell you?"

"Nothing."

"What the hell do you mean, *nothing?*" Cord asked savagely.

"Just that," she shot back, her voice as harsh as his. "Nothing! Not one damn thing. I haven't heard one word about or from you since you disappeared."

He closed his eyes for an instant, hardly able to believe. "Christ . . ." His eyes opened pale blue, very clear, blazing with life and hope. "Yet you ran to me."

"Yes," she said finally, because he waited for her to answer.

"You cried for me."

"Yes," she whispered.

"And you made love with me as though there was no tomorrow."

"There isn't."

"There is."

"Not for us. For us there's only today, now, this instant. In the next instant you could be gone, or the next."

"No." Cord's voice was quiet and very sure.

Raine turned away, not wanting to fight with him, not wanting to face the end of the dream so soon after its beginning. "Have you eaten anything?" she asked, moving to get out of bed.

His hand closed around her arm, chaining her.

She turned to him. "Coffee? Black, no sugar, right?"

"Are those the only questions you have for me?"

"No. But they're the only ones I'll ask."

"Don't you want to know why I'm here?"

She turned her face away, feeling shame crawl redly up her cheeks. "What do they call it?" she asked, her voice shaking. "R and R? Yes, that's it. Rest and Recuperation. You know, when the soldiers go to town and pick up women."

"Stop it."

She turned on him with more despair than anger. "Don't worry, I can stand the truth. I'm not going to throw you back out into the cold. I'll be here when you get back the next time, and the next, until you find a woman you want more or you're killed or I . . ." Her voice frayed into silence.

"Or what?" he demanded harshly. "Until

you find a *gentle*man?"

"Until I stop loving you," she said, her voice ragged, "whoever you are, whatever your name really is."

His expression changed, gentleness smoothing the rough edges of his mouth and voice. He pulled her close again, burying his lips in her hair, drinking her sweetness.

"My love, my love," he whispered, "didn't Blue tell you anything at all? I turned in my resignation the day after I made love to you the first time. I knew I had to have you, and I knew that you couldn't live with my work." He laughed curtly. "Neither could I. Not anymore. One too many battles, one too many wars."

For a long moment Raine stared into Cord's clear eyes, afraid to let herself believe. "Why didn't you tell me?"

"I couldn't quit immediately. Not until a certain matter was cleared up. I didn't know how long that would take." He closed his eyes briefly, remembering a ravine where darkness fell too slowly and death came too fast. "I was going to wait until after your ride. You had enough to handle with the Olympics. You didn't need to know that I was facing the most dangerous assignment of my life."

Her breath wedged. She touched his lips with a hesitant hand. There was no hesitation in the kiss he gave her fingertips.

"I wish I could have seen your gold medal ride," he said. "But it went blue all the way to the moon."

She saw the change in him, anger and grief and pain. "What is it? What's wrong? Do you have to go back soon? Isn't it finished?"

"It's finished."

He closed his eyes, remembering the friend who had fought beside him and lost, the man who would never again mangle Spanish phrases and ask after chess games. But Bonner hadn't died alone. Cord had made sure of that, despite the hot blood pumping out of the wound in his thigh.

"The terrorist I was after is dead," Cord said evenly. "Very dead. Another man died at the same time. A good man. The best. So we gave him my identity, and we buried him."

"I don't understand."

"According to official records, Robert Johnstone and an unidentified passenger died tragically in a light plane crash in the Mojave Desert."

Raine remembered the name Robert Johnstone and realized that her father had given the good-luck coin directly to Robert Johnstone, alias Cord Elliot. No wonder her father hadn't told her anything; if Cord hadn't mentioned his real name to her, her father never would.

"Who are you?" she asked, trying to keep her voice calm.

"Cord Elliot," he answered quickly, almost fiercely. "The man who loves you. The man who's going to marry you."

She stared at him, almost afraid to believe. "Are you sure?"

He smiled crookedly. "Yes, I'm sure I love you. Yes, I'm sure I'm going to marry you. And yes, I'm sure my name is Cord Elliot. I have the papers to prove it. Lots and lots of them."

Raine smiled despite the tears that suddenly appeared on her eyelashes. "Is the ink dry?"

"Of course. I worked for the guy who owns the presses." His smile faded. "Will you marry a man with no past, a man whose only marketable skill is a certain knack with knot-headed horses? Not that we'll starve. I haven't had much to spend my money on through the years."

She smiled, then kissed him slow and tender and deep. "I'll marry you on one condition."

His black eyebrows lifted. "What's that?"

"That you'll let me buy this ranch for us."

His expression changed.

"Don't you like it here?" she asked quickly. "It's so beautiful. And Dev loves it. We could buy a few mares and train the foals and — what's wrong?"

"Do you really like it here?" he asked.

"It was like coming home," she said simply. "If it hadn't been for the peace these mountains gave me, I would have gone crazy these last weeks. Can you understand that?"

"Oh yes," he said softly. "That's why I bought this ranch five years ago. It kept me sane until I could find you. Will you live here with me, raise four- and two-footed hellions with me?"

Raine bent over Cord, letting her kiss be her answer. When she shifted to lie beside him again, she saw the livid scar. She touched his leg carefully.

"Will you be able to ride?"

He laughed. His hand traced her spine, urging her closer. "In a few months, I'll be as good as ever. Better. I'll have you." He nuzzled against her neck, tickled her ear with the tip of his tongue.

"We'll spend a lot of time riding," she said dreamily.

"Yeah." His smile was slow and sexy. "And sometimes we'll even take horses along."

Her laugh sounded more like a purr. Her fingertips traced the tendons in his neck and settled on his pulse.

His expression changed as he watched her, saw her pleasure at simply touching him. "Come to me, love. I need that place by your fire."

"It's yours. It always has been. It always will be." She curled against him even as he gathered her close. "All those tomorrows finally belong to us."

We hope you have enjoyed this Large Print book. Other Thorndike, Wheeler, Kennebec, and Chivers Press Large Print books are available at your library or directly from the publishers.

For information about current and upcoming titles, please call or write, without obligation, to:

Publisher
Thorndike Press
10 Water St., Suite 310
Waterville, ME 04901
Tel. (800) 223-1244

or visit our Web site at:

http://gale.cengage.com/thorndike

OR

Chivers Large Print
published by AudioGO Ltd
St James House, The Square
Lower Bristol Road
Bath BA2 3SB
England
Tel. +44(0) 800 136919
email: info@audiogo.co.uk
www.audiogo.co.uk

All our Large Print titles are designed for easy reading, and all our books are made to last.